SHADOW UNBOUND

SHADOW UNBOUND

ANGIE DAY

Rahne Press is a publisher in the United States. The city of publication is Cedar City, Utah.

www.angiedayauthor.com

Cataloging-in-Publication Data is available upon request.

ISBN: 978-1-7338144-0-9 (hardcover)
ISBN: 978-1-7338144-5-4 (paperback)

Edited by Suzanne Johnson
Cover Design by Sarah Hansen at www.okaycreations.com

First printed in the United States of America.
10 9 8 7 6 5 4 3 2 1

To my husband.
Thank you for believing in me.

PREVIOUSLY IN

LEGEND UNDONE

Mara wasn't just a Legend who survived on human energy, she used to be a dangerous Shadow who wielded more power than she wanted. When she discovered that Alec, the leader of the Shadows and her childhood love, held a dark secret, she ran.

Mara must keep moving, hiding among the humans that every Legend learned to hate, while she searches to understand her past. Under the alias Kate, she meets Kylan and his way of life challenges everything she used to know. As she falls for Kylan, she finds clues about what happened before she became a Shadow.

But the closer she gets to an answer, the closer Alec can get to her and destroy everything she has grown to love.

NOW IN

SHADOW UNBOUND

Mara is a Legend, born with unmatched power. More than that, she is a Shadow: ruthless, feared, and lethal. But all of that changed when she became Kate and fell in love with a perfectly human life and the Legend that showed her how to live it: Kylan. After battling the Shadows and uncovering the memories they stole, she was free. Free to be with Kylan, his family, and the Rogue life they had chosen.

When a new human is brought into their lives, everything unravels. The family she has grown to love is thrown into chaos. Kate can't save any of them. But Mara can.

As Mara steps back into her previous life as a Shadow, it fits a little too well. The longer she walks with danger, the more she sees in common with the Shadows she left than the Rogue she was pretending to be.

When her two worlds collide, Mara should be faced with a choice. But a greater evil awaits her, one with the power to shatter both worlds.

CHAPTER ONE

"You're a what?" Cassie screeched as everyone's eyes widened.

Her red hair burned in the lights of Kylan's house as she waited impatiently for my answer. She had the hottest temper of his siblings, but Rachel definitely came in a close second.

The others had a similar look as Cassie, confirming that they heard me correctly.

I just waited for all of them to process it. I was still making sense of it myself. This was the first time that I had really said it out loud.

I am a Level Five. The only Level Five in existence as far as I knew.

"That's not possible." Cassie crossed her arms in front of her chest, looking me up and down to notice a change.

She wouldn't find anything. I looked exactly the same as I had before, and frankly, I looked exactly like all of them.

"Kylan, are you sure?" Rachel asked more calmly than her sister.

The two women stood together, and both looked between

me and Kylan. Rachel's hair was long, smooth, and a deeper red, but Cassie's skin was lighter and freckled.

"This is a joke, right?" Derek asked, waiting in vain for the punch line to drop.

He was Cassie's husband and the only person who could keep her remotely level-headed.

Kylan winced. "I wouldn't joke about this, and you know that."

He stood next to me as all of them continued to decide whether or not they were going to accept the new information.

"Prove it," Derek challenged.

I smiled, hoping someone would say that. While I didn't want to scare them, I was a little too eager to show off. As any Shadow would have been.

"Change," I said and touched the sleeve on my shirt.

The maroon fabric slowly darkened to black. The energy slowly left my body to perform the act. I still had plenty in my system, but after each stunt I would have less and less.

Most of them already knew I could change the physical nature of cells, so that part wasn't a surprise.

"Create," I said and turned my focus to the plant in the corner of the room.

I focused on the cells of the leaves and coached them to multiply. The leaves quickly doubled in size and almost toppled the plant over.

Everyone in the room focused on what I was doing, waiting for the next Level. I couldn't even hear any of them breathing.

"Destroy."

"No, no—" Kylan lunged and grabbed my arm just as the leaves curled, turning black.

The edges disintegrated into black dust while the rest of the plant withered. The particles fell to the beige carpet and piled in sad heaps.

"I liked that plant," Kylan said.

He released my arm, and I mouthed an apology to him.

"Read." I locked eyes with Derek.

His eyes widened and then slammed shut, but just a second too late. I had already made the connection into his mind. I searched for something that only he could have been thinking.

I laughed when I found my answer and judging by the look on Derek's face, he knew what I had found.

"Should I say it out loud?" I asked.

"Say what?" Kylan asked, eager for the dirt on his brother.

"The pattern of underwear you're wearing." I smiled even wider and kept my eyes glued to Derek.

His gaze ignited, and even his darker skin color turned a shade of red. After reading his mind, I could feel exactly how much he didn't want this revealed.

"Derek, honey." Cassie sighed and put her face in her palm. "I told you to get rid of those."

Everyone laughed. Rachel's breathy giggle even brought a grin to Cassie. Kylan lowered his head and tried to hide his laugh behind his hand.

Create, kill, change, read, and extract were the Five Levels. The first four Levels that I demonstrated had been the easiest, the ones that other strong Legends could expect to have.

The laughter died, and some other tightness thrummed through the room. The next Level was the one that all of them feared. Extract.

"Do you want to volunteer?" I stretched my hand out to Derek.

If he wanted to challenge me, then he should be the one to risk me actually being right.

Derek walked forward and looked at Kylan to check that it was all right. He nodded and the wary brother turned back to me.

Everyone watched Derek to see if he would actually go through with it. Fear flashed across his dark brown eyes before he took a breath in.

It was a risk for him to stand this close if I was telling the truth about being a Five. I was about to take his energy from his body. This type of power was extremely rare and Derek was taking the safe bet to assume I didn't have it.

"Extract."

I kept my hand raised, waiting for his hand.

He slowly lifted it and placed it in mine. His skin touched mine, and I didn't have to focus very hard to coax his energy out of his cells. The bright heat left his body and swirled into mine. I was expecting the same intensity as a human body would offer.

But this was nothing like a human. The energy seemed to spark and crackle through each cell in my body. My mind sharpened and honed in on the sweet rush that obliterated all my prior thoughts.

This energy was like pure magic.

Derek noticed the power seeping out of his body, and he yanked his hand back.

The connection broke, and the intense energy piercing through my skin halted. All that remained was empty air and my excited breath.

As soon as Derek took a step back, so did everyone else. This was exactly what I expected when I told a room full of Legends that I was an Extractor.

I knew it was coming, but it still hurt to see their faces change to look at me in fear.

"Dude…" Derek muttered, already reaching to nudge his brother.

"Don't say…" Kylan started.

Derek didn't stop. "She's an Extractor!"

He and Cassie shifted away from me. I caught Cassie glancing at the door and knew she was judging how fast they could exit if they needed to do so.

I would've done the same thing. Extractors were rare and incredibly dangerous. I had only ever known of two, besides myself.

The monster that murdered the closest thing to a father I had, and Kylan.

"We can't be safe around her," Cassie urged.

"I knew there was something off." Rachel shook her head and narrowed her eyes.

But she looked more interested than afraid. She didn't step away from me like Cassie did.

"She's actually a Five," Derek muttered to himself.

"She's not a threat to any of us," Kylan said in that same authoritative voice.

He raised his hands to quiet the rest of their complaints. Cassie wasn't up to being calmed by him.

"She can take our energy. How could you possibly say that?"

Kylan lowered his arms and walked over to Derek slowly. He snatched Derek's bare forearm. It looked like a comforting touch, but I knew what he was doing. If I was going to be revealing my darkest parts, then he wanted to as well.

"I know," Kylan said.

A faint yellow light swirled into Kylan's skin like mist threading through his veins. Derek looked down and noticed what was going on and jerked his arm back.

"You're a…"

Kylan was dangerous, an Extractor like me. But they had

known each other for centuries. That changed things. Derek's eyes softened. He wasn't looking at an enemy, he was looking at family.

"I'm sorry I haven't told any of you." Kylan put his hands back safely in his pockets.

Rachel was the first to step forward, kind and gentle.

I waited in agony as she walked up to Kylan. He didn't dare look at her either. But she silently put her arms around him. Kylan touched her arms tentatively, and when she didn't recoil, he hugged her tight.

"We love you. That shouldn't change because of what you can do," Rachel said into Kylan's shirt, and her warm eyes snapped up to mine. "That goes for both of you."

I nodded and Kylan pulled away from Rachel's arms to look at me. His smile lines crinkled around his green eyes, and a lump formed in my throat.

Cassie still seemed a little cautious of both of us. Derek cleared his throat as soon as he caught Cassie's eyes.

"We should be celebrating. Kylan scored the one and only Level Five. Nicely done, bro." Derek smiled at Kylan and they bumped fists.

Kylan's shoulders relaxed even further and the tension in Cassie's eyes softened. We all waited for her to speak what was racing through her mind. Her face didn't betray her thoughts enough for any of us to assume.

"I guess if anyone was going to, it would be Kylan." Cassie reluctantly broke into a smile.

Kylan and Derek both put their arms around her and, just like that, they looked like a family again.

My gaze moved to Rachel, who seemed to have her eyes trained on me instead of joining the group hug happening in front of us.

"Is there something else?" Rachel asked curiously.

She couldn't read minds, but her past in manipulating people with the best of the business world had taught her how to read faces. My time away from the Shadows had let my lying skills lapse.

I looked back at Rachel and my hand moved to the edge of my right sleeve, the place that proved my identity as a Shadow.

The part of my body I had hidden so no one would see the black dagger tattoo there. The dagger I hated.

"Kate, you don't have to," Kylan comforted and walked over to me.

He put his hand on my back tenderly. I looked into his warm eyes for the courage I needed to lift my sleeve. If I wanted to be a real part of his family, I would need to be honest.

Lies were what had gotten me kidnapped. Lies were what allowed Kylan to be dragged back to the mansion with me. I was done with lies. The more I told the truth, the less my past had a power over me.

"I want to," I said to Kylan and faced them again. "You're right. There is one more thing."

That slim fabric covering my arm was my shield, my reason that I felt safe around other Legends or humans. The idea of removing it was enough to make my breaths come in uneven spurts.

But I focused and pulled on the bottom of my sleeve. Kylan sucked in a breath through his teeth.

The cloth dragged up my skin, and I lost track of the seconds that passed. All I could do was watch their faces as the sleeve reached my elbow.

I knew as soon as they saw it. I recognized the drained complexions, the shocked breaths, and defensive hands.

They saw the dagger.

"Shadow," Rachel gasped.

CHAPTER TWO

Rachel and Cassie locked eyes with each other before they turned and glared at me. My skin lit up in fire under their scrutiny. My feet shifted uncomfortably as I waited.

I knew it was too much.

They leapt back. I tried to look away from the scared faces, but I couldn't force myself.

I was too much.

Their acceptance and love vanished in a matter of seconds.

"No…no…" Cassie shook her head, red hair shifting around her shoulders, and walked over to Rachel. "I'm sorry, Kylan. I can't do this."

"Cassie…" Kylan started and reached out toward her.

She ducked away from his hand and whipped back around to face him.

"No! You knew about her, didn't you? I can't believe you would let her back in this house. You know what the Shadows did to our parents." Her voice broke as she reached for her sister.

They put their arms around each other and looked at me as if I was personally responsible for whatever horrific death they must have endured.

I knew how Shadows treated other Legends, the Rogues. Humans were killed quickly. They weren't as fun to taunt. But with a defiant Legend who stood in their way, they took their time.

But I couldn't contain my morbid curiosity. I looked at Cassie and hoped she would explain.

I didn't ask. I just waited.

She stared back at me. I felt her trying to enter my mind. She was only a Two and wasn't going to get in without my cooperation. I knew I'd be opening myself up to whatever she wanted to inflict on me, but I thought I owed her at least a little respect.

I relaxed my shoulders and felt the connection between us solidify, allowing her to pass through like smoke through cracks.

My mind instantly lit up with images flickering into place. She was creating a thought in my mind to match the memory she held.

The coarse, unfamiliar feeling made my mind stagger to try and shove the image in my memory. But this memory didn't fit into anything.

It wasn't mine. It was hers.

A man with bright red hair and a petite woman held each other, their brown eyes both wide with fear. They clung to each other as if that was the only thing that would save them.

Menacing Legends encircled them, none of their arms bearing a mark. An obvious leader of the group took the first step forward. The couple remained frozen in place, holding their breath. I recognized the leader as soon as I saw his dark eyes and calculating grin.

It was Charles. Alec and Kylan's father, and the man that raised me.

The couple looked at him like he was the one they were most afraid of hurting them. He snarled, and they cowered even more. Tight, short breaths sputtered from the innocent pair of Legends.

Charles lunged for the couple.

The image disappeared.

Fear seeped through with the thought, leaving a lingering shudder. The memory was long before Alec created the mark to identify the Shadows. He only did that when he took over as leader of the Shadows after his father's death.

Then I thought about Charles, and my heart cracked.

He was the man I had always seen as my father. He and Alec took me into the Shadows when I was little. But Charles was also the one responsible for my mother's death, the reason I needed a home in the first place.

I had no idea what I thought about Charles now. The more I learned about him, the more the perfect picture I had in mind of a father scattered.

The images and feelings vanished to leave me looking at Cassie's reddened eyes filling with hot tears. The room fell silent.

"You have no idea how sorry I am," I whispered.

She stepped toward me, keeping her burning gaze on mine. The fresh anger flared in her spiteful brown eyes. Despite her petite frame, she seemed ready to tear my throat out.

"You're sorry? I watched them die in front of my eyes. Your Shadows followed me all the way home, where I had to tell my little sister that we had to run," Cassie said, her face cold and unchanging. "I don't care if you're sorry."

"Kate didn't kill your parents," Kylan whispered. "My father did."

The silence in the room could have shifted gravity itself. No one even dared take a breath.

"You're not..." Rachel looked at him and glanced down at his right arm.

The skin was bare, something that should've proved that he couldn't be affiliated with the Shadows.

"The name I was given at birth was Kylan Stone. Alec is my brother by blood." Kylan left the words in the air like even he was afraid to touch them.

I stepped forward and put my hand in Kylan's. His fingers wrapped around mine gently. He kept his gaze on his siblings. All of them were processing the sea of new information.

The selfless part of me didn't blame them. The opposite part of me wanted to already be past all of this.

"That's not possible." Rachel sucked in a breath.

She wasn't taking the news as hard as Cassie. Rachel had grown up and forgotten about Cassie and her parents. It must have been easier than wondering. Cassie saw them die.

That kind of heartbreak didn't go away. I knew that.

"You're telling the truth..." Cassie looked into Kylan's eyes. "How...how? You and he are so different."

"You don't get to choose your blood." He shook his head. "I was lucky enough to get away when I was young. I started my own life and found all of you. I've been happy. Kate wasn't so lucky."

Derek looked at me now. Cassie refused to meet my gaze.

"I was kidnapped by the Shadows when I was too little to remember anything else. They hid my identity and my abilities from me for centuries. I grew up believing they were my family." A sad smile passed my lips. "No kid wants to believe their family is evil."

Rachel lifted her hand to her mouth. The weight on

my chest lifted enough for me to remember what it felt like without it crushing me.

Everyone in the room understood the difference between living the life they were set on and choosing their own. Rachel had been a liar and manipulator. Derek had family running a lab.

But their pasts didn't include nearly as much death as mine. Especially not Cassie's.

"Kate didn't get to choose being a Shadow any more than you got to choose your red hair," Kylan gestured to Cassie.

"Genetics and murder are not the same thing," Cassie spat.

"Kylan's right," Rachel interrupted.

There was a warmth in her gaze. Another breath of confidence filled my lungs. Her sister whipped around faster than I could follow.

"Excuse me?" Cassie challenged.

"You can't choose your past. You can't change it either," Rachel said, understanding and calm. "She's no more a Shadow than Kylan is. Not anymore."

"Cassie, I'm truly sorry for what happened to your parents, but that wasn't me."

"Let's pretend it was you. That you were the one standing between them and getting home to two little girls. Can you tell me you would've spared their lives?" She looked at me for the answer she had been waiting to ask someone for too long.

It wasn't an answer she wanted. "No."

As a Shadow, I would have jumped at the chance to take down anyone Charles asked me to. Lies weren't going to save me anymore. I didn't want them to.

"But I was a different person back then." I stepped forward, hoping to explain.

"Different person? That makes it okay?" Cassie interrupted. "We had to run that night. The emergency plan was to split up and hide until it was safe. The second Rachel and I left each other, that's when the humans starting getting curious about Legends again. Witch trials, inquisitions, conspiracy theorists. It was never safe. I ran and ran until there wasn't anywhere on the earth that I hadn't tried to hide. It took me centuries to find my sister again. *Centuries.*"

Cassie glared at me with the years of hatred she'd held for any Shadow. She backed away and put her hands up like she wanted nothing to do with me. "But hey, you were a different person back then."

She left in a huff of strangled curses and fresh tears. Derek followed slowly, sending a glance to Kylan before he stepped out.

"I remember that day." Rachel swallowed. "Cassie ran in the house. She took three seconds to tell me that our parents were dead and that we needed to go. I heard them outside…the Shadows. It's different for Cassie, though. She watched…she saw them die. I'll never understand what that feels like."

My heart broke for them. I knew what it was like to lose a parent, to watch them die.

Kylan put an arm around his sister and pulled her into him. She leaned against him like her knees were going to buckle underneath her otherwise.

Her hand tucked her smooth hair behind her ear. She looked up at me with red tinging the corners of her eyes.

"I don't expect you to forgive me." I lowered my head, still keeping eye contact with her.

To my surprise, a smile spread across her face. Rachel looked up to Kylan and then looked back down to me. She shrugged her shoulders.

"If Kylan says you're worth it, then who am I to judge?" Rachel asked and smiled at me.

"Thanks," I answered her almost-compliment.

She left with a soft smile on her face, no doubt going after her sister. Kylan came up behind me and wrapped his arms around me.

"I'm sorry about Cassie." Kylan pulled me around to face him.

I glanced at the living room, formal and refined. Glistening pictures of their recent adventures filled the pristine walls. They were smiling, together, and happy.

"I want this," I whispered, almost scared to say it out loud. "I want this family. I want you."

"Give it time. They'll come around. Cassie too. Even if she is the most stubborn person I know," Kylan said, hiding a smile. "Other than you."

"Hey!" I smacked his arm.

He caught my hand and pulled me closer to him. "This family needs someone like you. I need you."

I smiled, relaxing into his arms.

Kylan reached forward and touched the gold locket around my neck. An unspoken question. The necklace belonged to my mother, Lydia. The only Level Five ever made.

The lab created her and realized she was too strong. They didn't want any Legend to have that kind of power. But it couldn't be undone. She escaped, and they never used the full strength of the serum again.

Then, she had me. As far as I knew, I was her only child.

But maybe even that wasn't true. Up until a couple days ago, I didn't even know about my connection to her, or my abilities.

The Shadows had kept all of that hidden from me in hopes that I would help them win the war with the new labs that were trying to replicate the original serum, as the documents and research were all burned to the ground courtesy of my mother.

The only tangible object I had that tied me to Lydia was this necklace.

She left a journal behind too, but that was still safely in Alec's grasp at the mansion, with the rest of the Shadows. Rumors said the inside of the necklace was supposed to hold the secret to how she was a Level Five.

I just had to open it.

"You don't have to if you aren't ready," Kylan said so sweetly as he held my hands.

We sat on the soft, sleek couches and toes of my shoes dug into the rug. After a week of crazy with the Shadows, the empty house felt like a warm, peaceful paradise.

"I want to, and I want you here. I love you," I said, sure and strong.

"I love you too."

His warm touch seeped into my shoulder. I took a deep breath and looked down at the ancient locket.

Whatever the risk, I wanted to know how she did it and I wanted to know the legacy she left behind.

My hands clutched the turmoil contained in the innocent metal. My eyes looked straight into the golden future in my hands. I took one last breath and pulled at the tiny clasp on the locket.

A shimmer of light traced the outside of the locket and the clasp released. The locket had been waiting for centuries to be opened by its rightful owner. Only her own child could access it.

I could almost hear it singing the praises of finally being freed.

My thumb pulled at the outer edge of the locket gently

as it unfolded in my hand just as I had pictured it would. I looked into the center of the open locket. The untouched gold sparkled in the light.

Three words were scripted in the center of polished gold. I held it closer to my eyes and saw the flowing letters, impossibly perfect.

"You are loved," I read aloud.

As my voice spoke the words, the locket answered.

A bright light flowed through my mind, healing as it went. A burst of emotion crashed through the mental walls that had stood for centuries. The walls Alec and his father created.

With the barriers crumbling, my mind was finally free. I could see everything. I realized what was held inside the locket all this time. It wasn't the code that Alec dreamt. It wasn't the secret the world fabled.

The reason only I could open it was because it was meant for only me.

My mother pushed me on a swing set, back and forth. The metal chains creaked against the frame. The sun warmed my back. She laughed as she caught me in her arms before letting me swing out again. We had the same bright blue eyes.

I felt the surge of joy flood my heart as it would've back then. Before I could tell Kylan what was happening, more images flooded in.

She was reading me a story as the moon rose in the night sky. Her hands pointed to the words as she taught me what they meant. The paper crunched in my hand, and the smell of the new ink on the pages lingered.

She held my hand as we walked in the garden, the smell of freshly cut grass surrounding us. The steps were familiar from walking the path nearly every day. She bent down to a bush and let me try a raspberry for the first time. The burst of tart flavor raced across my tongue.

She sang to me as I laid my head in her lap. My ears recognized the familiar voice. Her hand stroked through my blond hair. Her steady breathing lulled me into a daze. My eyes closed as I drifted off to sleep.

The light faded back into the unassuming necklace in my hand, and with it, the images. The few poignant memories remained on the front of my mind but what had flashed before me was decades of a lifetime.

It was everything I could recall from before the Shadows took me.

Legends lived much longer than humans. Our aging was different, slower. The Shadows may have taken me when I was young, but I had still spent so many years with her.

The locket held more than just moments frozen in time. It was my life.

My memories.

My mother.

Memories tied to a strong emotion are nearly impossible to forget. The more emotions I gathered across my life and tied them to memories with the Shadows, the more these old ones faded.

I never knew anything was wrong until their façade slipped long enough for me to understand what a prison the Shadows had created for me. When I went back to try and coax them up again on my own, I had nothing.

They were buried too deep to easily be resurfaced. They were gone.

Until that moment.

The locket taught me something that I never knew about myself. I had a mom who loved me, and I understood exactly how much. It showed me that I wasn't alone and that I never had been.

That was her great power, and it had nothing to do with her abilities as a Five.

The locket wasn't a secret. It was a lesson. I smiled at how useless this was to Alec, but how invaluable it was to me.

"What does it mean?" Kylan's voice broke my concentration.

I snapped back to reality and felt the simple weight of the locket in my hand. The fabric of my clothes touched my skin. The clean air filled my lungs.

"You'd have to be her child to understand," I muttered with a smile on my face.

Tears stung my eyes and I didn't bother blinking them away. I leaned my head onto Kylan's shoulder. He had given me a family that filled a void in my life. He had loved me unconditionally, even when he had every reason not to.

For that, I would be eternally grateful.

But what I wouldn't give for another moment with her. With Lydia. I knew her now. To be sitting on this couch with her stroking my hair. To have her blue eyes like mine look at me with pride and love. To have her soft arms around me.

In place of all of that, I had this locket. One little piece of her.

I wish I could tell her how much this meant to me. I was confused as to how she could have possibly known my intense need for exactly this.

But maybe she was like me. She knew I would need the same thing.

Kylan didn't talk anymore. He just reached forward and held me in his arms. My body curled into him and I held the locket close to my chest.

Right then, I held all the power in the world. True love. With that, there was nothing I couldn't do, nothing that could stand in my way. I was free.

My mind answered the call that echoed across centuries of time.

I love you too, Mom. I smiled.

A feeling of safety washed through me. Even if all my questions weren't answered yet. I looked at those beautiful green eyes next to me.

This was my life now. All of it. This beautiful family that was learning how to exist together. This past I had just been given back. All of us wandering through a world full of humans, together.

And not all humans were bad. My mind immediately thought of Lisa. Tomorrow would be the first time I would get to see her since leaving the Shadows' mansion.

I had risked everything when I challenged Alec the first time to leave the Shadows. I had risked my own life and Kylan's by challenging him again when I found out I was the Five.

Despite my victory, I didn't feel like it was over. Alec just gave up, and he never surrendered something he really wanted.

I wasn't sure how much of this I controlled and how much he still had planned for me.

I may be stepping forward into even more danger than before, but when Kylan had his arms around me, all I felt was safe. I sighed and laced my fingers in Kylan's.

Tomorrow would be a whole new day.

CHAPTER THREE

I shoved the plastic binders back on the thick, white shelf in my office and turned back to my smooth, uncluttered desk.

When I had started this analyst job, I was here to study the humans and hide. I stayed because I actually found myself enjoying it here.

I liked waking up every morning knowing I was going to see all of them. Lisa and the way she smiled at Chase and his baby face, Mr. Lyle and his monochromatic three-piece suits, John from accounting with a permanent hunch in his back from his computer that sat too low.

They weren't Shadows with fiery powers and tumultuous feuds between the different Levels. The creators and destroyers were the worst. As a changer, I hadn't bothered to involve myself in any politics there, I had just dominated whatever I tried in my own talent.

And I had been too obsessed with Alec to notice anyone else. Thayer came into view a couple of times, Nikki demanded her own attention from me. But it was mostly him.

This place was so different. Humans lived a completely different life than I had before. The type of life I wanted to involve myself in. I cared about the people here.

My mindless straightening of my already immaculate office and wandering thoughts were interrupted by a quiet knock on my doorframe. I turned to see Lisa's bright smile and tight curls fully unleashed around her face.

"Lisa," I smiled. "Come in."

"I just wanted to stop by and give you these." She walked over and handed me a small stack of papers.

"The reports from the other branches. Great, thank you," I said and set the papers down on my shiny desk.

"You're welcome," Lisa answered and stayed exactly where she stood.

Her hands swayed around her as her eyes wandered around the office. She bit her lip so slightly I almost missed it.

"Was there something else?"

"Oh, nothing," she sighed, trying to avoid my gaze.

I raised an eyebrow. "Okay, what's going on?"

She grimaced, hoping for a way out of saying whatever she was supposed to say.

"Mr. Lyle needs to speak with you," she muttered and stepped out of the doorway for me to exit.

I smiled at her and walked easily down the hall. Kylan was walking out of Mr. Lyle's office. He winked as I passed by him, and I thought about sticking my foot out to trip him.

The conversation was short and expected after my impromptu vacation time. At least that was the lie Kylan had told everyone when we came back.

Humans had rules we had to follow. Workplaces had procedures set in place for when two coworkers were in a relationship. All of it felt like it barely applied to us.

A vacation was hardly what I would call being kidnapped, brainwashed, and forced to torture Kylan by showing him that I would always be a Shadow at heart.

I doubted Kylan would actually associate being ripped away from home, drained of energy, and left for dead with the same thing as sitting on a beach to clear his head.

But that was the world we lived in. A world that sometimes collided with the schedule of the human world. It was far from a perfect fit, but it was good enough for now.

Lisa was waiting for me when I left Mr. Lyle's office and guided me to her own. She and Chase had just gone away together, and I could only imagine the news she had to spill.

I smiled and let her pull me in. But I caught a glimpse of Kylan at the end of the wide, bright hall. I could barely see his face past the light streaming through the floor-to-ceiling window behind him.

But his face had gone pale and his hand clutched his phone tight enough that it looked like it might shatter.

I glanced at Lisa, who followed my gaze and immediately backed off.

"I'll call you later," she said.

My hand waved at her, but I was already moving to Kylan. I pushed him back into his office and closed the door before he totally let loose whatever humanlike restraint he had.

Something told me this went far beyond the office and rules. This was more.

"Kylan?" I hesitated.

He was already pacing, way too fast. If anyone had been listening to the footsteps, it sounded more like running. I just stayed out of his path and kept one hand on the door.

His green eyes were wild as they searched on the carpet floor, up the walls, and finally back to my face.

"What's going on?" I lowered my voice.

"I need to…um…I need to talk to you," he blurted and ran his hand through his silky hair.

His fists tightened until his knuckles turned white. He was either nervous or angry. His feet pointed toward the door, so he didn't want to be here. He also avoided eye contact, which told me he was ashamed of what he was about to say.

"Sure, just tell me what's—" I started.

He stopped me and grabbed my wrist just below my fitted sleeve. His suit shifted with the movement and his eyes blazed with worry.

"Not here," he whispered and promptly led me out of the office.

He didn't speak or stop walking until we were outside. I tried to pull against him to slow him down as we made our way outside. If I hadn't dug my heels in, we would've moved too quickly for it be humanly possible. Something was definitely wrong and the only thing I could think of was his family.

He finally stopped when we reached the park with the shaded bench. The one where we had our first lunch together, both still pretending to be humans.

Everyone was still at work, so the passersby were limited. He warily watched everyone who strolled past. He finally released my wrist to let me sit on the bench. But he resumed pacing, a little slower this time.

"Kylan, talk to me," I finally asked in a hushed whisper. I was hoping he would explode and tell me what was happening.

"I got a call this morning, from Rachel," he started talking.

"Okay," I edged.

"She… I don't know how to say any of this," he said, so fast I could barely catch it.

I finally stood and caught his pacing body by the shoulders. I forced him to sit on the bench.

"Calm down and tell me what's happening."

He tapped his feet on the concrete nervously but remained seated.

"She's dating someone," he said, as if the words were like acid in his mouth.

I relaxed and realized that all of this was just a "big brother" reaction to Rachel bringing in someone new.

"Ah, and you don't like the guy?"

"Not for her." He clenched his teeth and shook his head.

Kylan was still on edge. This was more than just the normal reaction. I decided to push further.

"What's so wrong about him?" I laid my hand on his arm.

I could feel his pulse racing through his body. He shook his head and stared at the ground. He clasped his hands so tightly I thought he was going to break his own fingers.

"He's…" Kylan started.

"He's what? He's too tall, he's too nice, he's too old for her? What?" I said and instantly regretted the words as soon as they flew out of my mouth.

Kylan's seething gaze turned to finally meet mine. His eyes burned deep pools of guilt into mine.

"He's human," he finally managed to get out.

My jaw fell open. He shot back up and resumed pacing. This time, I didn't stop him. In fact, I thought about joining him.

"What?" I asked. "That's not—what?"

Not really wanting an answer, just no longer able to keep my thoughts to myself.

"I have spent years coexisting with humans and I still can't picture how someone could ever fall for such a…at least not in a romantic…" Kylan started, trying not to gag.

"How is that even going to work?" I wrinkled my nose.

My skin crawled just thinking about the two species together. It was like Rachel dating a baby. Humans seemed to be a lot like us, except they were weak, irrational, and their lives were so short.

Rachel would be at least a few centuries older than him. Centuries. It just felt wrong.

Kylan finished my rant. "What's she going to do when she gets hungry and desperate for energy? Or what happens when he gets old?"

"Okay, okay." I reached for him and dragged him back down to the bench. "Look, this isn't helping. The person we really need to talk to is—"

His phone rang with a sharp interruption. He turned the screen over and looked at the caller.

Rachel.

"I hung up on her after she told me the news. She hasn't stopped calling."

"Answer it," I coaxed.

Kylan looked at me and reluctantly tapped the answer key on the screen.

"Yes," he said through those same clenched teeth.

I motioned for him to take a deep breath and relax. He tried to follow. I rubbed his arm, trying to calm both of us. I couldn't hear Rachel's voice over Kylan's breathing and boiling blood.

"Does Cassie know?" he asked.

Another pause and a painful scowl on Kylan's face.

"Tonight? I don't think that's a good…" he started and, apparently, she cut him off.

To be fair, being patient wasn't Rachel's strong suit. She was accepting, kind, and adventurous. But she was also impulsive and every bit as stubborn as her sister.

"Fine, bring him over to my place tonight," he finished

and immediately ended the call. His eyes zeroed in on every business person enjoying a lunch break.

"She's bringing him to meet us?" I confirmed. That seemed worse than wrong. Why didn't she want to just run away with him, maybe have a few happy years, and then come back to reality?

It couldn't be serious. She couldn't be serious. With a human? Practically an infant? A shiver moved down my skin.

"Yes," Kylan answered curtly.

"I...I don't...I have no idea what to say here," I admitted, holding my own hands in my lap.

"I don't like the idea, but if this all ends badly, could you...could you change his memory?"

"Yes." My voice was heavy.

I had the ability to change a human's memories, but that was a lot of work. My changing talent had always centered on physical appearance. But I had done it before.

It took a significant amount of energy to do it properly. As a Shadow, I always had enough energy to complete a task like that, and still plenty to spare.

As a Rogue, a regular Legend, there was no way I could inconspicuously take that much energy from humans. I never carried around that much.

That wasn't the only hesitation. Taking away someone's memory can change them because it alters the way those experiences shaped them. Even if the memory was changed, it had a risk of returning.

Killing the parts of the brain that held those memories was even more dangerous, but definitely more final. When a human or Legend permanently loses parts of their mind, it can leave them altered in unpredictable ways.

Nikki had been the only one to successfully do it. I wondered if Alec had ever tried.

"Okay, good." He sighed out a breath of stress.

His shoulders relaxed slightly. We still had hours until tonight, and part of me wondered if Kylan's sanity would make it that far, or my own.

"You know what we need?" I perked up. Kylan looked at me.

His eyes were a swirling mess of worry and questions. I knew that look too well. I took his hand in mine and leaned in.

"A distraction."

Kylan's eyebrows pulled together and I smiled.

CHAPTER FOUR

"Kate, I'm not sure this is a good idea." Kylan looked around nervously.

I smiled and pulled on his hand. "Trust me, it's going to be fine."

In downtown Portland, a protest was erupting at Pioneer Courthouse Square. Humans covered the entire area, making the red brick underneath almost invisible.

This city was known for being loud and proud of its unique opinions. While most people were a bit strange, the city as a whole was the perfect place for an outsider to fit in.

As Legends, we were the definitions of outsiders in a human world.

"You want to walk into a horde of angry…people and stock up on energy. How is that going to be fine?" Kylan's eyes still bounced around wildly.

"Because there are so many of them," I started to explain.

"Exactly—there are so many of them," Kylan threw back at me, still standing firmly in his place.

Kylan eyed me nervously, clearly out of practice in taking energy from people. He told me that he had taken lives before. I still had not asked if they were Legend or human lives. Knowing he was an Extractor meant it could have been either.

Judging by his nervous stance and stuttered breathing, I would guess they were not human.

"Listen, we walk through the crowd, taking a little more than we normally would. It's warm outside and these people are either excited or angry. Which means that their energy is even better than if they were calm. It also means that they won't notice if a little bit goes missing," I coached and moved closer to the clamor, pulling Kylan behind me.

A group this large was like a goldmine for the Shadows. We could race through here without even killing anyone and come out with enough energy to last an entire day of using our abilities as much as we wanted.

I could taste the power in the humid air. I almost forgot I was still holding Kylan's hand at all.

But quietly, he asked, "How do you know when to stop?"

"I don't." I tried to hide my smile. "It's a guess every time."

"You're not exactly making me feel any better," Kylan grumbled.

Something about this moment was more thrilling than teaching any Shadow recruit. It wasn't about murder or vengeance. This was fun. It was all about having enough energy to breathe easily the rest of the day, maybe a bit more.

Kylan wasn't a random stranger that I was charged with teaching. He was the person that I saw my future with.

Until now, that future had included living on a meager energy amount and being closer to living a human life than a Legend one.

It was a little different now. It wouldn't be like the Shadows, but maybe it could be a happy medium between the two. A medium where I wouldn't have to restrain myself as much to appear normal.

"We need this, Kylan," I started my argument. "A human is coming to your home tonight. We have no idea what's going to happen or what we're going to have to do to fix it. We need as much preparation as possible."

"I know, but you're talking about taking more than just what's needed. Aren't you?"

Kylan's eyes darkened and his lips tightened. I forced a smile.

"I'm talking about being ready to protect your family."

I reached forward and touched the first human's hand. She was a slender redhead with sleeves that covered most of her arms, despite the warm weather.

She didn't notice when I touched her; others were pressing on her as they moved past too. So I let my finger stay connected to her skin longer than I should have.

The warm energy burst from the human's skin into mine. The power swirled into my muscles and even into my bones, making me forget about the thick, humid air. The sensation mixed with each breath I pulled in.

My eyes moved to Kylan in a bliss-fogged stare.

"Kate," Kylan warned, looking at the human.

I pulled my hand away and she didn't even flinch, just adjusted her stance and kept facing away.

I stepped back to Kylan, and he watched my eyes and the human girl. She did reach up to her shoulder and rub the muscle connecting to her neck. She was tired. Her body felt the lack of energy, but because of the crowd and the circumstance, she didn't even bother looking over at me.

"Trust me," I mouthed to Kylan.

His green eyes didn't relax. They lit up and looked around at the crowd. I felt the buzzing energy inside my body and all I wanted was just a little more.

"I'm probably going to regret this later." Kylan shook his head and stepped into the crowd with me.

We weaved in and out of the lines of people. They wore bright colors, and half of them carried signs. Their arms were tired, their bodies dehydrated, and their feet probably ached. Anything we stole exacerbated all of those symptoms.

Without energy fueling them, their bodies wilted as we walked by. No one was injured or missed the energy we took.

It was a rationalization.

I knew what I was allowing myself to do, and how much I had been wanting it for a long time. I knew it was wrong to take so much, to want so much. Every touch brought a flurry of exciting energy into my body. I wanted every moment to last forever.

If I held on too long, I could take it all.

The human would drop dead on the ground, and I'd be feeling too good to even fathom guilt. I knew I shouldn't do that, but the line between murder and safety blurred more and more with each step.

With each touch, I wanted more energy.

This kind of lifestyle was impossible to maintain on a daily basis, but that didn't stop me from thinking about it.

Today. I could do this today.

I slipped by hundreds of people, unnoticed, but glowing with warmth. Kylan walked behind me. I glanced back at him now and then.

His moves were deliberate. He controlled himself more than I could. He mouthed the number of seconds he held the connection before breaking the skin-to-skin contact.

No more than three or four seconds. Every time.

I stopped walking and instead turned to face him. People surrounded us on all sides, half of them shouting, the other half probably wondering why they were still standing out here.

"Do you ever just let go?" I asked, looking up at him.

It was a real question, honest. His green eyes squinted as he thought. That only twisted my stomach more.

"What do you mean?" he asked.

"I mean, do you ever just stop thinking about what you need. Do you ever just…take as much as you want?" I clarified, keeping my voice low for the humans bustling around us.

"Thinking like that can really hurt people." Kylan shook his head.

I refused to let the guilt penetrate me yet. He had to know exactly what I meant before he could really answer. Until then, I didn't know he was that much better than me. I opened my mouth once more, stepping even closer to him.

"What if it didn't hurt anyone? What if all it did was make you feel…better?" I asked again, hoping to get a different reaction.

"I've done that before." Kylan looked down at the ground and the faintest smile crossed his mouth.

I clung to that smile. To the person that could think about energy and not immediately back down. His eyes lit up even if he kept them focused on the bricks.

"With which kind?" I finally asked the question buzzing in my ignited mind.

His gaze wandered through mine as he looked at how excited I was, how happy I just became. He sucked in a sharp breath and closed his eyes.

Legends, he mouthed the answer.

"Wait, really?" I asked, suddenly interested in the past that Kylan never detailed for me.

Kylan didn't want to draw attention to us. He grabbed my hand and pulled me to the edge of the mass of people.

The few lingering humans were just out of earshot if we kept our voices down. Kylan released my hand and locked eyes with me.

I waited, waited to see that smile again. But it vanished as soon as he started talking.

"Think about the moment that you touched Derek. The feeling of that incredibly strong energy pouring into your body. Compared to normal energy, it's…it's like liquid bliss and power and excitement all mixed into one. So, yes. I have let go. I have taken everything I wanted. I have been so utterly high that the guilt couldn't even touch me," Kylan finished with a grim gaze. "I know what it's like to live without any restraint. I remember everything I'm missing."

"And?" I pressed, my nerves racing underneath my skin.

"It was the best and worst years of my life. And I decided that I never wanted to do it again. The more energy I had, the more I craved. It became excruciating to control myself at all," he whispered.

"But if you learned to control it, like Rachel or—" I started, my energized heart jumping at the opportunity.

"Rachel is using human energy. For me and you, that's not the same anymore. You have no idea how many people, Legends, would have to die before I figured out how to really control myself on that kind of power. How many lives is it worth for me to be more comfortable?" he hissed back, closing his eyes.

He ran his hand through his hair. He wasn't angry at me. He was angry at himself. Any rage that threatened to come out was quickly internalized.

"Look, I'm not sorry for asking. I'm just new to being an Extractor…kind of." I stepped back.

"Then remember this. Losing control is not safe for anyone. I don't want to live like that." He hung his head and kicked at the red bricks.

"Ever?" I confirmed.

"Not if it means hurting other people."

My heart split as his words sunk in. He never wanted to live on the edge. He never wanted to let go. He never wanted anything close to what I wanted.

Despite being surrounded by hundreds of people, I felt alone.

It may not be the life he wanted, but it also may not be the life I needed. I thought about how I was ready to give up looking for the locket just to stay with him.

It was a search that had consumed decades of my life and threatened my safety from Alec. I had left the Shadows to go on this search and hid from them for decades. I had raced across miles of the globe trying to track even a whiff of a lead.

But having Kylan was worth more to me than all of that.

My buzzing hand reached out to touch his. His eyes looked back up at me, hoping that I would drop the subject.

"Thank you for explaining that to me."

I tried to smile but the very energy threading through my body seemed to weigh me down.

"I know it's not the life you're used to," Kylan started. "If you want—"

"Stop right there," I raised my other hand. "If I wanted the life I had before I could run back to the Shadows. I left for a reason."

I had to say it. I had to think it. Kylan was everything good and warm and safe. I wanted him. As much as I wanted the energy I used to thrive on, it wasn't worth losing him.

If I had to choose, I already knew what I would pick. What I had to pick. It was Kylan. From the moment he looked at the dagger on my arm and chose to love me anyway. It was him.

But more than that, it was every wink in the hallway at the office. It was every smile he kept hidden from his family when he didn't want them to see him blush. It was even the way he stumbled around his power like he didn't remember he was a Four.

Even more, it was that when he held me in his arms, the rest of the world fell away.

Choosing between all of that or the high-inducing energy I had been trained to crave, it wasn't a real choice. At least not anymore.

When he saw the sympathy in my eyes, he relaxed. He turned my hand around in his, lacing his fingers with mine.

"I hope you know how much I love you." His green eyes locked onto mine.

The protest faded into the background. The city buildings surrounding the square could have been invisible. It was just the two of us, holding onto each other.

"You better," I joked, and a smiled finally released on his lips.

A familiar happiness sparked in his eyes. My heart sped in my chest. I stepped closer to him, placing a hand on the side of his face. His eyes never left mine.

He just tilted his head into my hand. A bright flutter released in my stomach.

"I have another idea." Kylan smiled.

CHAPTER FIVE

I could hardly breathe. Not that I wanted to.

Completely silent, I didn't even blink. I listened to my surroundings, hoping something would give him away. I waited. Then waited longer.

The extra energy whirred through my body. The rush awakened all of my senses. I could see, hear, and feel everything at a higher level. A pale comparison to me as a Shadow, but I was much higher than I normally allowed.

Then, I heard it.

The tiniest sound of a foot crushing the carpet. I knew exactly where he was. I smiled and shot up from my crouched stance.

The kitchen counter stood between me and Kylan's unsuspecting back in the living room. He had guessed my location wrong. I took the chance to shoot.

I sent a red Swedish fish directly toward the back of his head. He spun at the last second and caught it in his mouth.

Frustrated, I fired off three more, too quick for a human

to see. He moved even faster and caught the first two in his mouth. Before I saw him catch the third, I put my hand on the counter and threw myself over to the other side.

Midair, I tossed another candy at him. He snatched it. One more fired as I landed. Kylan leaned all the way down and caught that one too.

"Ha, victory!" Kylan threw his hands in the air, mouth full of red candy. I smirked and crossed my arms.

I walked toward him and slowly pointed behind him.

"Actually, I think you missed one," I said sweetly.

He turned, and we both looked down at one bright red fish lying on the white carpet.

"No!" Kylan shouted.

I laughed at how dramatically he was taking the loss. It was a simple game, too easy for the Shadows, but perfect for us. He whipped around and looked back at me.

"Hey, don't be a sore loser." I raised my hands in defense and smiled, stepping away.

"Too bad I don't know any other kind," he taunted and lunged for me.

I let him wrap his arms all the way around me. My feet left the floor and I landed gently on the couch behind him. I fell with my back to the couch, and he followed right on top of me.

His afternoon scruff brushed my cheek. His body pressed up against my front and the couch held me up from the back. My heart raced. All thoughts of any of the day's stress vanished as I looked into his hopeful eyes.

"Who's the real winner here?" Kylan asked playfully and leaned down.

Before his lips met mine, I locked one of my legs around his and pinned it down. Using that leverage, I threw him off and onto the floor next to me, flat on his back.

He huffed, trying to catch his breath. I twisted off the couch and leaned down. I laid my body on top of his. I was so small compared to him. Fire bloomed underneath those green eyes.

"Still me," I answered.

He pulled my face in close and kissed me. For that moment, our hands wrapped in each other's hair and our lips danced. Our bodies were brimming with energy and our hearts raced to keep up.

Those strong hands splayed across my back, taking up most of the space there. Nothing could hurt me while he held me like that.

"So, this was your big idea to avoid an argument?" I breathed against his mouth, "Distracting me?"

Kylan's lips spread into a smile. His heart raced under my chest. He opened his eyes long enough to let his gaze roam across my face. He lifted a hand under my chin and tilted my head to a better angle.

"It's working isn't it?" Kylan whispered, trying to steady his breath.

My mouth kissed his again. Soft and strong, warm and scorching all at the same time. His hand moved from my chin to the back of my neck. The only thing I wanted, the only thing I could think about, was Kylan.

Derek's booming voice ended that moment. "Oh, come on."

The door slammed into the wall so hard it would definitely leave a hole.

Kylan and I both looked at each other, savoring the last drop of the moment before we sat up.

"Rachel is clearly having a mental breakdown and you two are in here doing this?" Cassie's shrill voice started in before Derek touched her arm.

It was nice to hear her again. After the big secret reveal, she hadn't spoken a word to me. She had barely even spoken to Kylan. But her sister dating a human must have made her just desperate enough.

"Not that I don't approve," Derek muttered to Kylan and then snapped back to attention. "But we have been calling you guys all day."

I stepped off Kylan and he sat on the floor for a moment before standing up. Derek looked at Kylan and tried to hide his thumbs up gesture. I jerked my head and caught Kylan's smile in return as he straightened his shirt and stood.

No matter the tension, those two were always brothers. I tried not to laugh, guessing that their lightheartedness would send Cassie through the roof.

"Man, what are we going to do with you?" Derek's casual voice melted into a stressed tone.

Reality came ringing back into place. The distraction had worked, but we both knew it wasn't permanent.

"Well, until we talk to Rachel, there isn't much we can do," Kylan wisely answered.

He had a much clearer head than he did a few hours earlier. His voice was calm, and he even stood a little taller. I smiled at my accomplishment.

"She won't answer any of my calls," Cassie huffed and waited for Kylan to fix it.

"Rachel is bringing him over here. Tonight," Kylan announced. Everyone looked at each other and nobody knew what to say. "So, everyone just sit down and wait."

So we all sat.

And waited.

In the most awkwardly charged silence.

The second hand on the clock was louder than anyone's breath. We all wondered what would happen and if it would go well.

So when Rachel opened the front door it felt like more of

a relief. Cassie jumped out of Derek's arms and bolted to her sister.

"Whoa, sis." She laughed as she closed the door behind her. She was here alone.

"Why have you not been answering your phone?" Cassie's questions unloaded. "Did you finally come to the realization that dating a human is a terrible idea? Who is he? Wait, is he just outside?"

Rachel finally clapped her hand over Cassie's mouth. Once she was confident that the questions had stopped, Rachel released her sister.

"His name is Jacques, and he's waiting outside in the car," Rachel said slowly.

Even her breaths were careful. She understood the sea of eggshells she had just walked into.

Derek took over for Rachel and pinned Cassie by wrapping his arms around her from behind. Cassie waited in silence but with impatience brimming from her eyes.

"Rach..." Kylan sighed.

She took a moment before meeting Kylan's eyes. She finally looked at him and took a deep breath.

"Rachel, what were you thinking?" Derek asked, less accusatory than Cassie.

That didn't take her gaze away from Kylan. The look in her eyes showed her respect for Kylan and how she needed his approval for something.

I had promised myself I wouldn't reach into any of their minds. Now was especially a tough time to keep that promise. I settled for waiting for a verbal response like everyone else.

"Does he know about the rest of us?" Derek asked.

Rachel nodded and all of us took a step back from her.

Betrayal crept up through me, sending shivers down my arms. I couldn't imagine what her family of decades was feeling.

"He's not going to say anything to anyone. He knows how important it is for us to keep this a secret," she explained.

"From what? Your excellent example of keeping secrets?" Cassie bit the words, anger clouding her eyes.

"How could he understand? It's not him that'll be dragged off to a lab to be dissected, studied, or just straight-up killed." Derek interrupted. "He has nothing to lose compared to us. Trust me, I know exactly what happens to Legends who enter a lab, forcibly or not."

Derek's parents joined a lab in their efforts to recreate and improve Legends. The price of such research was the pain and suffering of countless existing Legends. When Derek wouldn't stand for it, his parents disowned him.

I hadn't thought about how deep this would cut for everyone in the family. Derek was insulted, to say the least. Cassie was shocked that Rachel would ever betray her trust. Kylan was disgusted at the thought of letting a human into the family.

"I'm sorry." Rachel's eyes glued themselves to the floor.

She crossed her hands in front of her in the humblest approach I had ever seen her take.

"Rachel, have you thought this through?" Kylan softened his tone.

"You can't actually have a future with him," Cassie said. "You're too different from each other."

"We are not all that different from humans." Rachel's eyes lit up at that comment.

"Not that different? Um, how about strength, abilities, the way you eat, his need for sleep, or even *aging*. How can you say we're not that different?" Derek finally burst, releasing

Cassie from his grip. "In twenty, thirty years, you two are really going to *look* different from each other. You'll look like you haven't aged a day and he'll have gray hairs coming in. Rachel. Think."

"I have been!" she shouted and balled her fists.

Kylan reached his hand up to block Derek. The movement earned him a glare but Derek relaxed on his heels.

"You think this was an easy decision for me? I never thought it was going to come to this point. But I love him. He is everything I have been looking for." Rachel's sweet voice made even me forget what was at stake.

I understood what it was like to love someone you shouldn't, someone that put you in danger.

"Except for the fact that he will be dead in sixty years," Derek muttered from the back of the room. Rachel didn't flinch.

"She heard you. Back off." Kylan shot him a glance and Derek shut his mouth.

"Kylan, what do you think? If you say I'm not allowed to bring him into our lives, then I won't. I trust your judgment more than my own right now." Rachel looked directly at Kylan.

Her happiness was hanging in his hands. His shoulders tensed as the responsibility settled in. I put my hand on his shoulder and felt him take a breath.

"Bring him in." Kylan nodded to Rachel.

The smile spread quickly on her face. She jumped forward and threw her arms around him briefly. All eyes were on Kylan. He reached up and patted her on the back. With that encouragement, she raced out the door. As soon as the door shut behind her, the second round of questions had begun.

"What do we do now?" Cassie asked Kylan for his advice.

"We are going to be polite and see how this thing goes tonight. I don't agree with Rachel's choice, but regardless, she has already made it. I think we all know how determined she can be sometimes. So, the way I see it, we can either try to get to know this guy or lose Rachel." Kylan looked at Cassie now. "And I don't think any of us want that."

Cassie nodded solemnly, still too shocked and angry to speak. Derek reached his arm around her, his touch calming her instantly. Cassie's eyebrows relaxed and she took her first full breath in minutes.

We looked out the glass of the front door. We could see the two of them approaching, hand in hand.

The two of them looked so unalike but the biggest difference was the obvious was he looked so utterly human. Softer, weaker, and somehow younger than the elegant, gorgeously sleek woman sauntering next to him.

"Well, here goes nothing." Derek cracked his neck.

CHAPTER SIX

Rachel stepped through first, and then came Jacques.

Everyone in the room tensed. Jacques shut the door behind him and took a look around at all of us.

None of us had the restraint to sit on the white, comfortable couches behind us. Instead, we huddled between the coffee table and door like the worst greeting crew ever.

He stood a few inches taller than Rachel, not quite as tall as Kylan or Derek. He had dark hair and brown skin. Compared to Rachel's fair complexion and red hair, they couldn't look more opposite. The only thing similar was their eyes. Both warm and brown.

It was difficult to not look at him as if he were a child. It was hard not to look at any human as inferior. He must have been a tenth of my age.

Jacques' eyes widened, trying to take everything in at once. He was nervous. Not only was he meeting his girlfriend's family, but they were all the deadly and infamous Legends that haunted the worst horror stories.

I almost felt sorry for him. Rachel held his hand proudly.

By the way they looked at each other, they were in love. It was like watching a train wreck happen. I just couldn't look away even if I tried.

"Everyone, this is Jacques," Rachel announced kindly.

She looked at him like he was what kept her steady. We all murmured our greetings to him in turn.

"Jacques, this is Cassie and Derek Challis, my biological sister and her husband." She motioned to the two of them first.

Cassie nodded and stood frozen in polite rage. Derek leaned forward and outstretched his hand to Jacques.

It was a normal gesture. But a Legend inviting a human to touch them was like asking them to play with fire. Without looking at Rachel for confirmation and almost without hesitation, Jacques took Derek's hand.

"Firm handshake." Derek laughed. "Rach, I like this guy already."

Rachel's shoulders softened. She smiled and mouthed *thank you* to Derek behind her boyfriend's back. Derek dropped the smile and nodded back to her. He wasn't doing her any favors; he just didn't want to give Jacques a reason to be scared.

"This is Kate Martin. She's fairly new here, but we like her." Rachel smiled.

I nodded, watching him carefully. His eyes lingered on me too.

"Then last, but certainly not least, Kylan…uh, Kylan Beck," Rachel paused on the name.

Kylan nodded his head at her assumption. This human probably knew nothing about Legend culture and didn't need to know that Kylan's true last name was Stone. For the moment, none of us needed the Shadow reminder.

They shook hands, and I watched Kylan's face. This was hard for him, but he allowed a smile to break through.

"Kylan, I think you are the one I've heard the most about. Rachel sings your praises all day long," Jacques said.

I watched Jacques now. Rachel's gaze made it obvious that she wanted him. I just needed to know why he would step into a den of Legends for a woman. It didn't seem like a good enough reason.

Jacques looked at Kylan in awe and also seemed relieved that Kylan looked fairly normal.

My mind blazed with the remaining energy. I tried to keep my focus, but everything seemed to shine for the first time in months. I narrowed my eyes and looked back at the green eyes that always brought me peace.

"Rachel is very kind." Kylan smiled. The couple relaxed now that the introductions were over.

"Well, come on in and sit down." Derek guided us. "Cassie has been dying to know more about you since Rachel first mentioned your name. You know, earlier today."

Rachel glared and Jacques gave a forced laugh as they sat on the couch. The awkward silence and pained stares ensued.

"Well, uh, how did you two meet?" I asked a seemingly harmless question.

Jacques answered. Bold. "We met at the hospital. Rachel was volunteering there and I was a patient for a brief while. I was in a car accident and needed to stay a few days to make sure everything healed. Rachel was the prettiest volunteer there. When I got out, I looked her up."

"He caught me off guard when he called. He made it sound like this was a pity date, so I thought there would be no harm in humoring him for a day," Rachel interjected. "We went out horseback riding and then swimming."

Cassie's eyes lit up as she looked at her sister. That was exactly something that Rachel would love, and Jacques had pegged that before even really knowing her at all. Observant.

"I think she was expecting dinner and a movie," Jacques added.

"I obviously did not dress appropriately. He kept it all a surprise," Rachel interjected, clearly embarrassed by that.

"You looked great." Jacques reached over and put his hand on Rachel's.

I still shuddered, thinking about how she could kill him right now and he wouldn't be able to stop her. She would never dare, and her self-control was impressive anyway. But that didn't stop my mind from reading this as a threat to him.

He smiled easily. Either stupid or trusting.

"It was the most exciting date I'd ever been on. Despite my better judgment, all I could think about was seeing him again," Rachel said.

"She handled everything so well. Best date in a long time. After I dropped her off, I was already planning the next one." Jacques looked at her the same way she gazed at him.

They were head over heels and I caught Kylan wincing.

"Sappy," Derek mocked quietly. Cassie shoved an elbow into his arm.

Kylan and I smiled. Rachel perked up out of her trance to roll her eyes and grumbled, "Very funny."

Jacques looked between her and Derek with furrowed brows. We all took a glance between each other. Then we looked at Rachel to see how she was going to handle this.

"Derek made a joke about how 'sappy' we sounded." She smiled and linked her arm in his.

"Oh, yeah." Jacques tried to brush it off.

The uncomfortable silence resumed. Everyone else in the room froze. In the presence of other Legends, these people were fun and witty, but enter a human and they all looked petrified. No one wanted to tread on the ice that just thinned.

I jumped in again, hoping to allow my mind to concentrate on something other than my fidgety energy.

"All right, Jacques, we know you're human. When did you figure out that Rachel wasn't?" I asked the question on everyone's mind.

"We went camping together, and she seemed a bit off. We had only been out a couple of days. I thought she was just cranky because she was sick of being out in the woods. She asked to take a walk by herself. I was worried she might get lost or hurt, so I followed to keep an eye on her. She went to a campground about a half mile away. I watched her…um…take energy from a couple that was sleeping outside," Jacques said with a struggle.

"She turned around and saw me standing there. The look on her face...She ran to me, like ran really fast. I was scared, and I had no idea what to do. I'd heard about Legend stories when I was in elementary school, as a joke. I just never imagined that I'd actually meet one. Ever."

Jacques stopped talking and looked around the room at all the Legends sitting in front of him now.

It looked like it was starting to sink in for him. He was surrounded by a group of superior beings that could end his life before he took his next breath. He didn't seem scared anymore though. He seemed…fascinated.

I narrowed my eyes at him.

"I had no choice but to tell him. It's not like he was going to forget," Rachel continued for him. She glanced at me briefly. "We spent the rest of the night talking about Legends, and I explained everything to him. I don't know how, but I knew I could trust him."

"She didn't kill them though, the couple. I should've said that. She told me that you guys don't take enough energy to actually hurt anyone," Jacques finally caught up to the conversation. Kylan couldn't help but crack a smile.

"Jacques, we know," Kylan laughed the words. "Rachel wouldn't hurt a fly, much less a human."

The laughs rippled through the rest of us. Even Jacques forced a smile.

"Do you have any questions you want to ask us?" I invited and held back a gag.

He looked at Rachel briefly before speaking. She nodded. He seemed like the type of person who took risks, yet in this situation, he backed off.

"Do you ever wish you were human?" Jacques asked.

His eyes stayed linked with Kylan. Kylan took a moment, and his head tilted to the side as he thought. My eyes locked back on Jacques. He was awfully curious.

I should have let this amount to him being a human who just wanted an answer, but I couldn't shake the weird feeling when I looked at his eager eyes.

Maybe too many years with the Shadows had made me paranoid.

"The thought has crossed my mind that it would be easier," Kylan began solemnly. "But I think it's a miserable existence to want to be something that you aren't. I find it better to make the most of what I am and where I am now."

The caution in his words to both Rachel and Jacques was obvious, even if only to the Legends in the room.

"Well spoken," Jacques commented.

"I have a question," Cassie perked up, and I already worried what she was going to say.

She scooted forward on the couch so she was within reaching distance of Jacques. The poor kid didn't even shy away from her.

"I want to know what it feels like," Cassie asked, raising her eyebrow.

"What do you mean?" Jacques asked.

"To lose your energy. I want you to describe what it's like for you." Cassie reached her hand out.

This was the moment where we got to see which one was the braver, or more stupid, out of the two of them. By the looks of it, Jacques wasn't going to back down from this seemingly unthreatening girl.

I had to admit, it was strange being so up close and personal with a human that knew I was a Legend. The others must have been feeling something similar. I had Lisa, but she thought I was human. It was easier.

Having Jacques know and having him sit right in front of us, unafraid, was surreal.

"Cassie, don't do anything stupid..." Rachel started.

"It's okay." Jacques nodded.

He didn't flinch at all as he grabbed Cassie's hand. Cassie didn't waste a second before she started pulling energy out of him. Judging by what I could see, she wasn't pulling very much at all.

"Um..." Jacques looked down at his hand. "I can't really feel anything. I think it tingles a little, but maybe tingle isn't the right word."

"Okay, what about now?" Cassie asked again, narrowing her brown eyes.

The wispy light around Jacques' hand brightened as Cassie tightened her grip. Jacques took a sharp breath in, still not moving away.

"Yeah, I definitely feel that." Jacques blinked, struggling to think. "It feels like I just got done hiking and the high is gone and now I can feel how tired I am. Except, I just keep getting more...more tired."

"What else?" Cassie prodded.

I kept to myself. I already knew the answer to that question. There had been quite a few times when Alec or I had asked my victims to describe what they felt. They had complied, all the way to the point that they no longer had enough energy to speak.

Jacques' eyes fluttered slightly, and Rachel grabbed Cassie's arm immediately.

"That's enough," Rachel ordered.

"Oh please, he's fine." She glared. "What else?"

"I…I'm not…" Jacques tried to pull his arm away weakly. Cassie held on and smiled.

"I said, that's enough." Rachel threw Cassie's hand off and put her arm in front of Jacques defensively. The human sat back into the couch, trying to catch his breath.

"You just saw me take a huge amount of energy and now you want to challenge me?" Cassie smiled, egging her sister on.

"Please," Rachel hissed and leaned forward, her straight teeth snapped at her sister. "You think that's anything compared to what I have?"

But the two women locked eyes, neither of them flinching. Derek looked like he was trying not to smile.

Rachel's smile widened as Cassie leaned back into the couch.

Cassie knew she couldn't take on Rachel, not without preparation first. Even though Cassie was a Two and Rachel was only a One, Rachel kept more energy in her system than anyone else in the family.

I admired her for it, while the rest of them condemned her.

Jacques' jaw had dropped when he saw Rachel's eyes flash yellow. He scooted back, taking sharp glances at Cassie.

That was the point of Cassie's little stunt.

It wasn't for Rachel, and it definitely wasn't for her own curiosity. Cassie wanted to make sure that Jacques knew he wasn't anything like us. She wanted him to know that he did not belong in the family.

It was a smart plan. If Rachel refused to think clearly, maybe Jacques would.

CHAPTER SEVEN

The door clicked shut behind the happy, now distressed, couple. They still held hands as they left.

All of us took a breath of relief now that he was gone. The silence filled the void that Rachel and Jacques had created. No one wanted to speak about what just happened.

"A human…" Cassie stood with hands like claws. "How can she be with a human?"

"Well, he was really nice," Derek offered and shrugged his shoulders.

"He did seem fairly smart," Kylan added.

"It wasn't as bad as I thought it was going to be," I chimed in.

Cassie ran her fingers through her already-wild red hair and froze in front of the door, snapping her eyes to us.

"It was awful," Kylan muttered. I nodded.

"Terrible." Derek shook his head.

"Thank you!" Cassie threw her hands up.

"But," Derek sighed and stared at the floor. "You know why it doesn't bother her that he's human."

We waited. A heavy weight settled on my stomach when he looked at me before anyone else. As if I knew the answer. "Think about it. He's probably not going to be human for very long."

"No." Cassie inhaled.

"She's gonna change him," Derek said and briefly glanced at the others.

"She can't do that," I muttered.

"She can," Derek's voice cut through the air. "The Louisiana lab had a successful trial serum ready about a few years ago. I have no doubt it's functioning now."

"Why would she?" Cassie wrinkled her nose. "I mean, there are plenty of Legend guys she could choose from."

"How do you know that?" I asked Derek, who seemed like the only one still on topic.

"One of the only perks of my parents working for a lab is that everyone trusts the Challis name and, coincidentally, my voice sounds exactly like my father's. I've kept tabs over the years." His dark eyes held back the rest of the explanation.

"That doesn't make sense," I thought out loud. "If the labs had a functional serum that could create other Level Fives, how have we not heard about it?"

"I haven't heard anything about the Levels they can create. Maybe they didn't make it to Five." Derek shook his head.

"Kate's right. The Shadows would be at their throats if Alec thought he could get that kind of power," Kylan added.

"They must not have created the complete serum," I said to myself.

"Either way, that doesn't change anything for Rachel," Derek redirected, looking tentatively at Cassie. "Legend is still Legend."

She shook her head. "No, no, that's…she wouldn't."

"Calm down. We don't even know what she's planning." Kylan raised his hands.

Derek looked pointedly at him. "I know. Cassie knows. So does your girlfriend."

"Not until I hear it from Rachel's mouth," Kylan answered him and Derek shrugged his shoulders, not backing down.

Cassie caught my eyes and nodded toward the door. I jumped at the chance for her to reach out to me for help.

"We're going to get some fresh air," I announced as she towed me along.

She bolted out faster than I expected and I followed. We dodged the few trees in our path to privacy. Once we were out of earshot, she stopped and turned around to face me.

"I don't...I do not have a good feeling about this," Cassie immediately sputtered. "Derek's probably right, but...but this is Rachel we are talking about. She'd be trusting a lab. We can't let her just walk in there. What if it's a trap?"

"Right, and Jacques is in on it? Cassie, that doesn't even make sense. You saw the kid. He was terrified of you," I said, trying to rationalize with her.

"He should be," she scoffed and rolled her eyes. "Anyway, I thought you were on my side?"

"Trust me, I am," I soothed. "I don't like the idea of her dating a human or turning him either."

As the words came out, I resisted shuddering. I didn't want to think of them together or of her walking in the front door of a lab and offering herself up to them.

"We've got to convince her otherwise." Cassie tapped her finger on her chin.

"Okay, but if we just sit her down, she'll feel ambushed." I folded my arms.

Nothing we did was going to change Rachel's mind. She was every bit as stubborn as her frantic sister.

"Girls' night," Cassie whispered and stopped. "Let's not lecture her, let's get her to talk about it. The three of us can hang out and relax, braid each other's hair, and get Rachel to realize she is making a big mistake."

"The two of us and her? She'll see right through that." I waited for her to try again.

"Well, if we don't come up with another option then I am prepared to kidnap her and strap her down in the basement until Jacques dies of old age," she snapped.

"Cassie..."

"Or of other causes. I'm flexible. Our basement is pretty sound—"

"Cassie!"

She threw her hands down. "She's my sister! You're telling me his life is worth more than hers?"

"Kylan's right," I said. "If you do something like that, you'll lose Rachel."

"Then help me fix this," she begged.

While she went back to pacing, an idea popped into my mind. The thought of saying it out loud made my stomach flip. But Cassie was on the verge of committing too many crimes to stay silent.

"I could invite Lisa," I offered and winced.

"Your human friend?" Cassie raised her eyebrow.

"My what?"

"Sorry, that's just what Kylan always calls her." Cassie shrugged her shoulders. "But yeah, that's perfect. Having a human there will make Rachel way more relaxed."

Lisa was so much more to me than just a token human. She was the one who convinced me to fall for Kylan. She helped me open up for the first time after leaving the Shadows.

Cassie's reaction drew my attention to everything I was keeping from Lisa.

"Well, I'll give her a call," I answered.

It was a simple girls' night. But something about this phone call seemed insurmountable. Whether that was putting Lisa too close to everything I wanted to keep secret, or feeling my two worlds cross paths, something felt wrong. I wanted them as separate as they could be.

I pulled out my phone and clicked on Lisa's contact. Her easy smile flashed in the picture. Each ring intensified my nerves until her bright voice answered.

We talked and I forgot why I was worried. Lisa had a calming effect on me, maybe because of how nervous she always was made me feel level-headed in comparison.

But she was coming. She would be there with all of us Legends, completely unaware.

I knew everything was going to be fine after talking to her. That was invaluable with Cassie next to me and fuming so much I wondered if she would explode.

We weren't of any threat to her, but being around us was dangerous. She had no idea what she was stepping into. Part of me felt like she had a right to know. It was a strange thought. I had never really considered humans' rights before.

She wasn't just a human, or a threat, or a food source, or anything like that. She was a friend.

CHAPTER EIGHT

A knock sounded at the door, and Cassie shot up from the couch. I stood slowly and caught her gaze as I shook my head.

"Sorry, this is your house," she said and gestured for me to answer the door.

"Keep it together. Rachel will sense a setup a mile away," I warned.

"I know, she's my sister, remember?" Cassie snarled.

I stopped and looked down at her. Cassie relinquished the nasty look on her face and faked a bow. I moved to the door and pulled it open.

The curly hair and bright smile waiting for me allowed me to relax.

"Hey, Kate." Lisa waved.

Her soft brown eyes seemed to dull the frayed, electrified ends of my nerves. I stepped to the side and let her in the house. Eager for her presence to calm Cassie as well, hopefully.

"I'm so glad you could make it," I said, and I honestly meant every word.

My eyes glanced at Cassie, who was trying to keep her hands to herself. Her palms were smashed together so hard they left white marks on the outer edges of her fingers.

"This is Cassie. She's Kylan's sister." I pointed and shut the door behind Lisa.

"Hi." Lisa put out her hand to Cassie and my body tensed.

It was an automatic reaction to a human offering bare skin to a Legend. But this was different now. After seeing what Cassie did to Jacques, I wondered who else could be collateral on her path to helping her sister.

I caught Cassie's eyes and watched her take a breath. She was supposed to be on her best behavior.

"Nice to meet you," Cassie answered and shook her hand lightly.

My eyes fixed where their skin met, and nothing happened. Lisa pulled her hand away and had a confused look on her face. My stomach knotted again when I flipped my stare back on Cassie.

"Don't take this the wrong way, but you don't look anything like Kylan," she observed and looked to me for an explanation.

"Oh…that's because…" I started.

"I'm married to his brother. Rachel, who you'll meet tonight, is my biological sister," Cassie answered smoothly.

That answer made sense. Of course it did. Maybe I was the one who needed to calm down and just let the night play out.

"Oh, that's great. I would have died to have a sister." Lisa shrugged and smiled.

I flinched at the poor choice of words. So did Cassie.

"Uh, do you want to come in? Rachel should be here any minute," I asked and pointed to the living room.

"Yeah, yes, thanks." Lisa walked in and looked around the house. "You have a beautiful home. It's really…"

"Clean?" I offered.

"Yeah." Lisa shied her eyes away from mine.

"Yes, I know," I sighed and looked around.

Few personal items lingered in plain sight. The walls were mostly empty, with only two photos that I actually cared about. One was of Alvie, my old dog. The other was Kylan and me sitting on our bench that Rachel had taken.

Besides that, the house was cold and hardly inviting, nothing like Kylan's home. He was the first person I allowed inside, and he mentioned the same thing.

Now, there were going to be three people in the place I kept so private. The vulnerability crawled on my skin like a bug I wanted to shake off. But this was a more neutral zone than Cassie's house.

Another knock sounded, and I looked at Cassie before I turned. She sat on the couch with Lisa, chatting but gripping the seat so hard that I thought she'd tear the fabric.

I opened the door and saw Rachel's auburn hair glinting in the last of the sunlight.

Showtime, I coached. Breathe.

"Rachel, come in." I stepped aside and she walked through the doorway

"Thanks," she said happily.

When I was about to shut the door, she caught my arm and pulled me toward her. Her lips brushed against my ear and her fingernails dug into my skin.

"Just between you and me," Rachel whispered and narrowed her eyes. "Did Cassie set this up?"

"No, I did. Hence, it is at my house. Look, even Lisa came, as promised." I looked to Lisa sitting happily on the couch.

The two of them were already giggling, however fake Cassie's must have been.

Rachel's shoulders relaxed slightly, and she warily stepped inside. I reached around her and took her coat from her hands. She shrugged it off slowly, keeping her eyes on her sister.

"I know she doesn't agree with me—" Rachel started and I interrupted.

"Rachel. Do you really think we'd invite a human to an intervention just for you?" I raised my eyebrows at her. "Get over yourself and come have some fun."

"You're right." She finally let go and stepped farther into the house.

Even Rachel knew she had a bigger ego than most. Telling her what she already knew was an easy way to lie. Something Thayer and Alec had taught me.

Before walking all the way into the house, she turned and looked at me. Her expression was too knowing and determined.

"You already know, don't you?" Rachel asked.

Her gaze was cold and unwavering. The decision to change Jacques. That was all the confirmation I needed. Derek was right, and Cassie was going to have a meltdown when she found out.

"It's not hard to put together," I answered her.

She must have known we'd suspect that she wanted to turn Jacques. If she really loved him, she would want to be with him longer than a handful of decades.

"You won't change my mind," she whispered back to me, still just out of earshot of Cassie.

"What if I'm not trying to?" I challenged.

She looked me up and down before walking into the living room.

We started off with painting our toenails. The most

human thing I could think of for a girls' night. Something about the scent of the polish and the ability to stare at the floor made all of us a little more open.

Every passing minute smoothed over whatever hard feelings we had when we came into the room. Even Rachel started to look relaxed.

"How long have you guys been dating?" Rachel asked Lisa.

She smiled when she talked, and it put me less on edge and Cassie more so. I could tell she was losing patience fast with the small talk, delaying any other agenda.

"Just under a year. I know it's a little early to be thinking like this, but there is just something about Chase that makes me feel..." Lisa tried to answer and looked up to find the right word.

"Makes you feel wanted," Rachel finished the sentence for her. "I get it."

"You two seem like such a good fit for each other," Cassie answered sweetly toward Lisa, but Rachel knew the comment was intended for her.

I silently begged for Cassie to keep it together a little longer. The last thing I wanted was her to lose it with Lisa in the room.

"That's the beautiful thing about love. No matter how different you are, it can still draw you together," Lisa answered innocently.

It was painful how unaware she was. Cassie's eyes flicked over to Rachel's growing smile.

"I couldn't have said it better myself." Rachel avoided Cassie's gaze and returned to the paintbrush in her hand.

"You know what this night needs?" Cassie perked up and quickly screwed on the lid. "Popcorn. Mom had this amazing recipe for the best caramel you've ever had. Pour a little on top of the popcorn, and you could be floating on a cloud. Lisa, would you come help me in the kitchen?"

"Uh, sure." Lisa tightened the lid on her own bottle.

"Great."

They linked arms and waddled to the kitchen, careful not to smudge their freshly painted nails. Cassie shot me a glance before she turned to face her distraction.

That was my cue.

But it was too obvious now. I held my breath and waited a few moments longer for us to be alone.

Thankfully, Rachel saved me by starting instead. "Can I ask you a question?"

"Of course." I kept my eyes on my drying nails.

"How did you know that you and Kylan could be together?" she started.

My mouth parted and nothing came out. She continued.

"I mean, you and he are very different. Different pasts, you know? What made you think that after all of it, you still loved him?" she clarified and finally looked up at me.

"It's okay to be different from each other," I started.

Her eyes lit up for a brief moment. I winced. I knew what I was about to say would crush whatever hope had just sparked inside of her.

"You just have to be moving in the same direction without trying to change things about each other," I added.

"Unlike me and Jacques." Her voice dropped and her eyes narrowed.

"Rachel, listen…" I started.

"I knew Cassie would try something. I just…" Rachel shook her head and errantly painted her toes. "I didn't think you would go along with it."

Her words sliced into me. She and I were similar. We both had sketchy pasts and were trying to be better. Both of us wanted a happy future, even if we didn't feel we deserved it.

The hurt in her eyes sealed the ache in my chest. I understood her more than anyone else in the family.

"I know how alluring it is to be with someone you aren't supposed to be with." I lowered my voice. "When I was with the Shadows, I was in love with someone. We were crazy about each other. You know, the kind where the sun rises and sets with them? Then I realized that I never really belonged there, and he still did. The only way we could be together was if one of us changed so drastically that we couldn't even recognize ourselves."

I paused, unsure how to finish. "It wasn't worth it, and in the end it really couldn't have worked."

"Well, if you were so in love with him, then what are you doing here with my brother?" She tossed back in my face.

I shook my head and changed the subject. "All of that was a long time ago, and not the point of the conversation. We are talking about you making a huge mistake."

There was too much of my relationship with Alec that she couldn't understand. Anything I said would either hurt me or Kylan, and none of it would help change Rachel's mind.

"I'm not an idiot. I've thought this though more than any of you can imagine. None of you, not even Cassie, can accept that I can make my own choices," she hissed at me.

I had never seen Rachel so fired up and seemingly careless. She was either crazy, or crazy in love. Neither of those options led to her having a sound mind if I tried to attack her any further.

"She's just worried about you," I tried to explain.

She rolled her eyes and clenched her fists. "I'm not dying."

"But you might. Trusting a lab is risky at best," I tried.

I reached forward and put my hand on her knee, just like I had back at the lake when she first told me about her business past.

"Wouldn't you risk it for Kylan?" she asked and locked her eyes on mine.

"That's not—"

"That's not the same thing? If Kylan was human and you could change him so he could be with you. Wouldn't you?"

The words caught in my throat. All the lines Cassie had been pounding in my head were stuck behind this logic barrier. As much as I didn't want to admit it, she had a point.

"Everyone is so quick to judge me without thinking what they would do in my shoes. Jacques is everything to me." She leaned forward and pleaded.

Those scared brown eyes, so similar to Cassie's. She needed at least one person on her side.

"You could find someone else. Someone better suited to your...lifestyle," I answered and instantly recognized how heartless it sounded.

"Because humans are so terrible? Need I point out that your best friend is a human too," Rachel threw back at me, nodding toward the kitchen, where Cassie and Lisa giggled about something.

"We aren't worried that he's human...Well, we are, but we're more worried about you dying in a lab trying to change him," I said.

"So you'd rather he stay human?" she asked.

But I knew she wasn't just talking about him. She meant Lisa too. Vulnerable. Weak. Unaware of the Legends around her. It was dangerous and heartbreaking to be close to us and never live on the same path.

"Yes. You two can be happy just the way you are, if that's what you really want," I answered in a hushed tone; our voices were getting almost loud enough to be heard over the sound of the popcorn popping.

"You really think the rest of the family would accept him if he wasn't like us? Did you not see how the other night went?" she asked.

"I'm saying it's not worth the risk..."

"Prove it then. Tell Lisa that you're a Legend, a former Shadow even. Then, assuming she accepts you, bring her to the family." Rachel lifted her eyebrow but her stare was serious.

"What would that prove?" I asked, already not having a good feeling about her answer.

"If you think that my human would be accepted, surely yours would too," she answered, and I didn't feel any better.

"That's not the same. Kylan already knows about her."

It was different. Totally different.

"And he's fine with her because she doesn't know anything about us. As soon as you tell her, everything changes," Rachel argued.

When I thought about her proposal, the pit in my stomach told me her logic was correct. She understood the impossibility of the challenge. She didn't actually want me to do it. She just wanted me to empathize with her.

"That would really change your mind?" I asked back with the same determination.

A glimmer of worry passed in her eyes, but she hid it quickly.

"I've spent centuries searching for anyone who could keep up with me, make me laugh, and give me a reason to be excited for a new day. Cassie was that for a while, but she has Derek and those two are always together. In fact, I'm surprised he's not here tonight." Rachel glanced at the kitchen where Cassie was.

"You can imagine Derek sitting here and painting his toes with us?" I raised an eyebrow at her.

"Hot pink. That idiot would do anything for Cassie," she said, staring at the carpet. "That's the kind of love I want. I want someone who would put me first, even above family."

"Someone to make me feel...wanted." Her fingers slowly closed the bottle she was holding and placed it back in the plastic container that held the rest of the tiny bottles.

"Jacques is that person for you?" I asked.

"Yes," she answered firmly. "If you can prove to me that we can exist as we are, then I won't go."

Cassie walked into the room holding a steaming bowl of popcorn. Her eyes found mine immediately and searched for reassurance. Lisa followed behind, happy and unburdened.

She had no idea the amount of confusion and danger I would rain down on her if I opened up about this. In that moment, I looked at her and mourned the relationship we had. If I told her, it'd be gone.

My hand touched the locket around my neck. I felt the rush of happiness as I remembered the unconditional love of family. Rachel was family to Kylan and she had become important to me. If I had a way to stop her from risking her life, then I had to try.

Cassie and Lisa stepped around the corner, still careful of the drying nail polish. Cassie held a bowl of steaming popcorn and Lisa laughed at a joke that I hadn't paid attention to hear. Lisa looked so innocent, so fragile, everything that I pictured a human to be.

My eyes found Rachel's one last time.

"Deal." I nodded.

She smiled darkly. She won this battle and now I had to decide if I was willing to put up a fight.

CHAPTER NINE

I paced back and forth in my office, crushing the soft carpet under my ballet flats. My hands clenched and released by my sides. My mind raced faster than I cared to follow. Instead, I stared blankly at the floor.

If I wanted Rachel to give up her idea of changing Jacques, I had to confess my story to Lisa. She seemed so loving and kind, but I had witnessed the kindest hearts turn bitter in the presence of a threat.

The second I revealed my past, that's exactly what I would become in her eyes.

"Kate?" Lisa's voice, along with her light knock on the door, interrupted my thoughts. "Can I talk to you?"

Perfect timing. I gulped down the rest of my nerves. Lisa waited patiently, her big eyes full of trust. She had no idea what was coming.

"Yeah, will you close the door?" I squinted and took a steadying breath.

Lisa came in the room and softly closed the door behind her. She turned around to face me again, relaxing her shoulders slightly.

"So this is kind of work-related," she observed and sat on one of the armchairs by the door.

I sat in the chair opposite her as she twirled her curly hair around her finger, her eyes looking at the floor instead of me.

"But you want it off the record?" I clarified and tried to find a starting point.

"Yes," she edged and looked up at me, trying to read my face.

She dropped her hand from her hair and settled it into her lap, shifting her position in the chair so she could sit straight.

"All right." I sat in the chair next to hers. "You may speak freely."

"I'm sure you have heard that Mr. Lyle is looking for a head of a new department," she asked slowly. The mood instantly shifted in the room.

"Yes, he is…" I spoke lightly.

"I'm thinking of applying," she blurted, and the surprise seemed to hit her as she finally heard those words out loud.

"That sounds great. Why would you not?" I asked, encouraging her to share.

"I've only been with the company for five years. It might be a little early. Plus, going from assistant to a department head is a huge step…" She trailed off.

"One that you are ready to take," I interjected.

Her eyes flashed an unexpected smile. The timid woman I had first met would hang her head and say as little as possible. This woman in front of me now almost looked eager for the challenge.

"Really?" she asked with her hopeful eyebrows raised.

"Absolutely. You can't stay an assistant forever, so why not now?" I answered and nodded.

"Do you think Mr. Lyle would take me seriously? I mean, I'm a woman and most of the department heads are male. I've also been working as his assistant, and he might not be able to see me in a leadership role," she said, voicing her real fear.

At first, I wanted to laugh off her concern. She was the most vital part of the company besides Mr. Lyle himself. She was the only one who didn't see that. But her shifting gaze and nervous hands in her lap meant she needed more than that. She needed honesty.

"You're going to have to show him that you can take charge. The first step is going to be applying for the job and taking yourself seriously," I advised.

"I think I can do that." She sat up straighter and lifted her chin.

"The application doesn't open for a few days so make sure you're prepared." I smiled at her.

Her eyes gleamed with plans and determination. Her biggest worries right now were whether or not she should be with Chase and if she could land a well-deserved promotion. Those were totally rational, human worries to have.

I mulled over flipping her world upside down by showing her what my world was like.

"I'm glad that we're friends," Lisa answered, looking at the ground now. "I don't know where I would be if you hadn't come along."

"You didn't need me. You just needed to believe in yourself," I corrected her.

"You keep pushing me to do that. Thanks." She looked up at me now with her big, yet sheepish grin.

"Don't thank me just yet."

"What?"

"It's nothing…I just…" I tried to start. "There is something that I need to tell you."

My hands came together in my lap automatically. I looked down at my nervous and twisting fingers instead of at her innocent eyes.

The black dagger etched in my arm, sitting just under my sleeve, itched. It burned. I was keenly reminded of its presence and what it meant. I had put my past behind me, and Kylan's family knew everything, but it still haunted me. I don't think I would ever really be able to shake the memories of the people I had hurt or the ingrained thrill of stealing energy.

But I thought about the locket. I ran my fingers across the metal that had warmed to my body temperature.

You are loved. The words written on the inside of the necklace echoed in my mind.

I can do this, I thought.

I forced myself to come back to the moment at hand. I felt the chair pressing against my back. I tasted the stale office air. Everything around me was normal and comfortable. Everything except me.

She put her hand over mine. "Kate, you can tell me anything. You know, despite seeing you every day at work, I don't actually know that much about you, but I want to. I wish you would let people see inside more often."

The honesty brimmed in her eyes. I looked deeper, wanting to infiltrate her mind and make sure she wasn't scared of what I said next. I knew that would only work for a little while. Eventually, everything about her would be altered by my influence. All the things that made her unique would diminish. It was impossible to truly change someone's mind without affecting other things.

If I told Lisa about me, she would have to accept me all on her own.

"You're right, there is a lot that you don't know

about me," I started, trying to ease into this as much as possible.

She waited patiently, unaware of the information I withheld. I felt her warm hand resting on mine. Her caring eyes looked into mine unapologetically. She felt safe with me, she felt close to me. She cared about me, and I cared about her.

"Before I came to Portland," I pushed on, hoping that I could rip through the explanation.

When I looked back at her, I realized that there wasn't anyone else in the world that I wanted to remain in the dark more. She was the one person I wanted to keep untouched and perfectly safe. Once she knew, I would lose her. I knew that.

I also knew that I wasn't willing to let this bright spot in my life go.

"I didn't have a friend that I felt as comfortable around as you," I sighed and relaxed back into the chair. "I'm really glad that I moved here, and that I met you."

She tilted her head to the side and smiled at me. Her arms wrapped around me and pulled me closer to her.

Me.

A Shadow.

Her not knowing was the only thing keeping this relationship together. A tear stung in my eye when I realized it.

"I'm really glad I met you too," she said into my ear.

I held on to her tightly, not wanting her to let go.

"You have no idea how much you mean to me," I managed to whisper.

She was the one spark of hope that I could really live amid humans. She was the face that reminded me that people had lives, lives that weren't mine for the taking. Lisa was my connection to the reality I now lived in.

I understood Rachel's perspective in a way I had not expected. It would've taken so much courage to share her identity with a human, especially one she loved.

She had risked all of that, and Jacques had stood by her. That was unimaginably valuable.

If Jacques had accepted her, that spoke mountains to his character. He had seen everything about her and decided to stay, decided to love her anyway. I couldn't force her to let that go or to watch him slowly die in front of her eyes. None of us should.

Lisa got up and left my office with a polite wave. The door swung open behind her. I nodded and pulled my phone out of my pocket. I quickly clicked the number I wanted and waited. After only one ring, she answered.

CHAPTER TEN

"Did you do it?" Rachel asked, without bothering with a greeting.

"Rachel, listen—"

"Did you do it?"

I paused. Anything I say before the answer she needed would just be ignored.

"You win," I answered her. I could picture her smug smile.

"Not so easy, is it? Thinking you're about to ruin someone's idea of you," she taunted slightly.

She had no idea how true that statement pierced into me. I risked it when I told Kylan's family about me. I'm not even sure if Cassie fully forgave me for my part in the Shadows.

But to take this leap was too much. I wanted to preserve the perfect dynamic that Lisa and I had. This kind of information would ruin everything.

"I understand why you want to do what you have planned." I stared ahead at my office. The words formed in my mouth and reached my ears faintly.

"And?" she asked, waiting for the approval she had been hoping for since she walked Jacques through the front door.

"I think you should go," I answered her.

I heard the sigh of relief passing her lips on the other end. Total opposite to the worry locking up my spine.

"You know Cassie won't approve, or Kylan, for that matter," she reasoned in a shady voice, leveraging the fact that I was the only one who knew for sure that she wanted to go to the lab. If I told them, they would stop her in any way they could.

"They don't need to know," I consoled her.

"What?"

"I will cover for you. You deserve the chance to be happy." I paused. *Even if it's with a human.*

I did want her to be happy, but I didn't know how high a price she would have to pay for what she thought was her one shot at attaining happiness.

I knew the betrayal that might be coming. When Rachel returned with a Legend Jacques, then everything would be all right again. For now, it was better for both of us to not say anything.

"Have I told you how much I like having you in the family?" she joked as her sweet tone returned.

"Listen carefully. I will keep the secret for one week. If you aren't back by then, I'm going to assume things went badly, and I will tell everyone where you went. Deal?" I challenged her.

The risk she was taking was immense, but to her, Jacques was worth it. At that moment, I didn't blame her. Jacques was worth it to her. Lisa was worth it to me. Kylan would be worth it to me. I understood Rachel, just like she wanted.

"Deal," she echoed back to me.

"Okay," I sighed.

"And Kate?"

"Yes?" I edged, almost not wanting to hear her ask for anything else.

"Thank you," she whispered with all the hope choking in her words.

"Thank me when you come home safe." I hated the words.

With that, she ended the call, and I didn't know the next time I'd talk to her.

Part of me wondered if she could just send Jacques on his own. It would keep her safe. He'd be taking all the danger. But I already knew that answer.

If it were me, I wouldn't leave Kylan. I'd walk with him the entire time. I'd be there when he woke up to an entirely new world. And he would be the only person that I want to spend the beginning of forever with.

Rachel had to go. At least, I kept telling myself that over and over.

I looked down at the phone in my hand and clutched it a little too tightly. This could either be really good or really bad. I was hoping for the former more than I could express. I looked out of my doorway and saw Kylan's office.

Please let her be all right, I wished.

CHAPTER ELEVEN

Stepping back into my apartment felt like walking into a museum.

I had been home for almost a week and I was still a stranger here. Every object remained exactly as I had left it. The damp air had the same thick smell. The locket hung around my neck, reminding me of everything I had learned, of how much I had changed.

I wandered around, trying to reacquaint myself with what should have been my home. It wasn't. It was four walls that held my belongings.

That was all.

I went to the window, looking out at the humans in the parking lot. Beyond them were parks and sidewalks that wound toward the city. All of them had people.

My body reminded me of a dull ache in my head and the restless muscles everywhere else.

I knew the feeling. I wanted energy. Or at least my body wanted energy.

Even though I had been at the mansion for only a few

days, I had spent most of those days on a high that I hadn't felt in decades. My body loved it.

Two people walked to their car; one looked tired and the other bounced with every step. Easy targets, even with witnesses.

That's the energy talking, I told myself.

The ache in my head turned to a throbbing pain. My hand clenched the string attached to the blinds so tightly that one wrong move would rip it off.

I couldn't tear my eyes away. I should. I should, right?

Guilt, shame, worry—any of those emotions should have stopped me. But I couldn't hear a single thought against walking outside.

I snapped the blinds closed, taking an actual step back.

The temptation waned and the pain subsided to a distant pang.

This should be easier, I wanted to tell myself.

I had done this before. I had stopped taking so much energy. The Rogue life wasn't as bad as it seemed when I got used to it.

But I wasn't used to it right now. I was a Shadow, wearing a Rogue's clothes and pretending to be a human to every stranger around me.

My body found a chair in the dining room without me consciously thinking to sit down. Arms resting on the wooden table, my gaze moved to my right arm.

A silky sleeve covered what was underneath.

I didn't need to see it to know it was there. The dagger. There were times that I wanted to tear it off my own arm. But Nikki had ensured that any removal of the mark would be impossible. All of my attempts proved it.

Maybe that wasn't such a bad thing? It was hard to be anything after growing up as a Shadow. The mark was a physical reminder of everything my body was already feeling.

"Once a Shadow, always a Shadow," I muttered.

No one was around to hear me, I knew that. I stared at the wall instead of my arm.

Cassie was right to hate me. Derek was right to fear me. Rachel should have never trusted me. I only knew how to bring pain.

I shook my head, hoping the negative thoughts would leave with the movement.

My hands shoved the table away from me, eager to stand or move away from the strangling reminders.

That's the energy, I retold myself.

I settled for pacing back and forth, moving closer and closer to the door with each pass.

A ring interrupted my movements.

I let out a huge breath, happy for the distraction. Energy no longer mattered for at least the next few seconds. That break would be enough. It needed to be.

The phone was cold from resting in my purse. I snatched it and noticed the number was blocked. I answered anyway. Even a scammer or salesman would be better to talk to than my own wall.

"Hi, this is Kate," I said, a little too eagerly.

No sound responded.

"Hello?" I tried again.

Nothing.

I pulled the phone away from my ear, looking to make sure the call was still live. It was. I put it back to my ear, listening harder.

Breathing. That was all I heard. There was definitely someone on the other end. So I waited, trying to ignore the eerie feeling that filled my apartment.

"Hello, Mara," a female voice said.

The blood slowed in my veins. The creeping feeling crashed in around me, constricting my breaths.

"Who is this?" I asked with a hardened voice.

Nothing again. The only people that called me Mara were the Shadows. Even Alec couldn't disguise his voice to sound that much like a woman, and it was too low-pitched to be Nikki.

This was someone else. Another Shadow? Who else would…

A low laugh came through the other end of the line. My hand clutched the phone so tightly that I heard the edges start to crack.

"Who. Is. This?"

The voice didn't answer. A beep sounded as the call ended.

I tossed the phone on the table and backed away. Mara. No one called me that. I wasn't Mara anymore. I was Kate. I needed to be.

The room seemed to close in around me. The windows were no longer views of the outside; they were entry points for an attack. I moved to the front door, remembering that I hadn't locked it behind me.

Before I reached it, the door opened.

My muscles braced to run.

CHAPTER TWELVE

"Hey, beautiful." Kylan stood in the doorway, leaning against the frame.

My muscles liquefied. He looked just like he had on our first date, all smiles and charm. His hands tucked in his front pockets of his jeans.

I forced a smile on my face as he stepped inside.

"Kylan," I sighed. "I know I told you that I wanted to be alone tonight—"

"I know, I know." Kylan interrupted. "I don't mean to bother you. But Derek has been jumping down my throat with the Rachel news, and I'm trying to stay out of sight."

He lifted his hands out of his front pockets and raised them in surrender. His big, wanting eyes were impossible to say no to. Success flickered across those green irises because he knew he was winning.

"You're fine." I waved my hand and stepped aside.

The cryptic phone call was the only thing on my mind. It was probably nothing more than a Shadow's attempt to rattle me. There were a few I could think of with a grudge.

Two words shouldn't be bothering me this much.

Hello, Mara. But I could feel them underneath my skin.

Kylan came in and kept talking. "I mean, you think Cassie is losing it? Derek is fit to be rolled up in a ball and tossed down a hill. Ugh, sometimes those two are the worst thing for each other. Why is Rachel doing this?"

I shut the door and interrupted, "I'm actually really glad you're here because there's—"

"Well, of course you are," Kylan smiled and pulled me in.

Both of us were instantly distracted. My heart launched into overdrive as his body pressed into mine. I wrapped my arms around him, grateful for a place where I finally felt at home.

He kissed me gently at first. Then it changed. His hands moved up to my face, angling my neck so he could kiss me deeper. My breath caught as I waited for what he would do next.

Kylan's phone rang in his pocket. Both of us halted. I could hardly hear past my own breathing and the roaring in my ears. I could smell him, in a way that made me want to taste more.

But another ring shattered the connection and I gave up. I sighed and pulled my face away from him.

"That's probably Cassie," Kylan complained and pulled out his phone.

"Why is she so worried?" I kept my voice even. "Rachel hasn't announced anything yet."

"It's just her. Any little thing can set her off, but normally she winds back down pretty easy after some time with Derek. But this is huge, and they're both losing it. One second," Kylan explained as he clicked to answer. "Hey Cass."

I relaxed into him, his one arm still wrapped around me. He rubbed his hand up and down my back.

The odd phone call mattered less and less with each pass of his hand.

"I know. She didn't. Yeah, I know," he said.

Another string of high-pitched words I couldn't follow.

"Fine, I'll swing by later," Kylan confirmed.

I smiled, thinking of Cassie's sharp voice asking him to be another shoulder to lean on. I could only imagine Derek in the back corner of that room, ready to pull his own hair out.

"Tell Derek I'll be there soon, I promise. Love you, bye," Kylan rushed and hung up the phone.

"Sounds like you need to leave." I nodded as I ran my hands up Kylan's chest.

His breathing paused when he smiled. His heart raced just as fast as mine. I smiled up at him, enjoying the moment of peace.

"We could both leave," Kylan tilted his head to the side.

I winced. "Cassie doesn't need me there."

I was the Shadow that killed her family and I was also the person who failed at convincing Rachel to drop her human. And I didn't want to face her knowing I had just sent Rachel off to a lab.

"I'm sure she'll come back around. But maybe a little time apart is a good thing." Kylan shrugged.

He backed away from me, a smile playing on his lips.

"This is good, though. I was thinking about going out tonight," I said easily.

Kylan gave a long look before he said, "You don't seem that tired."

I wasn't. I mean, I was dragging a little bit, but that wasn't what was bothering me. I could still taste the sensation of being high at the mansion. I missed it.

I didn't need more energy to survive. I wanted it to stop

the headache and the twitchy fingers. Kylan would have a hard time understanding that even if he could sympathize with an energy binge.

"Coming back has been a…transition for me. I just need to, uh, take the edge off?" I tried to explain.

He nodded with a flicker of doubt in his eyes. That vanished when his hands ran along my silky shirt and ended when they touched my jeans.

"There are other things to take the edge off," he said in a low voice.

He pushed me back slowly, watching my eyes the whole time. The wall pressed against my back, and I forgot the uncomfortable pain in my body.

"Are you sure you have time?"

I smiled up at him, waiting for him to remember that his sister had just called. The only goal in his focused gaze was me. A smile parted his lips.

Blood rushed loudly in my ears even though the room was utterly silent. He lifted his hand to the back of my head and leaned in slowly.

The phone rang in his pocket again.

His eyes narrowed as he considered the conflict. He looked at me again with determined eyes.

"I don't have to go," he whispered.

"They need you." I tried not to sound as breathless as I was. Kylan smiled at my attempt.

"I need you," Kylan argued and nipped at my ear.

The rings stopped and we were back to the pounding silence. I lifted my chin unintentionally at the same time that Kylan leaned up. His lips brushed mine and I didn't remember the words he said or anything I wanted to say.

I kissed him like he wasn't about to leave. My hands touched his soft hair and let themselves trail down his strong neck and shoulders. The wall and Kylan's arms held me firmly in place.

Heat flooded my cheeks and the muscles flexed in my fingers, pulling him closer to me.

Another ring pierced the air.

Kylan let out a breath as he lifted his hands off me. His forehead was still pressed to mine as he reached in his pocket and looked at the screen.

"It's Derek," he groaned and clicked the answer button.

My body relaxed against him. Kylan shifted so his head was resting against the wall, his lips so close to my ear.

"This better be good," he answered in a gruff voice.

While he waited, he kissed the corner of my ear, moving down the skin of my neck.

Derek's voice was talking too fast for me to follow, and with Kylan distracting me I doubted I'd be able to string the words together anyway.

"That hardly sounds like an emergency," Kylan said, and I remembered he was still on the phone.

He lifted his head and pressed a kiss to my forehead. Derek's voice had gotten louder.

"Fine...yes. Okay, I'm on my way. Yes, really. Bye." Kylan pulled away from me.

My hands fell to my sides and the ache of less energy washed back in. He shoved the phone back in his pocket and reached a hand up to smooth my hair.

"How do they know you haven't left already?" I asked, hoping that would buy a few minutes.

"Tracking app. We all have one. For safety reasons and because they are a little nosy, yes," Kylan joked. "But they can see that my phone is still in the same spot."

Thank me when you come home safe. The words wrenched in my chest.

"Go," I said before he tried to explain. "Your family needs you, and I wanted to go out anyway."

"I'm sorry. With all this new information, they just need a little more attention than normal. I swear, they aren't normally like this," he said.

Kylan leaned in again, and I kissed him gently.

"Go, before they call you again," I whispered.

He moaned and trudged to the door but smiled when he looked back at me. I leaned my head against the metal doorway and watched as he drove away.

I touched my fingers to my lips. I wanted Kylan in my life. That I was sure about. And Kylan came with a family.

One day I hoped to be a part of that family. But for right now, they needed each other. I understood that even if I didn't want to.

I walked outside and tried to enjoy the liberating feeling. Instead, all the emotions inside me had calmed and the only thing left was a burning desire for energy.

As much as I wanted to take a deep breath and push it away, the burn lingered.

When my eyes landed on a human, I expected there to be more restraint.

CHAPTER THIRTEEN

It took two days before Cassie even deigned to ask about me, and that was a breakthrough.

Kylan convinced me that it was finally time to see each other face-to-face. Even Derek said it would probably be fine. Not exactly the vote of confidence I wanted, but it was something.

Those few days were spent worrying about Rachel. She had been texting me every now and then with just long enough in between for me to jump to the worst conclusion.

But I hadn't gotten another mysterious call, and there wasn't a Shadow in sight. So I fell into a routine of complacency.

My main goal was to cover for Rachel, which presented just enough distraction from the energy cravings and haunting phone calls.

"Hiking?" Cassie asked, crossing her arms in front of her chest, tapping her foot furiously fast.

"Yes, hiking," I said. "Now get in the car!"

I sat behind the wheel with Kylan in the passenger seat.

Cassie and Derek needed to get out of the house and out of their own heads.

They had been stressing about Rachel ever since they laid eyes on Jacques, and poor Kylan couldn't take another lecture without bursting at the seams.

Kylan got out of the car and opened the back door for her before Cassie could open her mouth.

"Come on, it'll be fun," Kylan smiled at her.

"Well, you don't have to tell me twice." Derek grinned and slid in through the open door, all the way to the other side of the seat.

"Where are we going?" Derek leaned forward to my seat excitedly.

"We're going up Mount Hood," I added to the pitch and smiled. "Should take us less than an hour without those pesky trails in the way."

Derek smiled and let his head fall back against the leather headrest.

The thrill was already creeping up my arms. This endeavor was pretty selfish, but I needed a release for all my pent-up emotions. Derek looked eagerly toward the stubborn woman still standing outside.

"That does sound fun," Derek called out to her and patted the seat next to him.

I was anticipating taking my powers out for a spin in such a public place. Derek looked like he needed a break from life in general.

"Okay, let's go then," Cassie moaned as she dove into the car.

Kylan and Derek both breathed a sigh of relief.

"Excuse her, she had a little too much fun this morning," Derek mentioned as he put both his hands on Cassie's shoulders almost to hold her down to the seat.

If he didn't, it looked like she might bounce right out of the car.

I gripped the steering wheel as hard I could without leaving an indent to hide the excess energy of my own.

"I see what Rachel's been going on about," Cassie beamed and looked out the window. "Even the sun looks brighter."

Kylan glanced at Derek as he got in the car.

"Cassie was freakin' out again last night, so I took her out on the town." Derek shrugged his shoulders.

"Clearly, that was a good idea," Kylan scoffed at Cassie rolling down the window and sticking her head outside the car.

"Hey, you try living with little miss I-have-to-control-everything-in-the-universe. Eventually you'll get just as desperate. This is the most calm she's been in days," Derek leaned forward and talked in a hushed tone.

"I can hear you," Cassie sang into the air outside.

"No thanks, bro. She's all yours." Kylan smiled back at his brother and then looked back at me.

As Derek tried to pull Cassie back into the car, Kylan just smiled at me. My gaze ventured over. He winked.

With Kylan beside me, the two crazy Legends behind me, and the locket around my neck, I was at peace. To top it all off, I still had extra energy to burn.

My fingers tingled with anticipation. At least I was better at hiding a high than Cassie was. Although I doubt hers was as strong as mine.

After what seemed like a short drive, we pulled up to the trailhead. I threw the car in park, and Cassie's feet hit the ground before I had a chance to get the key out of the ignition.

"Who's ready to run?" Cassie announced the challenge. Derek stood out of the car and cracked his neck to either side.

"You're on, babe," Derek accepted her challenge.

She took off first and he went bolting after her. Less than a second had passed and they were already beyond the line of sight from the parking lot.

With a glance around the empty lot, Kylan and I took off after them.

We ran faster than a human could dream of doing. The trailhead led right and we headed left.

Cassie went up into the trees and swung along the tops of them. Derek barreled through the underbrush. Kylan ran after them, and I followed closely on his heels.

Eventually, we all made it to the hill leading up the backside of the mountain. We halted to scan what was in front of us. It wasn't so steep that we had to climb, but it was steep enough that this wasn't going to be a leisurely run, either.

A challenge. I grinned.

Kylan took off first and I followed right after him.

Freedom of running was just what I needed. The energy pumped through my veins, making me faster and more agile than I had been since I left the mansion.

I could grab a branch and swing myself ten feet in the air without worrying who was watching because no one was. I could run ahead of Kylan and show him the high he was missing. I could do anything because not even my body was stopping me.

This kind of freedom was bliss.

The mountain divided, and the hill continued around or the cliff led straight to the top. Kylan glanced at the cliff and looked at it as though he might attempt to scale it. He looked back at me.

"Ladies first," he challenged.

I focused on the cliff and took a running start without hesitation.

I jumped as high as I could and caught the small fingerhold

with one hand. I swung using the momentum from my jump and launched my other hand to the next hold.

Once I extended my arm, I knew I was an inch shy of actually reaching the hold. A second of focus and a new hold formed. The rock expanded, and my hand caught onto the newly created grip.

The adrenaline pumped through my body and powered my excitement. My feet caught up with me, and I clung to the cliffside. A smile broke across my face.

I secured my grip and looked down triumphantly at Kylan. His jaw hung down in shock. He stood there amazed that I had dared make the jump at all, or that I could think clearly enough to create the new hold in midair.

"Is this ladies first or ladies only?" I taunted him, and his expression became serious.

Kylan took his running start and I looked back at the cliff above me. I continued without him, grabbing a hold here and pushing from a foothold there.

Within a minute, I crested the cliff and pulled myself up and over. The unforgiving rock scraped against my stomach.

The breeze at the top of the mountain blew the smell of wet earth and open air. I inhaled as deeply as I could. Right now, with my body buzzing from the leftover energy splurge, I felt on top of the world.

I turned around to see Kylan climbing over the edge. The others must have taken the long way. Cassie needed the extra time to run for sure. Kylan walked to where I was and just stared at me.

"What?" I teased, not looking at him.

I noted his breathing was faster than mine and held back a smile.

"You keep impressing me. First, you're a Legend…then you're a Level Five no less, and not only that, you're a skilled

Five…and now you're an amazing climber." He threw his hands in the air. "I just don't know what to do with you."

"Oh, stop," I breathed. "You just made the same climb I did."

His blazing green eyes locked on mine. "Only after watching you do it, and using the new hold you made. A lot of those leaps I didn't think were possible until I watched you make them. Then, I had to try because I couldn't let you show me up without a fight."

"Well, how about we settle this?" I asked curiously.

"Okay, what'd you have in mind?" His eyes were intrigued.

I shrugged and stepped toward him. I put my hands on his chest and felt his breath catch.

"Cassie and Derek should be coming up the other side any moment. Let's say, first one to that side of the mountain wins?" I challenged with my eyebrows up.

"Ah, you think you can beat me in a race? I'd like to see you try." Kylan crouched low and leaned closer to my face.

Now my breath caught. He inched his face closer to mine until his lips hovered over mine. My heart launched in my chest, and I focused on his breath brushing my face.

His lips collided into mine before I could steady my stance. The surprise and rush of excitement nearly knocked me off my feet. Heat radiated through the clothing between us. My mind clouded as his hand brushed up my back, pulling up the hem of my shirt.

The world around me silenced, and all I heard was his breathing. But he stopped too soon.

My eyes opened in time to see him wink at me and take off running.

CHAPTER FOURTEEN

My mind yanked itself back into place and Kylan was almost out of sight before I had time to complain.

I tore after him through the tiny valley at the top of the mountain. I launched myself over the mound of rock standing between me and the next flat spot of ground. My feet pounded into the rock over and over until Kylan was in my sightline.

He made the mistake of taking the long way to keep him on flatter ground. I decided to take the harder route and go straight up.

When I dropped down to the other side, Kylan was racing around the corner a few steps behind me.

"Come on, Kate. You can't let me win just one thing," Kylan shouted after me.

I slowed my steps enough for him to catch up to me. Once he was within reaching distance, I threw my last advantage at him.

"If you aren't going to play fair, then why should I?" I asked and touched my hand to his arm.

A burst of chaotic, sensational energy illuminated my

senses. The world around me almost glittered. My muscles no longer felt an ache from working for the brief moment that I held my hand on his skin.

Kylan had the exact opposite reaction. He doubled over for a moment, but to his credit, he kept running. He sucked in a huge breath and yanked his arm away from me. When his eyes shot back up to mine, he looked ready to take me down.

"Oh, it is on." Kylan's eyes narrowed and he pumped his arms faster, forcing his body to match my pace.

"You want your energy back?" I turned and ran backward across the flat part of the mountain.

I raised my hands and felt way too satisfied at the frustration on Kylan's face.

"Come and get it," I whispered.

The other end of the mountain was in sight now. It was only about ten yards away. I didn't glance back at Kylan, as that would only slow me down. I tucked my head down and pushed my feet to go even faster.

The one thing I couldn't stop myself from doing was listening to his footsteps. In between each breath, I heard his feet hit the ground behind me, closer and closer.

After my next breath, I didn't hear anything.

I was only a few yards away when I felt Kylan's entire body weight crash into my back. His arms wrapped around me, and we both tumbled straight to the ground. We slid far enough to almost reach the edge of the next cliff.

The rock gashed against my skin, but with all the energy inside of me, I barely felt it.

"Cheater!" I screamed at Kylan as we halted.

"Oh, I'm the cheater?" Kylan released his arms around me and sat up.

The cuts on his arms were healing already. I lifted my

shirt and the wound was already changing from a deep red to pink. Mine faded faster than his and when it did, I lowered my shirt.

"Yes, you are the cheater. You can't just tackle me when I'm about to win." I tried to sound angry, but even I wasn't buying it.

"You're the one that stole my energy right out of me." Kylan moved closer and lowered his voice.

I offered my hand. "And now you want it back?"

"No, you can keep it," Kylan smiled and kissed the palm of my hand I raised. "This may sound strange, but the high... It looks good on you."

His hands wrapped around me and pulled my body closer to him. He looked at my eyes like he was holding the most precious thing in the world.

I bit my lip, trying to keep my comment to myself. I wanted to be immersed in the moment between us. But my curiosity got the best of me.

"I don't think I've ever seen you high," I blurted.

"No, you haven't." Kylan reached up and smoothed my hair that had been roughed up from the tumble.

"Will I ever?" I asked the most real question on my mind and I dreaded how long he paused.

His answer would tell me what kind of a future he saw for us. I assumed he wanted a little house on a hill, where we had monthly barbeques with our unaware, human neighbors.

I wanted a life that was quite similar to that, but with more adventure. More energy.

Growing up in constant danger and intrigue, part of me would always want that.

All I needed to know was that he and I were on the same track, just like I told Rachel.

Kylan looked at me for a second before lowering his face

to the ground. I didn't get to hear his response before the sound of footsteps invaded.

"That was awesome!" Derek bellowed. He barreled toward us with Cassie skipping behind him.

"Where did you learn to climb like that?" Cassie breathed, her eyes still sparkling.

"Instinct, I guess." I laughed it off as I stood and brushed off my clothes.

Kylan stood and shook his arms out like he was trying to rid the last bit of ache from the fall. An easy fix to that would be taking energy from any of us standing here. But one glance from him told me that wasn't going to happen.

"Oh, yeah—good job to you too, man," Derek added in a much less enthusiastic tone and slapped Kylan on the back.

Kylan narrowed his eyes at the mocking praise. He turned all at once and moved to tackle Derek, who stepped out of the way just in time.

That didn't stop Kylan's hand from reaching farther. This time Derek had already taken off in the other direction.

They chased each other around the open plane in front of us. I took the one opportunity I had to get Cassie to talk. But I wasn't sure where she stood.

Her brown eyes landed on me, and I tried not to move.

"Thanks," she said, barely loud enough for me to hear.

I smiled.

I knew what she meant. Getting out was good for all of us, but especially Cassie. She was worried too much about Rachel and at least for the last few minutes, she had been free.

I could understand needing a change of venue to steer thoughts in a better direction.

"Can I ask you a question?" I stepped closer to her.

"Sure." Cassie stretched her neck from side to side.

"Has Kylan...Has he ever been high around you guys?" I asked, looking at the ground so she couldn't guess what I wanted the answer to be.

"Kylan?" She laughed. "No way. The closest I've ever seen was when Derek took me to a concert and Kylan came along. There was a group of teenagers being so pushy. Kylan walked back toward them and after a few seconds, they quieted down."

My heart hammered in my chest when I glanced up at him tumbling his brother to the ground again.

She didn't seem to notice how much I hung on her words. "When he came back he was acting kinda strange, but I couldn't tell if it was from energy or not. He's not as obvious as Rachel, I guess. He finally told us that he was leaving, and walked off. That was the only time I can think of."

"So he's always been this way," I muttered.

Kylan was walking toward us until Derek tripped him and he snapped around again. They looked like Alec and Nikki fighting in the courtyard. Vicious and playful at the same time. Something told me they might be a while.

"At least as long as he's been with us." Cassie shrugged.

"Before that?" I avoided looking at her and just kept my eyes on Kylan.

"He doesn't talk about it much," Cassie mused. "Actually, knowing he's an Extractor makes a lot of sense now that I think about it. Whenever he talked about his past, he never felt bad about hurting humans, specifically. He just left that part out."

"He talks about it?" I pulled my eyebrows together.

Cassie shook her head and scoffed. "Oh, no. He doesn't. I only know what Derek tells me, and he won't even go into detail. I think Derek is the only one who actually knows anything about his past."

"Lucky him," I grumbled under my breath.

"I wouldn't say so," Cassie finally looked over to me. "Knowing about someone's past only means that you have to fight to see them the way they are now, and not the way they were. It's easier to just never know."

"Are you still talking about Kylan?" I asked, raising an eyebrow at her.

Her normally pale cheeks flushed. She forced a smile, and that must have been all she could muster.

She raced right toward Derek and jumped on his back. They spun around each other until they were both dizzy and laughing. Kylan backed off and looked at me.

Seeing his smile and his siblings made me happy. That was our now. My mind had always been trying to include my past into my future. Maybe I needed to focus on what I had right now.

As Kylan walked over to me, all I wanted was him in my arms. That was my now.

In that moment, it was all I wanted.

CHAPTER FIFTEEN

After a long walk back down the mountain, and an even longer car ride to drop Derek and Cassie off at their house, we were finally alone again.

"You know, Cassie brought up a good point," I started as soon as the door shut behind Derek.

"Uh oh. 'Cassie' and 'good point' don't normally go in a sentence together," Kylan laughed and leaned his head back on the headrest.

"No, I'm serious." I smiled back at him and he surrendered.

"Okay, I'm listening," he said, waiting.

"I think I've been judging you based on my past," I started and did not make it any further.

"Kate…" Kylan dropped his head.

"No, no, just hear me out. It's not fair. I've been wanting to live like nothing has changed. But really, everything about my life now is different, and I need to enjoy it. So, I'm sorry if you've been feeling pressure from me," I finished.

"You're not the only one that wants things from the past." Kylan still hung his head.

"What?" I looked at him.

"You're just the only one that's brave enough to say something, and brave enough to be willing to try it." Kylan finally raised his eyes to meet mine.

"What are you saying?" I asked, a flutter of hope rising.

"I'm saying that I don't think I will ever be like you, and I don't think you'll ever be like me. But I think we still work together really well. You challenge me, and frankly you scare me sometimes. But every day is a new adventure with you. It's exciting." Kylan shrugged, gazing out the windshield now.

I reached my hand over and laid it on his knee, just above a new tear in his jeans from our tumble on the mountain.

"You have no idea how good it feels to hear you say that," I whispered back to him as I pulled the car onto his street.

Kylan nodded his head and turned up the radio. He tried to sing along poorly to the music, but his skill was still apparent.

We both laughed at each other as I stopped the car outside of his house. He came around to my side of the car and opened my door too.

"Thanks for a fun date," he sighed and leaned against the car frame and the door.

"You're welcome," I said and stretched to kiss him. He reached over and unbuckled my seat belt.

"Aren't you going to walk me to the door?" He grinned. He would always walk me to the door when he drove. I smiled and rolled my eyes.

"What was I thinking?" I laughed under my breath.

I stepped out of the car and shut the door, shaking off some of the dust and dried flakes of blood. We wrapped our dirty arms around each other as we walked up to the side doors. I walked all the way up the wooden porch with him and I still didn't want to let go.

We arrived at the glass doors and just as Kylan was turning to face me and pull me closer, his phone rang. Again.

I wanted to shatter the phone with my own hand if it didn't stop interrupting every moment we had alone.

"Cassie can't already need you again," I groaned.

Kylan smiled and dug it out of his pocket. His eyes lit up when he saw the screen.

"It's Rachel," he said, already hitting the button and putting it on speaker this time. "Hey, there you are. Cassie has been worried si—"

"Kylan," Rachel said with a trembling voice.

Ice poured through my veins at the sound.

Kylan's face dropped. "Rach, are you okay?"

A silent pause was long enough for me to imagine all the terrible things that could have gone wrong.

"I'm so sorry," Rachel whimpered. "I didn't mean—"

Another voice took over. Female. Hostile. "Rachel's alive for now. You have until Friday at noon to deliver the Level Five to the Louisiana lab if you want her to remain alive."

I recognized the voice. *Hello, Mara.*

Kylan's eyes flicked up to me and my face drained. The lab. They had Rachel. I could tell Kylan wasn't breathing, but neither was I.

"Who is this?" Kylan asked.

I already knew how useless that question was. He didn't. I tried to reach for the phone but he yanked it away.

"We trust you know how to find us," the voice said, continuing the threat as if Kylan hadn't said anything.

"I'm not going anywhere until you tell me who this is. No, put Rachel back on the phone," Kylan commanded.

It was futile. I knotted my fingers together nervously.

"There's no need to waste time with questions that won't help you. Bring the Level Five or Rachel will die."

Kylan fumed. "If you even touch her—"

Rachel's scream cut through his words. A wail that would have made Cassie shoot off the porch, straight to the lab. But Kylan froze with calculating eyes.

"Friday at noon. The clock is ticking." The voice cut him off and ended the call.

When the screen changed, Kylan immediately tried to call her back. It went straight to voice mail.

Rachel was in danger.

And I was the one who told her to go. It was all my fault.

"She's gone," he breathed, barely above a whisper.

He clenched the phone in his hand, crumpling the metal. He didn't look at me. He didn't even look up from the porch.

"Kylan…I…" I tried to console him. My words fell flat when he raised his hand to stop me.

"She actually went through with it," his wispy voice was still barely audible. "She didn't even tell anyone she was leaving!"

"That's not true." The words tumbled out of my mouth.

I had promised not to keep anything from Kylan, and lying about this was included.

"What are you talking about?" he asked, glaring into my eyes.

"She came to me. She wanted to know if it was a bad idea for her to go. I told her that it was," I answered, and Kylan's shoulders relaxed slightly.

I winced for the rest of the story.

"I also told her that if Jacques meant as much to her as she said he did, then she should go," my voice said, feeling completely detached from me.

"You what?" he asked.

The phone didn't matter, and storming away no longer mattered. Because now he knew. I was the one who got his sister kidnapped.

Disgust flashed in Kylan's usually kind eyes, and my heart broke.

He yanked open the door and ducked inside. I should have taken that as a hint to leave him alone.

But I dared to follow him.

CHAPTER SIXTEEN

I tried to explain, but it didn't sound any better.

"She loved him, Kylan. She knew the risk," I said.

"She came to you for advice. Why not me? Why not Cassie?" He shook his head.

"I had no idea—" I started and he cut me off again.

"She's gone, Kate!"

The pain in his eyes was obvious. Pain I couldn't fix. Pain that I had caused instead.

I knew exactly what had just been ripped away from him. The way his hands shook when he tried to hold his face made my heart shatter.

"I'm sorry," I muttered.

The anger poured off his shoulders. His voice finally broke, and he collapsed onto the couch. "Sorry doesn't cut it. She's my sister."

"We will get her back," I mumbled as a comfort to myself.

Kylan took it as a personal goal, however impossible it was. The shaking slowed when he lifted his chin.

"Yes, we will." He stood from the couch and straightened his shoulders.

"Whoa, whoa, we need a plan first." I stood and raised my hands to stop him from darting out the door right then.

"I have a plan. We go over there and get Rachel back."

He looked down at me and almost dared me to defy him. I'd never been good at backing down from a dare.

"That's not a plan, that's a death wish. You have no idea what kind of defense they have," I insisted.

I thought through ways we could possibly pull this off. The technology and Legends would be impossible to surmount with just the four of us.

It wouldn't work.

"So, we'll gather the rest of my family and head out," he said with new hope in his voice.

Two more people. He thought two more people were going to solve this situation.

I shook my head. "That's not enough power."

Kylan ignored me as he brushed past to walk to the door.

We needed more power on our side. A lot more. My mind finally settled on one solution.

A solution that might get us more people, more talent, and more of a chance of bringing Rachel home.

My stomach sank.

"Well, it's a start," he continued, reaching for his dented phone and leaning toward the door.

"Kylan, stop." My voice was serious now.

Kylan whipped around and looked at me. My eyes were heavy and my smile was fake. It took him a few seconds to realize why I had hesitated.

"Kate," he started.

"I am going to fix this." I straightened my shoulders.

There was only one way I could feasibly fix this without turning myself in. He looked at me like I had transformed to something else, something dark and unwanted.

"No," he answered firmly.

"Do you have a better idea?" I edged, hoping he could come up with something.

"We can handle this on our own." He clenched his empty fists tightly.

"Kylan, be serious. We aren't going to the lost and found to get an old scarf. We are going up against a lab to sabotage a ransom for your sister," I said.

"We. Can. Handle. This," he said slower, shaking his head.

He was trying to ignore my logic. And it wasn't working.

"Cassie and Derek are Twos, and not even strong ones at that. That place will be packed with the smartest humans you've ever met and the Legends they devoted to them. We don't stand a chance on our own. You know it." I raced through the words before he could protest.

"Him. You would rather go back to him than stay here with us, and this is just a perfect excuse," he whispered, staring knives into my eyes.

The accusation stung. I hoped with all my heart he trusted me enough to believe me when I said, "This isn't about him."

I shook my head. Kylan didn't show signs of believing me.

"How can you say that? You loved him! And now all you can talk about is how much you want to have all the energy in the world. The humans won't even notice, right? You want all that energy? Go get it. Don't let us hold you back." Kylan glared down at me.

"I apologized for all of that." I stepped back but his rage and pain were undeniable.

"And one apology makes it better? He is my brother, and we are nothing alike. How could you want me when you've spent your whole life with someone like *him?*" Kylan looked at the floor and tugged on his hair.

My shoulders were heavy. "This is about family, and if you want yours back, we need their help."

His eyes did not sympathize, but they did change.

"I think you're right," Kylan finally spoke. His cold eyes cut into mine. "This is a family matter."

"What does that mean?" I hesitated to even ask it out loud.

"It means I am going out there to get *my* family and we are going rescue my little sister." The words seeped through his clenched teeth.

With that, he turned and left the house.

The door slammed behind him. I felt the cut that severed me from the rest of his family. He was very clear. I was no longer a part of that group.

One decision, one phone call, had ripped all of it away. I took a few short breaths and fought back the tears.

I clutched the locket around my neck.

I'm not alone. I comforted my mind. I let the strength fill the gaping holes from every rational doubt I could conjure. This task was hard, not impossible.

I had to fix this. And I knew exactly what I needed to do.

CHAPTER SEVENTEEN

The space between me and my destination closed quicker than I expected. Quicker than I hoped.

I fought to keep my feet moving and my mind clear. Ahead, the plains had turned into low hills. I was somewhere between where Montana met one of the Dakotas. A place so unpopulated no one had bothered to put up a sign for the state line.

Dry grass interrupted by patches of trees dipped into a valley, the valley I knew so well. I took one last breath and crested the hill. On the other side lay the one place I was hoping I would never see again.

The mansion. I remembered it all. Tall, glorious, and so out of place for the land around it. Ancient trees that didn't belong stretched around the perimeter.

I could see the tops of those trees now.

"You made this mess. You have to fix it," I coached myself.

I kept my mind focused on Kylan, on the defeat and agony in his eyes when the ransom words settled in.

My phone buzzed in my pocket. I yanked it from my jacket, hoping it was Kylan. I looked down and saw Lisa's bright smile staring back, and my stomach twisted in a knot.

She had no idea where Kylan or I were at the moment. I could imagine all her far-fetched scenarios about what happened to us.

"Hi, Lisa," I answered quickly, stopping my steps.

"Kate," she almost shouted. "Where have you been? I've been waiting to talk to you all day. Never mind. I'll just tell you now. So, I had my first interview with Mr. Lyle about the position and I think it went well. I talked to one of the hiring committee members and she said that Mr. Lyle was surprised I applied at all, but in a good way. A good way. Isn't that great?"

I smiled at her simple life. A job promotion. A boyfriend. No ransoms or threats. No looming mansion where entering could be the worst decision yet.

She needed her simple, seemingly human friend right now.

"That's incredible. I said you'd be a good candidate," I said.

"I know! When are you getting here? It's almost nine and you haven't shown up yet. Neither has Kylan, actually," Lisa said, and it sounded like she was pacing in the background, probably back and forth in her own office to calm her nerves.

"I'm not feeling well," I lied. "I don't think I'll be coming in today. Maybe for a couple of days."

My eyes wandered to the hill not too far away from me. Down that slope would be the mansion. A lavish nightmare filled with Shadows and one that Lisa couldn't handle hearing about.

"Aw, I'm sorry. Do you need anything?" she asked, her voice turning soft and breathy.

"No." I shook my head, biting back tears. "I just need to be alone."

All of it was lies. There was a lot that I needed, but none of it she could give me. Especially without knowing the biggest portion of my life. Legends. Shadows. I had to keep her protected from all of it.

"I'll call you later to check on you."

I nodded, even if she couldn't see it. "Okay."

I shoved the phone back in my pocket and any thoughts of my human-ish life aside.

Right now, I needed to be a Legend. Not just a Legend, a Shadow. I rolled my right sleeve up over my elbow, the mark of a dagger showing on my arm.

I marched forward and held my head high. My knees wanted to shake together, but I kept my outward appearance proud and strong. No one in there could know how desperately I needed this.

That would be my ace to keep.

The doors of the mansion loomed over me. I pressed my hand against the firm door and took my last calming breath.

I shoved hard and it swung open to reveal two Shadows on guard duty. Both of them straightened at the sight of me.

They took in my dark hair and soft complexion, but instantly recognized the locket hanging around my neck and the mark on my arm.

After that, they knew only one person could be standing there with it.

"Mara?" one of them asked.

Hearing my old name still felt strange. Even though I looked different as Kate, my eyes were still the same. So many things about me were still the same.

They both looked at each other, unaware of how to react.

"Take me to Alec," I ordered.

They paused just before obeying.

The guards each turned and almost ran into each other to lead the way. I smiled to myself at the power I still held. I may have given up that lifestyle, but the rewards were still exhilarating at times.

They led me down the familiar stone hallways, turning around every few seconds to keep a wary eye on me.

I kept my hands to myself, but my eyes wandered all over. Eventually, we turned the corner open to the courtyard, where plenty of Shadows were practicing their talents.

Keeping my eyes forward, I was determined not to make eye contact with anyone. Out of the corner of my eye, the Shadows we passed stood to gawk at me.

Whispers flew around the room the moment I stepped into view.

Everyone kept their distance and some even moved out of the way for the three of us.

I followed as they led me down the last hallway and finally stopped a few feet in front of the door. The Shadows looked at each other and then back at me. They stepped apart to signal that I was on my own from here.

Before I could move forward, I heard a rustle inside.

Alec rushed out of the open door just a few feet ahead.

He froze when he saw me and so did my heart.

The Shadow leader wore black jeans and a deep blue shirt that mirrored the color of his eyes. Alec always wore dark colors, dark enough to hide the blood and murder that covered every inch of him.

It made the pale shirt I wore seem too revealing, like it couldn't cover the blood on my hands.

My gaze fell on the black dagger on his arm.

I had just walked in, unsure if I could get out. My muscles

tensed and my eyes narrowed. Being here scared me deeper than I wanted to admit.

Alec looked me up and down slowly.

He stood tall, yet his face showed surprise. He took his time looking over my body and stepping forward toward me.

Every glance, every breath made me think this was a bad idea.

"Kate," Alec whispered my new name.

I stared back at him. An awkward feeling tickled down my arms at the sound of him saying that name. It was wrong. Or it felt wrong coming from him.

I ignored the onlookers behind me and the guards to either side of me.

"Can we talk?" I nodded my head to the room from which he had just stepped out.

He raised his hand toward the door to invite me in. I walked toward Alec and the door. Before I reached it, I turned to the two guarding Shadows already closing in.

In a dark, condescending tone, I threatened, "Don't let me catch you eavesdropping."

Both of their eyes lit up with fear and they automatically straightened their shoulders, freezing in place.

I smiled at both of them and walked through the doorway first. I listened carefully as Alec followed me into the room. The door clicked shut behind him, and I took a breath before I turned around to face him.

"To what do I owe this pleasure?" Alec asked and crossed his arms over his chest. I cringed at the smile creeping up his face.

"I need your help," I said curtly before he got any other ideas about why I was here.

After the words were out, I realized that was probably the

hardest part of this conversation. It certainly felt like the sting of a tape being ripped from skin, maybe worse.

"Interesting." He waited. His searching eyes were glued to me.

I fought not to squirm under his gaze. I was standing in Alec's presence of my own free will and my body was not acclimating well.

"Kylan's sister has been taken by a lab and is being held for ransom," I continued, swallowing the emotion in my voice.

"What's the ransom?" Alec asked, not flinching.

I lowered my gaze to the floor. "Me."

"Ah, and the altruistic Kate can't give up her life for someone she cares about?" Alec taunted me.

"You know I can't do that. I would be…" I shuddered inwardly at the thought.

"Torn apart."

My eyes flicked back up to his. For a moment, the sympathy I had been looking for flashed across his face. The corners of his eyes wrinkled because he wanted to fix it.

"Which lab?" Alec asked tentatively. He already had an answer in mind. "Just tell me it's not—"

"Louisiana," I finished.

He looked at me and let out a laugh. I glared, and he cut it off and rubbed the back of his neck instead. "More advanced, but less security than London. Could be worse."

I finally let my need show in my expression. Alec may not be a terribly emotional person, but he did care for me. I could still see that. He shook his head and stepped closer to me.

The air electrified with every step. I blinked, trying to focus enough to keep my breath from shuddering. I was scared, excited, nervous, and hopeful. All at once.

"I seem to remember you saying you'd never need my

help. That you never needed me at all." He stopped just inches in front of me.

"I'm here for Rachel," I answered and stepped back.

"Hmm. Is that why Kylan isn't here with you?" Alec questioned. I paused a moment too long, and Alec picked up on it.

"Are you going to help me or not?" I ignored his line of questions and his annoying smile.

I stared him in the eyes and waited for him to either give me what I wanted or throw me out.

Each second felt like needles pricking against my skin.

"I will help you," he conceded and crossed his arms over his chest. "Under one condition."

"I'm not coming back."

"That's not what I'm asking," he said.

He looked at my eyes and I couldn't tear them away from his gaze.

"What else could you possibly want?" My voice hardened.

I knew Alec and all his twisted schemes. I just hoped that this price wasn't too hefty to pay for Rachel. Or for Kylan.

"Your forgiveness," he almost whispered as his eyes turned soft.

CHAPTER EIGHTEEN

Alec was supposed to be cold and heartless. But that wasn't the person standing in front of me with open hands and hopeful eyes.

"What?" I mocked.

"If I help you, this represents a clean slate," he offered and raised his eyebrows.

He waited, hoping I would agree.

I paused and just looked at him in shock. I wanted to ask why. I waited for the punchline. The longer I waited, the more serious his eyes became. He held his breath and looked intently into my eyes.

"No." I shook my head. "You kidnapped me as a *child* and brainwashed me my entire life. You forced me to believe the Shadows were my only family. All along the way making sure I never caught on. If I did, you just changed my memory. All so that you could carry out your vengeance on the humans. Why, *why* should I forgive you?"

"Wait here." Alec raised a finger, not even considering my indignation.

He strode from the room. I didn't have time to process his words before he returned in a matter of seconds.

In his hands was the little blue book I'd seen in the safe that day. The day I found out that they had been lying to me, that my past was worth hiding.

"Lydia's journal. Consider it a peace offering," he said, holding the book in his hands.

I stepped away from him, not falling for whatever trick he thought he had me in. He watched me carefully before flipping to the first page of the journal.

"To my baby girl. I hope to tell you these stories myself one day, stories of our people, but for now I will keep them here. I love you more than you will ever know," Alec read aloud slowly.

His eyes flickered in the light. He waited to see my reaction.

To my baby girl. That was me.

The tears were automatic, uncontrollable. I wasn't standing in front of an enemy. I wasn't in hostile territory anymore. I was in a warm cloud, hearing my mother's words for the first time. The first time that I could remember.

My hands flew to my mouth to cover the strangled noise coming from me. My knees hit the floor. Alec dropped with me, still holding the little blue book.

Inside that journal was everything about her life, maybe about my life. She had addressed the entire thing to me. I caught my shuddering breaths and reached toward the seemingly insignificant book.

"This belongs to you. It always has." Alec closed the journal and held it out to me.

My fingers brushed the old cover. It was in pristine condition, waiting to be opened, to be read. The scent of the old paper drifted as I pulled the book to me.

The soft pages moved with my grip, and a shaky feeling moved down my spine. I wanted to hug the book as close to me as possible.

I lifted my eyes to him. He could have kept this book from me out of spite. It was a kind gesture, a little too kind for Alec.

"Why are you doing this?" I asked, expecting an honest answer but knowing that I might not get it.

"Those are my terms," he deflected my question.

I looked deeper into his eyes, hoping to see the trick in them. All I saw was the deep blue, more inviting than I had seen in a long time.

"I need one more thing," I edged.

"Risking my Shadows and giving you this journal back, that's not enough?" Alec raised an eyebrow at me.

"I need a moment of honesty from you." I stood, pinning the book to my chest like a shield.

"About what?" Alec stood with me.

"The lab in Louisiana," I started, watching every detail on his face. "Rachel left because she had a human that she wanted to turn Legend. Did you know they had a functional serum?"

Alec's eyes didn't shift at all. He just stared straight at me. A smile twitched on his mouth before he took a breath in.

"Yes," he answered.

"Yet, you haven't gone after them?" I asked.

"Their serum can create up to a Level Three. They haven't found a way to break through to a Four, let alone an actual Five. So, as of now, they have nothing I want," Alec explained calmly.

I watched his eyes, looking for any flicker of deceit. I watched his hands, relaxed at his sides. His breath, even and steady. He was telling the truth. But what Alec said was never really the problem. It was always what he didn't say.

"It doesn't make sense," I said. "Why would the humans running the lab even offer to turn another person into a Legend. What do they stand to gain?"

Alec was silent. I stared him down until he caved.

"You're asking the wrong question," he explained. "You want to know what the humans running the lab are thinking. But you don't need to know that."

I scowled. "Why not?"

"Because humans don't run the lab. Legends do, and they have plenty of reasons to create more Legends," Alec said.

My arms loosened at the news.

"Legends? If they run the labs, why would they be a threat to us? Why are they attacking us? They are the only reason acting out is such a danger. The only reason murdering in the Shadows is acceptable is because the labs haven't dared to take all us of on. But if that's—"

"Kate, Kate." Alec said my new name and I froze. "We can review politics or we can save your friend. All you have to do is say you want my help."

"How do I know you aren't lying?" I whispered.

He nodded. "Everything I just told you is true."

"The whole truth? You haven't conveniently left anything out?" I crossed my arms in front of my chest.

"You know me too well." Alec smiled. "But this time, I've fully answered your question."

I paused, looking him over like he would let something slip. "I don't know how to trust you."

Alec smiled widely now as his gaze roamed my face. Pride filled his eyes as he looked at the woman he trained so well. He knew exactly what he was missing and I knew he wanted it back.

"You can't," Alec answered easily. "You'll just have to risk it."

I had no other option. He knew that. He had to be manipulating me. I was sure of that, but I couldn't see how. I couldn't see why he wanted me to forgive, why he was being so kind.

It was a mistake. I was sure of that. But I said, "Fine. You have a deal."

I reached my hand out to him. He took a step closer to me, staring intently at my outstretched hand. He paused and looked back up to my eyes.

"You forgive me?" Alec confirmed before raising his hand.

"Yes." I nodded.

He reached out to me and took my hand in his.

My hand felt cold against his skin. He gave it a firm shake as his genuine smile brightened his expression.

Alec let his shoulders relax like they had been holding a physical weight. He moved to step toward the door. I used his hand to yank his attention back to me.

"Let me make one thing very clear. This doesn't mean I am back with the Shadows, or back with you," I threatened.

A dark smile spread on his lips. He didn't care what I thought this was or what I wanted. He knew what it meant for him, for that plan I knew he had formulating in his mind.

But I had to save Rachel. I had to prove to Kylan that I could protect him and his family.

Thank me when you come home safe.

"Understood." He shook my hand once more.

The light played in his eyes. It made me even more uncomfortable and I pulled my hand from his grip.

To avoid his gaze, I looked down at the old book in my hands. He nodded and left the room. I stood alone, nervous to see what was written on these pages.

I clutched the cover of the book, slowly pulling it open.

The paper crackled as it moved. The scent of dust filled the air. My hands flipped to the first page of the journal.

I read the opening statement in my mind. The same words Alec had just spoken. With the door closed and the room completely empty, I allowed myself to feel everything happening inside of me.

The words choked in my throat.

My breath shivered in and out of my lungs. My eyes darted across every particle of the page.

I turned the page to reveal the next entry, written in the most beautiful handwriting.

September 1777

Today is the best day of my life. Today you, my lovely daughter, were born. While this day is one to celebrate, I must admit that the world you have entered is not one I would have wished for you. You and I are quite different from the rest of them.

I'm not sure where to start our story, but it seems this is as good a place as any. The laboratory, as they called it. I have no idea how long I was there, as most of it was spent in utter delirium. Then the final tonic was ready. The one that would change the world, they told me. I will always remember the excruciating pain.

After a time, it finally stopped. I woke up and everything changed. I was changed.

A few weeks went by, and my body suffered. Food and water no longer satisfied me, not completely. I could not deny that they were right. I needed a human, if that was no longer what I was. I tried to fight it as long as I could.

Time passed along as if nothing had mattered. Everything in my life had fallen apart.

Then, you came. I feel as though I have a place to belong again. I swear to you, my daughter, I will do everything in my vast power to keep you safe.

I love you. Now and always.
Lydia

I held the book gently in my hands. The tears welled up in my eyes as I choked back a sob. My heart ached when I thought of how much my life had crumbled right in front of my eyes. Everything I had was hanging by a thread. Even through all this, I had her. Just like she had me.

"I miss you," I whispered to the inanimate journal. Still, a feeling of comfort wrapped around me.

I looked to the door that Alec exited. I wondered if he knew the gift he had given me. My forgiveness seemed like a fair trade for something as precious as this.

In fact, it seemed like more than a fair trade. I tucked the book in my arms and walked toward the door. I dried my tears and straightened my shoulders. This may have been a kind gesture, but Alec was still Alec.

Trusting him was a huge risk, and yet that was all I wanted to do right now.

He was playing me. I was not about to let him win.

CHAPTER NINETEEN

Around the corner, I followed Alec's commanding voice.

"The labs have taken a fellow Legend, and we are going to get her back," Alec announced to the group. The Shadows all looked between each other, holding back their one question.

"Why are we helping her?" Sage asked.

Her harsh voice rang out above the crowd. I looked back to see a pair of ruby eyes locked on me. Her tiny hand gave a wave from the shade under the balcony.

"Nice to see you too," I muttered to myself.

The few Shadows closest to me snickered. I glanced at their nervous eyes. They weren't sure how to act around me. I looked up at Alec and his eyes flew over to the petite yet threatening blonde leaning against a pillar.

"Once a Shadow, always a Shadow. Today, Kate has rendered us an invaluable service. We owe it to her to hold up our end of the bargain," he explained loudly so the rest of the group could hear his response.

Grumbles and complaints followed. But one stood out.

"Invaluable service. Ha. She never really was above sleeping her way to the top," a Shadow muttered in the far corner.

My ears perked up. I followed the sound and didn't recognize the face. It must be a new person.

Alec didn't waste a second as soon as his eyes narrowed in on the sound.

He leapt off the stage and through the crowd. His hand raised, now holding a dagger he had just created out of thin air.

The sound of the blade plunging into flesh rippled across the room.

The Shadow fell to the ground with the blade sticking out of his neck. Alec turned around and let the blood drip off his hand.

"Anyone else?" Alec offered and looked around.

The Shadows shook their heads. Silent and scared. Alec's word was law.

I looked at Alec and watched for any sign of a trick. The blaze in his eyes told me he was serious. I may have broken his heart, threatened his power, and beaten him in front of his own family, but he was still protecting me.

"Do we have to call her Kate?" Thayer's voice came from behind.

The one person who would dare to show up late to a meeting. A crazed excitement flew through my body and I knew it was him before I turned around. Thayer.

"Only if you want to sleep with both eyes closed," I said, not waiting for Alec.

Thayer's sappy brown eyes brightened at my threat. His brilliant smile stood out against his olive skin. I recognized every expression, every movement.

"It's good to see you again," he said like he was greeting an old friend.

He pulled me into a hug. I braced myself for some sort of emotional assault. Nothing came. He just held me close and then dropped his arms.

First came Alec with the peace offering, now Thayer. Both of them were being too nice. I settled my shoulders and promised myself I would stay alert regardless.

"The deadline is Friday at noon," Alec announced. "Thayer, Nikki, Sage, and I will be scouting out the location ahead of time. The rest of you will break up into three sections. Garth, Fiona, and Marshall will each be leading a group. I do not want the lab to know we're coming, so you will be taking different routes, traveling slowly and discreetly. No cars, no planes, and no humans. I want you on the ground."

Immediately, they divided themselves into groups upon his command. Their smiles and anticipation lit up the room.

"Allow me to repeat that last part. You will be traveling *discreetly*," Alec spoke slower this time and heads looked up at him again. "I don't want anyone to notice that you even exist when you pass them. Got it?"

A round of agreement came from the crowd. I noticed Grae wasn't anywhere to be seen.

He no doubt was tossed shortly after I left. I found myself hoping they took care of him quickly. Even if he didn't deserve it.

"The five of us will be leaving immediately; the rest of you will follow as your leader instructs. Leaders, see you on Friday," Alec finished, and a loud cheer erupted.

They all shouted to gear themselves up for a fight. The fight that most of them had been waiting on for a long time.

Alec stepped into the courtyard, giving specific instructions. Nikki came into view. She had been standing on the other side. As fellow Shadows, we were friends. Any superficial relationship ended when I walked out.

Nikki glared with her striking brown eyes. She turned her head and focused her attention on Alec. Her silky black hair fell around her shoulders with the motion.

I walked up to the both of them. Alec left to talk to another leader, Garth. He was tall and menacing, with sandy-blond hair and dark eyes. That left Nikki standing alone.

"Where's Grae?" I asked, already knowing the answer.

Nikki looked at me like I was the scum on the bottom of her shoe. Without answering, she moved her hands up to her hair and quickly tied a braid down her back as she walked away from me.

"Okay, never mind," I muttered to myself.

I looked over to Thayer, his lively brown eyes looking back at me already.

"Alec found out that he went after you with a dagger. He and I ended Grae right then and there," Thayer answered and stepped toward me.

"I'm sorry I wasn't there to see it." I smiled, hoping he would accept the sentiment.

The two emotions clashed inside of me as I so flippantly referred to someone's life and enjoyed the fact he had died, hopefully in pain.

"Nikki will get over herself eventually. It's going to take a lot of time before she sees you as a friend again. I did manage to convince her to tolerate you, though."

Tolerate, huh? I smiled back. I remembered back to a time when I would tease Thayer about the same thing.

An eerie feeling crept over me as I realized how deeply connected I was to this place. I didn't long for my old life, but my mind did feel at peace having the closure of seeing it in a less hostile situation.

Alec walked up and Thayer took the unspoken message and left to go stand with the others.

Nikki stood as close to Thayer as she could get. Her hands tied her long hair in a braid down her back all the while trying to keep her eyes off me.

Despite her jealousy and thinly veiled anger, she wasn't the person I was worried about.

"Sage is coming?" I leaned into Alec and whispered.

Her skin couldn't handle sunlight, courtesy of a lab experiment to improve Legends that went wrong. I didn't think she could make the long trek, especially not through the desert sun that waited for her outside.

"She'll be fine. As long as her skin stays out of the sun." He nodded over to her.

She put on a thick black jacket and gloves to match. She pulled the hood up around her face and tucked her white-blond hair behind her ear. Her vibrant red eyes shot over to me.

"I mean, is she going to create a barrier over her skin?" I asked, hushing my voice even further.

"A barrier," Alec pondered. "You mean like clothing?"

He smiled in a way that made me want to smack him. My hand twitched before I could stop it. He was actually making a joke. After everything we had been through, it seemed odd that he was so willing to get back to normal.

"She's not going to waste her energy by creating something that already exists," Alec explained. "By the way, she has excellent hearing."

I turned and looked at her. This time she stared back at me with her bright red eyes. She zipped up her jacket and didn't even flinch when Alec mentioned that she was listening.

"She better not slow us down." I looked back at Alec warily, hoping Sage heard that too.

"Speaking of clothes"—Alec reached behind him—"you might want to change."

He pulled out a small pile of clothing items that I instantly recognized. My hands reached out to touch the soft, pliable cotton and tight jeans. All the dark colors matched everyone around me.

"These are mine. You kept them?" I asked.

Alec simply shrugged his shoulders.

"Your whole room is exactly how you left it. Not touching anything was easier than throwing all of your stuff out," he explained without looking.

When I had changed into the dark clothing, I stood out less. Even when I left the mansion. I tucked the journal in the back of my pants, pulling my thin, charcoal shirt over it. I turned around and took one last look.

This place used to be home. It wasn't anymore, but it would always have left its mark on me. Literally, in my case. I looked down at my bare arm.

Today, I was running with the Shadows, and in order to get the job done, I had to be one.

I looked up to find Alec watching me. I tried to turn away before I saw his smile of satisfaction.

"Ready?" Alec called to me.

I looked back at his indigo eyes. They seemed brighter.

"Catch me if you can," I said, and my smile was automatic.

All my years of living and training flooded back into every atom of my body. Today, I was powerful, and that felt incredibly good compared to the powerless situation I had just left.

We both took off into the woods with the others trailing closely behind us. We ran as fast as our feet would carry us. The dirt parted under our shoes and the trees bent out of our way on my command. We ran past, completely unblocked.

"Show-off," Thayer called from behind me. I laughed.

"Jealous," I shot back at him.

I moved the next branch out of my way and then snapped it back just in time for it to hit Thayer. He ducked at the last second. I smiled. The adrenaline and using my talents easily brought joy bubbling up inside me. I couldn't deny, sometimes it felt great to live like a queen.

We ran all through the afternoon and into the evening. The sun began to dip behind the horizon. Trees turned into vast grasslands somewhere in Wyoming, or maybe we had crossed into Nebraska. As the light faded, I began to realize just how little energy I had.

I was exhausted and half limping with every pounding step. My head was splitting with an ache that traveled all the way down my spine. I needed energy. The rest of the group seemed to slow as well, but I was the weakest for sure.

I turned toward Alec and he caught my gaze immediately.

One glance and he understood what I wanted without me having to speak a word. Either I was that obvious or Alec was that in tune with me.

"Stop," he called and we all jogged to a halt. "Let's get something to eat."

Thayer grumbled, stretching out his barely challenged muscles. Nikki at least seemed a little relieved, even if she hid it.

The sun finished casting its brightest rays and settled into a warm pink. Alec pointed to the city lights glowing in the distance. We all caught our breath and walked to the awaiting city. As we got closer, there were far more lights than I was expecting.

An annoying tune carried in the air and the familiar scent of popcorn and grease hit me like a wall. A town carnival. Near the outside gates, we looked at the thumping, wild energy right in front of us.

My starved fingertips tingled just looking at the warm treat ahead.

"Mall and a carnival in one spot. I knew Norfolk was good for something," Thayer commented and was nearly drooling at the sight.

"We made it to Nebraska?" Sage asked, keeping her chin to her chest.

"Can't you tell by the smell?" Nikki asked with a disdainful glance around. "At least there's plenty of distraction. Sounds fun, doesn't it, Thayer?"

"I love carnivals," he moaned, his eyes already zoning out and lips curling into a salacious grin.

But I knew the Shadows making these comments, and they made my stomach turn now. To them, humans were mere toys and a crowded celebration was the perfect place to unleash.

This was different than Kylan and me in Portland. This was the Shadows, just like I used to be.

"No killing," I warned.

Thayer immediately looked back over to me and Nikki scoffed. I turned my gaze to Alec, the only one with real authority over them.

"Discreet," Alec commented back to him without even glancing at me. "No killing tonight."

"Fine." Nikki rolled her eyes as if my mere presence was already an inconvenience to her.

Thayer's gaze flicked between Alec and me. His brown eyes lingered on me before he turned to face the awaiting humans in the city.

"Whatever you say, boss," he said.

His smirk told Alec that even though he was in charge, I had been the one that just made that call. Thayer moved on easily and took Nikki by the hand. They both bolted toward the gate and leapt over it.

"Thanks," I nudged Alec with my arm. He still didn't look at me, he just smiled at the ground.

With the sun safely tucked under the mountains, the darkness of night overpowered the air. Sage reached up and tentatively removed her hood. Nothing happened. She looked up to us with a smile and walked toward the clamoring group of humans just on the other side of the gate.

"Won't the red eyes freak people out?" I asked quietly. I hardly knew anything about Sage, but I knew she would definitely draw attention.

"You see the red eyes?" Alec asked back to me. I looked back at him, confused.

"Doesn't everyone?" I asked.

"Sage has a rare level of talent for creating, especially things people see in their minds. The Sage everyone else sees looks completely normal. She only lets those she isn't afraid of see her eyes," Alec began to explain, still looking at Sage as she disappeared into the crowd.

Plenty of people glanced at her and nonchalantly looked away just as quickly.

"So she always blends in," I summed up his explanation. "How can she hold the illusion forever?"

"She doesn't. She's kind of a loner, and that means she only needs to hold it for a short period of time before she goes sulking somewhere. Now, please tell me you didn't make me stop the entire group just so we could stand here talking," Alec teased, and his excited eyes met mine.

"When have I ever wanted to just talk?" I asked, already regretting the way Alec could twist those words in his mind.

I didn't have time to see his smile before a loud ruckus broke out on the edge of the carnival scene. A team of high school football players were jumping up and down in their matching red letterman jackets. I didn't break my gaze from them.

The energy steamed off of their young, strong bodies. They weren't people, they were my next meal. Exhaustion tugged at my eyelids.

"Dibs on the football team," I muttered and stalked to the gate.

CHAPTER TWENTY

The young, athletic players were laced with adrenaline, hormones, and excitement. All of that entered my body, and I wanted to scream with joy.

The farther I got around the circle, the calmer each of them became.

My fingers tingled with the new energy as it sharpened every facet of my vision. Satisfied, I walked farther into the crowd. The young energy rushed through me, restoring my body. But for this trip, I wanted to be more than back to normal.

I actually had a reason to be high.

Despite the running that lay ahead of us, I knew I should take only the amount of energy that I truly needed.

It's what Kylan would do if he was here. I had to coach myself to remember that humans are people with lives. All of the mental effort didn't make the possibilities of energy sources dancing in front of me any less alluring.

I walked through the mass and touched as many people as I nonchalantly could. Most people didn't even notice because it was so crowded. I targeted the people who seemed the most energetic.

Flashes of Kylan and me doing the same thing at the square in Portland came back. A lump formed in my throat. I shook my head and instead tried to focus on the dirty ground.

My eyes caught a glimpse of Thayer sitting in front of a young girl at a kissing booth. She twirled her hair when he smiled at her, completely unaware.

Nikki was close by, giving the palm reader a back massage. Her hands lit up with energy as the man relaxed into her touch.

Her eyes caught me watching. She glanced at Thayer, who was too occupied making out with the human girl to notice anything around him. Nikki looked back at me and removed her hands from the palm reader.

He slumped forward, but kept his eyes open. She hadn't even knocked him unconscious. I stared as she walked toward me.

"I'm surprised you actually listened to Alec," I called out to her.

Nikki cracked a perfect smile and came to stand in front of me.

But she still didn't say anything. Her hand reached and pulled energy from the man standing next to her. He hardly even glanced at her.

She took a breath in and let the liquid power fuse into her body. Her hand pulled her black braid forward and smoothed some of the frays instead of looking at me.

"You're still going to ignore me?" I asked.

I tapped my foot on the ground, which caught her eye. She turned her head back to look at Thayer, who was now deeply invested in flirting with another human girl.

"Thayer thinks I shouldn't." Nikki's secretive eyes flashed back to me.

"What do you think?" I asked.

Nikki stared at me, unblinking. Her mouth pursed as she considered what I said. Her hand brushed another person next to her, allowing more energy into her body. She cracked her knuckles, covered in rings, before returning her stare back to me.

"I haven't made a decision yet. I understood the Mara who left. Her, I would want as my friend. But that's not you anymore. You're kind, even to *them*," Nikki spat as she glared at the humans around her. "It's disgusting."

"Not all of them are bad."

"Listen to yourself," she scoffed. "Have you even talked to one of them? Told them about what you are?"

"Those are two different questions," I answered as my eyes glanced to the ground.

I thought about Lisa. I had really talked to her and it was such a relief to have her listen. But she hardly knew anything about me. The guilt ripped through my chest.

"So you have to pretend to be like them? That sounds awful." Nikki stared at me, trying to see anything beyond my stoic gaze.

As a Shadow, I hardly regarded humans as living beings. They were toys at best, but in a moment of need they were nothing more than a meal. Nikki still thought of them that way. All the Shadows did.

"It's not as terrible as you think." I avoided her stare.

"I mean, you aren't actually friends with them are you?" Nikki asked, clearly appalled as her voice dropped even lower.

I looked up at her and waited. She looked for an answer that would prove I was still Mara in some way, to prove I was still like her. If my relationship with humans was all fake, maybe that would be enough for her.

She wouldn't find what she wanted. My pause told her my answer without me uttering a word. She stuck her finger in her open mouth and made a gagging sound.

"You really are too good now." Nikki shook her head at me as her shoulders fell.

My heart felt heavy in my chest as I understood what she saw when she looked at me. I shouldn't need her approval. I had convinced myself that I hardly cared about her. Seeing her in front of me, hating me, it hurt more than I had realized it could.

"So you and I are opposites now. You're completely bad, and I'm all good?" I asked.

Nikki shrugged her shoulders and continued to stare without an answer. I knew waiting wasn't what would make her talk.

"I don't believe it." I smirked and walked past her.

My shoulder brushed against hers as I walked away. She scoffed and her footsteps followed me.

"You can look all you want, but you won't find anything good in me," Nikki called out.

"I think if you look hard enough, you can find good in anyone," I said.

She just smiled at me with her arms still crossed in front of her. I took a step back when I realized what she was doing. She baited me to end up right where she wanted.

"Really? Even Alec?" Nikki challenged.

My mouth closed at the mention of his name. I glanced around, assuming he would be somewhere close and listening to every word. When I couldn't find him, I looked back at Nikki. She grinned and tapped her fingers on her arm.

"Yeah, maybe even Alec." I nodded.

"But he's a Shadow. Thayer is. I am. None of us will ever be good," Nikki glared.

The word *good* looked like it tasted of poison in her mouth.

"People change. Just look at me." I raised an eyebrow.

Another smile pulled at her lips. She mindlessly twisted one of the several diamond studs in her left ear. Nikki took a step away and looked down her nose at me.

"Part of me wonders if you actually have. You look different on the outside, but I'm pretty sure I saw you enjoying some high school kids over there."

I didn't answer. I didn't even flinch at the sound of her accusation, however right it was.

She whispered, "Either way, as long as you are this *Kate* person, and we're Shadows, you won't ever belong with us."

Nikki faded into the crowd behind her. I looked over and noticed Thayer was gone too. I wasn't a part of them anymore, and that was all that mattered to Nikki.

Every mile I had walked toward the mansion, I thought about how much I didn't want to be there and how terrible it was.

After a day with them, I didn't know anymore.

The conversation with Nikki didn't help either. She told me I couldn't have it, and now I caught myself wanting it just in spite of her. I could have assumed it was a trap, but I knew Nikki. She may be better at lying than I was, but I knew that she genuinely wanted me to choose them, to choose her.

I wasn't a good enough person for Kylan. But I wasn't a bad enough person for Nikki, either. It stung.

I slunk farther into the crowd, hoping to lose myself in the midst of energy and people.

My empty drifting led me over to the game booths, where

I finally noticed Alec. He walked along behind all the people playing the games. Each person would be teeming with adrenaline.

Smart choice. I smiled.

Alec hadn't seen me yet. He was too focused. He brushed past the people in front and the next ones in line. He touched each of their shoulders or necks as he walked past.

His hand landed on an old man trying to scrape gum off the bottom of his cane. I stepped forward to stop Alec from taking his energy as he barely had any to give.

Before I was even within sight, Alec stopped walking and looked at the man. Instead of siphoning his energy from the skin of the man's arm left open from his rolled-up flannel shirt, Alec reached down and took the cane from him.

I stopped in my tracks, puzzled at what I was watching.

Alec looked at the cane and held his other hand underneath the rubber base where the gum clung. He moved his fingers in the air until the gum gently was coaxed off the cane and fell into his open hand.

He handed the cane back to the old man and tossed the gum into the not-so-nearby trash can.

"Thank you, son," the old man had to almost shout over the sound of the crowd.

"Don't mention it." Alec patted him on the back and kept walking.

He didn't smile at his good deed. He just strode away like nothing had happened. My jaw was nearly brushing the ground, and my eyes gawked at what had just happened.

I composed myself enough to make my way to a bathroom long enough to change my clothes to new ones I had grabbed from a shop. I threw the others in the trash. The short-sleeved shirt left the mark on my arm totally exposed.

I should have felt uncomfortable, but I didn't. I had been Mara for too long.

I touched as many people as I could reach on the way out. My body was buzzing with the bright energy it now held. I could hardly keep my hands from shaking with the excitement coursing through me.

I walked to the iron gate and didn't even worry about the people watching as I jumped, twisted backward over the gate, and landed on my feet with ease. Not very discreet, but I was on a new mission. Alec was waiting at the rendezvous point.

"I saw your little act down there," I called to him.

"What are you talking—" he started and I held up my hand to stop him.

"Save it. You knew I was watching," I accused him.

He looked at me with bewildered eyes that stood out even more with a new gray shirt complementing the color. Alec looked back tentatively at the carnival. The old man was still in sight.

"Don't tell anyone," he whispered, begging.

Instead of defending himself or trying to convince me it was real, he asked for my silence. The others knowing that he had gone soft would jeopardize his leadership, which made me wonder if what I saw wasn't an act at all.

"You expect me to believe that you are suddenly nice to humans now?" I fired my question back at him.

He took his time before answering, so I encouraged him. "You're Alec Stone, leader of the Shadows, and the most ruthless killer I know. What changed?"

"Everything," he finally answered just to stop me from talking. "When you left, I wasn't just losing a fight. I watched my best friend walk out the door. Again. And I knew there was nothing in my power that could get her back."

My eyes went wide at his brutal honesty. His eyes shifted,

looking from me, to the ground, and then back at me again. This lack of composure wasn't like Alec at all.

"After that, the life I was living didn't mean as much without you. So, I started to..." he stammered, kicking the dirt with his boot so he didn't have to meet my judging eyes.

"Change?" I offered.

His dark blue eyes flicked up to mine one last time. The creases around his strained stare only deepened his sincerity.

Before I could respond, Thayer and Nikki came barreling toward us, also in a new set of clothes. Nikki's shirt was not her own. It was stolen from the girl who was working the kissing booth that Thayer had found. I didn't want to wonder about what happened there.

Both of them were almost flying they were so energized. Sage followed closely behind them. She walked calmly despite the new, flaring energy surrounding her bright eyes.

I looked away from the glimpse of the honesty I saw in Alec to the two bouncing idiots that interrupted.

Thayer stood next to me and took my hand. He laced his fingers with mine and leaned in close to me. I felt his hard muscles press up against my arm. His bright brown eyes were the color of sunlight shining through maple syrup, and the way the energy danced in them made me never want to look away.

"Are we ready to go?" Thayer asked sweetly.

I smiled back at him and gripped his hand tighter.

The smile dropped from his face a second too late. I twisted his hand around his back and pulled until his shoulder threatened to dislocate. He clenched his teeth together instead of yelping in pain.

"All right, all right, point taken," Thayer managed to speak.

I released my grip on him and watched as he stretched his shoulder back the other way. He turned to face me, still leaning in too close.

"Thank you." I nodded.

"Seems Alec is the only one that gets to hold your hand," Thayer teased.

He fluttered his eyebrows and darted in the other direction. I caught Nikki staring at Alec before she rushed after Thayer. I wondered so many things about her.

Alec looked over at me with the same pleading eyes as he had before. I nodded to let him know that I wouldn't tell anyone about the old man.

It felt odd, keeping a secret for him. It's what a friend would do. I didn't want to consider us friends, but here we were being honest and kind and trusting.

We both ran off into the dark after Thayer and Nikki.

CHAPTER TWENTY-ONE

We ran through the night and into the next day.

We had made it to a rocky patch of land between cities that barely had a tree every hundred meters. Hopefully, we'd made it through half of Oklahoma by now. We were too far away from city signs to tell anymore.

At least we didn't have to waste eight hours of the day on sleeping. That would really be inconvenient.

The afternoon sun hung in the air. We were less than a day away from Louisiana at this pace. My heart thumped at the goal being within reach.

I looked back and saw Thayer trying to trip Nikki by throwing a rock at her feet. At this speed, all it took was one wrong step and she would go tumbling for a while. I rolled my eyes and kept running.

Sage ran in front of them with her chin to her chest, allowing her hood to shade her face. Not a speck of her skin was touched by the sun as she ran.

Alec ran right next to me, taking glances every now and then. He wasn't watching to make sure I was still there. He was watching to make sure I was still doing well.

I avoided his eyes as much as possible, focusing ahead. I heard something connect with a body, and whipped around, still moving forward.

Nikki's body flew toward the ground as her feet twisted awkwardly beneath her. Thayer's smile sparkled in the sun. But she simply tucked into a front flip and landed back on her feet.

Thayer's smile widened instantly. She kept her fast pace and shoved Thayer.

He laughed as he stumbled but kept running. I tried to hide my smile as I looked forward again.

The next sound I heard was a thud, and then a tumble. The dead leaves crunched as I turned my head and saw platinum hair flying forward through the air. I flicked my gaze to Thayer, whose eyes were wide.

Sage catapulted forward as she bounced and skidded to a stop. We all stopped running and waited for her to move. As soon as Sage stirred and looked like she was trying to pick herself up, we all took a breath of relief. Except Thayer.

"Her skin," Thayer choked.

Sage's hood had fallen back and her face was completely uncovered. The tumble had ripped holes in her clothing and taken nearly her entire right sleeve off.

Her skin was already turning a bright shade of red. I focused back on Sage and we all ran toward her.

As we got close, the stench of burning flesh rose in the air.

Sage screamed, the sound ripping through the silence. She frantically searched for a place to hide her body from the sun. The fabric around her singed away, revealing even more skin for the sun to burn. Alec yanked her up from the ground.

Her red skin now blackened from the constant burning.

Alec raced her to the nearest hillside that offered a small spot of shade in an outcropping. Sage huddled close to the rock as the burning finally ceased. She immediately removed her coat so the fabric wouldn't press against her hot skin.

She looked down at the giant red welts and black scabs covering any piece of skin that was open to the sun.

"Sage, I'm so sorry," Thayer gushed.

"Shut it, Thayer," Alec threw back at him as he helped Sage finish removing her coat.

She was so weak, she could barely keep her eyes open. Her body immediately began to heal the burns, and it took almost all her energy to do it. All of us were already tired from the night and day of running.

I looked around at the group, and all eyes were intently fixed on Sage. Alec helped her lie down on the dirt and took caution with her burned skin. She winced as she finally got into a comfortable position. Thayer had knelt down beside her now.

"I told Alec not to bring her," Nikki sneered next to me and crossed her arms over her chest.

"Me too." I nodded.

Nikki glanced at me, surprised that I agreed with her. Then she flicked her gaze over to Alec and her eyes softened. An uncomfortable feeling edged into my stomach.

She turned her eyes to me. I shifted in place when she looked at me with an unsettling familiarity again. Hating that Sage's pain caused an inconvenience for me. That was something Mara would do.

Sage opened her eyes long enough to look at me, then look back at Alec, her mouth moving slightly. I'm not sure what she said, but Alec turned around to look at me. He left

Sage's side and Thayer stepped in to help her fall asleep. He concentrated on her red eyes.

"You're safe," Thayer whispered. "I've got you."

The fear in her eyes melted away. It almost looked like she was smiling as her eyes fluttered closed. As soon as she stopped stirring, Thayer and Nikki worked together to create water, dumping it on her smoldering body.

None of us were talented in creating when it came to human skin. They couldn't heal her, but they could cool the burn.

Conserving energy was her best bet right now, at least until the sun went down, which was still hours away.

"Alec, we can't stay here. We have to move on." I hated the words as soon as they left my mouth.

I felt heartless, the mark burned on my arm, but I had to focus on Rachel. I pictured her scared and waiting at the lab. I also thought of Kylan with his little family, and how they were nothing compared to the abilities of the lab Legends. They would all be slaughtered if we didn't have a solid plan, and for that we needed time.

Time that Sage was sucking away at this point.

"Sage could die out here, and you're willing to just walk away." Nikki quirked an eyebrow. "Careful now, that sounds like the old Mara talking."

She sauntered closer, watching me carefully with her glistening brown eyes. I glared back at her, hating that she wasn't entirely wrong.

"You could always stay behind with her," I offered.

Alec stiffened and glanced at Nikki. She just smiled at him and then moved her gaze back to me. Her slow steps toward me made the uncomfortable feeling in my stomach tighten.

"Not a shred of loyalty anymore. You want to leave two

people behind?" Nikki moved her judging eyes around my face before she leaned in to me and whispered, "Maybe you really aren't as good as you seem."

Nikki leaned away and walked toward Sage and Thayer. My eyes glued themselves on her. My fists clenched at my sides.

This is different. I wanted to console myself. I wasn't being cruel in asking to move on. I was being smart. Sage's limp body was covered in burns, utterly helpless.

She needed help that I didn't want to give.

"We are not leaving anyone," Alec answered me. "We'll have to wait here until nightfall and then Sage can have all the energy she needs."

"We don't have until night!" I tried not to shout, but my desperation was barely contained within my own body.

"Kate, we should still get there in plenty of time." Alec raised his voice with mine.

I shook my head.

Rachel was waiting in a lab for me, for us. She was scared and probably injured if she was even still alive. I could picture how Kylan would grimace at every bruise on her body when he got her back.

Time was running out. We needed a perfect plan, and we couldn't get that if we spent all of our time getting there instead of planning.

Sage was not worth my new family. She wasn't worth losing Kylan over.

I pointed in the direction of the lab and Alec shook his head again.

I shouted at him. "Alec, you're asking me to sacrifice my family!"

"And you're asking me to leave mine behind!" Alec roared and stepped as close as he could without touching me.

Determination, and even the loyalty to his precious Shadows, screamed in his eyes. I had never seen Alec have to choose between his goal and the Shadows. He chose them. I paused, my mind reeling.

We each took a step back from each other after an intense stare-down. We weren't getting anywhere.

"Mara, this is my fault. Her body will have had plenty of time to heal once it's night. Then, we can double the pace to Louisiana," Thayer said from beside Sage.

Her eyes had closed and her chest rose and fell steadily. I hated her, I blamed Thayer, and I just wanted Alec to listen to me so badly that I barely noticed Thayer used my old name. Thayer reached down and wrapped Sage's hand in his, careful not to touch the blisters on her skin.

I glared at his sweet, brown eyes for being the reason Sage fell in the first place. I wanted to hurt him, but then my mind changed.

I didn't want to cause him pain anymore.

I actually felt sorry for him. My heart melted looking at the two of them sitting there. His big eyes looked up at me for sympathy and that was exactly what mine returned. I forgot any reason that could possibly cause anger toward him.

But that was too easy. I closed my eyes and shook my head to rid Thayer's intrusive emotional tampering. When my eyes finally snapped back up to him, they were more furious than before.

"Stay out of my head," I threatened through clenched teeth.

I stepped forward, right into Alec's arms. His strong muscles flexed against me as he held me back from advancing any further.

"Come on, let's go for a walk." He spun me around and faced me in the opposite direction.

"No."

"Staying here and yelling at everyone won't fix this either. We have to wait for night so we might as well enjoy the view."

I didn't protest as much as I should have because, in truth, I didn't want to just stand around waiting for the sun to go down. It bothered me that Alec knew that, but he did. My body turned away from him, and he clamped his hands on my shoulders, pushing me away from the group.

"Stay here with them." Alec nodded to Nikki.

I smiled at that. At least Nikki still wasn't important enough in Alec's eyes to join us. I shouldn't care, but I couldn't deny that I loved seeing her being put in her place.

We both walked away together, our steps falling in line. Alec kept his hands on my shoulders, guiding me. I trudged forward, not wanting to look back at the person holding all of us up.

CHAPTER TWENTY-TWO

We walked around for an hour, partly in silence and partly filled with awkward conversation.

The sun didn't seem like it was any closer to the horizon. Every time I checked, I was disappointed. Each antsy step brought us no closer to nighttime. I sighed heavily and kept walking anyway, grateful for the distraction.

We were far away from the group at this point and long out of earshot. As we walked forward, Alec shifted the conversation.

"Why isn't Kylan here?" he asked me pointedly.

He kept his gaze on the ground, but I could sense the intrigue from here. I had avoided the answer back in the mansion as a power play. This seemed different.

"He will be. He's meeting us at the lab." I shrugged.

I hoped he would accept it and drop the subject. I knew he wouldn't, though—that would be too easy.

"He didn't want you to come," Alec gathered and kept walking forward.

I should have waited and planned my response. Or I

should have changed the subject and moved on. Alec poking holes in my status with Kylan wasn't helping anything.

The smug look he always had when he thought he was right would be waiting. I already knew.

"He wants to get Rachel back." I didn't meet his eyes.

"So you came back, even without his approval?" he continued.

I took a breath and decided there wasn't a reason Alec couldn't know what was going on, why I was here with the Shadows to begin with, or why I felt so guilty.

"I have to fix this," I muttered to myself.

I knew Alec heard me, but I didn't really care. He stopped walking, waiting for me to turn around and look at him.

"Because they are asking for you as ransom?" Alec started, "Kylan can't really be blaming you for—"

"Because I was the one who told her to go," I cut him off.

"You what?" Alec asked with wide eyes.

His shock seemed a little too overdone, but I ignored it. He should be surprised that I would suggest any Legend get involved with a lab.

"She asked if I thought she should go, and I told her yes. I sent her straight into their hands. I didn't even think…" I shook my head.

"That it was about you?" Alec finished for me.

I nodded. Alec let his eyebrows rise as he sighed.

"Wow, you really messed that one up, huh?"

His laugh broke my attention to my guilt. I raised my eyebrows.

"Aren't you supposed to tell me that it's not my fault? That I shouldn't blame myself? That would be the nice thing to do."

"I never got anything I wanted by being nice," Alec countered.

I looked at him, from his black leather boots and his slim-fit jeans to his crisp, dark gray shirt that made his eyes the brightest color on him. I thought about what he said, the way he moved, and the way he talked.

"You sound just like him, you know," I commented.

"Who?" he asked.

"Charles."

I watched him carefully. Charles was Alec's father, and the only parental figure I had ever known. Despite everything I knew about him, I still wanted to think of him as the precious parent that I lost.

"You remind me of him too. The day he died, we both changed," he said to the ground now.

"The labs became the enemy, ready to lock us up and torture us. The other Legends became a threat because it only singled out our lifestyle more. The Shadows were everything," I continued.

But I remembered the reason I never told the story to anyone else, why I never talked about it. Missing Charles meant that I missed everything he taught me to do.

"To defeat the monster," Alec quoted his father, waiting for me to finish.

"You must become the monster yourself," I said, words tumbling from my mouth.

I didn't even have to think to know how that sentence ended. Charles probably never went a day in his life without saying it.

"You don't have the luxury of blaming yourself. You made a mistake, and if you want to fix it, if you want to defeat that monster," he started again.

"No."

I was not a monster. Not anymore.

I tried to think of every reason to be good that Kylan had

showed me. No words came to my mouth, not while Alec was standing so close and staring at me that intensely.

"Fine." Alec narrowed his eyes at me. "Kate, you can't blame yourself. This isn't your fault. Everything will work out exactly as you want. Raquel will be fine—"

"Rachel," I snapped.

"Right. And Kylan will come running back to your arms and you two will live uneventful, happy lives from here on."

Alec stopped me from talking by grabbing either side of my face and forcing me to meet his eyes. It was a lie. Every word he just said. I didn't believe him, but that was the point. Alec could either tell me the hard truth or paint over the worry with lies.

I had always respected him for the former.

In his dark eyes, his admiration was evident, the way it always had been. I saw the little boy that I grew up with. I saw a teenager taking over a cause that was way beyond his years. I saw the man that relied on his father's advice even decades later.

His eyes softened and his touch lightened, but his hands still held me close. The way he touched me made me feel like the most fragile glass in the world, and it was his duty not to break me.

"Is that better?" he asked, leaning dangerously close.

His breath caressed the skin on my face. My eyes were glued into this deep blue stare. He didn't force me to stay, but I couldn't move.

"Alec," I only said his name, but he knew exactly what I was thinking.

The problem with knowing someone for so long is that he didn't need to read my mind. He knew me.

"Yes?" he waited.

I saw his thoughts written so clearly across his stunning eyes. There was also a benefit to knowing someone a long time. I knew him.

"You don't have a chance." I didn't sugarcoat the blow. I didn't need to.

Alec didn't take offense to hardly anything. I could speak my mind freely because he would only hear what he wanted to anyway.

"Do you want to tell your heart that?" Alec whispered gently as his sure smile flashed.

I listened as my heart rate betrayed me and sped up almost on his command. My body still reacted to Alec's touch. Centuries of training had taught me that being around him was a good thing. Decades away from him hadn't changed that yet.

"Just a biological reaction. I love him." I changed my approach and turned my head away from him.

I started walking again, finally allowing myself to think a coherent thought now that I was a little farther away from him.

"You love the idea of him," he asserted. I slowed my walk as he continued. "I know what it's like to be around him. We spent a couple of decades together before he left. Kylan is so annoyingly perfect. As a role model, he's great, but anything else…well, it's stifling."

I stopped my walk completely and faced him.

I thought of us at the riot. I remembered the red brick. I remembered the crowds of people. I remember looking at Kylan and feeling all alone. I remembered the shame for wanting more energy than I should, wanting to cause more pain than I should.

You want all that energy? Go get it. Don't let us hold you back.

"I don't know what you mean." I lied. Despite everything, I felt this growing urge to defend Kylan.

"Yes, you do. Admit it. He's just *too* good. It's an impossible standard to force on yourself," he said.

He didn't move. He just waited. That was so unlike Alec. All of this was. He was almost respectful of my personal space. He never acted this way unless he really wanted something.

He's manipulating me, I thought.

All I had to do was beat him at his own game. If he wanted to twist my emotions, then I wanted to return the favor.

"So, you're saying I'm not good enough for him?" My voice filled with anger.

"No." He rolled his eyes and waited for me to talk myself down.

He looked back up with blank eyes and waited for me to talk myself off the emotional ledge I was standing on.

"This is why you and I never worked. You never believed in me!" I threw my hands in the air.

"I didn't have to, I knew you. I knew you were amazing and had immense potential at your feet. When you walked in a room, silence followed. People looked up to you because you were incredible." Alec gestured toward my heart and held my eyes with his. "Even before you knew you were a Five."

My breath stopped. That was a genuine compliment, not empty flattery. Those were rare with Alec.

"I also knew the dark side of you," his voice smoothly dropped.

I couldn't look away. My mind struggled to keep functioning. Alec was being honest, and I didn't know how to process it.

"You created the dark side of me." I finally got the words out.

All these years, I had wanted to accuse him of exactly what he had done to me. If only I hadn't met him. My life could've been so different.

"We created the environment—you made the decisions,"

Alec corrected me. "I never influenced your choices when we were growing up."

He moved his hand to my face and lightly brushed his finger against my cheek. The skin under his touch ignited.

"Any of them," he whispered.

I knew exactly what he meant. He wanted me to know that I chose to fall for him all on my own. While that may have been true, the rest of our past together was riddled with his utter control over my life.

"Don't forget all the thoughts you did influence or just took control of completely. I couldn't make a decision without you changing how I thought and felt," I said, trying to control my breathing, not that it was helping my heart pounding out of my chest anyway.

I turned my face away from his hand. He dropped it to his side as his eyes hardened.

"Thayer was right next to me during all of that. Yet you have no problem hugging him and treating him like nothing happened," Alec growled.

I smiled at him. His anger didn't scare me at all, especially when it stemmed from a place of jealousy. In fact, seeing him so enraged only got me excited because I was winning.

"This isn't about him. This is about you. All the terrible things you've done—" I started.

"Match all of the terrible things you've done," he finished my sentence unexpectedly. "This isn't a contest for who's worse."

"If it was, you'd win," I bit.

I shoved his shoulders and he spun for me to kick my foot into the back of his knee. His legs buckled, but he caught my arms and wrapped them around his upper body and took me with him. He launched me over his back and I slammed into the dusty ground with him landing against my side.

He laughed. A deep, breathy laugh I couldn't forget. It was real. Another rare moment with Alec.

The redness in his cheeks, squinted eyes, and hand clutching his chest like he needed more air. It was impossible to hate him like that. My giggle slipped out.

"You're a hypocrite," Alec accused, still laughing.

He rolled over and faced me, lying on the ground. I slapped away his finger that he pointed in my face. He was breathing hard between smiles.

"You're a liar." I pushed him over.

"You promised a clean slate." He took the hit but rolled right back to face me.

"You promised I would be happy." I raised my eyebrow at him.

He winced and looked down at the dirt below us and then back at me. A hint of compassion brimmed in those harsh, crystal eyes.

"You were," Alec whispered, and I heard the honest catch in his voice over my pounding heart.

"We're both pretty messed up." I turned so I was facing the sky as I looked for a distraction.

The perfect, clear blue sky. It reminded me of Kylan. It was always too easy for him. He seemed impervious to temptation. Unblemished. Like the sky on a clear day.

"That's part of what makes us such a good team."

Alec casually moved a leaf on the ground to distract me from his overt flirting. He wasn't stupid. He wouldn't try if he didn't think there was a chance.

I looked inside myself for a reason to shut him down for good. I really looked. I sat up instead, brushing off his comment.

"We weren't a good anything," I said.

I crossed my legs and picked up a stick in front of me. I

needed something to touch or snap in half. Alec sat up with me, a little closer now.

He probably hoped I wouldn't notice the lack of distance. But I was a born Legend and a trained Shadow. I noticed the change in the temperature near my arm. I noticed the way his breath went off rhythm.

I noticed everything, and he knew that.

"We were good at some things," Alec whispered.

My mind followed along slowly, letting every word melt whatever shield I had put up against him.

Alec's hand brushed up my arm, lighting a trail of fire on its way up, just like it used to. My heart launched into a sprint and my mind reeled to keep up. Then the guilt came creeping in.

This shouldn't be happening.

"Alec, don't," I forced.

I turned my face away from him. The dried dirt crunched when either of us moved. His hand reached my shoulder and turned me around.

"You don't have to be so good all the time. Not with me," Alec said.

Being good was what I wanted, I knew that. But it was exhausting sometimes.

Sometimes, I couldn't help it. I just wanted to take the easy route. I no longer had the bloodthirsty rage that drove me to acts of insanity. I just had the lingering distaste for acting like I was an average person when I clearly wasn't.

I was the only Level Five. I had power beyond belief.

Yet there I was in Portland, playing house with a group of people that I really didn't know. I was trying to be a hero in a world that I still didn't feel like I fit into. I was surrounded by people that didn't understand.

Alec did, though.

He had been there from the beginning. Despite everything,

he was still my closest friend. That's also what made him so dangerous. He knew too much.

I focused back on the Alec sitting in front of me. I wanted to see a villain, but I couldn't. His eyes were sweet and he was totally honest. It didn't seem like he was playing. It seemed like he was genuinely reaching for what he wanted.

For me.

Alec leaned forward slowly and subtly.

"This is a game to you. It always is." I broke his gaze and looked down.

Seconds later, my eyes wandered back over to Alec. Not to his face, but everywhere else. His shoes, his legs, his chest, and up to his shoulders. I knew every curve of him.

Centuries together could do that.

"Maybe I don't have to be so bad. And you don't have to be so good," Alec breathed.

He brought his hand over to my face again. This time, I didn't pull away.

My heart ached with guilt, not just for my past but for who I was right now and the bad tendencies I still couldn't control. Like my desire for Alec.

His face drew closer to mine. His breath pulled me in.

"We could meet in the middle," he finished.

"Alec, why are you doing this?" I pulled away and asked him plainly. "Don't give me some sob story about being lonely or changing. I know you too well to fall for that. Tell me why you want—why you're doing this."

He waited a moment before speaking. With my forehead pressed to his, I waited for him to speak. Two heartbeats. Three heartbeats. Four.

I couldn't convince myself to move. All I could do was listen as his breath turned into words.

"I want you. I don't want you just because of your power.

I want *you.*" He held my face in his hands like I was the only thing in the world worth looking at. "I want my childhood friend. I want the girl who laughed so hard that milk came streaming out her nose."

I laughed, despite the whirlwind of conflicting emotions in me. He smiled when he saw that he'd made me happy, even if it was temporary.

"I want the fiery woman that knows what she wants and doesn't let anything stand in her way."

My smile stayed. So he stayed where he was, dragging his fingers down my neck.

"I want all of you, baby. The good and the bad."

His words sunk in. I looked at his eyes and wanted to know the absolute truth. I looked as deeply as I could, knowing Alec would never let me in. But he proved me wrong.

Images came flashing across my mind.

I was about seven Legend years old, playing hopscotch in the courtyard of the mansion. I had been here for less than a decade. I was laughing as my toes barely even touched the stones before my next leap. Curiosity flashed in my eyes.

I grew up. I was a teenager, alluring and reckless. I pranced through a training simulation, dodging the blows and ducking through the finish line. The only thing that held my attention was Alec. He walked up and I was falling too hard to catch.

But then, I was a woman with wild eyes and a strong heart. The woman I used to be. My blond hair spun all around as I danced in the courtyard. Dagger flashing on the arm raised above my head. The light glinted off my shiny locks and my laugh mixed with the sunshine.

I held my breath. The smiles, the laughs, all of them came from him. All preserved in his memory. That was how he saw me. I was glowing and perfect and there was nothing in the world he wanted more.

But that didn't change anything. He was infatuated with me and I was desperately entwined with him. We were still too different, even more so now.

Those were the happy times, the ones I could smile at. But he was leaving so much out. I started to pull away, but Alec snatched my wrist. I locked eyes with him again.

And the visions changed.

I dropped a human to the ground after I had just drained the life out of her. My smile grew on my face as the energy melded into my body. My eyes lit up with excitement. I burst through the front doors of the mansion, completely flying on the energy I consumed.

I taught another Shadow how to cause immense pain to others. The human example screaming on the floor only meant that I had succeeded. I laughed.

I pulled my hand up to my gaze, human blood dripping from my fingers. My face was blank as I pulled a drenched hand through my hair. The sticky warmth painted itself across my ear and down my neck. I looked at Alec, long enough for him to see the blood, long enough for me to drag a red finger across his lips. He stayed perfectly still as I kissed him. The blood and his lips mingling together in one metallic taste.

I sucked in a breath. I understood, even if I hadn't wanted to see it before. To Alec, I wasn't good or bad. I was both. I was just me.

I blinked and came back to the man sitting in front of me.

To Alec.

"You let me read your mind?" I gasped, still shocked by what I had just seen.

It was so personal and touching. It was completely raw emotion weaved into every image. Little pieces of Alec I had never been able to feel. In that second, he was too fragile for me to touch, too delicate for me to want to break.

"So you can believe me when I tell you," he said slowly, still trying to recover after exposing a part of him he probably hadn't ever done before.

"Please don't," I begged in a whisper.

Words were already forming on his mouth. His lips pulled up in a heartbreakingly honest smile. I looked up to his eyes, hoping he would keep his next words to himself.

"I love you," he whispered.

He said like it was painful to risk me not feeling the same way. He held his breath like it was the first time he had ever told me that.

I remembered a time when he'd said that for the first time. Back when everything between us was easy and fun. Our only problem was Charles' ever-abusive reign and having to conceal how much time we spent together.

The air pulsed around us in the sparse desert that felt like it wasn't hiding us enough. A cool, dusty wind brushed my arms, making me aware of how heated my skin had become. My entire body felt numb and crazed at the same time.

I knew I shouldn't. I knew I would regret this later. I knew I'd have to answer for the moment that came next. I bit my lip hoping the pain would bring me back to my senses.

Alec waited, so softly, so gently.

Instead of the guilt weighing me down, my mind shoved it aside. At least for now. For right now, there was one thing that I wanted. Nothing was stopping me but my conscience.

But that wasn't a good enough reason.

His lips met mine before I could take in my next breath. We fit perfectly together. We already knew our way around each other. I wanted him as much as he wanted me.

I missed my friend and how well he knew me. I missed the boy who was always up to something exciting or the young man with so much future ahead of him. I missed the man that had all the power in the world, but the one thing he couldn't live without was me.

I missed, missed, missed this Alec.

Regret was sure to follow, but for now, all I could feel was Alec in front of me and the burning ember inside of me roaring to a fire.

My hands reached up to either side of his face, pulling him into me. Our lips crashed together and we both forgot to breathe. My heart fluttered when I felt his lips move on mine. Every inch of me needed to be near him, to feel more.

This was when I understood Alec best, when I was so close to him. A part of me could feel he was still hiding something. He had to be.

Unfortunately, a larger part of me didn't care. It was too wrapped up in the scent of his breath to worry. Maybe it should have.

CHAPTER TWENTY-THREE

The sun finally went down behind the trees.

It was almost night, and Sage would be able to run again soon. Alec and I stood, neither one of us saying anything. We walked back to the group in long, slow steps.

As we neared the others, he didn't touch me. He didn't look up at me in confusion. I had to move on with reality. And for some reason he seemed willing to let me go.

So you can believe me when I tell you. I love you.

I shook my head. He was my past.

If anything, the kiss was more of a goodbye to the life I used to live. At least, that's what I told myself. I just hoped Alec saw it the same way.

"There you are," Nikki's annoyed voice broke through the silence.

"Good." Thayer looked up at us, still kneeling next to Sage.

She was sitting up and using his arm to steady her. Her burns had mostly changed to a deep shade of red, healed enough that she could bear to be touched.

Her gaze darted all around and her eyelids fluttered. She teetered between almost healed and all her energy depleted. She could hardly keep her eyes open long enough to make solid eye contact with anyone.

None of us were too worried. As long as she could get to a human energy source, she'd be fine.

"Is she ready to move?" Alec asked, snapping back to reality.

A few moments ago, he had been different. He was so purely my Alec. In front of the others, he changed to the leader they needed.

"Yeah." Thayer looked at Alec as he helped Sage stand up.

"There's a town a few miles east of us." Alec walked over to Sage and checked on her himself. He held her with the same gentle touch he had used with me.

"Is that what you found on your little *scouting* trip just now?" Nikki asked.

"Doesn't matter. Let's go," Sage grumbled and took a few shaky steps forward.

Before she fell, Thayer swooped down and picked her up. She weakly swatted at him, the errant annoyance hardly even fazing Thayer.

"Fight me all you want, princess." Thayer smiled and ran east.

Nikki took off running after them.

Alec looked over at me, a glimmer of confidence in his eyes. I knew what he was thinking. I also knew I had to say something if I wanted to stop that thought.

"What happened back there, can't happen again." I looked at him seriously and waited for his mood to fall.

It didn't. He kept smiling and moving toward me.

Just before I was about to run, he flashed forward and hovered his mouth above mine. He raised his hand to my face and brushed his finger along my cheek. I looked into his indigo eyes and saw all his thoughts swimming inside. He leaned in close to my ear, his excited breath hot against my skin.

"Catch me," he whispered and chills skittered down my spine.

My feet knocked out from under me and I fell. My back smashed into dirt, knocking the air out of my lungs. Alec took off without giving me a chance to regain my footing. He never fought fair.

A smile broke across my face as I shoved off the ground and used it to propel me forward.

The adrenaline spiked in my muscles as I chased after him like my pride depended on it. He didn't waste time looking back to judge his competition. He already knew everything he needed to know about me.

We reached the town—more thriving and buzzing than the last one, even with the carnival—in a few minutes, and the only one that was breathing hard was Thayer. He finally put Sage down and let her stand on her own.

Her obvious indignation gave her enough of an energy burst to be able to walk without help now. She stumbled into a homeless man and they both moved out of sight. I didn't bother following to check on him. Alec had given his order already.

We raced each other into the town without moving too quickly for the humans to notice. All of us smiled at the waiting energy ahead. Standing with the Shadows and descending into a town brought back a lot of memories as nostalgia washed over me.

Yet, things were different this time.

I knew the humans weren't going to be killed, I knew that I wasn't going to be manipulated, and I knew that Alec didn't care if I was good or bad.

For the first time in my centuries spent with the Shadows, it felt like home.

Alec and I walked together into the town. Both of us felt the exhaustion from running all day and waiting all afternoon. We immediately brushed the people that were closest to us.

I was holding on longer than I should have, but I justified it because my body ached from a lack of energy.

Alec spotted a bar that had people spilling out the front in a long line. He grabbed my hand and dragged me all the way to the entrance.

I saw the people dancing inside, and I didn't protest. The heat of their energies radiated all the way over here. We were stopped at the rope when the bouncer gave Alec a disapproving look.

"I don't think so," the burly worker scoffed.

Alec immediately pulled on my hand again and held me in front of him. The bouncer looked at me for far longer than was comfortable. A smile spread on his human face. I tried to hold back a gag.

He stepped aside and let us both through. Alec grabbed my hand again and starting walking both of us to the center of the group of people. I pulled on Alec's hand and brought him close enough to me so he could hear.

"Did you just use me as your ticket to get in?"

He smiled and winked at me. The loud music almost drowned out his voice. The smell of sweat and alcohol immediately filled the thrumming air as soon as we crossed the threshold.

"It was easy. You could get into any bar you wanted looking like Kate," he said.

He returned my smile. Almost automatically, we moved to the beat of the song, and the rest of the people in the room fell away. I leaned my head to his ear, noticing the brush of his skin against mine.

"You think Kate is pretty?" I asked.

Alec had always loved the way I looked as Mara. As her, I had shoulder-length blond hair and far more threatening features. Of course, my icy blue eyes were always the same. Unchangeable even for me.

Kate, on the other hand, was soft and approachable. Hardly a Shadow. I had dark, chocolate curls that reached almost to my waist like they did now.

He pulled back just enough so I could focus on his lips. The smoky air and flashing lights changed the color of his skin.

"Beautiful," he mouthed.

At the single word, none of the people, music, or lights around me mattered.

My eyes stayed with him until a man behind Alec bumped into him. Alec lurched into me and anger immediately flared in his eyes.

The person turned around and said nothing, too drunk to even offer his apology.

Alec pivoted on his heel and glared at the man. As large as this human was, he was completely useless against Alec. Especially against an angry Alec. I cringed, knowing his upcoming fate.

"Get out of here." I leaned forward and shouted a warning to the man.

"Make me," he challenged.

I grimaced as that was probably the worst thing he could've said just then.

Alec snapped his hand forward and latched onto the back of the man's neck. He pulled the man in closer. The faint glow of the energy coursed into Alec, but was easily lost in the misty light show of the bar.

The man tried to pull away from Alec, but his strength was fading fast.

His eyes drooped. Alec didn't care. I did the only thing I knew would stop him.

My hand shot forward and touched Alec's arm. I immediately pulled energy from Alec himself.

Alec felt the energy leaving and dropped his hold on the man, who quickly stumbled away. Confused, Alec looked down at my hand and the energy flowing out of him, then he looked back up at me in wonder.

He didn't stop me.

CHAPTER TWENTY-FOUR

I was utterly stunned.

The other times I had pulled energy from a Legend, I was fighting, proving a point, or running. Too guilty or distracted to enjoy it.

I thought it felt amazing then. But now, I was concentrating on the sheer bliss and exhilaration that filled my body.

What made it worse, or better I guess, was that it was purely Alec. The power was laced with everything I imagined him to be, everything I wanted to feel from him. I was literally pulling him into me.

My breathing sputtered and all I could focus on was Alec's adrenaline rising in his body, sending his energy into me faster. My heart raced at the same pace as his.

With my eyes locked on Alec's, he stepped closer.

His body being so close felt wrong. My mind screamed for me to step away. My body disagreed. It wanted more of the strong, vibrant energy. And more of him.

I reached my hand up and put it on his neck, and instantly more power jolted in. His face was close enough to mine that

I pressed my forehead against his, another point of heated contact.

My hands pulled him closer and my body was ablaze with his energy. I lost track of time and how much energy was now pouring into my system, until I felt Alec's knees wobble.

"Stop," he croaked out gently.

My eyes shot open and I saw what I was doing.

I lifted my hands off his skin, already sensing the guilt. But Alec smiled, weary and feeble and still grinning. He reached next to him and pulled energy from the woman dancing next to him. Little touches here and there. The pain I'd caused was nothing to a Shadow. I couldn't hurt him if I tried.

He reached his other hand up to my face. Alec was the one holding on to me now.

We both moved to the music, and pulled the crazed energy all from the humans around us, into our bodies.

I smiled and let my muscles relax as the song calmed my worrying thoughts. I saw Alec smile and noticed how tightly he held on to me. For a moment, I forgot where we were and what we were doing, and I just danced.

The music buzzed in my chest and my fingers stretched to the ceiling with power. I had my back to Alec now and he moved forward, placing a kiss on my neck.

"Seem familiar?" he whispered.

Then my mind forced me to remember. I stepped away and looked at him. His eyes searched my face for the same answer I gave a long time ago.

"We should get going." I nodded toward the door.

We had enough energy. I was ready to run for days. We didn't need to stay here.

"You sure you don't want to stay a little longer?"

His smile changed from soft to dark. He was at once a tender child I didn't want to hurt and now my dark, guilty pleasure. My lips parted as I tried to think of what words to say.

I saw my reflection in the windows just behind Alec's smile. Even in the dark and crowded club, I still remembered who I was.

Everything I had spent decades working toward came to my memory. I could still remember vividly the face of the person that I wanted more than anyone, and a life I wanted to fight for.

In the end, that wasn't Alec.

I shook my head. "I'm Kate now."

He knew that meant I was with Kylan, his brother. If Kylan still wanted me after all this was over.

Alec's eyes fell and then filled with understanding. It was the closest to empathy I had ever seen from him. I turned to leave the bar, looking forward to the clean air that could clear my thoughts.

A hand fell on my shoulder, stopping me. Alec spun me to face him, strong and unapologetic.

Before I could even breathe a word, his lips came down on mine.

He kissed with a force he had restrained earlier. He was desperate now.

Those strong hands kept me pinned. The deeper he kissed, the less I could divide us in my mind. We were barely two people anymore.

His breath mingled with mine. He needed this. He wanted me more than anything waiting outside. My mind raced and my heart struggled to keep up.

He paused briefly, breaking the connection. I wanted to lean forward and kiss him like that again. I couldn't fight the urge. The most I could do was freeze in place and wait for Alec to be the noble person and let me go.

Because as much as I knew I shouldn't, I wanted him too.

"No matter what you look like, you will always be my Mara," he whispered against my lips.

His hand held the back of my head so I couldn't move, even if I could convince my body to do so. He kissed me gently one more time and I realized I didn't want him to pull away just yet.

"Alec, you can't—" I started, taking advantage of the clear thought.

"I just needed to say it," he said and stepped back. He held his hands up in surrender. "You should know all your options. You always have a home with the Shadows."

I love you, were the words he didn't say.

A tear stung the corner of my eye. I remembered what Nikki said, that I'd have to choose who I wanted to be. If I ever came back to the Shadows, things would be different, things would be honest.

I had already forgiven, the original deal I had made with Alec, and now we could all forget together. Every bad thing I wanted but had been trying to train out of my system could exist there.

I wouldn't have to be so good, and they wouldn't have to be so bad, just like Alec had said. I held my lips tight, trying not to say anything.

Alec didn't stop me as I darted out of the bar and onto the street. I closed my eyes and gave in to the one urge I had been fighting this whole time.

I wanted energy. An extreme amount of energy.

I wanted to feel all of it charging through my body as it erased all my stress, just like it used to.

When I opened my eyes, the world in front of me changed. The people that walked on the streets became targets. The sidewalk spread out in front of me, begging me to follow it.

So, I ran.

I ran as fast I wanted to through the Midwestern town. The humans may have seen, but judging by how dark it was, they probably wouldn't. Either way, I didn't care. My mind was blazing with choices and I wanted anything to silence it.

Every person I passed walked away with less energy. As I ran, my body fed off of the abundant power around me. I ran up and down all the major streets with names of flowers or food that were supposed to seem quaint.

I didn't focus on the ornate street running through the center of town, the various museums to preserve the ancient history of only a couple hundred years. I was older than anything in those halls, stronger than anything they could have built.

Eventually, it felt like my feet weren't even touching the sidewalks anymore. My muscles finally relaxed. The bursting energy inside me was barely contained by my own skin. I was higher than I had been in years.

And it felt…it felt so incredibly good.

I met back up with the rest of the group outside of town, near the beginnings of miles of farmland. All of them looked like they had their fill of energy. Their bright eyes all watched me as I approached.

Sage's burns were gone almost completely. I wondered if her skin would return to the perfect porcelain color it was before.

She had a new jacket tied around her waist. When I looked closer, all of her clothes were new, with the wrinkles still in them from being folded in a store. All of them were still just as black as the previous ones.

Nikki admired her nails. She had her head lowered, but that still didn't hide the wicked grin on her face as she drawled, "What took you so long?"

"We all know what took so long," Thayer said with his arms crossed in front of his chest.

My smile gave me away a second too soon. I lunged for him, trying to kick his knee out from under him. He dodged at the last second.

"Look who finally learned." I applauded him. "Are you ready to go now?"

I smoothed my dark hair and walked through the group. He must have seen how fast I moved and saw how my eyes burned when I looked at him.

As I brushed by Thayer, my hand grazed his exposed neck. A small burst of energy flew from his body to mine. Touching Thayer was different than Alec. Different emotions, too twisted and vibrant to tell them apart, but still more exciting than a human's.

Thayer shoved my hand away from him and took a step back. I glanced back at him, waiting for his next remark.

"Are you high?" Thayer asked, a look of disbelief in his eyes.

"Why would that be so surprising?" I put my hand on my hip.

Alec stared at me with a flicker of admiration and question. He didn't say anything, waiting for me to answer for myself. I let my gaze travel back to Thayer.

"It's not…" Thayer edged.

"It's not surprising for Mara," Nikki muttered as she smoothed her long braid.

I didn't wait for her words to sink in. I took off running in the direction of our destination. Louisiana wouldn't stand a chance against me, not against me this high on energy.

It's something that Mara would have loved.

As Kate, I justified that I needed the energy. I was a good liar, but even I couldn't lie to myself about why I wanted the energy.

Whispers followed me through the trees.

"Boss, what did you do to her?" I heard Thayer's voice say.

"I kissed her," Alec admitted easily.

"Your brother is gonna kill you." Thayer's words were barely audible now.

"We'll see about that." Alec's voice was the last one I heard.

I listened in with more attention, but could only make out their running footsteps nearing me. It was strange to think that a little while ago, I didn't want anything to do with Alec or them.

Now, I ran with the Shadows without a thought of what would be the right thing to do.

CHAPTER TWENTY-FIVE

We arrived to the miles and miles of orchards that hid the lab from sight. Rumors were that this land was used for farming, and no one really bothered to ask much more than that. Plenty of other farms with barely any people were scattered in this area.

It was northwest of Baton Rouge and far away from any attraction that could draw a wandering human near.

Mounds of earth hardly big enough to call hills and endless trees stretched in every direction.

A perfect hiding place.

Far enough from humans, but not so far that energy was out of reach for anyone who could manage the trek to another farm or even farther to a city.

The land under our feet was soft, moist like the air we breathed. The trees in this fake orchard had grown unattended. They were too close together, the branches weaving a blanket of cover above us with swathes of moss stretching down.

The first glimmer of something other than nature came into view and we slowed. Alec looked at Nikki and after a few seconds, she changed direction. Then, he did the same to Thayer.

Kate, head to the south side. Alec spoke into my mind.

I had left my mind open and that was never safe around Alec, no matter how much he seemed to have changed.

Meet at the base of the hill at sunset, he finished. I nodded to him and snapped my guard back up.

I walked toward my lookout point, reminding myself to keep my guard up. Dodging the patches of standing water, I reached the top of the hill and crouched low.

The lab beneath me had dark windows and a mix of steel and concrete walls. I waited for hours, noting how many Legends or humans went in and out.

It was nearly sunset before I broke my concentration. I was about to turn and walk down to the meeting point when I saw a sleek, black limo pull up to the courtyard in front of the lab.

A few assistants near the door raced to the car. All of them kept their eyes to the ground. A woman stepped out slowly.

She had black, shiny hair that rivaled Nikki's and wore large sunglasses that concealed her face. She handed her bag to one of the assistants standing at her attention.

They all waited until she started walking forward. She meandered to the door, taking her time. She looked down at her glittering, diamond-studded watch just before entering the building.

"Sixteen more hours," she remarked.

She stopped and looked at the surrounding area as if she expected someone. I remained completely still, staring at my opponent. In sixteen hours was the ransom time. She was the one behind all of this. We were definitely in the right place.

What worried me was that her voice sounded eerily familiar. I had never met her before, but I couldn't shake the feeling that something was off. I tried to place her in my memory.

I pulled the journal from my waistband, flipping to the next entry.

June, 1779

We had to leave. The humans grow more restless with each passing day. The other people, the ones that are now like me, have started to cause unease. The people are scared. Stepping outside of the house has become dangerous. Too many humans believe we are a threat to them. They are right.

Our kind is far superior to them, but more importantly, we need them to survive. They have started hunting us down. I thought the threat would burn with the lab. It did not.

I want to be sympathetic to the humans. Even looking at myself, all I can see is a thief, a murderer. Then I look at you, my precious, perfect daughter.

You are no thief, you only take what you need. You are no murderer. I wish I could give you a different life, but I cannot. All I can do is teach you to be kind to the world. Maybe by the time you are grown, the world will have learned to be kind to you as well.

I love you. Now and always.
Lydia

I couldn't say that the world had become more kind. It was a dream to believe that the humans would ever knowingly coexist with us.

Just an impossible dream.

I felt a hand drop on my shoulder.

I spun and grabbed the person by the neck, slamming them up against a nearby tree. The loose leaves shook down, sending the moss swaying just as I was about to cause an undue amount of pain to whoever had come to find me.

But I realized who I was holding six inches in the air.

"Oh, it's you." I let out my breath and dropped my hold on Alec.

His feet hit the ground and he rubbed his neck, sucking in a distressed breath.

"Nice greeting." He strained to get the words out.

"You know better than to sneak up on me," I whispered and raised my chin.

"You didn't show up, so I came to check on you." He straightened and stopped exaggerating his pain.

He had already begun healing. The pain probably didn't even bother him anymore. I looked at the sky, realizing how dark it had actually gotten.

"You were worried about me?" I turned and looked at him, trying to study his face.

Alec always protected me when I was a Shadow, but so many things had changed between us.

"I'm always worried about you," Alec whispered and stepped closer, reaching his hands out to me. His fingers brushed my arm automatically, like he thought they belonged there.

My blood pumped so loudly that I could hardly hear the leaves shifting under his feet, or notice the added heat from his body getting closer to mine. I shook my head and looked for a way out of the situation.

"Sorry, I didn't realize it was this late. I got distracted," I muttered and breathed through my response.

I turned around to face the lab. Alec dropped his arms and stepped to stand beside me, looking down at the lab. I sighed in relief for the diversion.

"What did you see?" he asked, crouching down next to me.

"A woman with black hair and horrible fashion taste. I think she's the leader." I didn't bother pointing my finger. Alec could easily see who I was referring to.

"Good," Alec commented and nodded his head. I turned to see his smile. "Then we can get them all at once."

We both watched until the woman went inside, then turned to head back down the hill. We met up with the others to share intel. Tonight, we had to have a plan because tomorrow was the deadline.

"There are no scouts patrolling the north side of the building," Sage spoke up first.

Finally, she's useful on this trip, I grumbled to myself.

Hanging around Alec and being on a power trip had changed my attitude too much. I shook my head and took a breath. I was Kate, not Mara. I never had to be her again.

"That's good, we can start there," Alec said as he planned in his head.

"The east entrance has two guards placed at the door," Nikki shared next. "They never rotated. What's worse, the entrance requires a retinal scan."

We all groaned at that news. There was no way to fake a retinal scan. Eyes were permanent. The lab knew exactly who they would be going up against.

"Same with the west," Thayer said. "We aren't getting in a side entrance."

"And the back doesn't have any entrances?" Alec asked Sage.

"None except the windows on the fourth floor. Everything else is concrete and steel," Sage said, tentatively parting her sleeve from her glove to check the light. She hissed and shoved the fabric together.

So far, this plan was not looking good.

"Well, Mara, oh sorry, *Kate*, can change that," Nikki offered and tossed her braid over her shoulder.

"An entire building that we have no idea how thick the walls are?" I stepped toward her, Alec put a hand between us. "No, no I can't. The last time I even came close was the day Charles died and the whole building went up in flames. I won't be able to control it on that level."

A quick grunt from Thayer, and I raised my hands and stepped back.

"You won't have to change the whole building, just a doorway-sized hole. Or can you not handle that either, cupcake?" Nikki stepped forward and my anger flared.

"Someone is going to notice if a wall just dissolves. The whole plan will be blown." I clenched my fists, wishing they were around her neck already.

"Hey, hey." Alec stepped between us and looked at Nikki. "Back off. She's right. We can't force our way into the building; it will ruin any chance we have at surprise."

"The front has guards posted on the inside and I couldn't see a rotation," I shared and everyone's shoulders fell a little. Only one viable way in and out existed. The front door.

"We can't take them all at the front if they're coming one by one. We need them to have a reason for all of them to leave the building," Alec said more to himself than to anyone else.

He looked at the ground and pursed his lips. Then his eyes flashed up at me, and I was already worried by how hopeful they looked.

"They aren't expecting the Shadows, right?" Alec asked me.

I hadn't exactly broadcasted my plan. The only person who knew what I was up to was Kylan, and I highly doubted he told anyone but Cassie and Derek.

"Well, no..." I started.

"At the most, they are expecting Kylan's family...and you," he continued.

He smiled easily as the plan formed in his mind. I finally pieced together what he was suggesting.

"No—"

"But then we could still have the advantage of a surprise!" Alec held up his hands to restrain me.

"We are not offering them up as bait to bring the lab workers out." I gave him a stern look.

He didn't change his decision. I took a glance around at the others. I hoped to see at least one of them sided with me. But that was a long shot.

"We would get there before any of them even got close," Thayer spoke up and tried to soothe me.

I braced myself for a foreign feeling to come in and convince me to go along with the plan. It never came. Thayer wasn't influencing my decision at all. I narrowed my eyes at him, not believing he could actually be that altruistic.

"Yeah, if they show up without you, all the lab Legends will file out to punish them. They didn't get what they wanted, so of course they'd make a scene," Nikki agreed eagerly. "We certainly would."

"What if they don't?" I asked. "What if this doesn't work at all and instead they send a few Legends out to kill them all.

Kylan's family won't stand a chance against them." I looked directly at Alec.

He was the only one I really needed to convince. His face didn't change when he looked back at me. His sharply defined eyebrows lifted, waiting for me to conform to what he wanted.

"We will be there in time, I promise," Alec assured me.

The others got a little quieter at the last word.

"Then at least let me stand with them." I tried not to sound like I was begging.

"You can't," Thayer moaned. "If you go out with them, they'll snatch you too quickly for us to get there."

"He's right, Kate. For this to work, you have to be with us," Alec said softly.

He took my hand in his and held it tightly as he looked at me, his eyes wide with hope. I knew he was asking for more than just me staying back with them. I couldn't promise what he wanted.

I wasn't sure I still deserved Kylan, especially after how I had acted this week. I ruined his family, left him, kissed my ex, and got so high I barely cared about any of that. If anything, I deserved to be dumped and left alone.

With that weighing on me, I felt a new draw back to my old life.

Maybe I wasn't cut out to be so good. Maybe it just took me this long to understand that. And maybe, judging by the look on his face, Alec knew it all along.

He had let me go because he knew that eventually, I would come back, no matter how long that took.

I looked into his deep blue eyes, fighting the overwhelming urge to agree with him. His hand squeezed mine even tighter. I listened to the sound of his breath as my resolve fell.

"Fine, we can let them go out first," I muttered.

I already grimaced at the thought of their reactions when we told them that I agreed to offer them up.

"And what about you?" Alec asked, not taking his eyes off mine. I turned my eyes to the ground. I pulled my hand from his grasp

"I will stand with you," I said.

The words flowed comfortably from my mouth, far more comfortable than I wanted them to be.

"That's my girl." Alec smiled.

That's my girl. Those words echoed through my mind during the long night.

We all stayed in the sprawling, overgrown trees that night. Anyone walking on the wet ground wouldn't be able to see us up there, not through the thicket of leaves and moss.

The full moon shined bright enough to light up the area around us, peeking through the leaves like a kaleidoscope of blue light.

I read through another entry in the journal by the scarce glow of the moon. I wanted it to bring some clarity, maybe even hope that everything could work out.

The words spread out on the page and my eyes drank them in.

February, 1780

The whispers have followed us to the new land. Up and down the streets I can hear talk of a mythical creature that steals souls in the night. People wail of their lost loved ones. They ask questions. They talk when they think I cannot hear.

You are so young, and you have so much to learn. I try my best to teach you about taking energy. You don't understand yet how badly you can hurt people. I have to watch you always, never turn my back when other people are around.

The night before today, I awoke to shouts outside of our house. They came with torches to our front step. I gathered you up and took what I could carry. I ran into the night. I kept running until I no longer saw another living person. The farther away we are from them, the longer we have to walk to get energy. However, the closer we live to them, the more dangerous our lives become. There is no reasoning with the humans. They talk, they plan, but they do not think. They call us murderers as they do everything they can to kill our kind.

I will do whatever I must to keep you safe. You are the one thing that brings joy to my life. I will not lose you.

I love you. Now and always.
Lydia

She was right, even then. My heart twisted as I thought of her navigating through every turn of life on her own. She had a child that depended on her. She was forced on the run because of an ability she never wanted.

Tomorrow would be the first step in changing what should have been corrected centuries ago. Kylan would take Rachel, and Alec would take control of the lab.

We rounded up the groups of Shadows trickling in throughout the night. All of us took turns refreshing our energy supply in the nearby neighborhoods or cities. The plan of attack was whispered in the streets or between branches.

Each person had their own responsibility, and we needed the numbers to make this work.

Kylan and his family would walk out first, without me. Then, once most of the Legends had come out of the building, we would descend.

Best scenario, they'd be stupid enough to bring Rachel out to make them watch her die. We could grab her and take off.

Worst scenario…I didn't want to run it through my mind. There were so many holes in this plan and so many things that could happen.

After I returned from my trip into town, I felt the energy almost bursting through my skin. I wasn't as high as I was the night before, but I was pretty close. As close as I could get while still maintaining control.

Alec nodded when he saw me and walked over.

"Kylan's family is a couple of miles out," Alec whispered as he pointed to the west.

I listened closely, barely able to hear their voices in the distance. A smile spread across my mouth as I heard what I knew was Kylan's voice.

"Okay." I breathed in.

This was the moment I had been dreading. Telling Kylan about the plan we hatched, the plan to put them in as much danger as possible. Although, there were other things I was dreading too.

"Do you want to bring them in, or shall I?" Alec asked kindly, seeing what a dilemma this caused for me.

He was being too nice. Normally when he did this, he had either done something bad or was about to. But it had been going on long enough that I wanted to believe he might actually be genuinely trying.

"Follow me." I looked up at him but didn't wait for his response.

I started walking in the direction of Kylan. Of my Kylan.

Maybe he would understand. He knows how energy and power could change a person. He wasn't as pure as fallen snow like I thought he was. Maybe he would be reasonable. It was a stretch, but it was all I had to go on.

We ran until their voices were close enough that a human could hear them. Then, we stopped. I stopped. I looked ahead and waited for them to reach us, all the while trying to comfort myself.

Alec put his hand on my shoulder and rubbed gently. My muscles released as he applied pressure.

"It's going to be all right," Alec whispered.

But I didn't hear those words. *That's my girl.*

That was what he really meant. And I knew as soon as we saw Kylan, he would think the same thing.

Too nice again. It sent goosebumps down my arms. I nodded my head and stared in front of me, waiting.

CHAPTER TWENTY-SIX

Kylan

The trip was a long car ride followed by a long time of pacing back and forth in the various cities surrounding the lab.

I had no plan. I had no idea how to get Rachel out of the lab. I wouldn't hand Kate over, no matter what she had done. But I couldn't let Rachel die.

Every time I looked at Cassie shaking in the night, trying to console herself in Derek's arms. Every time I thought of Rachel's scream on the phone, I wanted to break something.

But all I could do was try, even if it was powerless. We were a family and we stuck together no matter what.

Family. That only made me think of Kate. I wanted her to be here. I wanted to tell her how angry I was for what she said to Rachel and how awful it was not seeing those exciting blue eyes next to me.

"You okay?" Derek asked.

We had walked through the miles of thick trees surrounding the lab. It looked like no one had pruned these trees in decades, maybe longer. But I was more concerned about Cassie, who clutched her arms, walking far away from either of us. I nodded to her.

"Is she?" I said

"I'm asking about you." Derek turned back to me.

"We'll get her back." I kept walking.

I didn't know if I was talking about Rachel or Kate more. Derek patted a hand on my back and went to Cassie, softly guiding the three of us together.

"What are you going to say?" Cassie whispered.

I peered down at her. Cassie nodded, and I knew who she was talking about.

"I don't know," I answered honestly. "She may not even be here."

"She said she had a plan. Maybe she's already here and she can help us fix this," Derek interrupted my thought.

"Maybe," I muttered.

We kept walking in silence. My heart was in my throat, making it hard to breathe.

I felt her before I saw anything. The air had changed around me. The wet wind carried a new smell, something familiar.

The scent changed when they became visible through the trees. They. The two of them waited at least a few meters away. I halted when I saw them. Together.

Those icy blue eyes were sharply trained on me. I saw her and I wanted to melt into the soil. The air tightened between us like hands pushing me away from her.

Seeing her stand next to my brother, dressed like him, marked like him, I felt too much to distinguish anything. All I could do was stand and stare.

She was the reason I was in this position, fighting for everything I loved, for my sister. We couldn't lose Rachel. Cassie couldn't lose Rachel.

I caught a glimpse of red hair moving in front of me before I could pull her back. Derek already had a hand clamped on her wrist.

"You're Alec Stone," Cassie gasped.

She looked at him and saw his black dagger showing proudly on his arm. Her face paled like she had just seen a nightmare.

"In the flesh," Alec said and smiled from the way she said his name.

I clenched my jaw and Kate grimaced at Alec's reaction. At least she wasn't totally brainwashed by him yet. Cassie didn't see the same thing. She looked at Kate like she was ready to tear her skin off.

"If he's here, the Shadows are here," Derek warned.

She broke her concentration on Kate and listened. They were quiet. Even if we listened hard enough we wouldn't be able to hear the rest of the Shadows despite the numbers.

"You brought your Shadows with you?" Cassie's voice spat out.

Derek and Cassie stood shoulder to shoulder as they looked at the two of them. They were protecting each other. I stood just to the side of them, looking directly at Shadow Kate.

I splayed my fingers and crouched just slightly, an automatic response to that dagger mark. I hated Alec, and I hated how much she looked like him.

She was a part of their family as much as ours, the only bridge to our divided worlds.

For the first time this week, I knew what I wanted. I knew that my family couldn't be complete unless everyone was there. Cassie. Derek. Rachel. And Kate.

I was fighting for two of my family members today.

One of them was trapped in a lab, and the other was

standing next to the leader of the Shadows wearing the same dagger as him.

"They aren't here to hurt you," Kate said and raised her hands. "They're here to help get Rachel back."

"Why would they help us?" Cassie asked and pointed an accusing finger at Alec.

"Our reasons for wanting to take down the lab are…" Alec glanced at her—of course it was her—"personal."

My stomach sank the second I saw Kate glance at Alec. The others flinched at the sound of his voice. But she seemed to be silencing him instead of encouraging him. She didn't care about him the way he was implying.

I stood straighter now and looked between the two of them.

"The Shadows have been waiting for an opportunity like this for a long time," Kate tried to explain further.

My eyes hardened. Alec wouldn't hand out free favors. He had to be getting something in return. Cassie and Derek looked at me to see if they should trust either of them.

"We have a plan, but we need your help," Alec offered slowly. "If this all goes well, you can take Rachel—"

"And you can take Kate?" Cassie interrupted.

"What? Why do you even—" Kate started, glancing at me.

My eyes went wide with hope.

"Kylan told us all about your *one true love*," she mocked the words.

I frowned. We had had a lot of talking time between Portland and here. Not all of that was as kind as I probably should have been. I was angry and giving Cassie way too much information that she couldn't wait to blow out of proportion.

Derek glanced at me, trying to understand if Cassie was wrong at all.

"Aw," Alec whispered to Kate and flashed a smile. "Nice to know you still talk about me."

My eyes slid to him and my fists tightened even more. Cassie's face twisted into a snarl as her assumption was confirmed by Alec.

"I don't," Kate threw back to Alec and opened her mouth to continue.

"Listen Cassie, there is—" Alec started.

"How do you know my name?" Cassie interrupted and froze in place. Her face went white.

I had never told Alec her name. No one should have. I put a hand on her arm, ready to pull her back and attack if I needed to. Derek did the same thing.

He wasn't touching Cassie with the two of us here. But he didn't make a move.

"How do you think?" Alec said slowly and raised an eyebrow at her. "Same way I know how much you blame Kate for this situation. Or how desperate you are to control everyone around you, including this cheap replica of a brother that Kylan's found. Derek, is it? Or how scared you are that you didn't even feel me enter your mind at all."

"Get out, get out!" Cassie shut her eyes and pressed her hands to her ears.

She walked back into the both of us. I kept my eyes on Alec. He raised his chin so he could look down his nose at the rest of us.

"As I was saying, the help from the Shadows is not contingent upon her choice."

Kate threw a glare at Alec. "There is no choice."

"I know there isn't." Alec winked at her. "But you can at least let the poor guy think he had a chance, baby."

I took a step forward and wanted to rip out his tongue for calling her that again. A nickname from when she was Mara. I remembered it from the dungeons, and from the forest when he took us both captive.

But she wasn't that person anymore, no matter how much she looked like it. I had to believe that.

Before I could say anything, she did.

"Do not call me that." She shoved a finger in his face, but that anger only made him smile more.

"What's the plan?" Derek interrupted.

Thank you. Sometimes he was the only sane one between Cassie and me.

Cassie saw his open-mindedness and gradually followed along. Each of them took turns staring at Alec, then staring at Kate. I listened to Alec's plan, trying to imagine it coming from her instead.

I never cracked a smile though. I had to keep my expression even in front of Alec. Instead, I tried to focus on what Alec was explaining.

After he was done, I took a moment to think about all the risks. There seemed to be too many, but our plan wasn't much better.

"You agreed to this?" Cassie asked, looking incredulously at Kate.

"I know how it sounds. But all of you will be completely safe," she assured, and my muscles loosened at the sound of her calm voice.

"Safe? You mean like how you promised Rachel that she would be safe?" Cassie challenged.

"I think we should do it," I said in a final tone.

My shoulders relaxed knowing I wasn't the only one who saw the faint amount of hope in the plan. Kate smiled at me, and I wanted to grab her and run as far away from here as we could. But both of us needed to stay right where we were.

"Great, I'll get them ready," Alec responded and turned back to the Shadows. "Kate, are you coming?"

I halted. That name sounded wrong in his mouth. Sounded like it meant something different than when I said it.

"I'll be there," she said without turning to face him.

I listened as Alec took off after the Shadows. But I kept my eyes on her. On my Kate.

"He calls you Kate now?" I asked.

"Uh...yeah," she rushed. "Please don't take anything he says seriously. I told him that my coming back to the Shadows had nothing to do with him and everything to do with Rachel."

I could already see it in her eyes, but hearing her say it made it even more real. She didn't want Alec anymore. This was a part she had to play and nothing more.

"Relax." I smiled. "I know desperation when I see it. Especially on my brother."

That allowed her to relax slightly. She glanced at where Alec had left and turned back to face me. Her eyes focused on mine.

"I'm sorry you're upset about my methods, but we'll get her back." She stepped forward.

"I know why you did it," I whispered.

My eyes flashed a brief moment of understanding and almost gratitude. Without the Shadows, we might not be able to get Rachel back without making the trade for Kate's life. We both knew it.

"Anything for you." She smiled weakly and tried to swallow the lump in her throat.

Seeing her so close made me want to fix every problem we had. She jumped forward and wrapped her arms around my neck. For a few seconds, I just wanted to hug her back. But I was frozen, feeling the way she held her breath too long and her soft arms pinning me to her body.

But this wasn't a Shadow holding on to me. This was Kate. My Kate. The one that somehow made the rest of the world make sense around me. The one that made all the pieces of my life fit together. The one that completed this family of mine.

I wrapped my arms around her, and she breathed a sigh of relief. I pulled her in tighter than I expected and my heart thumped loudly in my chest.

"I miss you," I breathed through her dark hair.

She held her breath again. Strings of fire burned through my chest. I glanced at Cassie and Derek, both of them trying to look away and give us some privacy. I smiled again, my mouth moving against Kate's hair.

"I'm not going anywhere." She held me close.

Feeling her body pressed against mine, both of us holding each other, made my entire body blaze. She was so small and fit perfectly under my arms…but I had other things to worry about today. Other plans and people that could ruin everything else.

I pulled away and took a step back. "I don't think you should trust him."

She smiled knowing that I was still concerned about her, that I missed her.

"I don't trust him. But we have to use him. We don't have another choice," she answered seriously.

My shoulders relaxed a little when she explained that she still sided with us completely. I took a glance around at the others.

"Everything is going to be okay," she said to the rest of them.

Derek's eyes softened slightly now that I had let her in this far. Cassie kept her glaring stare on Kate. But it didn't matter if Cassie was still mad. She knew we had to use the Shadows too.

The plan was risky and borderline insane. There was a chance that I may never see any of them again. So I wanted to make these last few seconds count.

I wanted to do what I should have done instead of sending her away. If we only had this moment, then I was going to use it.

"Kate," I called.

The second her eyes met mine, I had to move.

I kissed her like I hadn't seen her in years, like kissing her was more important than anything beyond the trees. She pressed against my chest and I couldn't believe how small and fragile she felt. But she was astonishingly strong if she could walk back into the mansion, if she could be around Alec and not turn into who she used to be, if she could fight for my family even when I rejected her.

She was the strongest person I knew, and I never wanted to let her go. I forgot about anyone else around us. I forgot the soppy ground we stood on.

Because for this moment, I was flying. I took in a breath and kissed her again, unable to hold myself back. I savored every second of her warm lips.

But seconds were all we had. I was too aware of the time. The ransom clock was ticking.

I pulled away too soon but left my forehead pressed to hers with her hands holding me as close as I could get.

"It's only a few hours until the ransom. You better get back to the Shadows." I glanced behind her, breathless.

The statement cut deep as I was reminded that for now, she was with the Shadows. I leaned back and hated that I needed to let her go. That I had to watch her return to my brother instead of asking her to stay.

"I'll see you when it's over," she promised.

I placed my hands in my pockets to keep from reaching

for her again. I moved my gaze to the ground. I was still breathing hard from the kiss. But I allowed myself one more look.

My fingers pulled at the air and felt a delicate flower stem form between them. A bright yellow daylily now rested in my palm. I lifted it to Kate and she smiled instantly.

She gently took the flower and took a step back to where she needed to go.

"See you when it's over." I winked and then turned around to face the others.

Derek was already smiling and Cassie was watching with sad eyes as Kate ran back toward the Shadows. I calmed my thoughts by telling myself that as soon as we got Rachel back, everything would go back to the way it was.

Everything about her eyes and body language told me she wanted it. We both wanted it. I smiled.

We could all be a family once this was over.

CHAPTER TWENTY-SEVEN

I tucked the daylily in the first few pages of the journal and secured both of them under my belt.

A flower that was hard to kill, that could survive a lot. That's what I was, that's what our love was. Something that was too strong to just wither and die.

I was still smiling when I walked into the middle of the Shadows and stood next to Alec. He looked at me and immediately noticed the grin.

"Things went well?" Alec whispered his question, trying not to look at me again.

I went to answer but instead he turned to the group leaders, making it a point to ignore me.

He gave an instruction, and they each left to disperse the information. When they turned away, Alec faced me again with eyes trying to look bored.

"Yes." I nodded my head and didn't elaborate from there.

Alec stared at me, his eyes roaming my entire face, suddenly interested.

The other remaining Shadows had either taken the hint that Alec wanted to be left alone or were already otherwise occupied. They moved around each other without a sound. They talked below a whisper and their steps were silent.

"Did you tell him?" he asked, leaning down to me.

His hopeful eyes gave away exactly what he meant. Alec needed to know that once this was all over, I was leaving.

"Kylan knows everything he needs to know," I answered vaguely, hoping that would hold.

I walked toward the top of the hill, careful in my steps. I wanted to be where we could keep an eye on Kylan's family. The rest of the Shadows were getting in place, going over the plan with each other.

We just needed Alec's signal to move and the ransom time to tick down.

"That's not exactly an answer," Alec whispered, following right behind me.

"It's not exactly your business," I retorted.

"You don't want him to know," Alec mouthed, barely even speaking.

He grabbed my arm and stopped me from walking. Alec looked across my face, observing carefully. He could always spot when I was lying to him.

"Know what?" I raised my eyebrows. "Nothing happened."

I waited for him to say that we were getting back together. After that, I could shoot him down and get him angry enough to fight.

Alec studied my eyes. "Why would you lie to him?"

If Alec had a stronger moral compass than I did, I knew I was making a mistake. I planned to tell the truth, once all of this was over.

"I don't have to discuss my every thought with you," I said.

"You're afraid to tell him," he said. "I can wait until you get over your feelings for my brother, but he would run away screaming, right?"

"That's not what this—"

"You know you can't hide what happened forever," Alec interrupted.

"What am I hiding?" I asked.

He shot forward and hovered his face a few inches from my face. I caught my breath, afraid to move too quickly and make a noise.

"That deep down, even you can't deny what you've been feeling ever since you saw me again," he responded carefully and brushed his hand along my face.

"Hmm…a mix of anger and disgust, with maybe just a dash of annoyance." I stared ahead, not looking at him or his hand.

I still felt the sparks along my jawbone. I fought the shudder already rocking down my arms.

"That we kissed," Alec continued, undeterred.

"Don't think—"

"Twice," Alec smiled at how frustrated I became.

"Telling him that would only hurt him more and he needs a clear head right now." I stared at him now, ignoring the way his hand fell from my face to my neck. "I will explain everything when the time is right."

"How are you going to explain to him you haven't been able to stop thinking about it? How you forgot exactly how good it felt to be with me and the Shadows, not because you had to but because you wanted to," he whispered and my heart fluttered. I swallowed and refused to flinch. "Or that it takes every ounce of self-control you have to stop yourself from kissing me again."

Alec stepped within a breath of me and I fought to keep my control.

I sucked in a breath and noticed how his blue eyes had lightened in the sun breaking through the clouds. His muscles tensed under his shirt and his chest rose with a new breath. I realized I had stared too long when I looked at Alec's mouth and saw his growing smile.

"How are you going to explain all that?" So quiet, so gentle.

His words were too accurate to be just a guess. He knew. I narrowed my eyes at him and took a step back from him, forgetting for a moment that I needed to be quiet.

Alec looked down and saw something under where my foot would have landed. He flashed his hand forward and pulled me back up on my other foot and into his body. His feet planted on soft, quiet dirt.

My breath stopped the moment I collided with him. He stared into my eyes, not needing to explain himself.

"Stay out of my mind."

"I didn't read your mind," Alec said while I stepped back slowly.

I opened my mouth to speak, but Alec got there first.

"Your friend Cassie is a Two. She couldn't even see it coming. You, on the other hand, a Level Five, you would've known," Alec explained. "Even if you are distracted."

"Then how…" I stopped talking, not wanting to say anything further.

"I saw it in your eyes. Thanks for confirming it, though." Alec winked again.

I didn't have a response for that, and Alec knew it. He smiled and turned his attention back to the lab.

"Whatever happened the last two days does not matter. I want to be with Kylan. The kiss didn't mean anything," I said, already regretting how heated my argument sounded. I should back off.

"Which kiss? The one where you couldn't help but jump on me in the forest? Or the one at the bar when your tongue—" Alec grinned.

"Both." I shook my head. "I mean, neither. Neither of them meant anything." I wanted to hit him, even if it made too much sound.

"I'm sure Kylan will see it that way too." Alec shrugged his shoulders without looking over at me.

"You arrogant little—" I hissed through gritted teeth.

I lunged for him, hoping I could crush the air out of his throat. Alec's gaze lit up as I reacted exactly how he wanted me to.

My arm flying toward his face stopped silently in the air when a strong hand grabbed me.

Thayer yanked me around to face him instead. His other hand clamped down on my other arm when it was within reach.

"What are you doing?" I whispered, trying to pry myself away from him.

"Helping you." Thayer smiled at me, pulling my arms farther away from Alec and closer to himself.

"This, this is not helping me," I whispered back. I moved my arms that were entangled in his hands.

"He's baiting you," Thayer coached quietly. "Take a breath and calm down."

He stared at me as he took a deep breath, and then held it as he waited for me to follow. I rolled my eyes and took a deep breath with him. He watched me, and we both released our breaths at the same time. A smooth, calm feeling cleared my mind.

"Now Thayer, don't tell her all my secrets." Alec's voice pricked against my ears. "You'll ruin the fun."

That calm feeling exploded, replaced by the surging anger that Alec brought out in me. I pulled at Thayer's grip again, trying to face myself toward Alec.

I didn't pay attention to my steps, or my voice. All I wanted was to gouge out his precious blue eyes.

"Okay, never mind. Let's get out of here before you blow the whole plan." Thayer decided and pulled me around to face away from Alec.

Without a second to get my footing, Thayer shoved me in the opposite direction of Alec. I scanned the ground, finding a soft place to land before my feet hit. I turned back to face him with an incredulous look on my face. He simply lifted his hand and motioned for me to turn around and start walking.

"Where are we going?" I asked, not moving at all.

"To get more energy." Thayer walked up to me. "You seem a little low."

"What makes you say that?" I raised an eyebrow at him.

He leaned in close to my ear as he took a step around me. His breath tickled the side of my face as I waited for him to speak.

"Because it was way too easy to hold you down," he whispered.

He smiled and quickly darted out of my reach. He turned back to face me, nodding his head away from the lab.

I ran after him, following closely on his heels. Both of us watching our steps until we were safely out of earshot of the lab.

Then we broke into a dead sprint toward the nearest city.

CHAPTER TWENTY-EIGHT

Anytime I got within reaching distance, he sped up again.

My muscles could never compare to his strength. His ancestors were one of the first experiments also involving human strength. None of the Shadows could outrun him.

We crossed into Baton Rouge, and instantly my body reacted to the warm energy beating within the people there. Thayer coasted to a stop and I went to stand next to him.

"Why didn't you pick New Orleans?" I asked, hoping to avoid the Alec conversation.

"Ah, already hit it twice." He waved a hand. "Plus, this is closer, and Alec will want you back soon."

"You don't have to save me from Alec. I can handle him," I chided him. He sauntered on like it didn't matter.

"I know. That's all you've been doing the past few days is *handle* him."

I shoved him and he stumbled a few steps before a smile unleashed on his lips. His eyes watched me, and then moved to the street we were about to enter.

"It's not like that anymore," I reminded as I spotted the first group of visible humans.

"That's exactly my point. If you really want things to be different, you are going to have to stop falling for his games. Fights with him always end up with you back in his arms. I've seen it one too many times." Thayer reached toward a man and brushed his finger down his arm.

The human looked up at him and blushed when Thayer smiled at him with that gleamingly white smile. I rolled my eyes and ran my hand across a woman's bare shoulder. She was already smiling at Thayer too.

"He just gets underneath my skin so easily. Whenever I think about his stupid, smug grin, ugh, I just want to scream." I kept walking, talking with my hands and looking for the next energy source.

"Trust me, you're not the only one." Thayer scoffed and turned toward a crowd of people waiting to cross the street.

"You too? Then why do you stay with him?" I asked.

"Why would I leave? The alternative is living my acquired lifestyle and just hoping a lab won't lock me up," Thayer explained, slowing his steps and eyeing the humans. "I know you volunteered to go out on your own, but I'm not about to risk my life just so I don't have to follow whatever Alec says."

"You know, you could live in a way that wouldn't attract a lab," I suggested.

"That's not me. Plus, the Shadows are my life. Alec, of course Nikki, even Sage is growing on me a little bit." Thayer glanced at me. "Oh, and you too."

I laughed and stepped in between the humans, touching as many as I could. Their energy rushed into my body, brightening everything around me.

The world separated from me. All I could think about was their energy filling every corner of my mind.

Maybe a little too long.

"What are you doing?" An unfamiliar voice asked.

My eyes shot open. I brought my hands back to myself, but it was too late. The suspicion flooded through everyone's eyes. I glanced at Thayer. He nodded his head in the direction he wanted to leave.

We left the group of people, too quickly and still listening to their voices behind us. My heart pumped blood through my ears so loudly that I was barely catching all their words.

"I feel…different," a man called.

"What just happened?" another man asked.

"Legends," a woman breathed.

"That's not possible."

I looked over at Thayer with worried eyes. He looked down at me with a wicked grin. He didn't care about what they said.

"Those people are Legends."

"What should we do?"

Without a second thought, he turned around and faced the group of wondering humans.

"Come and get us," Thayer challenged, holding his arms out wide.

Instantly, all of their eyes changed. Their stares locked on to us as anger twisted in their faces. Each one had the same reaction. Intense, unbridled revenge.

Thayer was doing this to them. On purpose.

The humans ran after us, not shouting or stalling at all. The humans each broke into a dead sprint as we turned and led them to an empty alleyway.

"This isn't very discreet," I said, glancing at Thayer.

He smiled. "The ransom's in less than an hour. What's the lab gonna do?"

"Kill us."

He laughed again. "We're Shadows. They won't touch us."

Once we crossed out of sight from everyone else, we faced them and waited for the humans to come crashing around the corner.

The first one stepped into view, and Thayer attacked him. He grabbed his arms and after a few moments, the man collapsed to the ground.

The woman came barreling right toward me before Thayer snatched her and dropped her to ground as well.

I caught the next person that raced toward us. My hands latched on to his arm and his neck. He struggled against me, until he was too weak to fight. His energy soared into my body, heating up every nerve ending.

I held on longer, taking far more energy than I would have been able to on the street.

The man's eyes fluttered closed as my breathing started to race.

The only thing that snapped me out of the haze was the sound of the man's faltering heartbeat. It sputtered on and on, trying to force the last bit of life to remain. I halted the energy flow and looked at the unconscious man in my hands. The last bit of energy lingered just beneath his skin.

It would be so easy, so sweet. The feeble human wouldn't even feel it. My mind battled against what my body so badly wanted to do.

"Take it," Thayer said as he walked closer.

I looked around and noticed that all the people were gone.

"You hid them already?" I asked him.

"Yeah, big cities are so easy," Thayer nodded toward the large brown dumpster behind him.

"You killed them all," I breathed, looking back at Thayer's seemingly harmless eyes.

"Just like you are about to do to him." Thayer nodded at the man I held.

I instantly dropped the man to the ground. His body thudded as it hit the hard concrete. I stepped back and looked back up at Thayer.

"I don't do that anymore." I shook my head, trying not to stare at the man on the ground.

I thought about the locket hanging around my neck as a reminder of everything past Legends have gone through to be kind to the human race. I thought about Lisa, and how this man was no different from her.

He probably had a family, a life, people who would miss him if he was gone.

Then, I thought about his energy. That final energy from a human. Desire raged through me, slicing apart any other thoughts. My body sensed the last remaining heat radiating from the human.

"So, you don't hear his human heartbeat? You don't sense his energy coursing through his veins? Or you don't feel that tingle in your hands drawing you closer and closer to what you want more than anything?" Thayer stepped toward me.

"I feel all of that." I struggled to focus, noticing everything Thayer was talking about.

"And yet you don't want to do anything about it." Thayer reached down and grabbed the man from the ground.

He hoisted him up as the man's body remained mostly limp in Thayer's grip. He watched me carefully with his bright eyes and stepped even closer to me.

"It's not that I don't want to." I stared at the man, feeling my blood pound in my ears.

"I won't tell anyone," Thayer whispered. "You can stay as perfect as you want to be."

I looked at the helpless human in Thayer's hands. I listened to his struggling heart and his shallow breathing. He may not live even if we do leave him here.

He definitely wouldn't feel me taking his energy now that he was unconscious.

All of these were rationalizations. But they were more convincing than anything else.

My hand reached forward slowly. I looked at the bare patch of skin on his arm, just above Thayer's hand. It was open, and so easy.

My fingers stalled just before I touched his warm body.

My eyes caught the yellow energy flowing from the man into Thayer. There was so little left that it was gone before I could blink. Thayer let the man fall, and looked straight at me.

"Too late," he said and smiled.

His eyes sparkled with the immense energy flowing inside of him. Thayer's eyes were easily the prettiest when he was high. It was like all the life and joy in the world swirled within his perfect brown irises.

"You took it all." I narrowed my eyes at him. "I hardly got any."

"Come take it." Thayer raised his bare hands.

His fingers wiggled, egging me on. I watched him carefully, judging if he was being sincere. Excitement flickered in his eyes as he crouched in a lower stance, bracing himself.

I stepped forward, close enough to touch him. I took another step, close enough to feel his breath. My hands reached up to him. His eyes watched me carefully. I smiled as I lay my hands on either side of his face. His breath hitched.

I closed my eyes and allowed his energy to flow into my body. All that joy and wonder I saw in his eyes raced through me now.

I held my breath, wanting to feel every sensation. The world around me faded. The heat from his energy ignited across my skin, burning deep into my entire body. A smile spread on my mouth as I felt every emotion rushing inside of him.

Tension. Excitement. Happiness. Curiosity.

They all crashed through me like a hurricane breaking glass. My heart raced as my eyes opened, looking at his trusting gaze.

I took a breath and tried to focus my mind long enough to pull my hands away from him.

I couldn't move them.

They felt like they were soldered to his skin. Like if I took them off, I would die.

My body forced me to hold on longer and longer. I looked back at him, with slight worry but it quickly faded to an all-encompassing pleasure.

I couldn't let go even if I wanted to. And I didn't want to.

The energy halted as Thayer stepped back, just out of my reach. I blinked as my body whirred with the new power.

"How did that feel?" Thayer asked, a smile forming on his mouth.

"Amazing," I answered honestly.

"Better than human energy?" he asked, stepping closer to me again.

"Imagine the best energy you've ever had," I gushed. "Think of how it made you shudder because it felt so good. The most intense, wonderful feeling."

He hung on every word I said. I smiled at how much I missed talking to him.

"That's not even close to what this feels like," I finished.

"You better stop," Thayer moaned. "You're making me jealous."

"Oh, my mouth is watering just thinking about it." I waved my hands in front of my face to try to cool my blazing skin.

"So, you must've had a really fun time after you left, knowing you were an Extractor," Thayer mused.

"Not really…" I shrugged my shoulders.

The reality I lived in instantly snapped back into place. I had taken energy from Derek to demonstrate that I was a Level Five. The other time was with Kylan on the mountain. Or Alec. Not nearly the kind of fun he was talking about.

"Don't tell me you had all this power and you didn't try it out." Thayer gawked.

"I did. A few times." I exaggerated.

It was two times. Derek for demonstration and Kylan for fun. Both were too quick to really notice.

"Being a Level Five is such a waste on you," Thayer scoffed as he looked me up and down, judging the whole way.

"Hey, back off. It's different when it's a Legend you're attacking. You wouldn't be racing to drain Nikki or Alec if you were an Extractor," I explained.

"Alec was right. You are different with them. With his brother." Thayer nodded as he reached down to the man on the ground.

"I just don't want the same things I wanted before." I shrugged.

He dragged the man over to the dumpster and flung him in. The body thudded against the others. He concentrated on the inside, focusing on the cells. Flames roared up over the top as each cell combusted. There wouldn't be anything left.

"Could've fooled me." Thayer leveled a stare on me, the flames glinting in his eyes.

"What happened with Alec was not what you think." I concentrated on the grimy asphalt.

"I'm not just talking about Alec. I'm talking about you. Being high on energy, all this power, being with the Shadows again. I see the fire burning in your eyes like nothing's changed." Thayer asked as he stepped closer and brushed off his hands. "You hide it when you're with the Rogues, don't you?"

"You don't know anything about who I am now." I narrowed my eyes at him, about to turn away.

Thayer rushed forward and grabbed my arm. I tensed.

"Relax, I'm not threatening you. I'm just trying to get you to understand what you want. I can see how much you care for Alec's brother, that's obvious." His eyes scanned mine.

"Then what's the problem? I'm happy with Kylan."

"That's not what I said. You care about him. But he must want you to give up the energy. You want to have as much as you used to. Am I wrong?" Thayer raised an eyebrow at me.

"No," I muttered.

Thayer stepped back, shaking his head. He looked back up at me. His dim eyes almost looked normal instead of their usual mesmerizing status. He was no longer high on energy because of the fire he started, and because of me.

"Come on, let's get you something to eat. I haven't seen you this tired in probably forty years." I smiled, keeping my chin down.

"I thought we promised not to talk about that," he grumbled.

"Nikki did," I started. "But I don't recall ever saying—"

"It was one bus and even *you* said it looked…" He stopped when he caught my smile. "Rude."

I shrugged and he laughed nervously until his genuine smile returned. I stretched to put my arm on his shoulder and walked the both of us out to the street.

"Do you regret it?" Thayer asked.

"Leaving the Shadows?" I asked, glancing each way down the street.

"Yeah. I'm gonna be honest, it's pretty difficult seeing you now." Thayer kept his eyes glued to the ground as we walked side by side. "I just picture you looking me in the eye and telling me that we aren't family anymore. I think of you storming out the front doors. I can't imagine what Alec is feeling. It's no wonder that he's tripping all over himself around you."

"Thayer, you know I couldn't stay. It was the only way to keep my memories, and find this." I pulled at the locket around my neck.

"I know I never actually said it, but I am sorry for what I did to you," he whispered, looking at me now.

"You mean how you trusted Alec over me." I smiled and elbowed him lightly in the ribs.

He faked a laugh, and then the thoughts clouded his expression again. Looking at his careful eyes, seeing him try to avoid getting close to me again, stung.

"You know how he can be. In the beginning, he made it sound like such a good idea, harmless even. We were just helping you. Knowing what happened in your past…it only would've hurt you." He winced. "Then, after a while, I couldn't stop. I knew if you ever found out, you'd hate me."

"I don't hate you." I forced a smile.

"But you don't like me either. Not the way you did before you left. You and I were best friends. It was always going to be the three of us. Me, you, and Alec. I mean, I guess, Nikki too. So really the four of us," Thayer laughed.

"Don't forget about Grae." I added, trying to hold down a laugh.

"Bite your tongue." Thayer pressed his fingers to the bridge of his nose.

I smiled. He stopped walking and looked seriously at me.

"Sometimes change is a good thing though." I shrugged, avoiding his gaze.

"It could still be that way, you know. You could come back, have all the energy you wanted, have all the respect you deserve as a Five. And all of us could still have each other," Thayer offered, taking my hand in his.

"So Alec can control me and you can just manipulate my emotions? No, thank you," I scoffed, trying to ease the tension.

"Fair enough." Thayer moved my hand in his so our pinkies wrapped around each other. "How about this? I promise that I won't change any of your emotions if Alec asks me to. Whatever you feel will be entirely of your own creation."

"Why would you give that up?" I asked, looking carefully in his eyes.

"Because I want you to honestly think about your choice. You don't have to be with Alec or Kylan. You can be whoever you want to be as a Shadow. Will you promise to consider it?" Thayer stared back at me, as confident as ever.

"You have a deal." I smiled and tightened my pinky around his.

Thayer smiled and released my hand. We walked toward the rumbling sound of people bustling and talking through the shopping street. Restaurants had their doors open and the smells of all the Southern food came wafting out in thick, spicy waves.

None of that mattered compared to the energy we had,

beautiful and vibrant and invigorating. After a few steps, Thayer put his arm around my shoulder.

"So, you know, if you find yourself falling madly in love with me, then you can rest easy knowing that is all because of you." He tried to hide his grin.

Annoyance flared inside of me. Completely genuine, just as Thayer had promised. His muscles braced for my reaction that he knew was coming. I smiled up at him instead.

"After all these years, Thayer Cade, I think it would've happened by now."

He relaxed and hugged me close for a moment. His dim eyes looked back up at the people waiting ahead of us.

"You're probably right." He smiled.

We walked together arm in arm through the alleyways and sidewalks. He touched as many people as he could possibly reach. None of them minded, especially the women. I watched his eyes light back up with new energy flowing through his body.

It was so easy to be around him. So easy to be with the Shadows again. Walking through the streets that turned into gravel roads and eventually empty land, it didn't really matter what I chose. We had to stick together through the fight, Shadows and Rogues, no matter what.

After it was over, then it mattered. But for now, I got to exist in my half-Shadow, half-Rogue world I had created.

Watching Thayer so happy and carefree, and thinking about what my life could be like if I could choose to skip any guilt, made me want to stop time.

I didn't want this moment to end.

CHAPTER TWENTY-NINE

"When you left, obviously Alec took it the worst of all. But Nikki, man, she threw a chair through a wall when I told her you weren't coming back." Thayer laughed at the memory.

"Are you serious?" I covered my mouth, enjoying the picture already.

The new energy radiated from his body. Both of us seemed to barely touch the ground as we weaved in and out of the trees and back to the lab. The power blazed in my body, fueling every sensation.

"You know how she is with her abandonment issues. She heard that you left, and she just…just lost it. It wasn't about Alec, or your memories, it was about her." Thayer rolled her eyes. "Everything is always about her."

I held back a laugh. I knew Nikki's tantrums. When she got angry enough, it was a full-on show. Nostalgia tinged the memory as it played in my mind. I looked at Thayer, his eyes on the ground.

No mental connection existed between us. It was just

me and my emotions that were too raw to name yet. He was being honest about not tampering with anything just to serve Alec.

I smiled.

"I wish I had left under less intense circumstances. I kinda wanted to say good-bye." I shrugged and looked up at him, waiting for him to look at me. "All of you deserved a better good-bye."

"You could give one to me now," Thayer dared, stopping his walk.

"What?" I asked, stopping as well.

"You heard me. It's back in 1990-something, you just found out about the safe, and you had those awful bell-bottom jeans…" He wrinkled his nose.

"Those were better than your rose-colored glasses that you said you wore when you wanted to look mysterious," I defended myself.

"I rocked those glasses, and you know it. But, focus. It's the day you decided to leave and you know that you're probably never going to see me again. What would you say to me?" Thayer offered.

"Okay, fine." I narrowed my eyes at him and took a breath.

I looked at his brown eyes and tried to picture myself back in that moment. Alec wasn't in the room, in this version. It was just me and Thayer.

In that moment, it felt real.

"You need to know that me leaving has nothing to do with you. I care about you more than you will ever understand, even if you can feel my emotions." I laughed. So did he. "I just can't stay here, and I wish I could take you with me. But I know you'd never leave. You're so loyal to Alec, to everything he's built with the Shadows. It's your home, your life. I know that."

His eyes softened as my words poured around him. His chest stopped moving when he held his breath. He just stared at me, waiting for the words he needed to hear.

When I was with the Shadows, Alec kept my past and my abilities a secret from me on purpose. Thayer helped him. With the two of them, I never suspected anything.

The weight of that decision rested on Thayer's shoulders. After all these years, it was time to let that weight go.

Especially because I knew what my choice would be at the end of all of this. I would choose Kylan.

I would always choose Kylan.

But leaving Alec meant leaving all the Shadows behind, including Thayer. For me, this good-bye wasn't for the '90s. It was for after the fight was over. It was for when I left the Shadows behind.

"I don't hold any malice toward you for what you did to me, for how you helped Alec. Because the truth is, despite all that, you're still one of my best friends. Whether we're together or apart, that won't ever change. So, thank you for all the good times. Those are the ones I'll remember always." I smiled at him.

His shoulders relaxed as his eyes widened. He finally released his breath.

"Thank you." Thayer reached for me and pulled me into his strong arms.

I wrapped my arms around him and held on tight. I felt his uneven breaths in his chest. His hand reached up and smoothed my hair as he pulled me closer.

"I've missed you, Thayer," I said into his shirt.

The warmth radiated from him into me.

I held on to him like he was the only friend I had left in the world. Kylan and I were on rocky ground at best. His family all but hated me. Lisa had no idea what my life was really like. None of the Shadows wanted me back, except Alec.

And then, there was Thayer. He was always the person I came to when I needed a comforting hug, or more than that. He was the person I relied on as a Shadow when I wasn't busy fawning over Alec.

I loved him more than any friend I'd made since I left. In that one regard, I almost did regret leaving because I lost him.

Thayer pulled his head back and looked down at me. I smiled up at him as he leaned closer. He moved his hands to either side of my face and pressed his lips to the top of my forehead.

"I've missed you too, Mara," he whispered against my skin before he stepped away.

"Kate," I stuttered, choking back the lump in my throat. "Remember, my name is Kate now."

"Alec's not here, so I don't have to obey him." Thayer smiled. "And it doesn't matter what you call yourself. You're Mara to me."

I rolled my eyes to keep the building tears from spilling over. I understood what he meant, though. If I stayed with the Shadows, I would always be Mara. I wouldn't be able to stay a good person if I was around them.

It would be too easy to become my old self.

A pit in my stomach grew. I knew that no matter what happened, I didn't want to live like a Shadow. Alec and Thayer could make all the promises they wanted, but Nikki was right.

If I chose them, I would become exactly like them again.

I avoided Thayer's eyes as we neared the lab. It was powerfully silent between the two of us. When I looked up, Alec was standing there, waiting.

The fun was over.

Alec looked between the two of us carefully. His eyes landed on me and the remnants of my smile. He looked back at Thayer with what almost looked like gratitude. If Thayer helped at all in convincing me to stay, then that meant Alec got to keep me.

I kept my smile glued to my face. I wanted him to fight for Rachel like I would be his prize if he won. I knew it was manipulative, and exactly what Alec himself would do. But I also knew that the other option was much worse.

"It's almost ransom time. Where have you been?"

"Relax, boss, we made it here in plenty of time." Thayer shrugged, his cool, casual demeanor back to normal.

Thayer winked at me and ran off to join the rest of the group. Alec surveyed me, trying to read my expression. This time I knew what he was looking for, and I fully planned on giving it to him.

"Are you ready for this?" Alec asked, lightly touching my shoulder.

I felt the ice from his touch cool my skin. I looked up to his eyes and that icy touch turned to fire. His deep eyes peered into mine like they were looking for something, reassurance of some kind.

So I let myself reach up and touch his cheek, my finger falling to his chin. Probably the last time anything tender or silent would be exchanged between us. I lifted my hand and softened my smile.

"I'm ready." *To leave. To be done with all of this.*

I brushed my shoulder against him as I started walking after Thayer. I felt Alec catch his breath as I walked by. My stomach knotted and my smile dropped now that he couldn't see my face.

He wanted to believe my lie.

My mind was spinning more than it was before. I thought

about Thayer and his promise to let me make my own choices. I thought about Kylan and the look of blind trust on his face. I thought about the Shadows, even Nikki, as the family I left behind.

I shook my head and focused on getting Rachel back. For now, that was all that mattered. Anything else would have to blow up later.

Alec and I walked to the hill where I had been originally posted to watch the front of the lab. It was the best view. When we got there, we both crouched down beneath the ridge.

I was careful not to touch Alec, while he tried to get as close to me as possible. I shuddered when his arm brushed mine.

"There's no turning back from here," Alec warned, his eyes wincing.

I wondered if he was talking to me or if he meant that toward himself. Before I responded, Alec looked to the east of the building, where Kylan's family should be standing. I glanced down at my watch.

It was 11:58 a.m.

Kylan and his family stepped into view, ready to start the feud we'd all been anticipating. His green eyes looked up at me.

Alec and I stood on the hill I had used to watch the front of the lab. Both of us monitored every movement from here.

Kylan waited for a signal to make sure everyone was ready.

I smiled back at him and waved him in. Before he turned his eyes away from me, I connected with his mind and sent him one last message.

I love you, I thought, and Kylan smiled.

He nodded his head and was about to turn his focus

toward the lab when his gaze shifted. He was still looking in our direction, but not quite at me.

His smile faded.

No. His face fell, and anger flooded his eyes.

I followed his gaze and noticed Alec staring directly back at him.

My eyes snapped back to Kylan, knowing exactly what Alec was showing him and knowing the memories would be tainted with Alec's emotion. I sucked in a breath.

Alec was showing Kylan everything he felt, along with the memories, and those emotions would be strong.

I wanted to shout an explanation to him, but we were too far away. I tried to plant a thought in his mind again, but he had created a block. Even against my strength, he was too talented of a creator for me to get around.

"Alec, stop it. This is none of your business." I shoved his shoulder, breaking his concentration.

"You kissed me. That is the definition of my business." Alec glared at me, a grin playing on the corner of his mouth.

"You can only show your side. That isn't everything and you know it," I growled at him.

"Maybe so, but he doesn't know that." He glanced back down at his brother.

I looked down at Kylan too, standing there as exposed as he could possibly be, anger twisting across his face. I begged for him to turn around and look at me.

Kylan's eyes did meet mine, one last time. When they did, I heard a faint whisper in my open mind.

Once we get her back, we're done. The words pierced into my thoughts and my heart.

I looked down at him and ached because I couldn't rush down there and explain everything. This wasn't the time or place for Kylan to be distracted.

I dug my nails into Alec's shoulder and forced him to turn and look at me. His eyes were flat and showed no remorse for what he had just done.

"I told you to let me handle this," I spat.

"He deserved to know," Alec threw back at me before I was finished talking.

"Are you that selfish that you couldn't wait until after the fight? Kylan is going in there with—"

"Yes, I'm that selfish." Alec cut me off again and, this time, his eyes finally showed emotion. "Especially when it comes to you."

The words caught in my throat. Alec looked at me like he was scared to death he was going to lose me. His eyes had just enough malice in them to make me think that he would make sure he wouldn't.

He turned back and watched as Kylan's family emerged from the tree line just as it turned to noon.

For the first time since I started this, I remembered exactly who I was putting my trust in. I wished I had heeded Kylan's warning to not go back to him.

Unfortunately, there was nothing I could do about that now.

I turned my eyes and watched as the leader of the lab exited the front door. Even from far away, she still looked familiar.

But I shook it off and held my breath as Kylan stepped out.

CHAPTER THIRTY

"You're on time. Poor Rachel was getting nervous," said the leader with black hair.

She spoke with such confidence. As she did, the Legends started filing down the steps and out of the lab, just as we had hoped.

"We're here to make a trade," Kylan said proudly. The woman smiled down at him.

"Have you brought what we asked?" The woman tilted her head and looked at everyone in the group, not seeing me.

For a moment, I was honestly worried that Kylan was going to offer me up anyway. He certainly was angry enough to do it.

"We have a new trade for you." Kylan crossed his arms over his chest. "Give us Rachel in exchange for your lives."

The woman laughed immediately. The rest of the lab Legends followed suit. The woman turned and spoke to the Legend nearest to her, and he quickly went inside.

"You mean to fight us?" the woman clarified, meaning that this was Kylan's last chance.

"No, we mean to kill you," Kylan said.

More Legends came out. Some of them looked scared to be there.

"So be it."

A sinister smile formed on the woman's face. The Legends around her rallied and at the nod of her head, they charged.

Alec raised his hand, and I watched as the Shadows feathered out of the trees. The lab Legends collided with Kylan's family and the Shadows were right there to rip them off again.

I moved to stand and Alec held me down.

"Wait," Alec hissed, watching the fight intensely.

Then, his eyes fell on the leader, who was looking around. He was waiting for the perfect moment to strike.

Derek fought two Legends at the same time, his strong arms snapping back and forth with all the fury of a man fighting for his sister. The first one took a solid punch to the face and the shorter, less threatening one was launched back by one quick blow.

I raised an eyebrow at how much more resourceful he proved than he seemed.

He took too long to turn back to the other one and that Legend had time to scoop up a sharp rock and slash it across Derek's back. The shorter one shoved a knee into his leg and he instantly buckled.

His scream shattered the air as he fell to the ground, his blood staining the back of his shirt. The first Legend that grabbed him wrapped his hands around Derek's face, to snap his neck.

Cassie heard his cry and rushed to grab the Legend holding him down.

At the last second, Thayer swooped in and peeled the other Legend off of Derek easily. Thayer slammed the Legend to the ground, fracturing his spine with a loud crack.

Thayer and Cassie both stood and looked at each other. They exchanged a brief nod before spinning to fight the next attackers.

I smiled. They weren't a Shadow and a Legend. They were two people fighting for the same goal.

Kylan moved through the lab Legends easily at first. He was standing closer to the front door than any of the rest of them had.

Any Legend he could get his hands on would drop to the ground after a few seconds.

Alec nodded, and we both stood.

We jumped off the hill as the fight turned in our favor. The second I set foot into the clearing, all the lab Legends' eyes were on me.

I was who they wanted. I was the distraction.

Alec and I stepped forward, and any of the remaining lab Legends came running toward us. The first three that approached dropped to the ground, clutching their heads in pain. Alec grinned as they crumpled in front of him.

I darted around them and went straight for the leader. With all the people in front of me, it was hard to get a good look at her.

A Legend came flying toward me, and I seized his arm and swung him around as his energy coursed into my body.

I released and he spun into the ground. He tried to push himself back up but was too weak. I stared into his eyes and stepped closer.

He tried to shuffle back, but I grabbed his arm. He braced himself, but instead of taking his energy, I waited. He looked up at me, confused.

I concentrated while he tried to figure out what I was doing. He would feel it soon.

Slowly, the temperature of his blood cells began to rise. I could feel the heat through his skin. As soon as he realized, he tried to pry my hand off, but I was much stronger than him without his energy.

He screamed as his face turned a bright red.

His body couldn't take the heat and shut down. His eyes fluttered closed as I dropped my grip on him. His body hit the ground with a thump, and I snapped my eyes up at my next target.

But my gaze caught Sage's brilliant eyes, fully red and threatening. She stood with three Legends surrounding her.

All of them battled a few feet away from her, shoving against an invisible wall. Every inch of her skin was covered in black clothing and her dark hood made her look more dangerous than she already was.

One of the lab Legends gave up and turned to Kylan, who already had his attention on someone else.

I moved but my arms were caught and yanked behind me. I scrambled to touch skin, but this Legend was more covered than the last one. I thrashed as the advancing blond Legend jerked Kylan around to face him.

Distracted, Kylan abandoned the Legend he had been fighting. The tall, skinny Legend was then free to pull out a thick, metal wire.

I struggled against the Legend holding me. Without being able to see his eyes or touch his skin, I'd have to be creative.

The tall, wire-wielding Legend threw it around Kylan and pulled it tight. Kylan's arms pinned down to his sides and the blond one smiled. The wire lit up to an intense red. Smoke rose where it touched Kylan's clothes and skin.

I tried to jump forward and help him. My arms threatened to tear out of place.

"Is that one your boyfriend?" the Legend sneered next to my ear as he hoisted me off the ground and dragged me to the lab.

The cord around Kylan turn white hot and his earsplitting scream filled the air.

Kylan was burning.

I closed my eyes and tried to concentrate enough to attack the Legend behind me but I couldn't focus. The Legend wrapped the hot cord around him once more. Another scream of pain.

Kylan was burning.

He dropped to the ground and writhed in agony. He tried to twist away or lift the cord, but it was too hot for him to touch and he was in too much pain to think straight.

I had to do something. I had to save him. I had to fix this. But I was stuck, my shoulders blaring in pain from my arms being pulled so hard.

I kicked in the air and hoped it might connect with the Legend dragging me. Nothing.

I had to do something.

Kylan was burning.

And even though it broke my heart, I cried, "Alec!"

The Shadow leader halted at the sound of my voice and saw me watching Kylan. He paused, probably deciding if he should let his source of competition for me die.

"Please," I begged, maybe too soft for him to hear.

The rage was choking in my chest. *Kylan was burning. Please.*

His eyes changed, and then he moved toward his brother. Only then, knowing help was on the way, could my heart relax enough to free my mind.

This time I closed my eyes and blocked out everything around me. When I opened my eyes, I locked them on a stocky man who made the mistake of watching me.

Once I had his attention, I smiled.

I reached into his mind and took control easily. The energy burning inside of me and the pain in my arms sharpened my attention.

His face twisted in confusion as he stared at his own limbs. He walked forward unwillingly. Following my mental command, he lunged for my captor and peeled his arms off my body.

As the pressure lifted, I couldn't help but smile at my own power.

The energy leaked from my body. It was slow at first, and then left with an aching, ripping feeling.

"What are you doing?" the Legend holding me shouted to his short comrade.

I kept my eyes focused on the one doing my bidding, ignoring my fleeting energy. His mind was fighting hard against me, but I kept eye contact and didn't falter.

I had too much to lose.

I whipped my body around and took the Legend that had restrained me, by his neck, the only exposed skin. His energy flowed until he was weak enough to release my other arm.

The submissive Legend walked to me willingly. Both of them sunk to the ground until their eyes shut.

I spun, searching for a white-hot cord or brilliantly green eyes. Alec had taken the Legend down to the ground and Kylan was peeling off the cord that had died down to a blackish red. Alec waited for Kylan to stand up, burns visible on his skin through his shredded clothing.

But he stood anyway. Alec grabbed the Legend at his feet and tossed him over to his brother. Kylan caught the cause of his pain by both arms. He stared straight into his eyes as the bright energy flowed into his body.

As it did, his burns healed and the Legend he held slumped.

I relaxed my shoulders and Alec turned around to look at me. I dipped my head, too conflicted to smile.

He could've let Kylan suffer and no one could blame him. No one would put it past him either. His eyes sank and I knew the reason Alec acted so out of character. He loved me. He saved Kylan for me.

I shook it off and moved on to my next target: the leader. My eyes focused on her small frame and shining black hair.

Standing next to her was Jacques.

I narrowed my eyes at him. Flaring fury made my hands shake at my sides.

He did this. The thought scorched in my mind.

Burning rage, seething vengeance, almost made me miss that he looked different, almost better. I watched his eyes and the way he held himself. There was something about him a little too perfect now.

He wasn't a human anymore.

I marched up to the steps and anyone that tried to stop me dropped to the ground.

Jacques stepped down to meet me. His gaze was level and unafraid of me. I smiled at how naïve he still was.

"All of this so you could be a Legend," I asked. He smiled a set of perfect white teeth. "Was it worth it?"

"Giving up a person I didn't care about in exchange for this," he said, marveling at his hands as if they held so much power now.

Compared to being a human, they did, but compared to me...not even close.

"Yeah, it was worth it." Not a hint of shame.

Didn't care about. He didn't care about her at all. Rachel in her shining, laughing beauty. He spent time with her. He had been welcomed into Kylan's home. She loved him.

And he didn't care. If he was already so cold, then I didn't mind acting like a Shadow from even his nightmares.

"Good." I smiled.

I looked into his eyes and created a block in his brain. It only took a few moments to infiltrate his entire mind.

Rookie, I scoffed.

With the block, his thoughts wouldn't be able to complete. He could send a signal to move, breathe, blink, or scream; nothing would reach the end. The new Legend was paralyzed in his own body.

My smile widened. Being this high on energy opened up a whole new arsenal of powers.

Footsteps came up behind me, and I recognized the walk. Jacques still had a blank stare. He was trying to think, it just wasn't working. I grabbed him by his shirt and pulled him down to my eye level.

"Why don't you tell that to him?" I snarled through my teeth.

I tossed his body directly back to Kylan who I knew was standing behind me. The block lifted from Jacques' mind in just enough time for the fear to flash in his eyes.

Kylan caught his airborne body with far more ease than I expected. We were still a good team in a fight, especially when both of us had so much energy to use.

Judging by how many Legends were on the ground, and the way his eyes lit up like green fire, he was obviously high on energy.

My heart leapt and blood rushed into my cheeks.

So this is what you look like? I smiled despite the chaos around us.

All I saw was him, so happy and strong. Even the clouded sunlight glinted off his brilliant eyes. He looked like a hero who just forgot his cape at home.

"You." Kylan glared down at Jacques, the reason all of us were here.

I smiled and left Jacques to face his punishment, satisfied that Kylan could take it from here. I turned my focus back on the woman with black hair.

She stood at the base of the steps with her arms crossed over her chest. She just stared, waiting for something.

A I got closer, my stomach twisted and I didn't feel like a powerful Five. I felt like I was staring into a nightmare.

I did know her.

CHAPTER THIRTY-ONE

"Raven Lancaster." I stared into her eyes and at her black hair pulled in a perfect bun.

She was the little girl I had met decades ago.

I'd killed her family and chose to leave her alive so she could live with the misery of growing up alone. She was only ten years old, and I still remembered how scared she looked even back then.

That expression of the helpless little girl was gone. Now this was a woman standing in a crisp, white lab coat with malice in her eyes.

"So you do remember me," she said, smiling.

I stopped walking at the sound of her voice. It called back the sharp memory of how young and devastated she was. Back then, her eyes had brimmed with tears as she cowered in the wooden chair next to the dinner table. Her family was scattered on the floor, and she couldn't peel her little eyes away from me.

I hated the memory now, but at the time, I was exactly as cruel as she remembered me to be.

"You're a Legend now. Aren't you?" I asked her plainly.

Something was off about her age.

She looked like she was maybe late thirties, when the last time I saw her was too long ago for that to make sense. She should have gray hair and wrinkled skin. But she had neither.

There was no way she could look this young when she should be double that age.

"Yes." She smiled at me with hate shining in her eyes.

"You should be…I mean, how can you look this young if the serum was just made functional?" I asked, both curious and hoping to stall for time so I could step closer.

"*Their* serum was ready about a year ago. That was about the same time that I joined the lab and handed over my serum that had been functional long before that." Her smile peeled back over her teeth.

"You? How could you have created that?" I asked, ignoring how rude it sounded.

She stood a little taller. "Never underestimate the power of proper motivation."

I narrowed my eyes. "That's not an answer."

"And I owe you a real one?"

She still hated me. Why wouldn't she? I still hated what I did to her.

"All of this, so you could get back at me?" I raised my eyebrows and lowered my head humbly.

I knew she wouldn't buy me acting weak, but I was hoping it would confuse her long enough.

"You think I'm overreacting?" She scowled. "How should one respond when they get a chance to take down the person that murdered their family in cold blood and left a ten-year-old girl alive to pick up the pieces?"

"I'm sorry," I blurted out. "I'm sorry for what I did to

you. I'm not the same person anymore. These people, and Rachel, did nothing to deserve any of this."

"Of course they did. They cared for you. They gave you a family when you were the last person that deserved one." Her voice filled with sharp darts of pain.

My eyes moved from her to the polished concrete steps. It hurt to see how much she hated me. It hurt even worse knowing that she had every right to detest me that much. That was Mara as a Shadow. That was me as a Shadow.

"If I could go back and change things, I would. Please don't tear apart an innocent family." I walked closer to her slowly.

Her eyes narrowed, and her grin pulled up the corner of her mouth. "Isn't that what Legends do best?"

I took a breath in and ignored the memory of the sweet little girl. This was war, and she was my opponent.

I lunged forward and grabbed her carelessly exposed arm. Her energy poured into my body. The sharp, bursting power revived every part of me. Legend energy fused into each of my cells. My mind exploded with power and excitement as the world around me began to sharpen.

This would've been an easy fight, if it weren't for what I saw next. It almost looked like she was smiling.

"Give us Rachel," I ordered.

Her knees buckled but her confident smile only widened. She reached her hand up and grabbed my wrist. As soon as her skin touched mine, bright energy coursed from me into her.

At first, I didn't feel anything. Then, every second her hand gripped on my arm, each cell ached as my energy screamed into her.

She was an Extractor too.

"No," she answered and stood.

The energy swirled like smooth fluid between my body and hers. Surprise crushed my thoughts and I froze. That was enough for her. I struggled back into reality but my energy was almost entirely gone.

I wasn't strong enough to stand anymore. My hands dove to break my impending fall. My open skin skid against the concrete steps.

"Did you think you were the only special one?" Raven hissed and released her hold on me.

I gasped as my vision divided into splotchy blurs of spinning colors. Darkness threatened at the corners. My blood sloshed through my body, trying to force me to stay alert.

I needed energy soon.

Raven knelt down beside me and patted the top of my head as if I was the child, not her. I wanted to be annoyed or angry, but everything was numb and fading.

"I may not be a Level Five, but with your help, we can change that," she said.

A quick motion of her hand, and a couple of Legends came to drag me the rest of the way inside. I tried to stand but slipped.

I turned my head and looked at the ensuing fight behind me. A Legend threw Cassie to the ground, snapping the bone in her right leg. She screamed, holding the injured limb as another Legend held Derek from behind.

"Stop, stop!" Derek cried and fought against the person who held him.

All he could do was watch his precious Cassie in pain.

Kylan saw the Legends grab my arms. He turned and looked at his family, in utter turmoil. His pained eyes looked back at me one last time before he decided.

His back turned to me as he ran toward his brother and sister.

My heart sank.

The Legends reached me and pulled me up, careful not to touch my skin. My eyes drooped and caught one last gaze. One last look at a pair of deep blue eyes.

Alec. I thought, unable to form any words.

He didn't hesitate. He dropped the Legend he was holding and sprinted toward me. The Legends holding me stopped to look, making my color-spotted vision shudder. I smiled wearily at their mistake.

Eye contact was exactly what he needed.

Both of their bodies went rigid as they screamed. I heard Raven screaming behind me. He must have gotten her too.

They dropped my arms and my body tumbled back to the steps. Each of them clutched their heads and fell forward.

Alec rushed to me and left them in lingering pain. He grabbed my hand and put it on his smooth face.

"Take it," he said.

His eyes looked at me desperately, like he would do anything to fix me. I pulled the energy from his body, into mine. All of Alec's fear and care was threaded through the energy. It was too raw of emotion, with long fingers that wrapped around all the parts of me that hurt.

As I awoke, he faded. I pulled my hand off of his face when I was strong enough to function on my own. Alec gasped, trying to let his body adjust to losing energy so quickly.

Both of us stood and looked at the open door. I turned to Alec for confirmation that he would come with me. He nodded.

"Let's go get her," I said and walked through the doorway.

He chose to follow me in. He chose to run to me when I needed him. There were too many reasons to be suspicious of Alec's help, but I needed him. And he was there.

"I'll go this way. You check down there." Alec

pointed down the hallway and we each took off in our own direction.

I searched an area filled with empty testing rooms. They looked like operation rooms in a hospital, with a table and equipment cluttering the space. I looked through each window, but all of the rooms were empty.

Alec's voice called from the other hallway. "I found her."

I took off running. Turning around three sharp corners until I reached the sound of Alec opening a metal door.

Rachel sat on the floor behind thick metal bars. She looked tired and had bruises all over her body. Her dark red hair looked like it hadn't seen a shower the entire time she had been here. Her brown eyes reminded me of Cassie, but hers were filled with fear.

Those brown eyes locked on Alec's right arm as he pulled the door open.

The dagger. She was staring at the mark that identified Alec as a Shadow, as her enemy. Fear drained the already-pale color from her face.

"Shadow," she breathed and scooted back to the far corner.

Her muscles tensed with whatever energy remained. She was totally defenseless in her current state.

The bars in her cell glowed with a faint white light. I recognized it from the cuffs Alec had put on Kylan when he had held Kylan hostage. The bars were tech-enhanced to sense when energy was used for a Legend's powers. Whenever someone tried, the energy seeped into the bars instead.

It was a perfect place to keep a Legend. Any attempt to escape would just drain them even more.

Rachel's eyes flicked over to me, and she relaxed her shoulders. A weak smile spread across her dry lips.

"Hey." I smiled at her.

"Kate, *Kate*. It's you." She shook with relief, lifting a weak hand to her mouth.

I walked forward to her, my feet scuffing against the tile floors. She remained frozen and her eyes still warily watched Alec.

"It's okay, he won't hurt you," I whispered.

Rachel looked back at Alec and took his outstretched hand. He helped her stand and she watched him warily the whole time. Something in her eyes changed when she looked at him and then looked at me.

She slogged out of the cell, came straight for me, and clumsily wrapped her arms around my neck. I caught her just before she fell and she buried her face into my shoulder.

"This is him, isn't it? The one you were talking about?" Rachel said in a breathy, trembling voice.

She remembered the story I told her about the man I loved when I was a Shadow. I never thought Alec would actually be standing here as an example.

The words caught in my throat.

I looked back at Alec standing there, watching me. His face lit up for a moment as he heard Rachel's question. All he waited for was my answer.

"Yeah, that's him," I whispered and looked at Alec.

A small wince tugged at the corner of his eyes. He looked like he was either sorry for something he had done or was about to do. I pulled my eyebrows together and he swallowed.

"Let's get out of here," Rachel sighed as she pulled away from me, her arms shaking.

I looked at her anxious and tired brown eyes. She dropped her arms to either side and her hands pressed against her legs like she needed something to hold onto.

Bruises scattered across her arms. Wrinkled clothes clung to her like they were sticky with sweat. She didn't stand straight and it looked like she hadn't eaten in a long time.

"Everything is going to be okay." I took her frail hand in mine and held it gently.

"Thank you." She shuddered when she spoke.

I shook my head. "Thank me when you come home safe."

A tear spilled down her cheek as she let out a shaky laugh. She nodded, and I turned to pull her toward the door.

A lump formed in my throat as I thought of Kylan's face when I would show him his rescued sister. I thought of Cassie and Derek. Everyone out there was waiting for this moment.

All I had to do was walk her to the door, and we were free.

My breath hitched. I could see it. I could feel it.

That was until I felt Rachel's hand pull against me. I turned, and my eyes widened.

A pair of hands wrapped around her head.

They yanked and Rachel's head snapped to the side. Her slick hair flipped with the motion and the bones in her neck fractured. Her hand went limp in mine instantly.

Her body fell to the white tiles with a sickening thud, red hair covering the floor around her head.

The next thing my eyes met was Alec standing directly behind her.

"I'm sorry," he mouthed.

CHAPTER THIRTY-TWO

Alec looked down at Rachel lying still on the cold floor.

Her tattered, worn body was twisted awkwardly and I wanted to fix it. I couldn't see her face. I snapped my eyes up and looked at him. I wish there was true remorse in his eyes, but it wasn't there.

"What did you do?" I asked, and then stopped immediately.

A distinct click sounded behind me.

I spun around and saw the bullet before the gun. I snatched the object flying toward my face.

I now held a tranquilizer dart with bright blue liquid. I assumed it was intended for a Legend. It looked deadly enough to bring one of us down.

Raven stood a few feet away, holding the gun pointed at me.

The weapon glowed with a white light, same as the cell that held Rachel, same as Kylan's cuffs. I couldn't attack the weapon—it would only siphon my energy. But I could attack her.

I didn't waste a second wondering how she got up so

quickly. I twirled the bullet in my fingers, about to launch it back at her.

A stabbing pain pricked into my back.

My muscles seized, and I turned around slowly. My entire body grew heavy, the dart doing its job. I looked at Alec standing exactly as he was before. Only this time with a glowing gun in his hands.

The sedative sent a slow-moving cloud of pain through my back.

"Why?" I choked out, blinking the drowsiness away.

I shifted my weight and still felt strong enough to stand on my own, maybe the one bullet wouldn't take me down. I blinked again, focusing my vision.

He didn't say anything. He shook his head gently and looked at me warily, still holding the gun in his hand.

"How long have you been working with them?" I asked through clenched teeth.

My sight clouded, putting a fuzzy ring of light around everything. As soon as I thought I could muster a step forward, another click sounded from Alec's gun.

The next bullet stabbed into my stomach, immediately releasing the narcotic liquid.

My hindered reaction time couldn't stop it. When my hand finally did reach it, all I could do was yank it back out and hear it clink as it hit the floor.

"Since you left," Alec answered.

I clutched my stomach and felt my knees finish buckling underneath me. Alec stepped over Rachel's dead body and caught me, lowering me to the floor. I tried to remain somewhat upright on my hands and knees.

The slow pain of the solution inside of me paled in comparison to the sting of betrayal flooding through my consciousness. Even touching him infuriated me.

"I will kill you for this," I said through the haze now enveloping me.

"No, you won't. You still care about me too much to really hurt me. The last few days were proof of that," he said and stood.

Raven walked around to stand next to Alec, nodding to the Legend that had followed her in. He immediately left the room as she held up a matching lab coat to Alec.

He slipped his arms through the stiff fabric easily, still watching me.

I sat on the ground and tried to hold myself up long enough for someone to come and find me. The last person I wanted to see Rachel lying on the ground next to me answered my wish.

Kylan rushed through the door. I looked at Rachel's body, my stomach still twisting at the sight. I lifted my gaze back to Kylan, grimacing at the effort.

"Rachel," he breathed, looking directly at her.

The color drained from Kylan's face. He stumbled forward and knelt down beside her. Tears welled in his eyes. But they turned dark and hard when they looked up at Alec. Both Raven and Alec had their guns pointed directly at Kylan's heart.

"Don't move. Or I won't be as lenient as I was last time," Alec said.

Kylan looked down at Rachel in his arms. He looked over at me and his eyes held the same disdain they did earlier. They traveled to look at the bullet sticking in my back and the other one lying on the floor in front of me.

Sympathy flashed briefly in his gaze. The slow pain shifted to a cold fire spreading through my body, numbing everything in its path.

"I'm so sorry," I huffed, trying to keep the words from crashing together.

My elbow buckled underneath me and I fell farther onto the floor. My heart pumped the serum through my veins, sending the numbing fire everywhere.

I'm burning, I begged.

Thayer ran in the room, already talking. "What's happening? The lab stopped fighting. They just—"

He stopped when he saw what was going on. *He didn't know*, I thought as the ache in my chest lifted from knowing Thayer didn't betray me too.

"Alec, what are you doing?" Thayer gasped.

"Getting the power I was meant to have," Alec quipped, looking back at me with icy determination in his eyes.

"By sacrificing her to the lab? You can't do this." He walked toward Alec.

"I *am* the lab. We'll talk about this later, Thayer," Alec ordered.

Thayer instinctively shut his mouth and looked at me with worry. He knew exactly what they would do to me here.

Derek stumbled in the room. Cassie balanced on his arm, limping and wincing with each step. Her eyes fell on Rachel, her freckled face washing white and her mouth falling open.

"No," she cried as her good leg buckled underneath her.

Derek reached another hand to catch her. His face twisted in pain as the wound in his back shifted.

"No, no, no," Cassie screamed into Derek's arm, tears already streaking down her face.

"Let me take Rachel and leave," Kylan offered up to Alec.

For a second, my heart stopped. The cold fire shifted. He was leaving. He wanted to leave.

But, I'm burning, I wanted to cry.

"You're just going to give up that easily?" Alec asked.

"Let me give my sister a proper burial. If you wanted to kill us, you wouldn't have stopped the fight."

"Fine," Alec said. "Take her and don't come back. Ever."

Kylan bent and picked up his sister, her slick red hair lifting from the shiny floor. He nodded toward Alec and stood.

The agreement was done.

Cassie reached a shaking hand out to her sister as they moved to the door. Kylan turned his eyes down toward me one last time.

The air choked in my throat. The freezing heat, spread across my chest, up my neck.

"I don't have a reason to come back," Kylan said.

His attention was focused on the exit now, on carrying his dead sister in his arms and supporting the weight of his grieving sister as she leaned on him.

Kylan walked out without looking back. He left me at the feet of my worst enemy, all alone.

Nikki and Sage came around the corner next. Eyes wandering, I could hardly think past the serum in my veins and the ache in my heart. My arms fell out from under me completely. I rolled over in time to land on my back. The ceiling swayed.

"Alec?" Nikki said warily and looked up at Alec.

He nodded. She relaxed her shoulders. The look in her eyes changed from cautious to triumphant as she stepped around me and went to stand next to Alec.

"Nikki… wh-why?" I asked up at her. My words were slurring together now.

"Alec has been there all along. He took care of us when

the rest of the world refused. If you wanted my sympathy, you should've never left," she spat at me.

I knew that my leaving years ago had hurt her. We had been friends. I just didn't know she felt the betrayal this deeply. But then again, it was Nikki. She had spent her entire time with the Shadows wanting what I had. Power. Respect. Alec.

Sage followed along with Nikki and went to stand by Alec too. Her mouth pulled in a tight line when her gaze shifted to me.

"Sage, you know wha…they'll do to me," I choked out.

But she didn't speak. She looked at the floor, her expression unchanging.

"Alec promised to fix her if she stood by us," Nikki answered for her.

That's why she had to come. I finally put it together.

If she was going to get what she wanted, she had to be here at the lab with them. That was why she risked everything. That's also why Alec wouldn't leave her when she slowed us down.

He always kept his promises.

Sage's eyes didn't even cringe as she heard the bargain she had made for my life.

Alec's smile widened as he saw my chances of getting away vanish. He tucked the gun in his waistband and knelt down next to me. I wanted to jerk away from him, but I could hardly find the connections to tell my arms to move.

"You've done an excellent job making enemies," Alec cooed and pulled up the back of my shirt, careful not to touch my skin when he took the journal and handed it to Nikki.

"You didn't tell me any of this," Thayer's voice almost broke.

Alec snapped a metal cuff on my wrist that lit up with an

inner white band. I wanted to protest, but my arms felt too heavy to shift.

Alec faced Thayer now. "I couldn't. You would've stopped me."

A hint of emotion tainted Alec's voice. He knew he would lose Thayer, so he chose to lie. Thayer meant too much to him to risk. I thought about my conversation with Thayer and how he promised never to help Alec hurt me again.

I waited to see how long that promise actually lasted.

"You're right, I would have. Because this is insane, even for you." Thayer jabbed a finger at Alec.

He reached for the Shadow leader, to fix my pain. Alec shoved him back and Thayer staggered away from both of us.

"Thayer, stop," Alec ordered.

"This is Mara we're talking about!" Thayer shouted back at Alec.

"I'm not going to kill her," Alec said and raised his hands in surrender.

"No, you're just going to make her wish she was dead. That's worse, Alec."

Alec reached behind his own coat and pulled the gun out again but this time he aimed the barrel directly at Thayer's chest.

"Don't make me do this. You've always been there through everything. Think about it. We could be Level Fives. Together. I have a plan for everything," Alec offered.

I watched Thayer's eyes change. I held my breath as I hoped the enticing power wouldn't be enough to sway him. It would break my heart if he turned against me too.

"To get that information you'd have to practically tear her apart. What makes you think that's okay?" Thayer asked, his voice changing.

Maybe this was the part where he sided with Alec again. This was the part where I saw just how much both of them could stand to hurt me.

"It's everything we ever wanted, and her pain won't last forever," Alec softened his tone.

"So, that's it then? You're really going to torture the girl you love?" Thayer pulled his eyebrows together and looked at Alec with disgust.

"I will do what I have to do." It almost sounded like there was a twinge of pain in his voice. But maybe I had moved to hallucinating.

"Then you're on your own." Thayer took a step back toward the exit.

"Wait. You're not going to stay?" Sage's voice cracked into the far corner of my blurry hearing.

"Thayer, that's crazy. You belong here!" Nikki shouted.

"Not like this."

Nikki kept her eyes glued to Thayer, refusing to glance down at me trying to hold my head up. Sage looked from Thayer to Alec, the first hint of worry in her eyes.

"She left us. Twice." Nikki's voice turned acidic. "Do you remember what that felt like? You trudged around the mansion for months after she left. She deserves everything that's coming to her."

I forced my eyes to look at Thayer, even with my vision swimming back and forth. Pain clouded his eyes as he clenched his fists.

"This isn't about me and it's definitely not about you. If you think Alec is doing any of this because he wants to enact your revenge on her, Nikki, you're wrong. He only cares about her," Thayer growled through his teeth. "And look what he's willing to do anyway."

"Thayer, please," Sage muttered.

"You're choosing her over me?" Alec's voice was almost too low to hear.

Maybe he honestly thought Thayer would have stayed.

"I'm choosing to be decent. I've followed you everywhere over the years and it was fun, but I don't think I can follow you this time."

Thayer turned around and walked toward the doorway without saying another word. Alec kept his gun lifted, just in case. My last loyal friend walked out of the room but looked at me before he turned the corner.

"I'm sorry," he whispered, and with that he left.

Between the guns, the cuff, and the cell, I was trapped. My eyes went back to the looming white coats over me. Nikki flipped through the journal and pulled out the wilted daylily, still clinging to its bright yellow color.

She grinned as she watched me struggle weakly. But she turned the flower into black dust, anyway. The crushed bits of hope fluttered down to meet me.

The entire room was swaying and the slow, burning pain had settled in every part of my body. I sucked in a final breath and let my eyes fall shut.

My body was dragged into the cell that Rachel had come from. The white light brightened the inside of my eyelids, reminding me that I wasn't getting out of this. The metal door clanked shut.

Just before I lost all consciousness, a hot tear spilled from my eye. I followed it all the way down my cheek and listened as it hit the polished floor.

That was the last thing I could focus on before everything faded.

CHAPTER THIRTY-THREE

Cold water crashed against my skin, jolting me awake.

My alert mind forced my eyelids to fly open. I blinked the water from my eyes and sat up. I saw a lab Legend holding the dripping bucket. Alec stood next to him.

"All right, get her out," Alec said, keeping his eyes on me.

I was awake, but hardly strong.

I had been at the lab for a few weeks now, I assumed. Every day was a new form of torture. They kept my energy levels low enough to make sure I was too weak to fight.

The lab Legend grabbed my arms with gloved hands. He pulled me up to him and smiled at me, wincing when he touched me. My body ached everywhere.

"Follow me," Alec said, holding a tablet in his hands.

He looked down at the screen and swiped at whatever it was showing him. On the outside, he didn't seem like he cared at all. Even if Alec was lying about everything, even if his grand plan was to make me a lab subject, I knew he still cared.

That was the part that hurt the worst.

I was walked down the hallway to the test room. The Legend finally released me so I could sit on the table.

A flurry of assistants filled the room. Human or Legend, I couldn't tell anymore. I was too tired to even think straight, let alone watch people carefully enough to decide.

Alec pulled out a small flashlight and clicked it on. The bright light flashed across my eyes, back and forth. Alec stood just behind the light, watching.

As he looked at me, I reached my shaking hand up to his wrist and touched his skin. The tiniest spark of energy warmed my body before he pulled his hand away.

I blinked hard and took the small amount of energy to change.

My hair lightened to blond and the features of my face changed to fierce and sharp in a matter of seconds. I looked like Mara, the woman he had fallen in love with.

He stopped looking at my eyes when he saw what I was doing. He stared at my face, my body, and paused for a moment. My wet hair sent cold droplets down my arms as I waited.

For that one second, he was hurt from seeing the bruises on my body and my exhausted eyes.

Then, in one shaky, cold breath, the moment was gone and his eyes hardened again.

"That's not going to work," Alec said with a blank stare. He shined the light in my eyes again.

"It will," I muttered.

I kept my appearance as it was. He would have to do this test with me looking like his true love.

"Not likely." Alec turned around to face the table behind him.

"Why did you do it?" I asked him.

"Do what?" he errantly asked as he lifted a needle to look at the empty case inside.

He handed it to Raven, who stood next to him. She walked it around the table and lowered it to my arm.

The previous day had been a series of needles and scraping blades, until I blacked out from the pain. They stopped and took me back to my cell to let me rest.

Today, they were out to finish what they started. I didn't keep track of the plans anymore.

"You know what I'm talking about. Why play nice if your plan was always to bring me here?" I asked. The thought had been burning for a while.

Why make me fall for you again? The question I didn't want to ask.

"I tried forcing you to do what I wanted last time and that didn't work. I needed you to walk in the door willingly," Alec answered quickly and tried to keep his eyes away from me.

He set the tablet down on the table next to me and rested his hands on the metal. His fingers reached for my restraint and adjusted it to be one notch tighter, the leather nearly slicing into my skin.

"I was already going to do that. You didn't have to do everything else," I said.

Alec shook his head as he shifted my metal cuff higher so he could tighten the strap even more.

"I know you fell too," I whispered.

He froze, too stubborn to look at me.

"I have a hard time controlling myself when I'm around you," Alec whispered back, barely even moving his mouth.

Raven stiffened behind him. Alec's finger slid from the restraint to touch my hand. It was the tiniest connection possible, but I wasted no time pulling as much energy as I could through that small opening.

His finger stayed, his eyes avoiding mine.

Warm, bursting energy screeched through his skin into mine. Even if the energy was Alec's, I wasn't about to turn it down when I was starving. I moved my hand to try and add another point of contact.

Raven cleared her throat from the back corner of the room. Alec blinked and snapped out of whatever trance he had been in. He lifted his hand out of my reach. My body screamed as soon as the energy pulled away.

I needed more. But I knew Alec wasn't stupid enough to give me any more, so I'd have to use what I had. My cuff was turned off and I wasn't going to waste this chance.

I focused on his eyes and flashed a memory into his mind. Back to when we had been running all day to get to the lab, then waiting for Sage to heal, and had finally made it to people.

The loud music boomed in the air. The excited and inebriated people bumped lightly against our bodies as we danced. My brown curls swayed with each motion of my body. Alec pulled me so close to him, close enough for me to feel his chest rise and fall with each breath.

It felt like his hands would never let me go.

Then, he kissed me and every thought in my mind obliterated. I could taste his happiness on his lips.

"No matter what you look like, you will always be my Mara," Alec promised.

I projected the images and the feelings entirely into him.

It took a significant amount of energy to enter his mind, my body cried for me to stop wasting what little power I had left. My sputtering heart trudged forward, trying to keep me alive.

It should've been harder to plant that powerful of a thought, but Alec had left a crack in his defense and I found it.

He shut his eyes and clutched the tablet he was holding. The memory had pulled on a seemingly nonexistent heartstring of his. When his eyes opened, they narrowed at me.

The Legend holding the syringe had pushed the needle against my arm, not quite breaking the skin. Alec raised his hand to stop her.

"You know what, I think she's had enough energy to go straight to the biopsies," he said, and the Legend immediately nodded.

The needle was gone from my arm.

My body tensed at the impending pain. The locket lay limply against my neck. I read the words in my mind again.

You are loved. A tear stung the corner of my eye.

I may not have enough energy to be able to withstand this pain or get out of my situation. Every scientific reason said I should just give up trying.

But the necklace reminded me that I was stronger than I thought. It wasn't just my own strength I was drawing on.

I focused my adrenaline and forced my energy to allow me to get into Alec's mind one more time.

It was a memory of us growing up together.

Alec had been struggling to get the Shadows together and willing to follow him. He was so young, and the only reason they trusted him at all was because of his last name. I found him alone in his room, staring at a wall. I walked over to the bed and sat next to him. When I put my arm around him, that was when I saw the first shimmering tear fall from his eye.

I wrapped both my arms around him, feeling his shaky breath. That was the only time he had ever cried in front of me. My heart filled with empathy. He trusted me more than anyone in the world—that moment was proof.

"I don't know what I'd do without you." Alec's voice choked.

The hurt in his eyes was as obvious as the relief of having me take care of him.

"You'll never have to find out," I promised.

"Enough!" Alec shut his eyes again and put his hands to his head.

He forced my touch out of his mind and glared back at me. He reached behind him and raised the scalpel he was admiring earlier.

More energy faded from my body. All the pains and discomforts that were masked before blared back into my consciousness.

"Am I bothering you?" I asked darkly.

"All of this bothers me. I don't want to hurt you. I love you." The metal scalpel glinted in Alec's hand.

"You can't love me and hurt me at the same time," I muttered, trying to ignore the water sticking to my shirt or the various, gleaming metal instruments behind the white coats.

"I know this doesn't make sense, but I promise it will." Alec closed his eyes.

"Does that mean you're going to stop?" I asked, not even hoping that he would actually agree.

When his eyes snapped back open, they shifted in the light. The cold, uncaring nature of Alec blared through his dark eyes.

"No," he answered. "Not until I get what we need."

That could be months. Years. Far longer than my mind could handle. Far longer than I wanted to live through.

I shuddered, feeling the cold now and the weight of the aching from previous days. I couldn't do this. Not for myself.

But I thought of everyone else that might be harmed in Alec's wake. Everyone else that had something to lose.

I could keep fighting for them.

"So you can turn every L-Legend into a Five? Reveal us to the world? That plan d-doesn't work." I shook my head.

Pain clattered in my head as I moved. I looked at Alec's skin. It was so close to me. With the restraints on, I would never reach it.

But that didn't stop me from craving it so badly.

"Of course it will. You'll see." Alec nodded back to me.

"You're setting up the humans to become prey." I narrowed my eyes.

Alec's mouth thinned. "That's what they are."

I looked in his cold, blue eyes and a monster with too much power at his fingertips stared back. I thought about Lisa, the one human that made their kind make sense. A human that Alec wouldn't think twice about calling *prey*.

My heart twisted.

A deep ache clawed at my entire body from a lack of energy. Alec's cruel hand gripped the scalpel again, turning it around. The metal gleamed in the harsh light. His dark eyes never left mine as he lowered the blade to my upper arm.

I forced my eyes to look away. I stared at the light above me instead, hoping that it would blind me so I never had to see his face again.

I tried to hold my tongue as the pain sliced through me. I knew I had provoked him, but I couldn't resist hurting him. If my pride had been silent for a few wise moments, this would hurt a lot less.

After a few seconds, I couldn't hold back the scream any longer.

CHAPTER THIRTY-FOUR

I lay in the corner of my cell with filthy, blond hair serving as the only pillow between my head and my arm.

My hand rested on the floor next to the iron bars with glowing white strips. I stared at the polished tile and the harsh reflection of the lights.

Alone and exposed, I had nothing but the sound of my breath and the buzz of the lights to keep me company.

It was miserable, aching in the spaces where my muscles and bones scraped together. It had been days, or weeks. I wasn't sure.

This level of exhaustion could make you see things. I knew that.

I should have known it wasn't real. Because I looked like Kate. Sweet, innocent, loveable Kate. That wasn't my reality anymore.

My hand warmed. I didn't feel a touch, just the warmth. I sighed, grateful for the minimal change in my environment. The heat spread up my arm and into my shoulder, enough encouragement for me to lift my head.

A pair of familiar green eyes met mine. His hand touched the tip of my finger, allowing his energy to flood into my system. My heart raced and my breath stopped in the air. I stood slowly, not wanting to take my eyes off of him.

As I stood, his hand fell away. I reached forward and wrapped my hand around that bar that stood between us. He was calm and I knew everything would be all right.

"Kate," he called.

The name sounded wrong. I shook my head, unsure if that was even my name. My feet shifted underneath me. My name didn't matter. He was here. I was safe.

"You're here," I sighed, a smile cracking across my dry lips.

Kylan tilted his head to the side as his eyes looked me up and down. He didn't move, he just waited. Then, he smiled.

"I came to save you," he said and lifted his head straight up again.

His words hit my ears and relief flooded through my body. The sheer amount of force released from my muscles shook through me. My hand still gripped the bar, and even it shook against my palm.

"Although, it looks like you don't need me for that. You can save yourself." Kylan smiled.

The bar shattered in my grip. The pieces shot apart, breaking the other bars. Within seconds, the cell collapsed around me. The glowing light that held me back scattered in broken shards on the floor.

I looked at my hands. Why could I break the bars now and not before? It didn't matter.

"I'm free." I looked up. "I beat Alec."

Kylan nodded.

I rushed forward to throw my arms around him. I was free. We could leave. I could leave. Kylan stepped back.

I halted. He tilted his head to the side again. This time a smile crawled up his mouth.

"But, what if it was me you were going up against?" Kylan raised his eyebrow.

I stepped back as Kylan turned and pulled a white coat from behind him. He shrugged his arms through it easily before his green eyes stared back at me again.

My breath stuttered in my chest. I stepped back onto the broken shards of light and metal. Kylan stepped forward and straightened the coat.

My hand was warm, just like it was when Kylan showed up. It wasn't just warm, it burned. My hand shook.

The broken light around me vibrated. I looked around and the world around me began to tremble.

"What's the matter?" Kylan laughed. "Don't you think you can beat me?"

My eyes shot open.

Just like in the dream, my hand laid next to the bars. But I looked like Mara. My blond hair twisted at the ends from a lack of showering. My skin was covered in a thin coat of grime and sweat.

A small, brown hand touched my fingers.

I yanked my arm back and stared at Nikki crouched on the other side of the bars.

"Nightmares again?" Nikki asked.

"Not important," I grumbled and sat up on the cold floor.

"That bad, huh?" She smiled.

"Why do you care?" I snarled, pushing my blond hair behind my shoulders and grateful for the air against my skin.

"I like seeing you this way." Nikki's eyes crawled over my entire body.

The harsh light from the bars reflected against Nikki's

brown eyes. Her smile gleamed even whiter than normal. She dragged her finger down one of the bars as her eyes moved back to mine.

"What? Watching me suffer?" I scoffed and tried to steady my breaths.

She smiled with her usual wicked grin before she lowered her gaze to the ground. She moved to sit down and cross her legs in front of her.

"I never got it, you know. The reason why everyone was so fascinated with you. Alec is nothing short of obsessed with you, and yet you managed to snag his goody-goody brother anyway. Thayer even hopped over to the good side for now." Nikki trailed a finger along the tile lines.

"For now? You think he's coming back, don't you?" I asked in a raspy voice.

Her eyes flicked up to me. I almost felt bad for her. Everyone she thought cared about her left. I left. Thayer left. Alec was the only one who had stayed.

"Not important." Nikki sighed and looked at me with cold eyes. "I think I figured it out. The reason everyone's obsessed with you."

"Because I'm more interesting than you?" I taunted.

The only reason she cared about the attention on me was because it wasn't on her. She needed to be important, and I was in the way.

"Because you're proof that people can change." Nikki stared at me like I was everything she could never be. "You grew up as a Shadow, the baddest of the bad. And yet, you came out with what looked like a family who wanted nothing more than world peace. It was sweet. Now, you're here, back to contemplating ways to escape and kill anyone in your path to do so."

"I wouldn't kill people." I shook my head.

The motion made the pain bounce around inside my skull. I winced and moved my hand, feeling the sore muscles aching at every contraction.

"Because you're too perfect?" Nikki glared at me.

"Because I'm not you."

I hoped to look intimidating. My clothes clung to my dried sweat that covered my body. I knew I must have a mark on my face from laying on my arm. I looked insane.

"Not everyone has the luxury of people lining up to protect them," Nikki snarled. "I've only ever had myself to rely on. I'm not stupid. I knew Alec wanted you more than he needed me. I knew Thayer was shifting his loyalty from Alec and that I wasn't a good enough reason for him to stick around, either. I'm not surprised that he left, or surprised that Alec let him go. As long as you're here, nothing else matters."

"What about when I left?" I asked. "You had more than twenty years to make other friends, but you didn't. You couldn't. You're cold and cruel and no one could care about someone as heartless as you."

"Take a look in the mirror, Mara. You're the one who used Alec's love for you to get him to come to the lab. You're the one who manipulated that sweet little Rachel girl to walk into the lab in the first place. You couldn't resist playing the brothers against each other. You are the reason for everyone's pain, and you still expected them to want to save you." Nikki smiled at me. "You're the most heartless person I know."

Guilt crushed my chest. My hands trembled as they wiped the stray hairs falling in my face. She was wrong. She had to be. I touched the locket around my neck.

"You don't know what you're talking about." I shook my head again.

"Don't I? I watched everything happen in front of my

own eyes." Nikki pulled her hair to the side and started weaving the strands together in a braid.

That wasn't good. "What do you want?" I gasped.

I let the pain show through my eyes as I clawed at the cuff on my wrist.

I understood that everything was my fault. I replayed the choice of asking Alec for help, of talking to Rachel, even of kissing Kylan for the first time.

Every decision I made led me here.

"You know, Alec didn't even blink when Thayer told him that Grae tried to kill you. He and Thayer just left the room, and I never saw Grae again." Nikki continued braiding her hair.

"Tell me what you want." I clenched my jaw, not wanting to think about another life I had inadvertently taken. Another person who died because of me.

"I have no idea what Thayer's doing out there. You remember how excited he was when he came to the Shadows? His parents were long dead, his uncle that raised him was gone too. He wanted a family, and he found that in Alec. He needed someone to follow. He always does. But, he's alone now." Nikki ignored me and continued talking. "Also your fault, by the way."

Her hands had reached the end of her hair.

"Nikki, look at me!" I shouted.

She released her hair without tying the end of the braid. The shiny black hair untangled itself and laid on her shoulder and arm. Her sharp brown eyes looked at me finally.

"You want to know what happened when you left?" Nikki asked, leaning forward. "Nothing. Thayer and Alec started searching for you. They were always gone. Grae spent all his time talking to the other Shadows, convincing them to like him. It took me years to persuade Alec to let me come along.

That's when we found you in Denmark. Up until then, they didn't even see me. They only came to me when they needed to mark a new Shadow. I was alone."

Nikki wasn't doing this for attention. She was doing this to get rid of me. She couldn't kill me. Alec would just retaliate the way he had with Grae. So causing me pain was the next-best thing.

I looked at where I sat. On a hard floor, inside a cramped cell, wishing that I could die.

This was her next-best thing.

"That's how Alec got you to go along with the plan to work with the lab," I said, letting my shoulders fall. "He promised it would hurt me."

"Exactly. He said he would make you suffer so much that you'd scream even in your sleep."

"All you care about is watching my pain?" I already knew the answer.

Nikki let her eyes roam up and down my body. She couldn't hold back the smile. She stood from the floor. I stayed and looked up at her. I had no pride left to lose.

She looked down at me like I was nothing to her, like she didn't even know me.

"I wanna watch you not matter," Nikki answered. "Once Alec gets what he wants, he won't need you anymore. If you happened to die just as the tests prove successful, he might not even be mad."

Death wasn't enough, though. She wanted me forgotten.

"Grae never hated me, did he?" I pulled my eyebrows together, not wanting to say my true thoughts aloud.

"No, he didn't," Nikki said.

"But you did. You used him. You knew Alec would try to kill the person who attacked me. So you sent Grae instead," I accused.

"Grae wanted to be in charge. But he needed to replace Thayer to get close enough to Alec," Nikki sighed as she explained. "Problem was, everyone *loves* Thayer. So I convinced him that if he killed you, Alec would be vulnerable and would need someone else to rely on. Thayer would be a basket case. And I may have promised to help sway the rest of the Shadows in his favor."

"You knew it would get Grae killed. But as long as he took me out with him, then you didn't mind," I said.

"Nope." Nikki shrugged.

"You were only friends with me so you could plan my death?" I looked at the floor, my eyes darting around like they could somehow find how I missed all of this.

But everyone missed it. Alec and Thayer never talked about it. Sage didn't say anything. Nikki was right. She was invisible to everyone else.

"Pot, meet kettle." She pointed to me. "You were only friends with me so you could make sure Alec never got feelings for me."

"Yeah, don't know what I was worried about," I muttered.

When I looked at Nikki, I saw a heartless person who loved hurting other people. Honestly, I saw the female version of Alec.

Except, she didn't have her own Mara. Maybe that was Alec?

But it didn't matter. Nothing really mattered anymore. Least of all me.

I moved my eyes back up to Nikki and slowly stood. I had to lean on the bars for support as my leg muscles tried to hold me up. I clenched my hands around the iron bars and stared at her.

"I'm sorry," I whispered, feeling the locket's weight on my neck.

I needed to make this right. I needed to try.

My voice choked on the lump in my throat. Nikki's cold gaze faltered. She looked confused, but didn't say anything yet.

I wanted to give an apology that might make her change her mind. Her silence dared me to try.

"You're right about everything. I used you, and I never really cared about you. I should have noticed how important you were. I always knew you were powerful and determined." I stammered through the words. "I'm honestly sorry. Maybe once I'm gone, you'll get everything you want."

Nikki was frozen in place, not even moving her chest to breathe.

"Even you deserve for someone to love you," I finished.

She nodded and didn't say a word as she turned around to leave the room. I watched as she walked away from me, her steps perfectly timed. She didn't want me to know that anything I said had affected her.

Maybe it didn't. Either way, I felt a twinge of relief in my chest.

I held the locket in my fingers, feeling the warm metal. My eyes closed as my head lowered. No matter what happened, I still wanted to be a good person.

Someone my mother would have been proud to call her daughter.

"That was big of you," Alec's voice shattered my temporarily happy trance.

My head snapped up in the direction of the sound. Alec leaned against a metal doorway while he stared at me.

"How much did you hear?" I asked.

"Enough to know that you just listened to her tell you how much she hates you, and yet *you* apologized to *her*. Now, I'm just trying to understand why," Alec mused as he walked toward my cell.

"Why would you keep her around if you knew she wanted to hurt me?" I asked. "I mean, I guess I shouldn't be surprised considering your definition of love includes physical harm."

"I knew she wanted to kill you. She knew I would kill her if she tried. You were never in any real danger." Alec shrugged.

I waited for the rest of the story.

"And I needed someone to support this whole plan. Someone who didn't like you. Nikki was the perfect choice. All I had to do was ignore her long enough to get her angry and then make her feel wanted when I needed her. I convinced Sage to go along with it too and here we are." Alec gestured to the shiny lab around us.

White, gleaming, and cold. I shuddered.

"Is she the one that convinced you not to tell Thayer?" I asked.

"That took a long time, but I knew Nikki was right. Thayer cared about you too much to obey me anymore. I noticed it during your last few decades as a Shadow. I had to use Thayer to convince you that killing other Legends was normal, and Thayer started asking too many questions." Alec looked pointedly at me. "He told me he couldn't keep manipulating you, and I knew his loyalty had shifted."

"But when you found me with Kylan…he was helping you. He still brought me back to the mansion anyway?" I shook my head.

"Thayer has a hard time saying no to a pretty face, and Sage can be oh so persuasive once she gets in your head." Alec smiled.

"That was her audition, wasn't it? To get into the Shadows, she had to convince Thayer to follow you one more time."

"Knew you'd put it together eventually." Alec's smile

grew even wider, and he stepped almost within reaching distance of the bars.

"You've been planning this for so long. Why? Level Five power couldn't be worth this much to you," I asked, feeling my knees shake beneath me.

Alec leaned in closer to the bars, careful to watch every motion of my hands.

"If I explain it to you now, you wouldn't appreciate it," Alec whispered. "Now, why are you being so nice to Nikki?"

"I know that nice is an impossible word for you, but I'm not like you anymore. I care about people and I care about being a good person," I answered.

"And that's what you believe you are? A good person?" Alec asked.

"I want to be." I stared straight back at him.

Alec looked at me for a moment, searching for something. When he didn't find it, he took a step back and changed the subject.

"Get some rest. Because tomorrow, the real pain begins," Alec muttered.

His cold eyes drove knives through my skin. I didn't want tomorrow to come.

CHAPTER THIRTY-FIVE

Kylan

Icy drops of rain pattered down on my shoulders.

We stood in a circle, all of us looking down at the saddest sight we had ever seen. One that we hoped wouldn't be coming for centuries.

Rachel's casket lowered into the perfectly rectangular hole at a painfully slow rate. The more it dipped out of view, the more the pain banged through my chest.

I thought back to the day that Rachel joined our family. Cassie had found her in New York. Her lifestyle there consisted of cheating the market and getting rich off of other people's losses. She was ridiculously wealthy and also achingly lonely there.

But Cassie had finally found her sister. They were separated as kids and it took them centuries to find each other.

The day she brought Rachel to the door, we all knew how important it was to her. Her eyes had never shined so brightly as the day she introduced us.

"This is Rachel," her voice trilled with glee. "My sister."

"Nice to meet you," She looked shocked and out of place. But judging by the way she held herself, she was used to feeling confident.

I stepped forward and her nervous eyes fell on me. My hand stretched out to her in an offer of peace. Her eyes sharpened at the sight of my movement. I watched her breath, her eyes, everything.

She was full of energy. It meant one of two things. She was either scared to meet us, or she always lived like this. Rachel's eyes watched mine. She knew what I saw in her. Her head lowered.

My eyes flicked over to Cassie. Her eyes pleaded with me to ignore it. One stipulation of being a part of the family is that we kept each other safe. Safe from humans, safe from the world. Having someone running around and taking energy from too many people put all of that in jeopardy.

This girl was a risk. I knew it. Cassie knew it.

"Please," Cassie whispered.

I looked back at the sister Cassie had been waiting for. Cassie had searched countries and continents for years. After their parents were killed, the two of them ran. Cassie kept searching, and Rachel accepted a life alone.

It wasn't her fault she was this way. She could learn to live like we did. When I looked at Cassie, I saw all the hope in the world. I wasn't about to rip that away from her.

"Welcome to the family." I stretched my hand out again.

She took my hand, but didn't seem convinced. I wouldn't be either. Maybe I could approach this in a different way. Instead, I concentrated on her wary, brown eyes.

It's okay to be scared. I created the words in her mind.

The energy faded in my body. I was out of practice, and did not have very much energy stored up.

Rachel's face fell in shock. My hand waited in the air. Her smile brightened on her face. I laughed at how she reminded me of Cassie more than I expected.

She glanced down at my hand and considered the offer. When her determined eyes flashed back up to mine, she took my hand. She gave it a firm shake and finally let a smile crack.

"Thank you." Rachel's smooth voice sounded like her sister's.

That was the best day of Cassie's life. This was the worst.

A sad song played through the rain, and none of us held back our tears. They mingled in the rain, both falling to the wet ground.

The sleek, black coffin lowered completely out of view now. The second it was gone, Cassie collapsed into Derek's arms, sobbing. He looked up at me, and I nodded.

They both turned and walked to the car. Her sobs shattered through the sound of the rain. This was as much as she could handle. I understood her. She spent years trying to find Rachel and was thrilled when she wanted to become a permanent part of the family.

That was all gone now.

Rachel was gone now.

I knelt on the muddy grass and put my hand next to the edge of her grave. The warm water felt odd against the cold earth. My shoulders hunched as I looked into the final resting place of a dear friend.

"You came to our family for Cassie, for love," I started, not knowing how any of it would end. "We promised to care for you and protect you. We failed. I failed. You have no idea how sorry I am. I should have never brought her into our lives."

The pain of hearing Kate say she needed to go back to the Shadows resurfaced. My fingers clenched into a fist, trapping the mud inside my palm.

"She was reckless. Crazy. Unreliable. Dishonest. She was everything that I should have avoided. She never fit in our family no matter how hard I tried…tried to force it."

The tears poured from my eyes. The sobs shook through my chest.

"She betrayed all of us." I gritted my teeth.

I looked up, hoping to see someone there. Hoping someone would tell me that this wasn't all my fault for bringing her in.

"You know what the worst part is?" I asked, and I could almost see Rachel looking back at me with her warm brown eyes. "No matter how much I hate her. No matter how much I think she got what she deserved. I still love her. I still regret leaving her there. I still wanted to choose her, instead of you. Maybe that's been the problem all along. I kept choosing her over everyone. But this time, I could only take one of you and I finally made the right choice."

I tried to laugh, but it brought more pain. I stood from the ground, the mud dripping from my knees and my hands.

"You'll never know how sorry I am. I will miss you so much, little sis." I smiled through the tears falling down my cheeks, blending with the cold rain.

I turned and walked to my own car and wondered how long it would take to fill the void she left behind. Regret raced through my mind as I thought of how close we were. Seconds sooner, and Rachel could have walked out alive.

No matter how many times I replayed it, the outcome didn't change. Despite having all this power, no one had figured out how to stop death. Right now, I felt as powerless as a human.

I yanked open the door and as I sat, I noticed a paper folder on the floor of the passenger side. I already knew what was in there. I snatched it from the ground and yanked open the front. I pulled out a photo of all of us.

Me, Derek, Cassie, Rachel…and Kate.

I had printed it off to give it to her. I wanted her to have something on the bare walls of her house. I wanted her to have a family.

Now the photo just pushed my anger over the edge. My hand clenched around the paper, crinkling the photo. I looked up at Rachel's gravesite. It looked so empty and lonely.

I pushed the car door open farther, letting the rain inside. My hand brought the photo out into the threatening drops.

"A life for a life," I muttered as the photo fell from my hand.

Before the paper even hit the ground, I shut the door and started the car. I wanted to hate her. I wanted to know that she was hating every sensation of her new existence. I wanted to wish her a life of misery with my brother.

But I couldn't.

I may have left the photo behind in the rain, but Kate was always there in my mind. She never left. Everywhere I looked, I always hoped I would see her.

The part that scared me the most was I didn't know if that would ever go away.

CHAPTER THIRTY-SIX

Just as the pain edged away, that terrible word pierced my reality.

"Again," Alec's voice ordered.

Another excruciating shock jolted into my body.

I tried to hide the pain, but my eyes betrayed me. I had been sitting here for almost an hour and I was exhausted.

The machine had been cranked up at intervals of twenty or thirty volts at a time. Each press of a button sent a shock into my body via the metal plates attached to my arms and back.

"Level of pain?" Alec asked calmly as he stared at his tablet, ready to enter the information.

He did this after every shock. Today started with him injecting something into me that he never explained. I lost count of the time I had been sitting in this chair, smoldering from the electricity combining with the serum in my body.

I gritted my teeth and covered the expression on my face. I looked up at him and he avoided my gaze, which was probably smart considering all the tricks I had been playing on his mind lately.

My eyes glanced toward Raven eagerly standing at the machine causing all of my pain.

Next to her was Sage. Her red eyes filled with discomfort as she watched. The other lab might have used a similar treatment on her to test her skin sensitivity.

I knew how much she wanted her freedom. I also wanted her to see every second of my pain. She should know just how much this was costing.

"One," I answered through my clenched teeth, delaying the results even further.

Sage's eyes fell as she heard my answer. Every moment I dragged this out was another moment of agonizing pain for me and another moment that she didn't get what she wanted either.

"How long are you going to let them do this?" I looked directly at her.

Sage's eyes went wide and she looked between Alec and Raven. Neither of them even budged.

"I know you don't understand. But I need this," she said and held her hands firm at her sides.

"You need this? You need to watch me scream? You need to hear me cry in my cell every night? You need to allow them to do to me exactly what the others did to you?" I didn't have the will to scream at her. All I could muster was a threatening glare and a few choked words.

"I haven't stood in the sun in centuries. Anywhere I am becomes a new prison for me during the day. You don't know what it's like to be that stuck. It slowly kills every single piece of you." She lowered her chin, avoiding my gaze.

"And this is worth it to you?" I challenged.

"Your pain is temporary." She closed her eyes and recited the words.

It sounded like she had heard that line a million times. I

imagined the people who took her said something very similar when she begged to be released.

"Guilt is forever. You'll always remember the pain you had to inflict because of the life you wanted." I looked at Raven now.

My words applied to both of them, but they were meant for Raven. I wanted her to understand how much I hated myself for what I did to her. Raven's cold eyes softened for a moment. She cleared her throat and looked away from me.

"You will never know what I went through in those cells. I was there for fifteen years. So if you think that I am going to feel sorry for you over your few weeks of discomfort, then you're wrong. Nothing you could say would make me trade my well-deserved happiness for you." Sage narrowed her red eyes. "Nothing."

The all-powerful Legend that Alec had hunted for in order to help him change my memory raised her chin.

Her eyes glowed in the fluorescent lights and her mouth formed a tight line that swore she would never waver on her decision. She spent centuries honing her skill, her only skill. She was a Level One, probably the strongest I had ever met.

In her burning gaze, it was the one thing that finally made her valuable. Deep down, she was just like me. She did what she thought was best in the moment.

I wanted to hate her. But I understood her more than she knew.

Alec stopped looking at the screen and finally looked at me. He could see how tired and worn I really was, and I saw the sympathy flutter across his eyes. Then they hardened again.

"You said your pain was only at a one. We are up to four hundred volts. You should be well above that," Alec interrupted my thoughts.

He walked forward and knelt in front of me. His dark eyes looked curiously into mine. The remaining energy pumped slowly in my body. Still, I wanted to squirm away from his stare.

"Maybe I'm stronger than you thought."

"No. You're just stubborn."

His eyes moved from mine, to my mouth, to my neck, and then back up. Feeling his stare all over me made my skin crawl. I didn't look away from his gaze, but I realized quickly that I should have.

Burning agony shot into my mind.

Every nerve lit up simultaneously with a pain signal to my brain. I wanted to clutch my head and curl into a ball but my restraints held me in place. My hands clenched and my breath seized.

I tried not to shout, but I couldn't hold it back anymore. I shut my eyes and tried to force him out of my mind.

The pain just kept coming, growing stronger.

"Stop!" I begged, and his power instantly vanished.

I blinked the last of the lingering pain away. My eyes looked up at Alec just in time to see his sick smile spreading on his lips.

"Level Five or not, you're still too strong," Alec judged, pursing his lips and looking for another answer.

"Thank you." I hung my head and closed my eyes.

"It's not a compliment." Alec shook his head, looking down at my neck.

My dark curls fell all around me, covering some of my skin from his gaze. I realized that I bothered Alec more when I looked like Kate, so I had changed back into that form a few days ago when a Legend's glove slipped and touched my skin.

I relaxed my arms and shoulders into the chair. My chest

heaved, trying to get the new air to force out any connection between me and him.

A speck of light glinted across Alec's face, my necklace reflecting in the fluorescents. His attention left my eyes instantly as his gaze lowered to my chest.

"This…" he wondered.

Alec stared at the simple string of gold around my neck. His eyes narrowed and he leaned forward. His hand snatched the locket from my neck as the chain snapped.

"What are you doing?" My words came out slow.

My eyes grew heavy as soon as he pulled the necklace off me.

"You shouldn't be able to do half the things you've done with the amount of energy in your system." Alec raised the necklace to me.

The edges glowed faintly when he moved it closer to me, and my eyes brightened. Only a Legend would catch the difference and Alec was carefully watching.

He moved the necklace away, and I felt my eyes turn weary again. Eyelids heavy and cold.

It wasn't power in a sense that could help him. It was a reminder to me that no matter how bad things got, I still had someone on my side. Having him hold that reminder in his hands felt like a dagger in my chest.

My mind was going to break.

"It really is a power source."

"Alec, it's not what you think," I tried and pulled against the restraints.

My body ached from a lack of energy. My breaths came in scattered and shallow spurts. My eyes ran wild, trying to focus on anything.

"Then, open it and show me," Alec offered.

I looked at the necklace, dangling innocently in his

fingers. The locket could only be opened by me. Alec needed me and he needed the necklace. He thought it was the answer to everything. He thought it was the reason they had not found the link yet.

As long as he hoped I would open it, he wouldn't destroy it. My mind was already spinning from not having it on. If it was gone completely, I don't know if I could recover from that.

Especially not here, with everything stacked against me.

"No. It's useless to you anyway," I gasped, feeling the loss of the locket.

Every happy memory I wanted to hold onto. Every thought of anyone I cared about vanished as the locket landed in the bottom of his pocket. I would never see it again. I would never see them again. Every person I loved, I ended up losing.

With the locket out of sight, any shred of hope vanished.

My body shrunk into the chair. My chest heaved up and down, each movement bringing a crippling ache to my sides. I felt every single nerve screaming in pain. My mind ignited in a flurry of frayed ends and broken connections.

"Well, now it's useless to you."

"W-why are you..." I tried to talk before the machine started up again.

The dull whirring sound of the charge came anyway. The whine grew higher in pitch as the machine readied for the next jolt.

"Don't try to be strong. It will only make this hurt worse," he cautioned with actual concern in his eyes.

His gloved hands moved forward and a finger brushed under my chin as he looked at me.

I glared at him and wished I could gouge those perfect blue eyes out with my bare hands. I took a breath and tried a new approach. The fury in my eyes faded to show the amount of agony I was in. I let Alec see just how much my body ached.

"Please," I quietly asked.

I watched Alec's eyes as he followed the tear that brimmed in my eyes and slid down my cheek.

My breathing quickened as my body finally released all the throbbing pain it had been holding back. I focused back on Alec and saw the remorse in his face.

His hand lowered and he brushed his finger along my arm, and Raven instantly powered the machine down again. When he reached the place where the metal plate touched my burned skin, he pressed his hand against my skin harder.

I cried out and tried to pull away from him.

"You're in pain. Now, tell me exactly how much," his voice mingled remorse and determination.

I knew the sooner I answered him, the sooner this would all be over.

"Six," I finally croaked.

My mind was a blaze of disjointed signals and thoughts. A new tear burned in my eye. I kept my gaze on him even though he was the last person I wanted to be seeing. I knew that him seeing my pain was hurting him, and if that was the only way I could cause him harm, then I would.

"Thank you," he answered and stood.

He looked down at me, holding the tablet in his right hand. The muscle under his dagger mark flexed. I took a shaky breath in and waited for him to tell me it was over.

That whirring charge sound didn't stop.

"Again," his icy voice called.

I didn't have time to say anything before the next resounding shock burned into my body. My scream shot into the air without a single hesitation.

I didn't care if Alec saw my pain. I didn't care about anything that happened after this.

All I felt was pain.

My muscles spasmed and my back arched against the chair. It stung and burned until it was gone. But the sensation still lingered. It even hurt to breathe.

"That was five hundred volts," Alec's voice said as Raven hastily recorded it.

I could feel Alec's eyes on me even though I couldn't lift my head to look back at him. My eyes focused past my bruised, too-thin legs and on the floor.

"I can't...I can't take anymore." I tried to lift my head and form a complete sentence.

I couldn't even hear the words coming out of my mouth, the blood was pumping in my ears so loudly.

"Then give me an honest answer," Alec asked gently.

He pulled off his gloves before he removed the cuffs holding my arms to the chair. My muscles were withered and fried and I wasn't going to be moving anytime soon.

Alec touched my arm gently and I could barely even feel it. My skin was singed and blaring in pain. He put his finger under my chin and lifted my head high enough to meet his gaze.

I hardly had to concentrate to pull energy from his body. His skin touched mine and my body immediately reacted. His energy warmed my already burning skin as it poured in through the tiny connection of his finger on my chin.

I looked him in the eye and wished I could hurt him like he was hurting me. I had no cards to play with, though. The only thing I could do was give him what he wanted.

"Ten," I pleaded.

He smiled just before he let my head fall back down. The energy halted, and my body was left scrambling to find more.

Alec picked up a small electronic light from the table next to me. He turned on the switch, the light glowing a dark purple.

Ultraviolet rays.

He moved the light toward my arm, watching carefully. The second the light touched my skin, I felt the heat. At first, it was uncomfortable on my already-burned arm. Then, the heat increased. The warmth changed to a searing scorch.

A sharp scream burst out. I yanked my arm away from the light, grateful that Alec had removed the cuffs.

My arm was out of the light but the burn remained, barely cooling at all. I looked down at the red blisters forming on my skin. The energy that Alec had transferred to me was now being used to heal the injury.

"You made me like h-her," I stuttered, dropping my arms into my lap and staring back at Alec.

"This was a test to see if we could recreate the condition. For you, it's only temporary. It only works when your skin is completely overwhelmed. But it should give us enough to make Sage's condition temporary too."

Alec gave the tablet to the eager blonde waiting in the corner. Her red eyes lit up with excitement as she walked forward and took the tablet from Alec. Her hands held it as if she was afraid to break it. The answer to her questions lay in her fingertips.

Alec smiled at Sage and then looked back to me. "Congratulations. You just gave a woman her life back."

"I hope it was worth it." I didn't lift my eyes up to her.

"If this works?" She held up the tablet. "It was worth every second."

She stopped and looked at my damaged body in the shiny chair.

Her red eyes met mine one last time before she left the

room. She was still apathetic even though I had just sacrificed to give her the key to her freedom.

She left the room without another glance back.

"Hand me the needle," Alec asked with an outstretched hand.

I watched him take a needle from Raven and adjust it so his finger was ready to push the plunger. He lowered the needle to my left arm.

"Wh-what is that?" I asked him.

My mind tried to send a signal that I should be worried. It never reached its target. I was curious, maybe even wondering.

But I wasn't scared.

There was nothing he could do to me to make any of this worse.

"Insurance," he said.

The clear serum tingled as it entered my body.

With that, I closed my eyes and my muscles went limp against the chair. My breathing slowed as my mind drifted off somewhere.

Every aching cell inside of me hoped I would never come back.

CHAPTER THIRTY-SEVEN

Kylan

The flowers scattered in my house had begun to wilt weeks after the funeral.

Despite the house teeming with gifts and flowers, it felt utterly empty. Portland seemed entirely different. Empty and frozen in time.

Years could have passed, and I might not have noticed. The facial hair growing in was my only clue of how long it had been.

I sat on the couch and watched TV as I had most days since we got back. My phone had too many voice mails from work and friends for me to even dare pick it up.

The only thing I used it for now was to order in food. The human would drop off the delivery and leave feeling a little more tired.

I kept myself alive. Barely.

I had to be careful. Whenever I saw a human, all I could think of was Jacques. I pictured his smug smile when he stepped out of the lab. I saw the fear in his eyes when he landed in my hands. I felt his new Legend energy racing into my body.

My family and I had kept in touch, but not closely. Cassie was the one I heard from the least. Any communication to me came through Derek. I had been alone for days, without uttering a single word to a person.

The silence almost felt normal to me.

Maybe being alone wasn't the worst thing. I lied.

Even I didn't believe me.

The silence broke when I heard a knock at the front door. All my family knew to use the side door, so this must have been someone else. I stood from the couch.

Normally, I would just let them think that no one was home, but this time I didn't. I actually craved to see another person.

Just not the person standing on the other side of the door.

"What are you doing here?" I asked, staring at his familiar eyes. I wanted to throw him off the steps the second I saw him.

"I know how we can get her back," Thayer said, holding his hands out like he was ready to catch the door I was about to slam in his face.

"I don't care." I stared back at him.

I didn't move or shut the door. I thought about how I left Kate, alone and in pain. I could guess the agony she must have been in the last few weeks.

But I still couldn't shake the images of her and Alec kissing. Dancing, laughing, and kissing. Not as Mara, but as Kate.

My Kate.

She chose him, and I thought it was only fitting for her to live with that choice. I still couldn't ignore the ache I felt in my stomach at what I had done to her.

"I can see that's not true." Thayer cocked his head to the

side, calling my bluff.

"She made her choice," I said through clenched teeth.

"No, she didn't. Alec is way too good at playing with her heart. I know because I'm the one that helped him do it. He knew the hold he had on her and he used it," Thayer explained.

A small amount of hope surfaced that maybe she did still care about me. Maybe she didn't know what she was doing.

"Why are you defending her?" I asked him straight. "Why are you not standing by his side right now?"

"Because I don't think what's happening to her is right. I care about her," he said and stared right back at me.

"Of course you do. That's what she does, right? She makes people care about her."

He didn't flinch. One look at his determined eyes meant he wasn't going to move until he got what he came for.

"Oh, get over yourself. You should have seen her when she came back to the mansion that day." Thayer stood tall and I couldn't help but want to listen. "I watched her walk in. I hadn't seen her since she left, and even then she wasn't really…herself. But when she came in that day, she looked like Kate, but she also looked like the person I had known all along. She was determined, she was brave, and she was a little scared. But you know what else? She was in love."

"Look, I don't need you to rub it in. I know what happened between them while she was gone," I started, trying to shut him up.

It didn't work.

"I'm not talking about Alec. She never acted so devoted with him. What I saw that day was how much she cared about you. So much that she walked back into her own personal hell. She asked the one person she hates more than anyone for help. When Mara left, she never had that kind of courage. That was because of you," he continued.

For a moment, I was almost ready to listen. Hearing him talk about her brought back all the memories of why I loved her. She was strong, brave, kind, and selfless when she needed to be. All she wanted was to be happy and belong.

But then images of her and Alec resurfaced in my mind again. I saw him hold her close. I saw her reach for him. I saw them kiss. I *felt* how enticing she was to him. I felt exactly how much he wanted it to happen.

She gave him what he wanted.

"I know that she doesn't just hate Alec. She's in love with him," I spat.

"You know, I've heard very little about you, but I've been told you're smart. Although I am beginning to doubt that because even an idiot knows the difference between love and lust. She's attracted to the freedom and excitement that Alec promises, but she knows it can't ever last," Thayer explained in a slow voice.

I wanted to smack him. I raised a hand to stop him from talking, but he reached into my mind faster than I could blink. An overwhelming feeling crept into my body.

All I wanted was to be silent. I couldn't move. I could hardly breathe. All I could do was listen. Every cell in my body begged to hear his voice.

Once he knew he had my attention, he continued.

"What she really wants is you," he said like he was trying to keep control of his own words. "She wanted it the day she walked in the mansion, begging for help. She wanted it when she trekked across the country on a stealth mission to risk her life and possibly save a woman she hardly knew. She wanted it when she stormed into a lab that turned out to be a special trap set up just for her. She knew what she was risking, but all of it was worth it because she wanted you."

As the last word came out, the hold on my body lifted. I took a deep breath and the relief spread across my shoulders. My chest breathed easy again.

"As much as I want to believe you. I can't." I didn't hide the pain in my eyes this time.

His perspective was touching, but it didn't change the facts. She chose him. It was a mistake, and we all knew it. But she still chose him. Even if I could bring her back, I don't know if I could ever shake that from my mind.

"I know nothing I say will convince you," Thayer said, but didn't leave.

I stared at him, waiting for him to make another move. The man just stared right back at me.

"You'd be right," I answered him through clenched teeth.

He still didn't move.

"That's why I brought a reinforcement," Thayer announced and stepped through the doorway without hesitation.

I turned to see if anyone was following him, but I couldn't see anyone. I moved to throw him out of my house when I heard the voice coming from the doorway.

"I think you should listen to him," Derek said before I got my hands on Thayer.

I turned to look at my brother standing with his hands in his pockets. He looked up at me carefully and stood while I decided what to do.

I looked back at Thayer's glib smile and fought the urge to punch it straight off his face. When I looked back at Derek, I knew what my decision would be. No matter how far off the deep end I had gone, Derek always had a way of bringing me back.

"Fine, you have two minutes," I said and stepped aside to invite them in the house.

They both started talking at the same time. I tried to focus on their words as much as possible, but my mind was already trailing off on the idea of actually getting Kate back.

The tiniest stitch of emotion returned to my numbed body. It crept in so quietly, I had barely noticed it was there.

Hope.

CHAPTER THIRTY-EIGHT

My body jumped at the sound of shouting coming from a familiar voice.

My weary gaze shifted toward the sound. Two people held Nikki in between them, her black hair snapping back and forth in the air. She dug her heels against the tile as they forced her down the hallway, away from the testing rooms.

They must have been Legends if they were holding her down, but I couldn't tell. I could barely see straight, let alone concentrate enough to distinguish a Legend from a human.

"You said it would work! You promised that it was ready!" Nikki screamed at Alec as the Legends tried to wrangle her away from him.

"Everything said it would be successful," Alec ran his hand angrily through his hair.

"You call this successful? I am nothing!"

"I'll find a way to fix this. I will," Alec promised as Nikki's guards carried her around the corner.

"I will kill her, Alec!" Her scream echoed down the hall.

A door slammed, sending another echo. My eyes blinked slowly before they landed back on Alec.

He clenched his fists, and a few sharp breaths filled his chest. Alec reached down and grabbed the table in front of him.

With a loud bang, the table flipped over and hit the opposite wall. His hands shot to his hair and yanked through his dark blond locks, freeing his face from any distraction. His eyes went wide as they darted across the floor like he was trying to think through what just happened.

I stared at him just a little too long.

His eyes snapped up to look at me through the glass window, and the shock melted into burning rage. He caught me looking at him and charged out of the room, nearly ripping the door off its hinges.

All that stood between him and me was empty air, not even a sheet of glass to protect me anymore. His eyes seethed, and I was actually grateful for the bars.

"How are you doing this?" Alec asked me with a wild anger in his eyes.

I didn't dare to speak yet. I just twisted the cuff nervously on my wrist.

"We have spent the last few weeks combing through every possibility. Pages and pages of charts and predictions and calculations. We looked at everything! It should have worked," he started scolding himself instead of me.

"You tried to change Nikki," I guessed.

"We ran every test we could without trying it on an actual Legend. Nikki didn't hesitate to volunteer, especially not when I told her how sure I was that it would work," Alec grimaced.

I wanted to roll my eyes at her stubbornness and sense of invincibility, but I didn't. I kept my gaze focused completely on Alec. He paced back and forth, slowly moving closer to me.

"Apparently, it didn't go well." My dry lips pulled into a tiny smile.

Alec halted and let out a strained laugh.

"Didn't go well?" he mocked. "Instead of changing her into a Five, it took everything away."

"Wait…is she human?" I asked.

"No, she can still take energy and is way too strong for her size. She's a Legend. Just a Legend with no power," Alec clarified. "She's a Zero."

"How is that even possible?" I asked, honestly wondering what he had done wrong.

"It shouldn't be!" Alec shouted back. "We can change humans to Legends, but we can't add a Level onto an already-existing Legend. It doesn't make any sense."

I had never seen him come so undone before. Normally, even in his anger, he was cool and calculating. This was just blind rage.

He slammed his fists against the bars of my cell. I instinctively took a step back at the loud sound.

"You're going to help me fix this, even if it's the last thing you do." His eyes burned into mine.

I waited for pain to come, but none did. He wasn't hurting me yet. The cool and calculating part of his personality resumed control. Ice spread through my veins, slowing every breath as I looked at his obliterating eyes. He was much scarier this way.

"Why is this so important to you?"

He froze just as he was about to turn away. I stepped closer to the bars, and Alec pulled his hands out of reach.

"Excuse me?" he asked slowly as he narrowed his eyes.

"You are the strongest Legend I've ever known. Everyone

cowers at the sound of your name. You couldn't become much more powerful than you already are. You're *Alec Stone*. Why do you need this?"

I watched carefully as my words took effect on him.

"Because all of that wasn't enough," he answered back.

His mouth turned down instead of spreading out into his usual crooked grin. His eyes flickered with a fleeting softness before they turned cold again.

"For who? For your father?" I asked.

"You. It wasn't enough for you," he answered and straightened the lapels on his white lab coat. "Maybe if I could have offered you everything, you never would have left. We could've been all-powerful together if we'd both been Fives."

"I didn't leave because of what you couldn't do. I left because of what you did do," I said calmly.

I talked like I was trying to reason with Alec, not as the great and powerful leader of the Shadows but as Alec.

"I lied about your past because I knew you would have been disgusted if you found out what we'd done. I was right, wasn't I?" he said just as calmly back, stepping away from the bars again.

He didn't show any signs that my words were reaching him at all.

I filled my eyes with fake sympathy, hoping he would let his guard down again. Hoping he would approach the bars one more time.

"I was desperately in love with you. If you had been honest, I may have forgiven you," I said, and for the first time, he was actually listening.

For one precious moment, I had his undivided attention in an empty room. Alec may be smart, but he always said I was his greatest weakness. I was about to prove it.

"That's easy to say now." He tried to wave my reason away.

I kept looking at him and begged him with my eyes to step closer. Surprisingly, he did.

"You didn't give me a chance back then." I slowed my words and tried to look as enticing as possible.

Which was hard considering I was weak, bruised, and covered in dried sweat. But a few steps closer and I would be able to touch him.

"It wouldn't have changed anything," he answered slowly and took another tentative step closer.

I hid the smile pulling at my mouth. Instead, I returned his blank face with my open, innocent eyes. Alec knew in his mind that I wasn't about to profess my love.

But under every layer of anger, power, lust, and everything else that gave him his reputation, the little boy who fell in love with me wanted to believe I still cared for him.

"What if it did?" I asked and watched his tough façade begin to melt away.

The boy hiding inside of his manipulative personality flashed in his expression. The boy that a long time ago, I did fall for. He was also the boy that would do anything for me, including stepping forward when he knew that he should keep his distance.

"What are you saying?" he asked gently.

His hands reached out toward the bars that held me back. He was just barely within my reach.

"I'm saying…" I stalled as he took the last step I needed him to.

His eyes looked at me with a bright flare of hope. His body leaned closer to the bars that stood between me and him. A small smile almost flashed on his lips.

My hand shot forward through the bars and clamped tightly around his neck. The only exposed skin on his body.

His energy burst from his cells into my aching ones.

I expected to feel a warm rush of energy that would allow my body to operate properly, but what I received was so much more.

My body had been dying, slowly. The lab assistants had all kept me on the brink of consciousness. When his energy hit my body, it wasn't human energy that swirled gently through my veins. This was Legend energy.

Alec's energy.

Every nerve in my body ignited. Every cell buzzed with new life. Every breath rejuvenated my mind. The room around me crystalized into perfect clarity.

I turned my bright gaze back to Alec's shocked eyes and watched as his hand fumbled to shove me away. With how fast I was siphoning him, there was no way he'd be strong enough to pry me off his body.

As he pointed out, he was no Level Five, and until he was, he couldn't stop me.

My eyes locked onto him as his face twisted in fear, fell in defeat, and pulled together in shock all in a matter of seconds. The energy roared in my body. If these bars weren't blocking my power, I could snap them in half without thinking.

"I'm saying that you are a manipulative, egotistical piece of scum that doesn't deserve a shred of the power you already have. As long as I have an ability to think clearly, I will never choose you again. Now, hand me the key," I snarled, so close to his face that I could see the reflection of myself in his eyes.

I pulled him into the bars and took way too much pleasure at the surprise in his expression.

He struggled to breathe, and the energy faded from his eyes. He had less than a minute of consciousness left but instead of handing me the keys, he smiled.

"You won't kill me." His strained voice was barely audible.

"You have been torturing me for more days than I can coherently string together in my mind. I am emotionally and physically destroyed. Do you really want to take the risk that I can make a good decision right now?"

"I didn't think you were that cruel." Alec smiled, his eyes fluttering.

The energy poured into my body, singing through every particle of my skin. I couldn't slow it down even if I wanted. My body had been so desperate for too long.

"The only thing I can think about is your energy in my body. I want it all." I enunciated every syllable. "Unless you give me a reason to spare your life, I will drain every breath out of you."

Alec's eyes widened with fascination as he watched me.

"I'm not cruel, Alec. I'm desperate," I growled.

Alec reached in his perfectly white pocket and pulled a key out. His hand shook as he passed the key through the bar.

The second my fingers wrapped around the cool metal of the key, I released Alec. His body fell to the floor. His muscles shook as he struggled to lift himself up on his hands and knees.

I quickly turned the key in the lock, knowing that all I had to do was get far enough away from the bars to use my powers and break out of here. I had the energy and the opportunity.

The key clicked in my hand as the lock released. I immediately shoved the door open. Hope surged through my entire body. I'd have to figure out a way to get the limiting cuff removed, find some shoes, and the nearest energy source possible.

But all of those could wait until I breathed fresh air miles away from this lab. My muscles primed to race toward the door.

That was until I heard Alec's voice behind me.

"What? No good-bye kiss?" his voice taunted, and I froze.

I turned around slowly, amazed that he could still be so arrogant, or even talk at all.

My anger spread even more when I saw his sadistic smile in sharp clarity from the new energy. I wondered if he was really that delusional to think he still had any upper hand.

I narrowed my eyes at him and fought the urge to rip the last of his energy from him.

The desire tingled in my fingertips. One more touch and I could feel the incredible burst of final energy from Alec himself.

My mind raced. It was almost more than I could handle. My eyes looked down at the person responsible for every unhappy moment in my life. My hands curled into fists.

In my anger, I didn't hear what was going on around me. Alec's smile rushed my mind. Rage overwhelmed my senses.

"Don't move," Raven called from behind me.

My ears burned at the sound of her voice, of her threat. I turned to face her in all her bravery. I saw three people, clearly Legends, standing with guns raised. In the middle of them was Raven.

I noticed another person, also a Legend, closing the door to the outside hallway. I noticed everything and processed it all at once. It was amazing how much I could perceive with enough energy.

It was like I had been blind, deaf, and drugged all at the same time, but now I had all of those abilities back.

With my only exit blocked, I stood to face my enemies. A human assistant scrambled to Alec's side. She reached her hand out to him to help him up.

Idiot. I sighed as Alec reached his hand up to hers.

Within a few seconds, she fell to the ground. I didn't wait to see if she was still breathing. Alec slowly stood, and I turned to fix my eyes on Raven.

"Thank you, sweetheart," Alec said to the girl on the floor.

"You didn't honestly think you could just walk out of here, did you?" Raven sighed, her hands not loosening on the gun.

"You can't stop me," I said.

"No, but he can." She smiled as her eyes moved to behind me.

I didn't have time to turn before Alec's gloved hands wrapped around me. One hand pinned my body close to his, the other shoved a needle directly into my neck. I grabbed both of his arms and threw his body over mine and sent him crashing into Raven.

My body reacted to whatever Alec had injected into me. I took a step forward and stumbled. I had enough energy to keep moving, but at this rate, I'd barely make it to the door. I heard Alec's laugh as he stood and helped Raven up.

"You know, you actually had me for a minute." Alec clapped as my legs wobbled and I tried to blink the darkness away.

He looked at my weakness with pride. Discomfort crawled all over me under his gaze.

"I learned from the best," I threw back at him.

"Yes, you did. You and I really are a perfect fit." He smiled, his eyes still dim from a lack of energy.

I clenched my fist and tried to hold back my anger. With

all the energy spinning inside of me, I couldn't think past that moment. Right then, I just wanted my hands around his throat.

Alec laughed at my struggle. A tiny, insignificant laugh. But at that sound, I snapped. I lunged for him.

My body stopped at Raven's next bullet. The tranquilizer flowed into my body immediately. I could no longer stand, so I dropped to my knees right in front of Alec. My stomach twisted at how much he was enjoying this.

I watched him squat down enough that his eyes were level with mine. His smile made me want to scream.

"When are you going to see that you can't beat me?" he whispered and bumps rose on my neck.

I tried not to show how scared I was of what he would do in retaliation. My head swirled with the sleep drug, and I forced my eyes open.

"Once you have what you want, what are you going to do with me?" I whispered.

I had to focus on his white coat or on the sound of his breath to stay alert. I needed to hear his response.

"That depends," he answered. I looked at him, confused.

"You're gonna let Nikki kill me," I answered for him instead, an answer that actually made sense.

I had disrespected and manipulated him in every way possible. Even he wasn't stupid enough to leave the one person alive that could actually bring him down.

"No, I'll just let Nikki think that. But I should make you wish you were dead," Alec tilted his head to the side, just like Kylan used to do.

The painful reminder of him panged in my memory. Chills raced across my skin at how much Alec looked like his brother in this moment. My eyes drooped, and my weak breaths trembled.

"Should?"

"Depends on if you decide to play nice or not," he finished his statement with, "Do you think you can do that?"

"Burn in hell," I seethed as my eyes finally shut.

With those last words, I collapsed forward, right into his open arms. My consciousness waned, and all I could feel was the warmth from his body.

"Baby, as long as you're there with me," I heard him whisper just as the last of my consciousness faded.

One warm tear slipped out of my eye. I was stuck here in this place for the rest of my miserable, and long, life. Stuck forever with Alec. I couldn't think of anything worse in the world.

CHAPTER THIRTY-NINE

Kylan

"Are you sure about this?" I asked, looking at both of them.

Thayer stood next to me, a little too close for my own comfort. Derek stood across from me, his arms crossed over his chest.

"No, but it's our best shot," Thayer answered.

I was a little surprised he didn't just lie to me. That's something Alec would've definitely trained him to do. As kids, he said he would practice telling people a similar version to the truth.

That way, when he really needed to lie, it came naturally to him. It scared me, especially at such a young age, how much he had reminded me of Father.

"It makes sense." Derek nodded toward Thayer.

"How do we even know if they'll join us?" I asked.

Thayer had pitched a plan involving a sneak attack on the lab. Whatever Shadows refused to stay with Alec were supposed to be willing to help us, but I had yet to see any sign of that commitment.

"Not all of us agree with what Alec is doing," Thayer answered my real question.

"And you're going to lead the stragglers?" I asked him back.

I narrowed my eyes at him as I tried to decide if all of this was just a trap. I had no reason to think that. Alec got what he wanted, so he wouldn't have any motive to come after me or my family again.

However, Thayer had done the unexpected thing and left. Maybe that's why I struggled to trust him.

"No." Thayer put a hand on my shoulder. "We are."

I took a glance at Derek, who shrugged. "It's worth trying. We need to get her back."

"We?" I asked.

"Yes, all of us. You're not the same without her. I want my brother back," Derek answered firmly with a hint of a smile.

"How can you be so happy? Rachel is dead. She's gone," I challenged him.

His brown eyes looked back at me with a new fire of anger.

A snarl pulled at his top lip. "You don't think I'm sad? I have to go home to her blood sister every day and remind her that Rachel isn't coming home. I have been nothing but sad since the second you walked out of the lab with her body."

Heartbreak flooded his eyes. His shoulders slumped forward. I put my hand on his shoulder, hoping to take some of the pain away but knowing I couldn't.

"But it's time for us to stop wallowing and do something," Derek finished as he lifted his head to meet my gaze.

He looked at me with a determination I had only seen when he was trying to get Cassie to fall for him. He tried for a solid decade before she even gave him the time of day.

When I had asked him why he focused so much on her, he always gave me the same answer.

She has a power like no other Legend. When I'm around her, time stops. I can't just let her go. That was all he would say.

That line made me chuckle every time I looked at him and Cassie. The two lived their lives teetering on the line between ripping each other's head off and being crazy in love with each other. Their whole relationship made me believe that miracles were indeed real.

"I'm sure I could get over it eventually," I answered a completely honest response, no matter how heartless it sounded.

"Not this one, bro. This one is different." Derek shook his head at me.

"I know. You have no idea how badly I want to march in those doors, tell her I'm sorry, and carry her out in my arms. But every time I think about it, I see Rachel lying there on the ground. I see Alec, smiling at her. I see that dagger on Kate's arm and I remember that she and I are more different than we will ever be similar." I looked at the ground, not wanting to see Derek's face when I told him what I thought.

Derek shook my shoulder to get my attention. I reluctantly pulled my eyes up to look at him. His eyes locked on mine and didn't move.

"You know how I don't like to get touchy-feely, so I am only going to say this once," Derek started, with a smile on his face. "She's your Cassie. You can't just let her go."

I stared back at him. Before I asked my next question, Thayer spoke up.

"She needs you. She doesn't stand a chance against Alec and the entire lab," Thayer said so fervently it was obvious how much he cared about her, even loved her.

Then again, Kate had told me about how he enjoyed

messing with people's emotions. I had just seen how easy it was for him firsthand. The thought of his level of skill made me shudder.

He was the perfect example of what I could have been had I stayed with the Shadows. A little bit of good, mostly bad, and extremely powerful.

"How long will it take to round everyone up?" I asked, and breathed out any doubt I had.

I wanted Kate in my life, and I couldn't leave her stranded with Alec. The time for grieving was over. I knew she cared about me, and anything else I could forgive.

"They're already here," Thayer smiled and looked toward the front door.

I walked back to the door. When I opened it, I saw at least ten Shadows standing in my front yard, along with Cassie standing a safe distance away from them.

It was an odd sight to see them all standing together.

My sister looked up at me. The Shadows looked at Thayer like a sea of awaiting dark soldiers.

For the first time since the two of them knocked on the door, I actually thought we had a chance.

"You knew." I glanced back at Derek.

He knew me better than almost anyone else. When I looked at him, I didn't see a stranger I picked up along the way. I saw a brother, in every sense of the word.

"Yup." He slapped his hand on my shoulder and I looked out at all the people waiting to mobilize.

"So why not just use the people outside as motivation instead of getting all...sappy on me." I punched him lightly on the arm.

"You needed to hear it. And you better remember it, because I meant it when I said I'm only saying it once, bro."

I couldn't help but notice the redhead standing off from the rest of the threatening Shadows. Cassie kept her arms crossed and took glances often at the others.

"What about her?" I nodded toward her.

"I can hear you, you know," Cassie called, still not moving.

"She'll be okay…eventually," Derek shrugged.

He stepped off the porch and walked out to meet his Cassie. To meet the person that stops time for him. She welcomed him with open arms, and he melted into her. Her eyes glanced up to me, and she offered the slightest smile.

Cassie and Derek walked up to us, holding hands. Derek could try to hide his soft side all he wanted, but it oozed out whenever he was around Cassie.

"Even with all of these people, we can't run a full attack like we did last time. Someone has to open the doors." I tried to deny the hope burning inside of me.

"I've got that part covered." Thayer smiled. "I have someone inside."

"Who?" I immediately asked.

"How do you know they aren't trying to trick us again?" Derek asked my next question.

His confidence was contagious. Out of all the people in the world, he would know what going up against Alec would take. We had seen what a lab was like, and this would be the next level of impossible.

But if Thayer actually thought we could do this, then maybe we did stand a chance.

"You'll just have to trust me on this one." Thayer crossed his arms. "The less you guys know, the better."

"You want us to walk in there blind?" I asked with raised eyebrows.

"I want you to trust me. If you know the whole plan, Alec will sense it from a mile out. He's never been in my mind before. I'm the only safe person to keep a secret," he explained, still smiling.

"Wow, no offense," Cassie scoffed at Thayer's insult.

"No, I hope you take offense to that." Thayer leveled his gaze on her. "You guys are Twos, and Alec could get in your mind even if you were actively trying to keep him out. In his sleep. It's that easy. You, however, happen to be a Four. Congrats on that. But Alec's your brother, and your minds are way more alike than you'd ever want to admit. So yeah, you need to trust me because I'm your only option."

This kid was way too prideful, considering the suicide mission we were about to undertake. I had a feeling that this would annoy me all the way to Louisiana. As smug as he was, he was also right.

"All right, let's go get her," I said with a smile for the first time.

I pictured holding Kate in my arms and carrying her out of the lab. The hope flared inside of me.

This was going to work.

I was going to get her back.

My fingers tingled at the thought of having her with me again. In that moment, it felt like time stood still, just like Derek always said it would.

CHAPTER

FORTY

The sound of footsteps fractured through my bleary mind. My eyes fluttered open and the harsh light broke through. I turned my head and forced my eyes to focus on something, anything.

A pair of black shoes stood in front of my bars. My eyes rolled around until I finally made contact with the one face that was etched perfectly into my mind.

His cold blue eyes were locked onto me as well. They always were.

"Good morning, baby." A smile slithered across Alec's face.

"It's morning?" I asked, trying to blink away any of the last confusion.

A couple of lab Legends almost ran down the hallway. I squinted to see what they were running toward before I realized that it wasn't worth my energy to care.

"No, but that doesn't really matter to you." He shrugged a shoulder and grinned.

Familiar and cold anger laced through my chest at that

smile. He knew what he was doing. He wanted me angry for some reason. I didn't have time to care, though. I was too flooded with resentment to think straight.

"I am done with your jokes and the needles and the pain and the pounding inside my head," I growled and slammed my hands against the bars. "Let me go."

The bars lit up, and my energy pulled from my body. I shook my head at the loss. Now I knew how a human felt. This was just *annoying*.

Despite the setback, I heaved myself back to the bars. The remaining people in the room backed off, looking at Alec with worried faces.

"When we are so close? That would be extremely anticlimactic," Alec taunted.

"You aren't any closer than when I walked in here. Face it, you're just not everything that these people thought you would be," I sneered at him.

"We'll see about that." Alec smiled in a way that made my bones freeze in place.

"What?" I asked, not wanting the answer, but the unknown was far scarier.

"I have a proposition for you," Alec offered and reached in his pocket.

His hand drew out a delicate gold chain with the locket I thought I'd never see again. Without saying anything else, he dangled the locket through the bars and dropped it in my open hand.

I touched the soft gold and the comfort my body needed flooded in, uncontrollable and cascading.

You are loved. You will be okay.

My muscles relaxed against my aching bones. My breath penetrated deep enough to stretch the bottom of my lungs. My heart beat in a renewed, strong rhythm.

The intricate locket face and gold chain were too delicate in my hands. But with it, I remembered that somehow, I could get through this. Even if things were never okay again, I could survive.

"Open it," Alec said.

My eyes shot up to his relentless gaze. I brought the locket to my chest, clutching my hand around it as tightly as my weak muscles allowed.

"That's not a proposition, that's an order. There's nothing you could offer me that would make me willing to do that," I snarled at him and backed into the cell wall of solid concrete.

Breaths shuddered through me as I clutched the locket to my heart.

"Not even the life of someone you care about?" Alec raised his eyebrow.

I smiled, hating the sting from moving my chapped lips. "You're bluffing."

No one I knew could be in danger from Alec because they wouldn't risk coming here. Kylan hated me. Thayer left me. Lisa never even knew I was in danger. Any other Shadows that left knew Alec too well to be stupid enough to attack him.

I was completely alone in this. For once that brought me comfort.

"Am I?" Alec smiled back.

I heard the sound of a voice I recognized, a voice I hadn't heard in so long.

She screamed, and even her scream sounded fragile.

My heart dropped in my chest. I knew who it was before the lab assistants even opened the door to drag the unlucky person out.

"You see, your Legend 'friends' aren't stupid enough to walk back in here. But you know who is just dimwitted enough to call your phone and ask where you are?" Alec smiled and held up my phone in his hand.

My eyes snapped over to two assistants walking with a person tossing between the two of them, trying to get away.

Another scream came from the person they held. I raced to the front of the bars, my metal cuff clinking against even more lights. Somehow, if I was closer, maybe I could make this better. All I could do was watch as a set of tight brown curls bounced with every step, and listen to her high-pitched protest.

"Stop it. Let me go! You can't just hold me against my will," she screamed.

What a perfectly human thing to say. I grimaced.

Those kinds of laws didn't reign in my world. My hands tightened against the bars, the necklace chain threaded through my fingers. The inside light cutting into my vision reminded me that I was trapped.

I wanted to do something, I wanted to fix this, but I couldn't. I didn't have enough energy and the bars would just absorb anything I tried.

"That's right, a human who just couldn't wait to come to her friend's rescue when I told her that you were in a hospital in Louisiana. All I had to do was give her the location and she brought herself right to me," Alec finished.

The two captors turned her around and my eyes looked at the last person I wanted to see in these walls.

"Lisa," I breathed.

Her bright, delicate eyes snapped up to look at the person behind the bars. Me.

Well, what was left of me at least.

My dirty, skimpy clothing matched my messed-up hair and tired eyes. I hardly even recognized me anymore through the bruises and cuts.

"Kate?" She heaved a breath. "Did they take you too? Do you know what's going on?"

Her sweet plea shot straight into my heart.

There was no way to explain this to her without sounding completely crazy, or utterly heartless. As much as I wanted to fix this, I couldn't.

"So do you want to tell her why she's here? Or should I?" Alec asked, like this was a normal situation for him.

"Lisa, I…I'm the reason you are here," I admitted, wishing I had more time to explain this in a comfy living room instead of a cold prison.

"Do you know these people?" Lisa asked, as she took the final steps to stand next to Alec.

"Come on, it's not that hard to put together is it?" Alec asked and rolled up his sleeve and tapped his dagger mark for her to see.

She looked at Alec's arm, and then her gaze followed his eyes over to me. My skin needed to be exposed for the experiments, so my arm was no longer covered by my usual long sleeves. I couldn't hide it if I wanted to.

One look at my arm in those white lights and she had all the answers she needed.

"You're one of them," she breathed, and her eyes widened.

She was shocked, and I could handle that. What I couldn't handle was the way she shoved away from me, farther into the arms of the lab Legends. I was a bigger threat than them.

The look of betrayal in her eyes broke me more. I put her in this danger, and I couldn't get her out. Just by knowing me, her life was more dangerous and, until then, she had no idea.

This was the reaction I feared. It's the reason that Rachel

came marching into a trap. The reason we all followed her. My own cowardice had caused every moment leading up to this.

"The human can think!" Alec raised his arms in triumph.

Alec pulled the glove from his right hand, exposing his hand. His eyes watched me carefully as he did. My gaze shot between him and Lisa. I knew exactly why she was here.

"I don't understand why I'm here." Lisa looked back at Alec, not trusting me anymore.

"I know you don't. It's okay." Alec patted her on the head and then let his bare hand trail down her cheek.

A bright flicker of energy flashed between her skin and his hand. I yanked on the bars, turning my knuckles white. I cringed as the little but precious energy ripped away from my body.

One of my knees buckled as I sucked in a breath to steady my stance.

Alec wasn't draining a human, he was killing my friend.

"Stop!" I begged, my voice breaking.

He lifted his hand from her skin immediately but took his sweet time turning around to face me.

"I'm sure you've figured out my proposition." He smiled at me. "Open the locket, or watch your human friend die, right in front of your eyes."

"No, no please, don't do this…" Lisa started, shaking her head.

Alec smacked the back of his hand across her cheek that he had just caressed.

Another flash of energy fluttered into him as their skin connected briefly. Her mouth closed, and when she turned her face back to him, tears shimmered down her cheeks.

"I have a very low tolerance for humans, especially those that don't know when to be quiet," Alec threatened with a haunting look.

Lisa's sob pulled her lips into a tight line. She couldn't stop the streaming tears, wet trails falling down both of her cheeks. The left side of her face had turned red from Alec's hit.

She looked back at him and nodded her head as her lip quivered.

He restrained himself from hurting her again, so instead he turned his threat to me. "So, what will it be? You give me the necklace and your friend lives."

"Alec, please. The necklace won't help you. You don't need to do this," I tried to explain.

But it was selfish. I had just gotten the locket back. I didn't want to give it up again. It was the only thing that had kept me sane while I had it. I already felt myself slipping into mental oblivion.

If I had ever really needed it, that time had come. I clutched it tighter to my chest.

"I'm not a very patient person. And your friend's scared energy is almost too enticing to pass up." Alec glared down at me.

"I can't. I need it," I sobbed as I gripped the locket and looked at Lisa.

Alec's eyes flickered with irritation. He already knew how much the necklace meant to me, and he wanted the same kind of power. His fingers wiggled by his sides, itching to touch the human standing next to him.

My eyes darted back to Lisa. She looked like she wanted to scream. I seemed to be trading her life for a necklace. As if I wasn't heartless enough. She clenched her fists and remained quiet, afraid of Alec.

It was more though. Surely, the price of her life was not less than my sanity. I knew I had made too many choices based on what would be best for me. Any selflessness was truly centered more around my own happiness.

Flashes of Rachel lying dead on the floor pushed into my mind. Kylan's heart breaking when he saw Alec's memories. Thayer's eyes welling up when I said a new farewell. Then Lisa. My choices had always been about me.

"Choose," Alec growled.

His hand latched onto the back of Lisa's neck. The energy immediately started draining from her eyes. The wispy, yellow light of her energy swirled around Alec's vise-like grip.

Within seconds, her knees buckled. My eyes flashed back and forth between Alec's hungry gaze and Lisa's scared desperation.

A few seconds more, and her eyes drooped.

"Now," Alec ordered again.

I looked at the necklace in my hand. It radiated the dim warmth that helped remind me everything was going to be okay. I would lose the one form of comfort I had left in this cold cage.

With a faint click, the locket released, and I pulled it open.

I'm sorry. I thought to my mother, to myself.

I knew what I was handing over. Every day was a waking nightmare, one that would never end.

I was already close to breaking into a million pieces. If the torture continued any longer, I would shatter.

This necklace was the last thing standing between me and total insanity.

But Lisa was worth more. I held the chain and let the open locket fall into the air. It bounced as it reached the end of the slack, and shined in the lights from the bars.

Alec let go of Lisa the second he saw the two faces of the

locket parted. Her head fell to the side as she drew a slow, feeble breath. The assistants holding her watched Alec for the next command. He rushed forward to the bars of my cell.

I pulled the locket back to me and waited for his eyes to meet mine.

"I give you this, and she lives. Promise me," my voice cracked.

Alec's eager eyes lit up as his smile widened. The creases formed around his eyes, and my stomach twisted in a knot. He was hiding something else, I knew it.

It was so obvious.

But my head hurt. My body ached. My eyes couldn't focus on anything for longer than a few seconds. Even my hands shook. I couldn't make a sound decision if I tried.

Most of all, though, I couldn't watch Lisa die.

"I promise," Alec answered, hand out just on the other side of the bars.

I glanced behind him at Lisa. Her reddened eyes glistened with tears, and her brown skin stood out against their perfectly white lab coats. Her frail body was suspended between the two assistants.

She was human and entirely harmless. Something I no longer saw in myself. Something I wanted to protect.

My eyes, fluttering with exhaustion, snapped back to Alec. I moved my hand forward and the locket swung as it passed between the bars. My heart was heavy in my chest as I held onto my last strand of humanity.

"You win," I admitted and looked up to his eager eyes.

"Finally," he muttered and stared at the gold in his hands.

His face dropped and he held it closer, like the words would change. He read the simple words over and over before setting a confused stare on me. I shrugged and focused on Lisa.

"You got what you wanted. Now let her go," I begged again.

I knew it wasn't what he wanted. And now he knew it too.

Those cold eyes narrowed on me. The smile that spread across his face made my stomach sink.

"Oh come on, baby." Alec yanked his hand and backed away from the cell, smiling even wider. "You know me. Did you actually think I was going to let a human walk out of here after seeing everything?"

I tugged against the bars. "No, no, no. You said if I gave you the necklace that she would live."

"I did say that." Alec nodded, still backing up toward Lisa.

"You pride yourself on keeping your promises. Why risk your reputation now?" I asked, grasping at anything that might catch his attention.

"I would never do that. And she will live," Alec finally answered me.

I let out the breath that had been stuck in my lungs. My hands relaxed on the bars and I finally looked back to Lisa. The mild relief on her face could barely be seen through all the fear.

"Just not as a human," Alec finished.

A cold dagger of fear stabbed into my ribs. "What?"

The two people holding her revealed a set of needles. Inside the syringes must have held the serums that could turn her.

A Legend. She'd be a Legend.

I was already shaking my head as a third assistant pulled her tight curls out of the way. She was either too scared or too weak to fight them. Probably both.

With her bare neck exposed, they waited on Alec for the final word.

"No. She is a good person," I rushed. "You can't just sentence her to this kind of life. She doesn't deserve this!"

"Kate, w-what's he...what..." Lisa stuttered, tears flowing from wide eyes.

"Talking again." Alec glared at her and nodded his head to the two assistants.

I didn't get a chance to answer before the needles plunged into the base of her skull. Her eyes rolled into the back of her head as her face twisted in pain.

"No!" I screamed.

Lisa's body went rigid like she wanted to scream. She pulled in a sharp breath and fell limp in their hands.

As she was lowered to the floor, I sunk down with her, trying to be as close to her as possible. I reached my arm through the bars, knowing I couldn't reach her.

Her eyes remained closed as the vicious serum ripped apart every shred of her DNA to recreate her very being. Tears flooded my eyes as I gripped the bars in front of me.

Alec knelt down in front of me, blocking my view of Lisa. I had no choice but to look at him.

"I always keep my promises. But you should know best of all that I don't always tell you everything. And you never ask the right questions," Alec taunted again.

I could barely hear him through my ragged breaths.

"No," I muttered to myself.

He was right.

I had only asked about keeping her alive, but not in what state. Just like I didn't ask if he was working with the labs and their serum back at the mansion. I had only asked if he had known about them.

He did answer honestly. He always did. I should have seen this coming.

They dragged Lisa off to the room she came from while her body finished the change.

When she awoke, she'd be a Legend. She would be scared and have no idea what to do. She'd be alone as she adjusted to her new reality.

All of it was my fault.

"Look at it this way—now I have everything I need. I have the locket. I have you. And soon enough, I'll have the power to be a Level Five." Alec lowered himself to the floor.

I dug my fingers against the tile, not saying anything yet.

"You love me," Alec whispered, gentle again. "So shouldn't you want me to be happy?"

"I do not love you," I growled directly into his face.

"You're getting a little better at lying. That was almost convincing." Alec smiled.

My hands slammed against the bars in front of me. Alec didn't flinch. The energy from my effort launched into the bars. My body cried as the energy left my cells.

I needed every bit of power I could get. But I didn't care anymore.

I had nothing, and no one, to lose anymore.

I grabbed the bars and yanked on them, wishing I could crush them in my hands. I concentrated on the cells of the iron, willing them to rip apart, or melt, or destroy them in front of me.

More energy poured from my body and crashed into the bars, causing them to glow even brighter. My eyelids felt too heavy to hold up but I yanked them open.

I punched my fist directly into the iron bar. The metal clanged, and I shrieked as the pain split up my arm.

"You've been fighting so hard." Alec smiled. "You're exhausted. Just let go."

"Never," I gasped as I kicked my foot against the bar.

Energy ripped from my body again. My vision blackened in the corners; white flashes spotted in the air. I thought it was from the glowing light on the bars until I felt the heaviness descend on my shoulders.

"Everything will be so much easier. Let go," Alec said.

His voice sounded muffled, like it was under water. My ears pounded and my entire body felt like it was on fire.

Every nerve in me screamed in pain.

My feet stumbled underneath me. I reached forward and grabbed onto the metal bar to catch myself. That last little bit of effort left me and sucked into the very bar I held.

"Give in to me."

The last thing I saw was Alec, smiling at me.

His perfect smile. His hand clutching the open locket. His eyes trained on only me. I wished that it was all a dream, a nightmare.

My body crashed against the cold floor. Everything was gone. Every tie to reality faded as I slipped off into the most painful sleep.

CHAPTER
FORTY-ONE

Kylan

It took a few days to run to the lab, but we arrived in one piece and undetected.

We, mostly Thayer, had been formulating plans along the way. That kid did not stop talking. Ever.

We stopped in a town just outside of Louisiana to stock up on energy before we hit the lab. I was careful about my consumption. I was always careful.

I took an inventory of myself and how much energy I needed. Even Cassie and Derek had mentioned all the running had made them weaker. I wanted to be as alert as possible while still having a sound mind not clouded by energy racing through me.

Being high meant being strong, but it also made me want more. Not just human energy. I'd want Legend energy. I would crave it. The nearest Legends around were my family, and there was no way I was putting them in danger.

But if Thayer didn't stop chattering, he would rise to the top of my hit list. I shook my head, focusing on the city instead.

I refused to let anything ruin this day.

Today was the day. The day Kate was going to be coming home with us.

I nodded to the Shadows, and they all dispersed among the crowd. My eyes lingered on Thayer. He was smiling at a Shadow with black curls and spun her away from him. Then he turned back to me with a curious gaze.

"Why are you doing all of this?" I asked the question that I should've asked as soon as he showed up at my door.

"Don't worry," he laughed easily. "I'm not out to steal your girl."

Cassie ran up behind us, with Derek bouncing eagerly after her. He wasn't taking a risk of low energy today. Cassie and I didn't have the heart to stop him.

"That's comforting," I mumbled and kept walking, glancing at the other two and hoping Thayer would talk to them instead.

"Look." He ran up to me. "Even when she was Mara, we were never anything more than friends with a few benefits."

His smug smile wasn't helping my attempts at altruistic thoughts.

The black-haired Shadow overheard us and turned her head toward the conversation. I think Thayer had said her name was Fiona. I wasn't sure though.

"A few?" Fiona laughed.

Thayer shot a glance over to her immediately. She blushed and looked at the ground before responding.

"Try one more word, Fiona, and I swear I'll make you in love with your brother." Thayer glared at her.

Fiona's light eyes widened. Thayer lunged toward her and she threw up her hands in surrender. Before he moved any closer, she took off running toward the town. I opened my mouth to talk and Thayer turned held up his hand to stop me.

"Mara is gorgeous and fun and strong and so many other things," he started.

"Not helping," Derek sighed.

"But we've never had real feelings for each other. That's the truth. I know how she looks at someone she's in love with. Trust me, to her, there was only Alec." He stared at me intently, as if that would calm me.

"Still not helping." Derek swatted a hand at Thayer, which he dodged.

"It's fine. Sometimes I forget that she lived an entire lifetime before I met her," I said, turning my gaze to the moist ground.

"That's the downside of such a long life. We have to carry the baggage for much longer than the humans do," he said.

I ignored how much I appreciated that comment. We walked along the street together, brushing people as we went by. Cassie and Derek walked on their own, mostly so Derek wouldn't be around any more humans.

Thayer made an apparent effort to flirt with every attractive human we passed. I didn't know if he was doing that to prove a point, or if that was just him.

I was a little surprised at his well-placed thought. Most of me judged him as arrogant and an idiot. But I knew he at least wasn't an idiot.

"Do you honestly think this plan will work?" I asked him. "I remember Alec to be suspicious to the point of paranoia, but also too smart for his own good. But you seem to know Alec better than anyone."

"Nah, Mara knows him way better…" I threw a glance at him and he cleared his throat. "Uh, never mind."

Scratch that not-an-idiot comment. I fought to keep my stare even.

"How do I know Alec won't suspect you walking right in

there as a trap?" I asked an easier question for him.

"Alec wants this. Me asking to come back will be exactly what he was looking for. He'll be too happy to suspect anything," Thayer answered me calmly before he winked at a human girl walking past.

He touched her arm and the energy flowed into his skin easily. The girl blushed when she looked up at him. He smiled at her as if he were not in the middle of a conversation with me.

"Won't he question the reason you left in the first place?" I asked again.

I needed him to think about this as carefully as possible. Our entire plan hinged around him and a few Shadows walking into the lab completely undeterred.

"I'll take care of that." He nodded.

He kept walking, taking easy steps as he looked at the ground to avoid my gaze. He was still being so cagey about the information. Cassie even tried to talk something out of him without any results.

I stopped walking and grabbed his shirt to face him toward me.

"You have to tell me something. Is this about your inside person?" I asked.

Thayer shrugged his shoulders and pushed my hand away from him. "The person will be there to let the rest of you in and help me convince Alec that my intentions are pure."

"That's not very specific."

"That's as specific as it's going to get."

"I need a straight answer. We could all be killed if this doesn't work out," I said through clenched teeth.

Maybe he finally saw how nervous I was about all of this. Thayer smoothed his shirt and looked around to make sure no one was watching too closely.

"Alec won't think I'm lying," Thayer said in a hushed voice. "I know exactly how to make people believe that emotions exist when they really don't. He's never put up a guard against me, and even though I left him, I'm the last person he would expect to side with a few Rogues instead of my own family."

His voice was firm and his eyes were cold. Even I, of what I assumed was my own accord, believed him.

"Rogues? Is that what they call us?" I asked.

He smiled. "Thanks to me. I like to think of it as the Shadows are the real Legends and you guys are the ones that defected from the cause. The ones the labs can pick off when they misbehave instead of coming after us."

I rolled my eyes at him. So many things were still wrong with his point of view, but I didn't bother to address any of them at the moment.

"How do you know that you can convince Alec?" I redirected.

"Alec has no idea what it's like to be against me in a fight. Trust me when I tell you this—he won't know what hit him," Thayer finished as he stared at me. "You want me to show you?"

I saw his determination in his eyes and knew he was just as committed to this as I was. It must have been the way he held himself or how every person who got near him seemed to melt into whatever he wanted, but I actually trusted he'd do what he was touting.

"I'll see you at the edge of town," I said and moved to run in the opposite direction.

"Wait, where are you going?"

Man, he was used to being somebody's right hand. I smiled to myself as I looked at his eager posture, ready to follow.

"I'm not Alec. I don't like people watching me eat," I called back at him and ran.

I raced through the town, taking as much energy as my body could hold. I recognized the high feeling that I almost never let myself feel. I had to be on top of my game if I was going to take Alec down.

This time, I didn't plan on leaving my brother alive.

CHAPTER FORTY-TWO

My bare feet dragged on the floor, slick with my sweat.

The Legend assistant hoisted me up, and my face smashed into his shoulder. He walked both of us out of the testing room and Alec followed close behind.

I was still shaking from the tests. Alec was sure he knew what the problem was with Nikki's transition. The serum caused too much pain to allow a full transition. I still had no idea how that translated to putting me in agony either.

But I had stopped trying to follow his plans a long time ago.

My hands rested at my side as I pulled in slow breaths. They hurt. Everything hurt. Alec's tablet pinged, and it felt like a knife slicing through my skull.

"Nikki," Alec grumbled and stopped walking.

The lab assistant stopped. The stillness was incredible. No shifting, or moving, just resting against this person's body.

"Problem?" the assistant asked.

Alec shook his head, looking at the screen. "Probably not. But I better check it out anyway."

I kept my eyes on the white tile. Alec needed to leave, which meant it was only me and this Legend. My heart jumped in response, but I forced myself to stay still.

"Take her straight to the cell. We'll start the next tests in an hour," Alec ordered.

The assistant nodded and turned both of us back around. Alec walked off and my heart pounded out of my chest.

Adrenaline flooded. This was my chance. I was way too tired to be feeling anything, but my entire body was hyperaware of my surroundings and the lack of eyes on me.

This Legend carrying me didn't say anything, which was perfect. Every step we took away from Alec, away from the testing rooms, I needed.

A right turn on a corner.

Rooms on my left had lights coming through the windows. The others were dark. *Fewer people.*

A door opened.

She looked Legend, but she could be human. I didn't recognize her. She walked straight past us, not even looking up from her case of filled vials. *Alone again.*

The last corner.

Just ahead, the glow from my awaiting cell reflected on the floor. We weren't quite to that open room yet, the one that held my cage. I had to move soon. That room had too many cameras, and I couldn't guess who would be watching.

I didn't hear anyone behind us. *Almost there.*

My feet had been taking slow, staggering steps so he didn't have to carry me completely. Another way they wanted to wear my energy down before putting me away.

Now. I stopped walking and let my body fall forward.

His hands tightened around me, catching my waist in front of him. He was off balance, and holding most of my weight. I wrapped a foot around one of his legs and yanked as hard as I could.

At the same time, I grabbed his shoulders and pulled toward the floor. He didn't have the stance to catch himself before he fell over my back and onto the tile.

His body smacked against the floor. My senses ignited at the noise. *Too loud. Too loud.*

He had landed on his back and didn't get his breath back before I knelt over him. I leaned close to his ear with both of my cold hands clamped on his neck. His energy was already pouring into my body and he failed at trying to throw me off.

"Make a sound and I won't leave you with enough energy to breathe," I whispered.

His hands still pawed at me as if he would suddenly get the strength to push me over. My fingers had gone from aching and icy to burning with power.

The energy smoothed over all the parts of my body that were screaming in pain.

I pulled my head away to watch his eyes. They were scared. His hands stopped moving even though he was still awake. He wanted me to spare his life. Inside, I probably wanted to do that.

But my body didn't.

His energy was like liquid bliss. I shuddered. I needed all of it. Especially the last part. That was selfish, and I knew it.

I also wasn't planning on walking myself back to my cell and enjoying my extra power until the next test. I wanted to end it all.

That wasn't as selfish. I would be stopping Alec from creating a Level Five. I would be stopping him from unleashing Legend power on the world and enslaving the humans underneath him.

That was noble.

His eyes finally closed, and I could sense the end was coming. His breaths barely moved his chest against me anymore.

This was noble. I repeated.

It had to be. I let my eyes stray to my hands, still glowing yellow. Then to my arm with the dagger mark.

I was no better than a Shadow. No better than Alec himself. Why did I even try to be? I failed miserably and everyone knew it.

No.

My hands lifted from his skin. They felt heavier than my entire bodyweight.

His chest rose, just enough to tell me he was still alive.

Alec would kill him for letting me go. Either way he was already dead. But I didn't need to be the one to take his life.

I didn't waste another second. I stood and crept down a different hallway, one that I hadn't noticed cameras in. An exit wasn't connected to my cell room, but it might be to this hallway.

My ears noted every sound around me. My body wasn't operating at full capacity, but it was far more able than I had been before.

The sound of footsteps sent me skittering into the corner of the hallway. I didn't dare breathe until they passed.

I turned the corner and ventured a gaze down the open stretch. Nothing. I turned and looked at the other end and saw two large metal doors.

The exit.

I could have waited or watched or studied a better escape plan. But the exit was in front of me, and all the gut-wrenching memories behind me shoved me forward.

I still had a cuff around my wrist. I'd have to deal with that later. But I barely even noticed the warm metal.

Nothing mattered except getting out.

That's why my breath caught in my chest when I saw the door open in front of me. The sunlight cascaded onto the floor. The breeze touched my cheeks and I wanted to cry.

Nothing mattered except getting out.

I took a shaky step forward, my hands already reaching for the sunlight. That was the moment I was going to be freed. It was right in front of me. Too easy to even explain.

But it was too easy. And the explanation stepped around the door, blocking the only freedom I had seen in too long.

The woman was dressed in black, with a strappy top that revealed her tattoos. Her hands pulled a black braid over her shoulder.

"Going somewhere?" Nikki asked.

Any hope turned to a pile of useless dust. The muscles in my body seized as my eyes still wanted to look past Nikki. Outside was so close.

"Alec was holding you…how did you escape?" I focused back on her.

"People are easily manipulated, even without my powers," Nikki said and revealed a long bar that was bent on the end into a point.

She spun it in her hand even though it was as tall as her body. My eyes darted from the bar, to her face, to the sunlit forest behind her.

Her eyes burned too bright. I couldn't take her, not by force.

"You don't want to kill me, Nikki. Alec would know it was you and he'd hate you forever," I said.

She narrowed her gaze.

Nikki stopped spinning the bar, gripping it tighter in her hand. I didn't have time to take a breath before she snapped the bar across my legs, knocking me to the floor.

My hands and knees hit the tile just as the next blow pierced into my right arm.

Blood spread down my skin, joined by another stab on my left arm. I rolled to my back and looked up at Nikki's burning eyes.

"Maybe that's a chance I'm willing to take," she said.

The makeshift spear was now aimed at my heart. Even with energy in my body, I wouldn't recover from that.

My hands grabbed the spear, trying to force it away.

But I wasn't strong enough to fight her forever. The only thing that could save me was if Alec caught us. And that wouldn't be saving at all.

Sweat built on my palms and my grip was slipping. The wounds in my arms burned. Blood stuck to my back pressed against the floor. It was impossible for me to hold her back even this long.

Which meant she wasn't trying to kill me.

"You can't afford to lose the last person on Earth that cares about you." I shook my head. "Where would you go from there?"

"You're right," she said.

That was too simple. But she dropped the bar. It clanged to the floor and it sent a shockwave up my spine. That was way too loud, and I had been gone for too long. Alec wouldn't be far behind.

I only had the next minute to finish this. I sat up, ignoring the pain in my arms.

Nikki smiled in a way that made my stomach flip. She pulled a thin syringe from behind her.

"But if you suddenly became a Zero. What could Alec be mad about? Anyone could've made that mistake," she explained.

I closed my eyes and let my head fall back. That was a way more feasible plan. Knock me out with the serum, drag me back to my cell, and when I woke up I'd be powerless.

Alec might not connect that to her. Especially if she already framed someone, which I'm sure she had done.

When I opened my eyes, my muscles tensed, ready to spring. Surprise and force was all I had. There was a slim chance I might be able to get to Nikki and get the serum out of her hand before she could respond.

I had to take that chance.

My heel lifted from the floor, ready to strike at her stomach, but everything inside of me froze when a tall man stepped in from the outside.

"Thayer," I whispered.

Nikki shot a confused look at me.

His hand snapped forward and flicked the syringe out of Nikki's grip. It shattered when it hit the hard floor. He grabbed her wrist and shoved her back against the wall.

He had come back. He was here to rescue me. My tensed muscles relaxed and my shoulders fell. I wanted to sink into the floor.

I was getting out. *Nothing mattered except getting out.*

He looked down at me with a soft gaze. But he didn't smile, not the way Thayer normally would. There was something off about him. His eyes were different.

"What did you say?" Nikki asked, her eyes traveling from me back to him.

Thayer pulled Nikki closer to him and stepped behind her, keeping his hands locked on her arms. As he moved to the other side, it wasn't him anymore.

The skin lightened, the eyes changed from familiar brown to a warm green. Those eyes. I knew those eyes.

As soon as I saw them, I straightened, forgetting the blood trickling down my arms. Swaying from the injuries, I caught myself with my hands, not wanting to look away from Kylan.

But it couldn't be him. He was just Thayer. This was a game. Someone shifting in front of me, or altering something in my mind.

"Kylan?" I asked, not believing it this time.

He smiled down at me.

The smile was wrong. It didn't reach his eyes, not in the kind, carefree way that I remembered.

Nikki's eyes widened in smug surprise. When she glanced back at the Kylan holding her, she wasn't shocked or intimidated.

"Impressive," Nikki nudged her elbow to the fake Kylan.

I shook my head and forced my eyes closed. This was a trick. Another form of torture. My hands clawed at the sides of my face, wanting to get the image out of my head.

It's not him.

It's not him.

"It's not him," I muttered aloud.

The green eyes flashed in and out of my conscious mind. His smile brought a stinging pain racing into my chest.

"Don't you want to fight?" Kylan's voice asked.

My eyes shot open. He waited for the answer, like it was an easy thing to say. The truth was, I couldn't fight even if I wanted to. I was scared, exhausted, and breaking inside.

I let my gaze wander between their legs and to the forest outside. It was no longer calling to me. If I did get out, I'd be alone and wandering with a purposeless existence.

Why did I want to leave?

But that couldn't be Kylan's voice. Someone changing to look like him shouldn't be able to copy his voice.

When I glanced back up to him, I knew who it was. The only person capable of creating a vivid enough image for me to believe it was real. So real I could touch it.

"Sage." I clenched my teeth.

The façade of Kylan smiled again before the image melted. A tiny, white hand clamped around Nikki's arm instead of his. The green eyes were replaced by a slithering red.

"Don't you want to fight?" Sage asked in her own voice.

I let my chin fall to my chest. The slimmest chance still existed that I could get past both of them. It should be worth fighting for.

A sharp pain broke across my shoulder. When my hand reached back, I felt a tiny metal object. But more so I felt the tranquilizing serum rushing down my back like cold fire.

I looked up at Nikki's innocent smile as she stared at the person who had fired the bullet. Alec must have found us.

Then I moved my gaze to Sage, her face sullen and empty.

Should I fight?

No one needed to hear those words but me. I could fight to get out, I could give it everything I had. My body would fight until they killed me.

But my mind was breaking.

Nothing mattered. Not even getting out. The freezing fire spread across my chest and up to my already weary eyes.

CHAPTER FORTY-THREE

They kept me up night and day to perform the tests. Punishment for my escape attempt.

It had been two days. Maybe three. I couldn't really tell.

Exhaustion pulled at my eyelids. They had scraped at every cell in my body and tested every reaction. My muscles ached and my skin felt as thin as paper.

A pair of arms hoisted me up. I looked up and saw the same lab assistant that Alec normally had carry me from place to place. Alec was the gracious new lab leader and was letting me live and this assistant was his new pawn. I smiled at the thought that this poor guy was probably Thayer's replacement.

The assistant walked me through the door and set me down. I tried to stand on my own but couldn't.

"Sir?" he looked up at Alec and waited for the nod.

When Alec gave it to him, the Legend took off his glove and lightly touched my arm.

Warmth. Energy. I needed it. I tried to pull as much as

possible, but hardly got anything before he ripped his hand away as if he had touched something hot.

I now had enough energy to fully smile.

The assistant quickly replaced his glove and walked me over to the bed. I watched the way the assistant moved around Alec, much like someone else I knew.

"What's your name?" I asked.

I had said hardly anything to him since I got here. The Legend looked at Alec for approval. He seemed a much more compliant lap dog than Thayer. Alec looked at me, confused, but didn't say anything.

"Will," the Legend answered curtly.

As soon as the word was out of his mouth, he quickly looked to see Alec's reaction to him speaking to me. I smiled again at the familiar sight of a Legend looking to Alec for every command.

"Will," I repeated. "What a nice name. Not quite as nice as Thayer, but…" I waited for Alec.

His eyes shot up to mine, finally looking away from the tablet in his hands. I smiled, knowing I struck a nerve.

"Don't talk about him," Alec cut me off.

"You're just going to forget he ever existed? Forget that he was your best friend and you pulled a gun on him and forced him out the door?" I said.

"Not another word." Alec's cold voice rang in a final tone.

He walked over to me to put the restraints on my arms. If he was stooping to actually do the work himself, then I definitely had made him angry.

"Maybe I should have dated him instead." I looked away from Alec and up at the ceiling.

My mind errantly paid attention to his reaction. Teasing him, hurting him had become automatic over the past weeks, and especially in the last few days.

Anger fumed through him, turning his face to a strangled, red.

"I said not another word," Alec repeated.

I giggled. "I mean, don't get me wrong, you're really pretty. But Thayer, wow. He's got the looks and that Thayer personality that just makes you wanna—"

"Stop saying his name." Alec slammed his fists on the table next to me and all it did was encourage me.

I smiled even wider and looked into his eyes. His anger blinded him for a brief moment, and I loved playing tricks on him. He should have seen it coming.

My cuff must have been off because I was able to force my way into his mind again and plant a strong thought. He didn't have time to block it. The thought played and his jaw tightened.

"Stop it!" I smacked Thayer playfully and sidestepped him.

His hand swiped at the empty air where I used to stand. I turned to face him. His eyes lit up at the challenge.

"What, are you worried Alec's gonna catch us?" Thayer asked, relaxing his stance and stepping closer to me.

One slow step at a time. His bright brown eyes pored over me and I smiled at whatever was racing in his mind.

"No, Alec's not here," I answered him in a low voice.

I let him take a step closer to me, watching his eyes carefully.

"No, he's not." Thayer smiled and put his hands on my waist.

He pulled me in quick and held me tight. His lips landed on mine before I could finish smiling. The longer we kissed, the tighter we held each other...

Alec shut his eyes before the memory finished.

My body should have ached from the pain of losing more energy.

I hardly noticed anything at all. My entire body tingled with an irritating numbness.

When his eyes opened, they glared down at me. The anger that used to scare me didn't even raise my heart rate. I looked back at his gorgeous blue eyes and wasn't worried at all. The only thing I had to lose was whatever was left of my sanity.

That didn't seem like a good-enough reason to care.

"If memories won't make me change, what makes you think a lie would either?" he asked coldly.

He stared at my face, looking for the one thing he hoped wasn't there.

My smile.

"Baby," I cooed. "That was from 1858. You were gone on a trip that day with Grae, and Nikki was furious. You of all people should know the difference between a thought and a memory."

Alec's jaw fell slack.

His eyes clouded as he realized that what I just showed him actually happened.

When I was with the Shadows, I didn't exactly have strong morals and occasionally fooling around with Alec's best friend fell into a gray area.

I should feel ashamed for what I had done. I should feel guilty for causing Alec pain. My brain searched for any emotion to project. All it found was recognition of hurting someone and an overwhelming numbness.

"It doesn't matter who caught your eye before," Alec walked forward.

"You mean Thayer." I smiled. "Or did you mean Kylan? You know what? I may have even had feelings for—"

Alec cut me off by grabbing my hand and twisting my arm. My wrist moved under the restraint and my shoulder burst into a bonfire of pain.

"You belong with me." Alec leaned in closer as he said each individual word.

I saw the fury in his eyes and knew that there was nothing worse he could do to me that he wasn't already doing. The pain didn't bother me as much as it should have.

In fact, it almost felt good.

I laughed. What could he do to retaliate? I had nothing to lose. Absolutely nothing.

"Aw, I love you too," I sneered and watched him try to get ahold of his anger.

He took a breath and had to look away from me for a moment. Days of endless pain had crushed my sanity. I hardly recognized what I looked like on the outside or the inside.

I had become the person Alec was forcing me into, the psychotic villain.

Despite what I wanted to think, Kate was fading fast. The only person that remained now was Mara.

Maybe this was exactly what he wanted. Maybe if I became twisted just like he already was, we could ride off into the sunset together.

And when this was all over, I wouldn't *want* anything good. So, that just left him.

Alec released my arm.

"I know what you were doing. Before we came here," I started mumbling. "That was all so I would trust you, feel safe with you."

Alec waited in anticipation for me to finish connecting the dots. Judging by the light in his eyes, I was nearly there.

"Then all of this." I pulled against the restraint on my arm. "You aren't trying to make me angry or push me away. You're trying to break me."

Alec wasn't crazy. He was a genius. He knew exactly what he wanted and knew it didn't work when he had tried to force me to be like him. He knew I had to do it on my own.

"I lost Kylan. I watched Rachel die. I loved you, then I hated you. I lost my freedom. All in one day. And every day after that…all because of you." I looked over at him with new, understanding eyes.

He watched with thinly veiled triumph in his eyes. I wanted to cringe at seeing him so happy. I wanted to look away and feel sorry about my fate.

I couldn't.

Deep down, I wasn't sad that he won. I wasn't mad that he tricked me. The only thing I felt was a smug lift that I had successfully caused him pain. The only thing I understood anymore was pain.

My emotions were gone. All of them had been scraped, cut, shocked, or ripped out of me.

I was a hollow shell. The only thing big enough to fill the void was vengeance. The one thing I had tried to train out of my personality was the only thing left now. All it took was unending torture, fleeting hope, and crushed dreams.

All it took was Alec.

"This was what you wanted," I muttered, my voice empty.

I couldn't be angry at him. My emotions were too confused. When I looked at Alec now, I didn't hate him because of how much pain he caused—I admired him because of the entire plan that had been calculated to the insignificant details.

"Yes, it was," he answered and let a smile creep up his face.

He clicked a button that turned the cuff dark around my wrist and I could almost sense the buzzing weight lift.

To defeat the monster, you must become the monster yourself.

I looked back at him and didn't see the boy with a cold

father anymore. I saw the man who had shaped himself into what he is now. I looked at my reflection in his dark eyes, and though I was looking at my own face, all I could see was him.

I was his monster. He was mine. After a lifetime of trying, he finally defeated me.

"Well, if it's a monster you want." I snaked my hand around his wrist.

The slightest bit of skin peeked out, enough to allow a burst of fresh energy into my system. Power charged up my arms. I ripped my hands out of the restraints on the table.

I shot up and ran to the one person in the room that I had wanted dead since I woke up the first morning in that cell.

"What are you doing?" Alec asked, with hands raised to stop me.

"What I should've done all those years ago," I mumbled, and Raven's eyes widened.

I grabbed the back of her neck and threw her forward. She crashed into the closed door with a loud yelp. Most of her skin was protected by her coat and gloves. I couldn't pull her energy, but she couldn't take mine either.

Instead, I yanked the needle from my arm and clutched the cold metal turning warm in my hands.

"You've always wanted me to be a Shadow right?" I asked back to Alec.

I didn't take my eyes off Raven as the syringe changed to a small, sleek dagger. A Shadow's dagger. The one burned into my arm.

"And you. You wished all those years that I had killed you along with the rest of your family. Now I can hold up my end of the promise." I glared down at Raven's scared eyes.

"Alec!" she cried, her eyes darting back and forth.

"He won't save you. He wants this. What's it been, Raven, about sixty years? It's time to join the rest of them," I snarled at her.

Images of the terrified little girl cowering in her chair flashed through my mind. Emotions across her eyes.

I smiled when I realized that I didn't feel anything.

I understood what was happening, I just didn't care.

At all.

Without hesitation, I jammed the dagger into her artery. The metal buried deep in her neck. I pulled it down farther, splitting her entire artery open.

Her blood covered my hands within seconds. No matter how much energy she was on, she wouldn't be able to heal this in time. Especially not as I cut the knife down her neck.

Blood coated her limp body. She had assumed Alec was going to save her.

She had made the mistake that everyone did. She thought Alec cared about her. But Alec only cared about two things. His power and me.

She stopped moving, finally gone.

At least you can be with your family. I thought and grinned down at her pristine white lab coat now drenched in blood. *Not that they would want you now.*

I sat back against the door, exhausted. Alec looked at me in wonder. I smiled through the lingering pain that my energy was trying to heal.

"I was wondering what would break first." Alec shook his head and gazed at me proudly. "Your body or your mind."

"I'm a Legend. You can't break my body," I muttered and looked up into the glaring lights.

Alec turned away from the tablets, the syringes, and the scalpels.

He leaned down and gently brushed my hair away from my face. He pulled me up to stand with him, his hands still protected by gloves. The sticky blood that covered my hands and stained my clothes brushed onto Alec.

"Come, lay down." Alec guided me back to the metal table.

My wet fingers slipped on the smooth surface. I laid my aching body down and stared up at the bright lights. The cold metal pressed into my back.

"It's brilliant, you know. All of this. You can start over. We can start over. Well played," I said.

"Do you know how hard it's been to keep this from you?" Alec twirled my hair in his fingers.

"What makes you so sure I'll forgive you after all of this?" I asked, allowing my head to roll to the side.

"I'm not. But as you can see, you are the only thing I really want. Before we came to the lab, anything that happened between us on the road, I knew it didn't matter. You were always going to choose him." Alec tilted his head to the side gently.

That head tilt.

But it wasn't Kylan I saw anymore. It was Alec. Only Alec.

"So you didn't have anything to lose by hurting me. It wasn't really a risk." I turned my head back to the lights above me.

"It'll all be worth it in the end. We're almost there." Alec looked down at me warily.

I looked up into his eyes with a blank stare. My entire body buzzed with a throbbing numbness. I barely even felt him touch my arm, or move my hair.

When he looked at me, I wasn't angry. I wasn't scared. I was nothing.

"It doesn't matter. I don't feel a thing anymore." The words slipped out of my mouth.

"It'll be over soon. I promise, baby." Alec leaned down slowly.

His voice should have angered me. His pet name should have annoyed me. His unrelenting optimism and delusional goals should have set fire to my mind.

But they didn't.

I looked at him, and nothing happened. My heart continued to beat. My breath continued to flow in and out. Anything besides that was irrelevant.

"I don't care," I whispered.

His lips kissed mine and I instantly pulled energy from him. I didn't need to think about it. My body just took over for me.

I didn't stop him from kissing me. I just let him live out his fantasy.

Instead of power, I felt my body grow more and more numb. A strange, grasping tie to Alec and his energy bonded me even more to him.

I used Alec's energy to change my body into who I should have been all along.

If I had never become Kate, I never would've had to endure all this pain.

My hair lightened until it reached the striking blond it was before. It made the blood on me look even brighter. Other small changes pulled at my face.

His energy healed my bruised body, even if my mind had been training to shut out the pain. My muscles revived and I finally released the tenseness I had been holding in my shoulders since I stepped through the door of the lab.

When Alec finally pulled away, he looked down at exactly who he had been wanting all this time.

"Mara. Baby, it's so good to see you." Alec smiled like a little boy, unabashed and hopeful.

He left the restraints open around my wrists, but I didn't move.

I had nowhere to go.

The last of Kate inside of me fell away without a sound. The last tear I would probably ever cry stung in the corner of my eye. When I blinked, it was gone, and so was the worry. Everything was gone, everything but him.

Good-bye. I thought to myself. Well, to her.

CHAPTER FORTY-FOUR

Kylan

Thayer hopped out from the alley with brighter eyes than before. I trudged behind him, checking to make sure the people he left behind still lived while trying to get my own energy.

Making it to the lab was only a small part of the plan. Getting in and getting out would be the much harder part.

Cassie raced up to me, Derek following quickly behind her.

"You." She pointed at Thayer. "You said each of us had our own part of the plan, but mine and Derek's are the same. What is everyone else doing?"

Thayer's face fell slightly when he looked between her and Derek. "You weren't supposed to share."

"Why? Because you don't want us to realize you have no idea what you're doing?" Cassie stomped up to the Shadow.

Fiona came out of nowhere, flanked by two other Shadows. "Take a step back, Rogue."

Cassie stopped but didn't retreat. Derek came up behind

her, a hand placed over her arm in case he needed to shove her out of the way.

Thayer raised his hand at Fiona and stepped in front of Cassie. "The whole idea of this plan is that everyone only knows their own part. That way if you get caught or cornered, you can't reveal anything because you don't know the whole plan."

"That..." Cassie lifted a finger, but stopped. "That's actually not such a bad idea."

Thayer winked at her, letting a smile reach his lips.

"Did she actually just compliment him?" Derek leaned in and whispered in my ear.

"No, you must be hearing things," I muttered back, trying not to move my mouth. Cassie heard anyway and landed a punch on my arm. I laughed it off. "Wait, then, what was your part?"

Derek opened his mouth to answer.

"No!" Thayer shouted. "No sharing. Seriously, does your family not keep secrets?"

All of us shook our heads. Thayer let his head fall back as he let out a sigh. "Okay, for today, you do. It's safer, trust me. The only people who know the entire plan are me, Fiona, and my inside person."

"Wait, what?" I asked, my eyes landing on the Shadow girl next to him.

Thayer kept his mouth in a tight line, like he was still trying to keep a secret. After a few seconds, he let out a burst of air.

"Yes, fine! I had to tell someone, and Fiona was the next safest bet."

I rested my weight on my back foot and heard Derek stand behind me. Cassie was already at my side within a breath.

"I thought that would blow the whole thing? Why did you—" she started.

Thayer raised a hand and Cassie actually stopped talking. "She is the second-best reader in the Shadows. Actually, the best now that Alec's out."

Fiona smiled. "He's never read my mind. That was my audition to get in."

"See?" Thayer pointed at her but still tensed his shoulders. "So everyone just chill, go off on your separate ways, get energy, and meet back on the east side of the lab. Until then, no talking."

Derek grabbed Cassie's hand and pulled her away with him. The two were out of sight even before Fiona and the other Shadows could leave. But sooner than I wanted, it was just the two of us again.

Thayer lingered, eyeing me.

"Fiona, huh?" I asked.

His face twisted in discomfort. "I don't work well alone. And you are too chatty with your siblings."

"Still," I said, watching where she had left. "You'd risk the entire plan because you think Alec won't read her mind. What if she's not as strong as you think she is?"

It was too big of a gamble. I didn't know if it was normal for Thayer or not, but he seemed like he thought things out better than that.

"Well," Thayer edged, biting his lip. "There's more, but I don't know if you want to hear it."

My family, Kate, and everything I loved was on the line. I needed to hear it. "Tell me."

Thayer grinned now, taking an easy stance. "People tend to find me especially charming, irresistible even. That extends to the Shadows with us."

"I don't find you anything close to irresistible," I muttered.

"That's because I'm not trying," Thayer said easily. "With Fiona, I have tried. Quite a few times, and she still has the willpower to turn me down. Strangely enough, that's made me trust her all the more."

"She won't sleep with you?" I asked, hoping he would correct me. He just smiled. "You laid out a plan that has to be secret, but you told it all to that girl because she said no?"

"It's not an easy feat," Thayer said, walking again and waiting for me to follow.

"Did you…" I started, uneasy already. "Did Kate ever…"

"You don't want to hear it," Thayer answered softer.

The two of us continued siphoning energy from wandering city dwellers in silence. Thayer got higher and higher, almost to an impossible amount.

As energy came into my system, I felt myself reaching the edge of having too much. I needed to stop. That invisible line I never wanted to cross threatened to send me careening out of control.

Thayer had already run into a department store, through it, and back out by the time I realized it was getting close to strike time.

"Ready?" he asked in a jittery, excited voice.

I nodded. I couldn't look away from his brilliant eyes, at his energy. I could sense it from here.

"Okay, we'll need to meet her on the outside of town. She's waiting to let the first group in," Thayer said, already leading the way.

"She?"

He nodded. "No point in hiding it now, she'll have to lead you inside. As long as you promise not to let Tweedledee and Tweedlered know."

"Derek and Cassie," I corrected.

"Semantics." Thayer waved the comment away. "Just up here."

We were long past occupied buildings and roads that weren't falling apart. Ivy grew on the outside of a store made of concrete that looked vacant for so long.

I kept my gaze on the surroundings—it was too quiet. Thayer stopped in front of the door, checking his phone. When he saw the time, he started looking around too.

"Hmm." He pursed his lips.

"Problem?" I asked, following his gaze.

There was nothing. We were all alone. Whatever inside person he had promised, she wasn't here.

Thayer turned to face me, stepping close and lowering his chin to give me hushed instructions. Before he could say anything, three Legends stepped around the corner. One of them had a black dagger on his arm.

"Look who it is," the Shadow said and Thayer turned back around. "You two in town for a friendly visit?"

"Garth." Thayer whipped out a charming smile. "I didn't expect you to be on patrol duty. Nikki's always been the better destroyer between the two of you."

"Someone had to step up and take responsibility to make up for those who bailed," he said.

Something flickered in Thayer's eyes. Nikki wasn't around, and that was important to him. I shuddered, thinking of her and that potent destroying power I still couldn't shake from memory. I hoped she wasn't his person.

Not missing a beat, Thayer snapped, "You bailed."

Garth waved a finger at him. "Not in the slightest. And you know what? We're this close to getting a Level Five serum ready. Mara might be torn to shreds, but we'll be the first in line for that kind of power."

"After Alec, you mean. And Nikki. And Sage. And almost anyone else, and then you," Thayer said.

"Shreds?" I interrupted, focusing on the only important part of that statement.

Garth clicked his tongue. "I hoped there would be something of her old personality left when we were done. All of us are going to miss her."

"What are you saying?" I stepped forward. Thayer stayed perfectly still.

"She's broken. Mara. Kate. Everything about her," Garth answered. "She didn't make it through last night."

I couldn't hear anymore. I lunged for them. The only thing that stopped me was Thayer's arm shoving me back. He spun and threw a punch at the first assistant. The guy dropped with a sickening crack.

I launched back at them, taking the other assistant in my grip.

Thayer turned but not in time to block Garth's blow. The sound of bone connecting with bone echoed down the alley. He fell to the ground just as I sucked the energy from the assistant in my hands.

I had to act. Thayer was sprawled on the concrete, trying to stand before Garth could advance. I dropped the assistant I had been draining. He wasn't dead, or even unconscious yet.

We couldn't have a witness telling Alec about our presence, but I'd be able to reach that Legend if he tried to get away. I couldn't fix a dead Thayer.

Garth tossed Thayer against the tattered brick wall. I followed and snatched the collar of Garth's shirt and threw him to the ground. His back cracked against the shabby asphalt.

Thayer shook it off, still trying to stand while I knelt and wrapped my hand around the Shadow's neck. His energy flowed as he tried to catch his breath. His eyes flew open and his hands latched onto my arm.

But his strength didn't matter, not when so much of his energy was already in my body. That line I didn't want to cross was obliterated.

My eyes caught the assistant getting up. I could stop and chase after him. That would leave the Shadow alive and still stop the witness. But my hand stayed still, even if my eyes watched the running figure.

Thayer groaned, forcing himself to stand. His pain was masked with determination. I let my eyes wander back to Garth and met a blank stare with shallow breathing. He was fading fast, but his energy was feeling better and better.

She's broken. She didn't make it through last night, the words resonated painfully.

I had to save her, broken already or not. I needed the energy.

The adrenaline in my body told me to hold on. I set my eyes back on where the assistant should be. Instead, I saw him toppling over with a dagger in his chest.

Behind him stood a petite blonde. Her red eyes flared in the overcast sunlight.

"You can't handle one simple instruction, can you?" she said, hoisting Thayer up. "That just sped up the timeline. Alec will know these guys are gone soon. Thayer, we need to get you inside."

She kept glancing at me, and I didn't know why.

Thayer smiled, and I was surprised to see her standing there. Out of everyone in the lab, I didn't think this creepy one would be the first traitor.

But I was distracted too long. The only thing that drew me back to the Shadow beneath me was his final energy shooting up my arms.

I lifted my hand, but it was too late. He was dead, and my mind was swirling with power.

"No," I whispered, looking at my own hand.

I knew the feeling. Final Legend energy, impossibly strong and savory and fluid all at the same time. I knew that feeling all too well.

I stood, desperate to get away from the murder. Thayer and Sage had walked up to me, both with empty eyes that didn't understand.

"Are you ready?" Thayer asked, clearly sensing the turmoil inside of me.

"Don't," I raised a hand at him.

"Kylan, you took out a Shadow. You saved my life. This is not a bad thing," he said, and his words sounded like a vise tightening around my chest.

Took out a Shadow. I shook my head. *I killed him.*

His energy raced through my veins, strengthening and exciting every part of my body. His cold body was only steps away from me. My mouth went dry and a deep hunger sat on my chest like a boulder.

That Legend energy I recognized. I needed more of it.

"We don't have time for this, we need to get you and Thayer ready," Sage interrupted.

I didn't even glance at either of them before I turned away. They called my name, but I didn't answer. I knew what time it was. I knew we had a few minutes to prepare before going to the lab. I fully understood my part in the plan.

But I also needed to fix this screaming joy in my mind from the final energy. My hands pressed to my temples.

I hadn't drained anyone since those years I had chosen to forget. Not even when we came for Rachel.

Shadows wouldn't understand this. They'd brush it off and move on. Another death. But I wasn't a Shadow. I never wanted to be. I couldn't be a murderer again. And if I walked into the lab like this, with this craving, I'd become exactly that.

Murderer.

Murderer.

Murderer. Something needed to ground me.

"Kylan, wait," Thayer said. He whispered something, but not to me, then it was silence.

I glanced back at him. He was looking at Sage. My eyes followed to her red stare. Her face was blank, concentrating. But nothing happened.

"Give me two minutes," I muttered and turned to leave. I wanted to race down the streets, away from them. Away from the body.

I took a step and froze when a bright flare of red hair and a huge man walked around the corner.

"Cassie?" I asked.

She wasn't supposed to be here. Neither of them were. They'd see Sage, blow the plan.

I glanced back at Thayer and he nodded at me.

"What happened?' Derek asked. "Are you all right?"

I didn't answer the question. I walked up to him, but stopped when my body sensed their energy. The hunger spread.

Murderer.

I couldn't meet either of their eyes. Cassie moved forward. She wrapped her arms gently around my waist.

A shudder rocked through me. Her brilliant energy was overwhelming. Different than the Shadow's, this energy would be more familiar, inviting.

I shook my head, forcing the thought away.

"Don't," I said, stepping back. "I don't want to hurt you."

"I'm your sister," she said with a soft smile. "You won't hurt me."

She moved forward again. Every muscle in my body locked in place as she touched my back. Her movement was so slow, I almost couldn't feel it. I met Derek's sympathetic gaze. He laid a hand on my shoulder.

I finally let a hand rest on Cassie's back. "I…I just…"

"You don't need to say," Derek said.

Cassie nodded, and I automatically pulled her closer to me. Her soft red hair brushed my chin as I tucked my head down. Derek squeezed my shoulder.

"We love you," Cassie whispered, and I broke.

They were my family. The people who loved me no matter what. Their energy didn't matter. Legend energy didn't matter. Everyone was a person with their own life. A life that didn't belong to me.

I sucked in a breath and held on to the two of them as long as I could. When it finally came time to leave, I didn't want to peel myself away.

But I did. I stepped away from Cassie and let Derek's hand fall. Her cute smile sent a flood of peace through me.

"Let's go get our family back," Derek said.

I nodded. I was ready to go get the final member of my family. Kate was inside and the time was now. We had everything we needed to break her out.

Before I turned to leave them, the two of them dissolved into thin air.

Impossible, I thought.

I spun on my heel to face Thayer with a pained look on his face.

"You did this?" I charged toward him.

Thayer didn't answer. He didn't say anything when I

grabbed him by the shirt and shoved him against the wall. He even kept a groan stifled through his clenched teeth.

"You created this?" I demanded. "How could you have done that?"

"He didn't," Sage said quietly.

I dropped Thayer from my grip and moved to the little woman who had slithered in my head. Thayer grabbed my shoulder before I turned.

"You told her to play me," I said.

Thayer nodded. "I can't risk you throwing everything away. Not when we're this close. Think about it. Isn't all of that what Cassie and Derek would say if they were here? You didn't need them. You needed a reminder."

The words caught in my throat.

I looked back to where the vision of Cassie and Derek had been, that same peace followed when I thought of them.

He was right, even if I hated to admit it.

But neither Shadow berated me with questions or demands. They waited. For all their manipulating, they still wanted it to be my decision.

I glanced at Sage. "No more tricks."

She flicked her mistrusting gaze at Thayer and must have seen what she needed to. When she turned back to me, her shoulders relaxed and she extended a hand.

I shook it and followed them into the building, searching for the first part of the plan.

"You know what you're doing?" I asked to Thayer, not looking away from Sage and what she now stood next to.

"Pretty sure," he said.

That was hardly comforting, but it was all I had at the moment. I reached forward and Sage handed me a white lab coat.

"And she's gonna need one more thing from you," Thayer said.

I pulled the coat over my shoulders and noted the other racks of white behind us. The cool fabric felt foreign against my skin. But I straightened my shoulders as Sage guided Thayer out of the concrete building.

The only thing I focused on were those icy blue eyes I loved so much. And the person I would do anything for.

CHAPTER FORTY-FIVE

Another dawn broke through the small windows of the lab.

The floor was smooth against my bare feet. My hand wrapped in Alec's as we moved down the hall. He wanted to touch me, and I didn't object.

At least they didn't make me wear the cuffs anymore between rooms. My own comfort was the only thing I could bring myself to care about. Alec could think or do whatever he wanted to me now.

The last of the tests this morning needed time to be studied. Alec was excited about this round. He was so sure this time. He kept promising that we were so close.

Once he got what he wanted, he could be a Level Five with me. Any Legend could be. We could all live on energy from humans and we would hold all the power.

"Alec?" Sage called from around the corner.

"What?" Alec asked curtly.

Her red eyes stared at him, reading his expression. She held her breath as she tried to form the words.

"Don't be angry." Sage hung her head, taking a step back.

She glanced up at me nervously and then back down to the shiny floor. Her movements were a little too shifty, especially for Sage.

"What did you do?" Alec stopped moving, looking her up and down.

"I've been talking with Thayer." Sage let the words fly out of her mouth.

Alec's eyes narrowed. My breath stopped.

"Excuse me?" Alec stepped forward. Sage didn't budge. "Sage, he left. How could you even think that—"

"He wants to come back," Sage blurted.

Alec stopped talking. He stopped breathing too. I looked at Sage, reading every movement on her face. She seemed worried.

"Well you can tell him that we don't need him here," Alec scoffed.

"Why don't you tell him yourself?" Sage asked, raising one eyebrow over her creepy eyes.

"You don't have to keep me waiting at the door like some thief. I'm just here to see Alec," Thayer's voice announced from around the corner.

I followed the sound of his voice and guessed he was stopped at the front door. My mind lazily flipped through reasons he might be here.

When he left, he walked out on me crumpled on the floor. I waited to feel the anger of hearing his traitorous voice again, but it never came.

"What makes you think he wants to see you?" a male assistant responded to him.

"Trust me. He does," Thayer said.

Silence followed down the hall. I knew that silence.

I could only imagine the emotional trauma that assistant was feeling from Thayer. The fact that the assistant was a male didn't really change anything. Thayer definitely preferred girls, but his powers of persuasion worked on any gender.

Alec immediately handed me off to Sage and walked toward the front door. Her cold, gloved hand wrapped around my upper arm. She quickly turned, pulling me with her toward my cell.

"What's going on?" I asked.

My voice sounded monotone and callous. It was becoming the new normal for my tone. I sensed Sage knew more than she was telling Alec. When I looked down at her, her red eyes looked anywhere besides up at me.

"I'm as clueless as you." That was a lie.

She wasn't even trying to hide it. I watched her, hoping she would accidentally give me a clue. The metal door creaked open and before I stepped in, Sage gripped my arm tighter, still watching the floor with a calculating look.

"You've never asked about why the lab took me in the first place, turned me into this," she muttered.

Her face was still smooth, like she was waiting for me to invite her to share. I stayed silent, shifting my weight to the other hip because it seemed like I might be inconveniently standing for a while.

She continued. "A man had been watching me, following me home. Then it was two. Then three. They pointed and whispered, but everyone did. I was different. The hair, the eyes…"

I sighed loudly, hoping she'd stop and I could sit down.

That red gaze landed on me now. "I looked different from everyone else. So when they needed a random target, I was the one that stood out. And when they needed a person to try the skin experiment on, guess who they picked first?"

I narrowed my gaze at her. She was playing up the pain in her eyes. She was spilling this on purpose. She was looking for something.

"Torture and isolation and loneliness," she whispered, leaning closer.

She didn't break her stare. I tilted my chin down. "Sounds awful. Can I go?"

Her light eyebrows lifted as she scanned my blank face. She settled her stare on mine again.

Images flashed in my mind. None of them connected, and none of them belonged to me. She was creating the images in my head, and I didn't have enough energy to stop her.

White lab coats on a rack. She pushed them into a concrete room that they didn't belong in, all the while glancing over her shoulder. She was nervous.

A phone call. She held her phone to her ear, her voice was too muffled to understand. Although the hope in her eyes was incredibly obvious.

A retinal scan. Her bright red eyes lowered to the machine. The lights swirled around her eyes before finally beeping and flashing green. The lock released and she stood back up to face the door.

"Hold on," Sage muttered and nudged me forward into the cell.

I stumbled forward and let myself fall to a sitting position. Before closing the door, she bent down and touched her finger to the floor.

A green stem grew from under her touch, the tip peeling out into a small white daylily. I glanced up at her, but her expression was cold as stone.

I looked back down at the flower, daring to pick it up. It was so delicate it might have crumbled in my hand.

She locked the door quickly, though I didn't protest. I just stared at her. She left in a flurry of white-blond hair.

It was just the flower and me. I remembered that it used to mean something, something important and tender and riveting. But it was just a flower now. Simple white petals and a stem barely strong enough to support it.

The showdown between Alec and Thayer pulled at my attention. I couldn't deny that this was something I had always wanted to see.

Alec stood in the middle of the room, always the center of attention. Thayer stood at the door, daring to take slow steps forward. Infuriation steamed off Alec's charged body. I smiled at Thayer's fate ahead.

I looked at Thayer and immediately gauged his reaction to seeing us. He seemed happy to see Alec.

When his eyes fell on me, I noticed a hint of surprise. He must have been expecting my darker haired counterpart. I brushed my tussled, blond hair out of my eyes and folded my arms across my chest, still clutching the flower. He looked me up and down before he focused back on Alec.

"Thayer?" Alec said and glanced cautiously at me. He was protecting me.

"I shouldn't have left," Thayer said.

He was trying to focus on his words and ignore me entirely. Trying a little too hard.

Alec advanced toward his best friend, or what used to be his best friend. He lunged and grabbed Thayer's neck in his hands. Before I blinked, Thayer was pinned against the wall with Alec closing off his airway.

"What are you doing here?" Alec asked suspiciously.

"I ca...came back for you," Thayer choked out underneath his hand.

Thayer didn't move to counter Alec's attack. He didn't move at all. He just stood as still as possible.

"I'm supposed to believe you just had a change of heart? Come on, Thayer, I'm not stupid," Alec spat back at him and tightened his grip.

Thayer clenched his fists, fighting the urge to overpower Alec. Either with emotions or physical strength, he had Alec beat. But the second Alec got into his mind, Thayer would be done. He seemed to be settling for not attacking.

"If I wanted to hurt you, I would have," Thayer choked and raised his hands in surrender.

Smart move. I thought.

I wondered if Thayer was playing him. Alec knew Thayer was much stronger, and not attacking gave Alec the confirmation he needed. He dropped his hand and Thayer sucked in a breath.

He still wasn't fighting back. Sage was the person that brought him in, Alec had said that Sage was in charge of changing Thayer's loyalty before they kidnapped me. She must have been better than we all thought if Thayer came back despite the obvious danger.

"What changed your mind?" Alec asked. Doubt still shaded his eyes.

"You're my best friend and have been ever since I came to the Shadows. When Mara left the first time, I stayed," Thayer said and Alec listened warily. "I chose you then and I'm choosing you now."

Alec looked back at me with curious eyes. He wanted to believe what Thayer was saying. I knew that anyway, but seeing him told me he was falling for it.

I watched Thayer.

I didn't quite believe him yet. Something was still too strange. I glanced at the daylily. He shouldn't have come back now if all of this disgusted him before.

"Although it doesn't look like you two are at odds anymore." Thayer pointed a finger between the two of us and his smile flared back into place.

"Not anymore," Alec confirmed and turned to wink at me. A smile turned up the corner of my mouth.

"Good, because that was going to make this a lot harder." Thayer laughed and relaxed for the first time since he laid eyes on us.

His feet pointed away from Alec. He ran a hand through his hair. His breathing had a slight shake with each inhale.

He's lying. I narrowed my eyes slightly.

The last strand of doubt in Alec's eyes faded away. I flicked my eyes back to Thayer, looking him up and down. Without emotions tying me up, I saw every flaw of this conversation.

I wasn't on Alec's side and I wasn't rooting for Thayer. I was just watching.

"You don't care that I kept this from you?" Alec asked, looking intently at Thayer.

"You're not the only one with secrets. I can't hold it against you forever," he answered and masked a smile.

"She told me, you know." Alec kept his stare on his former second.

I knew exactly what he meant. I looked up at Thayer's reaction to me spilling the secret we had both vowed to keep. He just laughed and shrugged his shoulders.

"I figured she would eventually. I knew you wouldn't care since she never did," Thayer scoffed and looked up at me with his best sexy expression. "It didn't mean anything, did it, Mara?"

I expected a flurry of angst or at least a tinge of desire. Nothing came. The bars around me would protect any influence from Thayer, but I should've felt those emotions on my own anyway. I shut my eyes and took a breath.

He couldn't play me anymore. When I opened them again, I smiled.

"Not a thing." I leaned forward against the bars as the white light glowed against my skin.

I waited for Alec to accept my answer. I wouldn't apologize, and he knew that. His dark blue eyes softened a little more. Thayer was winning.

"You didn't come back for her?" Alec edged.

"I came back for my friend," Thayer answered.

The words were carefully chosen. But they were true. Thayer tapped the black dagger that had been there since he joined.

Alec looked down at it and smiled. All three of us shared the same mark.

"Welcome back." Alec stretched out his arms.

They embraced like brothers and when they were done, Alec looked back to me. Thayer's eyes followed, looking at the bars that surrounded me. His eyebrows pulled together as a smile crossed his face.

"Are you okay? What's up with the cage?" Thayer asked, stepping closer to me.

I lifted the flower toward the light of the bars. It rested in my palm for only a second before I closed my fist and felt the fine pieces crushing in my grip.

Flower or not. Kylan or not. I wasn't holding my breath for someone to save me. I had done that too many times before and woken up screaming the next day anyway.

Thayer's face fell. I smiled. I allowed my body to relax against the bars.

“Never better,” I said.

“She’s…in transition,” Alec explained, not catching what I had just shown Thayer.

“Transition to what?” he asked.

“Back to who I was always meant to be.” I shrugged my shoulders, and Thayer’s brown eyes flipped through emotions faster than I could read.

“Boss, you already tried wiping her memory and…” Thayer started.

“I haven’t touched her memory. She’s doing this to herself,” Alec said.

He had won. For the first time in centuries, I was actually happy about that. This life was easier than pretending to be good or masquerading as a human, easier than feeling everything. This future was much more enticing.

“What’d you do to her?” Thayer asked.

“I made her more…like me,” Alec muttered to himself.

With that he turned around and gave Thayer a tour of the lab, explaining everything. He was filling Thayer in on what happened to Nikki when they left down the hall.

I was alone again in the cell. I opened my hand to see the ruined daylily. It should have broken my heart. I should have cried as soon as I saw it.

But I didn’t.

I picked it up and held the broken pieces barely clinging together. It probably wasn’t real. Probably a cruel torture tactic Sage had made up. Either way, it didn’t matter.

Nothing outside of this lab mattered. Nothing besides Alec mattered.

Alec had me on his right hand and Thayer on the other. The deadly trio. He was just handed everything he ever wanted. The only thing missing was power.

Pretty soon, he’d have that too.

CHAPTER FORTY-SIX

I lay awake all night, waiting for the sun to rise or Alec to come back.

Seeing Thayer should've hurt a lot more than it did. He left me here too. Maybe he was manipulating our emotions, but Alec and I were both glad to have him back.

Seeing the flower should have hurt too.

But it didn't. If Kylan wanted to be here, he could've been. It had been weeks, maybe months since he left me.

So the flower didn't mean anything. A trick I was sure Sage had played on me. It was too late. I didn't care anymore.

The longer I was here, the less I wanted to leave. An eternity with Alec started to sound more tolerable with each passing hour.

After all, he loved me more than anyone I had ever known, including Kylan.

"Are you ready for this morning?" Alec asked as he walked by.

"For what?" I muttered, sitting on the floor with my legs crossed.

"Another test. But I think this is the last one we'll need," Alec explained.

It was a dazzling plan, Alec's idea.

I fell for his charade before we even arrived at the lab. I fell for it all. All he needed was Kylan to leave and that was enough to seal my fate. And he did leave.

Alec knelt down on the floor outside of my cell. Both of our eyes on almost the same level as we peered through the iron bars and the annoying light coming from them.

"Then can I get out of here?" I reached over and tapped on the bar.

"We're so close, baby. Just a little longer and we can go anywhere in the world," Alec promised.

I nodded.

"Mr. Stone?" a human assistant called from behind him.

Alec stiffened into a more perfect posture. "Give me a moment," he whispered to me.

I relaxed and let my eyes drag over to the human. Alec stood to face her. "What is it?"

The girl mumbled, "I just need to know when you want us to administer the 17B antidote? The subject does appear to be contained, so I thought—"

"Subject?" I scoffed and stood. "Contained? You want to step a little closer and say that again?"

I moved to the front of the bars and moved my finger to call her over. She took a step back instead and looked up at Alec with scared eyes. Her mouth hung open as if she was trying to find any words to fix my building rage.

"Mara, calm down," Alec warned.

"Ugh, I'm not mad. I just don't like humans talking about me like I'm not even here." I shoved my arm in the assistant's direction.

Alec looked down at the girl, who was flapping her mouth in an attempt to form an apology. He looked back up at me with his iconic wicked smile.

It made me smile too. His eyes flashed with excitement when he looked back down to the human girl standing in front of him.

"You know, I think you're right," Alec agreed and grabbed the girl's shoulders.

The girl's eyes went wide and her breath came in fast spurts.

Adrenaline. I smiled at the thought. The warmth of her spiking energy penetrated the air even around me. I could almost taste the satisfaction on my tongue.

"Careful, darling. I don't think you should walk so closely to her cell," Alec warned, holding the girl firmly in his grasp.

"No, no. I'm not—" she started before Alec tossed her straight over to me.

Her body slammed against the bars just as my hands grabbed her. I pinned her to the metal with one arm and yanked up her sleeve with the other hand.

My cells craved the heat radiating from her body.

I latched my hand around her arm and within a few moments, she stopped struggling.

"I wish I was sorry," I whispered to her.

It seemed honest. I thought I wanted to feel the pain of hurting her or remorse for ripping her energy right out of her body. I wanted to feel something.

But I didn't feel any of that. A gaping hole in my chest burned where my heart should have been.

The light drained from her eyes as the bright energy swirled around my hand. The glow from the bars looked even paler compared to her warm, yellow energy. It was a beautiful sight, a beautiful feeling.

My body relaxed as the new energy flowed all around. When the energy stopped, I let the girl fall to the floor. Her body flopped down, and I stretched my muscles, allowing the power to mingle inside of me.

I sighed and looked back at Alec.

His eyes were full of awe. I sat on the floor again, and then allowed myself to fall on my back, peaceful and satiated.

My blond hair spread out around me, my arms and legs relaxed. I stared up at the pattern of the ceiling, enjoying the temporary high I now had.

"Try not to do anything too crazy while I'm gone," Alec called as he picked up the girl and threw her over his shoulder.

I raised my hand in the air and gave him a thumbs up. His footsteps walked out of the room and left me in silence. In a room that glowed from the bars around me. I was still in a cage, but it didn't bother me at all.

I didn't want to leave. I didn't want to do anything.

I counted my breaths to pass the time. I traced every line on the ceiling. I tapped my fingers on the floor, feeling the silence.

Slow footsteps creeped behind me. I listened long enough to know they didn't belong to Alec, so I ignored them. People always walked past my cell. But these footsteps didn't stop.

"Kate?" his voice whispered.

I recognized the owner as soon as the sound hit my ears. I sat up slowly and turned to see exactly who I thought was standing there.

I waited for the happiness to rush in, but it never came. My body felt as numb as it had been before.

The only thing I felt staring at those green eyes was annoyance—maybe even that was too strong of a word.

"It's you," Kylan whispered.

He knelt down in front of the bars, in front of me, right where Alec had sat a moment ago. The two of them looked so much like each other now that I had seen them together. Part of Kylan would always remind me of Alec.

"Kylan?" I asked, confirming that I wasn't just dreaming this.

I had lost count of all the times I imagined Kylan swooping in to save me. None of them ever turned out to be real.

Having him standing in front of me ignited emotions that I thought were long dead. But they never fanned into a flame. They only ached inside of me, just out of reach.

"Yeah, it's me," he answered.

His smile spread across his face.

My eyes traveled down from his face to his body. Instead of Kylan's usual fashion-forward attire, he wore a crisp, unblemished fabric covering his clothing.

A white lab coat.

"You're not real. You're another nightmare," I realized as my shoulders slumped.

Another trick of Sage's.

I shook my head to get the image of him standing in front of me to go away. It had to be a dream. Those eyes were too bright. The lab coat was too new.

But I dreamt of this. Kylan saving me, Alec letting me go, or anyone taking me from this place. All of them ended with betrayal, with me being thrown back into this cell.

This was no different.

Nikki enjoyed every time she saw me wake from one of those familiar dreams. I glanced around the room, waiting for her to saunter in to sneer at me.

"I'm real. I'm here," he said, quickly pulling off the

lab coat. "This was just a cover to get in and walk around unnoticed."

He touched the side of my face. His energy began to flow slowly into my body. The second his skin made contact with mine I recognized that energy.

It wasn't a dream. Not even my most potent nightmares felt this real.

"So, you're here to save me?" I said, glaring.

My voice cut through the air in front of me, right into him. He pulled his hand back immediately like I'd bitten him.

"Yes…" he started, but his eyebrows pulled together.

"You're confused?" I asked in an apathetic voice.

The answer was written in his eyes. They darted back and forth between my eyes, searching for an explanation. He was looking for Kate in my eyes. But he couldn't find her.

Good, I thought to myself.

I wanted him to feel as hurt and confused as I did when he walked out. All the loving feelings I used to feel when I saw him were replaced with an acidic disdain.

"Yeah, I'm confused. I'm here to get you out of this cell. I'm here to save you," he started his hero's speech.

My eyes narrowed. This wasn't about him. It never should have been.

"What if I don't want to be saved?" I asked with my sharp eyebrow raised.

His face froze in shock. My smile pulled back over my teeth when he took a step back and dropped his hand.

"What? No…" His face dropped.

"You want to bring me home and have me turn back into the perfect girl you left behind, into whoever you want me to be," I mused, running my fingers along the iron bars that had become more of a friend than a threat to me.

He gawked at me, not able to even form a response yet.

"Am I wrong?" I asked, locking my eyes on him now.

"Kate, you're not thinking clearly." He raised his hands and stepped closer to me.

He moved slow enough not to spook me. Judging by the way he looked at me, I seemed like a bomb ready to detonate.

"What if I don't want to be good anymore?" I clarified the question, still waiting for an answer from him.

He came here to be a hero, but he hadn't thought through what he would do if I didn't need one. I watched him think about what I was saying, then I watched him shake it off.

"You don't mean that," he consoled himself and stood.

But his words meant nothing, like the daylily. They didn't spark any reaction inside of me. I stood from the shiny floor and stared back into his eyes.

"Says who?" I asked him again.

Kylan shook his head and dropped the careful stance he held. He tensed his muscles and took a breath to calm his frustration. Those gorgeous green eyes looked like they were trying to reason with an insane person, fighting to get his Kate back.

He was losing. "In case you've forgotten, you're being held hostage and tortured. I can't even imagine the kind of pain he's caused you. Now you're telling me that you don't want out?"

Kylan's eyes were glued to me.

Behind him, Alec finally entered the room and upon seeing Kylan, stopped in his tracks. He raised a finger to his mouth and stepped forward silently. Thayer walked around the corner next. Both of them crept farther into the room.

Alec's eyes glanced quickly to Kylan and then focused in on me. He must have found what he wanted. I watched a knowing smile split across his face.

Kylan was crumbling in front of me. Like we both wanted. Alec was winning. I just waited for the final strand of hope to break in his eyes, like it already had in mine.

He was still naïve enough to think that all this time alone with Alec wouldn't have an impact on what I wanted. He should have known better.

He should've thought of this before he left me here.

"What did he do to you?" Kylan asked, looking honestly concerned for me.

I smiled, his sentiment meaning so little to me now. Worry filled his beautifully green eyes, and it didn't set off any kind of response in me.

"I showed her what it's like to be good and what it's like to be bad." Alec smiled and Kylan whipped around to face Alec and Thayer standing there.

My gaze moved to the two Shadows staring down at their next victim. Alec sized up his little brother as a smile peeled across his mouth.

"She chose the latter."

Kylan's eyes shifted back to my blank stare. His idea of Kate was long gone.

I turned back to Alec and winked at him. He smiled. If there was anyone that really understood what I was feeling, it was him. He may have hurt me in the past, but he did teach me the most valuable lesson.

Feelings hurt. Being good hurts.

Letting go was the only thing that brought me relief.

Thayer looked at me with a worried expression before glancing to Kylan. I scanned his face and suspected there was more going on inside his mind than he had told us.

Alec turned to face him and Thayer immediately changed his face to show the same evil grin that Alec had.

A little too fast of an emotional change, even for Thayer.

"Look who came to visit," Alec said to Thayer even as he turned back at Kylan.

"He did come back for her. I wasn't sure if he still cared," Thayer said carefully.

"Will you please take her to another room? My brother and I need to have a little chat." Alec glared down at Kylan, extending the key to Thayer.

Thayer nodded and took the key from his hand. A small smile flashed on his lips. I stood, ready to leave the cell, but still watched Thayer. Something wasn't right.

The key clicked in the lock and Thayer yanked the heavy door open. He turned his back to me, and I followed him to the middle of the room. Once we were out of Alec's gaze, and a good distance away from the bars, Thayer turned on me.

I looked at his face and narrowed my eyes again. *He's hiding something.*

Thayer focused his gaze on me instead of Kylan. Alec was too preoccupied deciding how to kill his brother to pay attention. Thayer's brown eyes buried into mine for longer than normal.

I recognized the slight clench of his jaw and hands balling into fists at his sides.

"Thayer, don't—" I warned a moment too late.

Forced emotions crashed into me without hesitation.

Bars weren't protecting me now, so I couldn't force him out again. He was connected, and so incredibly strong.

He used to target specific responses in the mind that triggered only one or two emotions. Usually, just one emotion was overwhelming enough on its own.

This was nothing like that.

I felt everything. My knees hit the hard floor with a thud. I couldn't even find the breath to scream.

My hands flew to my head, trying to rip his connection to my mind. I looked up to Alec, knowing he wouldn't want this.

But Alec wasn't watching me. He was watching Kylan.

Thayer took a step toward me, his brown eyes watching me. My hands crashed into the floor to hold up my body as the first emotion collided into me.

Rage. It burned through to my fingertips.

Kylan lunged for Alec and brushed his hand against Alec's only exposed skin. Alec dodged and pulled a gun from his coat.

The bullet flew into Kylan before he had the chance to turn around. Kylan ripped it out immediately, but the bright blue liquid had mostly emptied into his body.

Another step brought Thayer closer to me. His brown eyes straining to stay focused as his mind ignited the next feeling.

Pain. The deep ache sliced into my muscles.

Alec kicked Kylan's feet out from under him and Kylan landed flat on his back. He didn't stand.

The serum would have been coursing through his veins, slowing every possible thought and movement. It was distracting and overwhelming, especially with a Shadow attacking you.

Alec stood directly, forming a dagger in his hand. It matched the one on his arm perfectly. If Kylan didn't move he would feel exactly what it's like to die a Shadow's death.

"I was worried I'd have to track you down myself, but instead you made it easy for me," Alec gloated and lowered himself to the floor, bringing the knife closer and closer to Kylan.

Thayer was close enough to touch me now. He dropped his knees to the ground next to me, still keeping his eyes trained on me.

Love. It ignited in my chest and the flames spread.

"I thought you didn't want to do anything to hurt your precious Mara," Kylan spat, using the name that Alec called me. That he probably always would call me, despite where I stood.

"Hurt her? Trust me, she won't feel a thing," Alec happily answered.

The knife dropped even closer to Kylan's chest. Each breath made his skin touch the tip of the dark metal.

"How can you be so sure that watching the love of her life die in front of her eyes won't bother her?" Kylan still held strong.

Thayer grabbed my clothed shoulder, sweat beading on his forehead. When I looked back up into his brown eyes, I felt my heart crack.

Sadness. The chill creeped up my skin.

"Love of her life?" Alec laughed.

"What, you thought that was you?" Kylan taunted.

"I'm sure she wouldn't stop me. See the best part about Mara is that now, she doesn't care," Alec finished and tipped the knife up under Kylan's chin.

Thayer sucked in a breath. I tried to brace myself for what came next.

My overwhelmed body could barely handle the emptiness I had chosen before they arrived, but these emotions made me want to curl up and die on the cold floor.

Thayer's eyes seemed to fill with sorrow for what he was about to make me feel. He knew more than anyone that there was one emotion I always chose to reject.

It was my fatal flaw as Mara. I always ignored one emotion so I could live the life that I thought I wanted.

Fear. It crushed into every individual cell.

My mind reeled. My elbows hit the floor. My back arched.

My muscles seized. My breath stopped. I never let myself be truly afraid of anything because I knew it would cripple me, it would destroy me.

I was right.

My eyes looked up to the source of all my fear. Alec himself. He stood over the man I thought I hated but now I couldn't bear to see die.

Alec watched his brother, sickly interested in the anticipation of killing his greatest threat. Victory flashed in Alec's eyes.

Kylan just looked at me and gave a weak smile. This may be the end for him, but that didn't scare him. I was here. One glance into those weary green eyes, and my body took over the feelings from there.

Alec raised the knife and as his fingers tightened around the glinting blade, the fear wrenched around my heart.

Before he plunged it down, I knew exactly what I wanted to do, what I needed to do. Because the only one that could save Kylan was me.

"No!" I heard my own voice shout, full of worry. *Worry.*

Thayer finally drew a deep breath and released his grip on me. He sat back on his knees as he gasped for more air to help his body adjust. Thayer's muscles tightened, trying to force himself to be okay with how much energy he just spent.

He wasn't forcing anything now. This was me.

I was feeling.

CHAPTER FORTY-SEVEN

Alec froze, dagger hovering over Kylan as those indigo eyes snapped to me.

After a second of studying my face and Thayer gasping next to me, those same dark eyes widened. Alec looked from me to Thayer, finally putting together the reason his best friend had returned.

"What did you do?" Alec growled.

"Something…something only Mara's been brave enough to do," Thayer responded in short gasps. "I defied you."

A smile pulled at my mouth. Thayer was too dramatic, and it was funny. I actually wanted to laugh.

Fire burned in Alec's eyes.

His best friend had walked back into his life, just to betray him. Alec's grip on the dagger faltered. His relationship with Thayer was disintegrating.

Alec's eyes looked to me for sympathy. I was his place to go for a safe landing. But when he looked at me now, he couldn't even see that anymore.

He was completely and utterly alone.

"So much for not caring." Kylan smiled and threw Alec off.

Alec's body hit the wall and knocked the air out of him. Kylan didn't waste time to appreciate that he was now winning. That was something a Shadow would do. Instead, he stood to finish the fight of centuries.

In a few shaky steps, Kylan was standing over Alec. Kylan was energy-deprived and angrier than I had ever seen him. In one motion, Kylan ripped Alec's sleeves up and grabbed bare skin.

Kylan's hands clamped around his brother and surprise turned to fear in Alec's eyes.

The bright energy rippled between the two of them.

As Alec drooped, Kylan strengthened. I knew what it was like to take energy from a Legend. You felt everything about them. You understood them. I wondered what Kylan felt when he sucked the essence out of his brother.

I could tell he wanted to drain every ounce of energy from the person he held in his hands. I couldn't deny that I also wanted to walk away and leave Alec's cold, dead body on the floor.

The only thing that pulled me out of my wrath was Alec whispering, "You are your father's son."

His tired eyes looked over at me and smiled. I was trading one villain, only to create another. Thayer looked up at Kylan with a worried expression.

"The only way to defeat the monster," Thayer muttered under his breath.

I knew the grim expression in his gaze. Alec was the monster that no one had defeated. Kylan was becoming the one to replace him.

I walked forward, painfully aware of every sensation. My hand reached and rested on Kylan's shoulder. A shock of warmth and caring flooded in through my arm.

"Kylan, don't," my voice called to him. It almost felt detached from my body. I couldn't tell if I really meant the words or not.

He held on anyway and watched as more energy poured from Alec's body into his. Alec struggled less and eventually stopped moving almost entirely.

"He deserves this," Kylan growled to the biological brother that he hadn't considered family for centuries.

"But you don't," I whispered again. His eyes snapped up to mine. "Don't turn yourself into him."

His grip loosened. He watched my blue eyes as everything else about my appearance changed in front of him. The slight energy I had went into changing back into the woman he remembered.

"Kate," he breathed like he couldn't stop himself from saying my name.

His hands released Alec and moved to hold me instead. He hugged me close like he never wanted to let go. I didn't want to either.

"Take me home," I said into his shirt.

The warmth of his breath filtered in through my hair. He pulled back and kissed me. My body ached at how much we both needed this.

We each took the pain and despair of the last few weeks and emptied it into each other. I felt my body pulling his energy. He let me take it. My skin felt pliable again, my muscles warm and moveable. I broke the kiss and stood to my full height.

Thayer stepped forward, and I turned to face him.

"Thank you," I said in the soft, kind voice I had grown used to as Kate.

I jumped forward and hugged him tight. He could have stayed with Alec. He could have not come back after he left. He could have walked away from it all. But he didn't.

He never gave up on me. And I never wanted to let him go again.

"I'm sorry for everything you've gone through. I…I felt it all," he whispered into my neck. "You're much stronger than I thought you were."

Energy flowed into my skin. My body must have been really deprived if I wasn't even trying to take it.

I smiled at my old friend. A loyal friend. So happy that he was there for me.

His weak smile turned into a smirk just fast enough for me to still recognize him as the Thayer I knew.

I took one glance as Alec's unconscious body on the cold floor, feeble and uncomfortable. Before the anger tinged this moment, I turned my eyes to the door. I walked forward, leading the way out.

"Okay, there's a hallway just past here…" I started talking.

"Wait," Sage called as she stepped into the doorway.

I froze in place. Her red eyes looked at me differently. A half smile formed on her mouth as she looked at me.

"Listen, before you go all crazy revenge on her," Thayer jumped in, "you should know that she's the reason any of us were able to get inside."

"What are you talking about?" I asked him, not taking my eyes off Sage.

"She's been working with me the whole time. She opened the doors. She gave everyone lab coats and guns," Thayer continued.

I stopped. "What do you mean everyone?"

A few more people stepped around the corner, dressed in white, just like the rest of the assistants.

I recognized their faces—Shadows. The ones that I hadn't seen walking around, so I assumed they'd left. I recognized

Fiona stepping through the rest of the group, a white lab coat on.

She grinned at me and then her eyes fell on Thayer, waiting on his command.

Some of the Shadows still cared for me, or for Thayer, enough to leave Alec. I smiled.

"I couldn't find it, you know," Sage said.

"Couldn't find…oh. The locket," I muttered and started looking around the room like it would be hiding somewhere in sight.

"I've looked over every inch of this lab. I can't find it. Alec never told anyone where he put it." Sage hung her head.

"Okay." I nodded, hearing the rush of hate, fury, and everything else that now pounded in my ears. Kylan's hand reached for mine.

Safe, home, tender, kind, every feeling so tangible I could taste the sweetness in my mouth.

Energy raced across his touch. Hot, rushing, and strong filtered into my skin. Everything that made Kylan, all the kindness and bravery and forgiveness, all flowed into me. I never wanted him to let go.

"I did find this, though," Sage said.

I glanced at her tiny hand. In it was a small, blue book with yellowed pages. The journal. She held it out to me with a soft smile. I grabbed the book and tried to pull it toward me. Her grip didn't release.

"I'm sorry," Sage whispered, "for most of it."

"I know." I smiled back at her.

I pulled the journal toward me and she let her hands fall away. I clutched it near my chest. It wasn't the same as the locket, but it was still a part of her. Peace flooded through my body. My reminder of family was still tangible, that was what mattered.

Then I remembered that I wasn't the only one with family.

"Wait," I looked at Kylan, "What about Cassie and Derek?"

Before he opened his mouth, I heard a booming voice behind me.

"See? I told you she was going to ask about us," Derek called.

I spun around and he stood in the doorway to the other holding rooms. Cassie stood next to him. She glanced at me and then back at the floor.

I knew she was trying, but more importantly, she was here.

My smile dropped when I saw a woman draped in Derek's arms. Her head lay against his chest, as her arms hung by her side. I recognized her tight curls covering her face.

"Lisa," I whispered and rushed forward. "Is she all right?"

"She's alive. It looks like they haven't been giving her enough energy. But we can fix that," Cassie explained quietly.

I nodded. I had never known her to be quiet before. I had to check and make sure I was talking to the right person.

"How did you know she was here?" I asked.

"We didn't," Cassie answered, a little more confident this time. "We searched every room, looking for you. But I recognized her. She was laying on the floor in one of the rooms with a bunch of sharp tools and a metal table. Honestly, it was creepy. She didn't even move when we walked in."

Cassie lifted her head to finally meet my eyes. I let all the gratitude wash over my face. Her mouth twitched in a smile. I wrapped my arms around her and pulled her in. Her head fit just underneath my chin.

"Thank you," I whispered.

"I knew how important she was to you. Your little human friend," Cassie whispered back to me. "I know what it's like to lose someone important."

One last squeeze and I let her go. Derek was smiling now, even if his eyes were still sad.

I grimaced at the word *human*. I'd have to explain that to all of them. Worse still, I'd have to explain it to Lisa when she woke up.

"I know how important Rachel was to you," I started. "I can't say enough to express how sorry I am. I sent her right into this trap, and I couldn't save her."

"I forgive you," Cassie muttered.

"What?" My head snapped up, my eyes searching her face.

It was almost too quick for me to hear. Almost too impossible for me to comprehend. She looked at the floor and kicked her feet together to avoid looking at me.

"Come on, don't make me say it again." Cassie smiled.

I took a step away from her, appreciating everything she had done for me. Then, I looked at Derek standing next to her, holding Lisa in his big arms. He was standing in the very place he swore he never wanted to step foot.

"You." I looked up at Derek. "You walked into a lab for me?"

Knowing about his parents, I was surprised that he would dare set foot in here. He was willing to do it for Rachel, but he never got the chance.

"Well, that's what family's for." Derek looked down at me with all the love of a big brother.

"You're family to us," Cassie said clearly.

My heart swelled and tears already brimmed in my eyes. Whether she meant it for Kylan or for me, it didn't matter. My mind finally realized that I was safe.

I was safe.

Raven was dead. Alec was out. Nikki was trapped.

After the worst torture of my life. After everything being taken away from me. After all of it. Kylan was here. My family was here. I was free.

Without warning, Kylan scooped me up into his strong arms. I lifted my head up and kissed him, in front of everyone else. His energy flooded into me again.

He broke the kiss and started walking to the door. As soon as I felt that we were moving, I struggled to get out of his hold.

"Okay, I appreciate the gesture." I squirmed. "But I am capable of walking on my own."

"I've pictured this moment for so long. Will you just let me be the hero?" Kylan asked as he held my body close.

I didn't see the desire for control that always burned in Alec's eyes. Kylan was helping because he wanted to, not because he thought I couldn't take care of myself. He was looking out for me.

"Fine," I sighed, and he smiled.

I narrowed my eyes at him and leaned my head into his chest and cuddled in close.

"What made you come back?" I asked.

"An old friend of yours told me I was being an idiot. He was right," he chuckled and kept looking ahead.

My gaze flicked back to Thayer walking behind us. He gave me a sheepish grin as he looked up at me with those brown puppy dog eyes, big and innocent.

"Sounds like someone I know." I smiled.

We stepped out of the lab and into the sunshine. I blinked as I looked up at the open sky for the first time in so long. Relief washed into my heart. I took a breath of the fresh air. I turned, and Sage stepped out of the doors and into the sun.

She closed her red eyes and lifted her face. She took a deep breath, her chest filling with fresh air. The sun reflected off her porcelain skin, but she didn't cringe.

"You deserve this, princess." Thayer smiled at her. "We couldn't have done it without you."

She immediately looked at me with worry filling her eyes. I thought back to the words I screamed at her.

Guilt is forever. You'll always remember the pain you caused because of the life you wanted.

Sage was a mix of sorrow and remorse. That was all I needed to see. I knew why she did it. I was the price to pay for her standing free like she was now. In truth, I might have done the same thing in her shoes.

"He's right." I nodded to her.

Sage relaxed her shoulders and threw her arms around Thayer. He picked her up and spun her around, laughing. He tripped off the steps and they both tumbled to the ground. Laughing, and falling, and careless.

I smiled. The part that broke my heart was Thayer's smile. He didn't have anyone else now.

Nikki was insane, Alec was a traitor, and the other Shadows were never on his Level of power. That mattered to someone like him. So, to him, I was all he had.

But now he had Sage too, as harsh and cold as she was. She could make him smile too.

"I can't believe we made it!" Derek laughed.

Cassie bounced next to him. "Seriously, you would not believe what Thayer had us all do. We were in charge of…"

I looked at them and stopped listening to the story. I just wanted to see them. Two people who had just faced their biggest fears all because their brother asked them to. They'd do anything for him, and today proved that.

They were a family, a seamless little family.

Kylan took off running. Everyone else followed along at their own pace. He held me for only a few miles before I begged him to let me run on my own.

He argued, I argued better, and he put me down.

My feet hit the ground, and we ran through the night and into the next day. We weren't rushing to get anywhere in particular. We were just putting as much distance between ourselves and that lab.

As we ran, I watched everything. The trees, the dirt, the grass, the cities, the roads. I saw it all like I was looking at everything for the first time.

Maybe one day I'd tell them everything that happened there or maybe it was best to keep it buried.

But in this second, in this carefree breath of time, I only thought about the soft dirt under my feet and the sun on my back.

Step after step, the lab faded and the day brightened.

CHAPTER FORTY-EIGHT

The hot water ran against my skin, commanding my muscles to relax.

I breathed in the damp, clean air around me. My body slowly swayed with the rhythm of the water hitting the shower floor. My mind cleared for the first time in months.

One breath in. I watched the grime of the lab and the dust from the run back to Kylan's house swirl in the water at my feet.

Another breath in. I touched my fingers to my arms and closed my eyes. I avoided any thoughts of Alec, the lab, or the endless experiments. I focused my mind on the one thing that got me through it all.

The locket.

I tried to picture holding it in my hand. I tried to allow the feeling of warmth to fill my body the way it did when I held the gold chain in my fingers. I tried everything. All I could muster was a few flickers of hope that quickly faded when I felt the empty space around my neck.

It was gone.

I choked back a sob, knowing Kylan was just outside and probably listening. I trained my eyes on the silver knob of the blue-tiled shower, trying to think of anything to stop the tears from burning streams down my face.

One big breath.

I closed my eyes again and focused on my heart still beating in my chest. I knew the support the locket had given me. In all my time, I had never relied on anyone enough to really miss them being gone.

These past few years, I had started to do just that. I smiled when I thought of how many people I now loved.

Cassie and Derek lost a lot, but they followed Kylan to come back for me. According to Kylan, Derek even encouraged it.

Lisa was sleeping in the other room, close by, and I'd have to explain everything to her tomorrow. For now she needed to sleep. She had been forced out of her human life to enter my world. Yet when we came back, she still trusted me.

I guess she really didn't have a choice.

Sage even came back with us. She may have been a part of the original torture, but in the end, she was the reason I was standing in this immaculate bathroom with a breakable, glass-encased shower instead of a cell..

Thayer did so much. He challenged his best friend, and lost him in the process. Everything in his life told him not to help me, but he did. Without him, I'd be facedown on a cold floor still, counting the seconds to give my existence a shred of purpose.

And then there was Kylan, pacing outside the bathroom door, straining to give me privacy but also wanting to be there for me. I had done so much to ruin his life, but he stayed anyway. He stayed.

Despite all of that, there was one thing I still wanted. I reached up and touched the place on my skin where the locket had rested.

I hung my head and let the water sift through my dark hair. There wasn't a way to win. There never was with Alec involved. He always did.

The locket was never coming back.

Alec would've hidden it or destroyed it the moment he woke up. My hands would always be empty, and my heart would always want that connection restored. My mind would always wonder.

But focusing on that would only drive me mad. I turned off the water and focused back on my life that I had now. I pulled my long hair into a bun, happy to have it off my shoulders.

I dried off and put on fresh clothes. Compared to the ragged, scanty clothing I had worn the entire time I was at the lab, the cotton slipped across my skin like the finest silk.

Feelings of comfort from a mother to her daughter washed through me and then vanished as if they had nothing to stick to, no reason to stay. One final tear crept out of my eye when I thought of everything Lydia had left me in that locket, and how I traded all of it away.

Steam followed me out of the bathroom into the bedroom. I looked at the meager pile of belongings that came with me from the lab.

The sweat-stained, blood-tipped clothes that I wanted to burn and never think of again and the small, blue journal.

New tears filled my eyes as I reached for the last shred of connection I had to my past. The journal held an entire lifetime of stories for me to catch up on.

I grabbed the book and flipped to the next journal entry.

April 1787

I hope we are able to stay in this place forever. The grass, the trees, and the little town at the top of the hill. You and I are happy here. It has been three years, and I have heard no suspicions or whisperings. The humans focus on their new country, and we can finally live in peace. I do not know how long it will stay this way, this quiet.

I watch every morning before we leave the house. I pace the floors every night before I close my eyes. All the while, you sleep and play and grow older each day. You mature much faster than I have aged since the experiment. I still remember the first time you said my name. You looked up at me with your gorgeous blue eyes and called me "Mom." My ears had not heard a sweeter sound.

We may be alone in this world, but we have each other. When I look at you, I cannot picture a better existence. Our life may be simple, but it is our life. My perfect daughter and me.

I love you. Now and always.
Lydia

"I'm sorry," I muttered through my sobs.

I placed the journal back on the bed, setting it apart from the things I didn't want to remember. Her one joy in life was being with me, and all that was gone. I was grateful that I at least had her journal to comfort me, to hear her words.

I dried my tears and once I felt composed enough, I opened the door to see Kylan standing in the kitchen. He immediately looked up and smiled.

"Feel better?" he asked.

"Yes, much." I nodded and looked at the closed bedroom door a few feet away. "How's Lisa doing?"

"Still asleep," Kylan answered and stepped around the counter.

"She's probably so confused and terrified. She doesn't know anything and that's all my fault." I hung my head and watched a drip of water fall from my wet hair.

"None of this is your fault. Alec had no right to go after her. When she wakes up, we can explain everything better, slower. We can walk her through whatever she needs to know," Kylan explained and touched either side of my clothed arms.

"She picked the wrong person to be friends with." I looked at the door again.

"Don't say that." Kylan rubbed his hands up and down my arms.

"Speaking of which, where did Thayer run off to?" I asked again, realizing how much I was not paying attention when we came home.

"He and Sage took the rest of the Shadows back to the mansion. He said he'd come back after he showed her what a life in the sun could feel like. His words, not mine." Kylan smiled.

"That sounds like something he would say." I laughed.

"Come on, come sit down." Kylan motioned to the couch. "I have something that will make you feel better."

I walked over to the couch and sank into the soft cushions. My toes tucked between the seams. I gazed out the pristine glass windows. From the comfort of Kylan's warm house, the icy air outside changed.

The tiniest flakes of white ice fluttered down from the sky. It was the first snow of the year. I had made it back just in time to see it.

"Here you go." Kylan walked over to me with a steaming cup in his hand.

He sat next to me, transferring the cup. I raised it to my mouth, enjoying the heat spreading through my hands. "Thank you."

Kylan smiled down at his lap before lifting his gaze to me. "Whenever it was cold outside and I had a bad day, my mom would always bring me a cup of hot chocolate and tell me everything would work out. And I know you've had more than a bad day, but I thought this would be a good start."

A sip of the drink sent cozy shivers down my back. I shoved my toes further into the couch and looked back up at Kylan.

I thought about everything I'd missed growing up. All these simple things replaced with daggers and murder and energy. Now, I didn't have to miss anything. I had a family right here.

"You have no idea how much this means to me," I said as I lowered the cup onto the glass table.

When I turned back to him, I let my gaze drag along his strong jaw and his soft lips curling around his straight smile. I scooted myself closer to him on the couch and lifted myself up on my knees so I could be at his height.

Kylan's eyes looked me up and down before his mouth

fell open slightly. His breathing stopped, and a spark ignited his gaze.

"Kate, I can only imagine what you've been through, and I want you to know that I totally understand if you need some time," he rushed, his eyes darting back and forth as he remained a statue on the couch.

"I don't want time." I leaned forward and ran my hands across his shoulders. "I want you."

I pulled myself forward and kissed him.

My hands tugged on his shoulders to bring him closer. Warmth encircled me, and the only thing I wanted was more of it. I kissed him and wanted to sink into his arms.

He had seen the absolute worst of me, and he still wanted me.

I held onto him like my life depended on it. My breath caught as he leaned closer to me. My heart raced as his hands felt up my back and he let out a low moan. I was on top of the world.

That was when I noticed that I was taking his energy. The slow burn of intense, crazed power was unmistakable. I tried to ignore how badly I wanted to keep that energy flowing into my body. I tried to turn it off.

I couldn't.

"Kate," Kylan said between his next kiss. "Hey, you've had your fun."

He wanted me to stop taking his energy. I wanted to stop. *Why didn't I?*

His lips met mine again, and the energy continued. I pulled my mouth away from his and still felt the wispy warmth creeping in where my hand touched the skin on the back of his neck. I lifted it off gently, staring at my own hand like I had no control over it.

As soon as the connection broke, the energy stopped.

"What's wrong?" Kylan huffed, still holding me as close to him as I could get, but no longer touching my skin.

"I'm taking your energy." I pulled my eyebrows together.

I put my hand back on his cheek, purposely concentrating as hard as I could. I didn't want to take his energy. I thought it as loudly as possible. As soon as my skin touched his, the energy resumed trickling in without permission.

That didn't make sense.

"Yeah, you're gonna need to stop if you want this to go much further." Kylan smiled and gently pulled his face away from my hand.

The energy finally stopped again.

I lifted myself off him and sat back down on the couch. I stared at my hands in disbelief.

"I can't," I whispered.

Insurance. I remembered.

Alec had injected me with something that he considered a backup plan. This was it. This was the thing that would make sure that I would never leave.

I had no control over my ability to take energy. I couldn't stop myself. Whatever off switch had existed before was gone, or blocked, or something. The most I could do was slow it down and even that was barely different.

I looked up at Kylan and winced when I saw his eyes searching for an answer.

"What do you mean you can't?" Kylan asked and touched my hand with his finger.

Another stream of energy immediately started. The power flooded into me. I grimaced as that confirmed my suspicion.

"That, that right there. I can't stop taking your energy. I'm trying to, but it just won't," I muttered, pulling away from him. "It won't stop."

"How is that possible? Every Legend can choose whether to take energy or not," Kylan started, trying to fix this.

A sinking feeling in my stomach told me there was no easy fix to this.

"I'm not like everyone else. I'm broken now." I flexed my fingers and I could almost hear them hissing for more. As if when they touched something, they wanted everything they could take. I warned, "Get away from me."

I raised my hands and scooted away. His face dropped and he reached for me. I jerked my arm out of his reach.

"Alec did this," Kylan clenched his teeth. "If he can't have you, then no one can."

I leaned my head back on the couch, staring up at the ceiling. My mind raced through possibilities of antidotes or ways to cope with this new reality. But I had no idea what he had done.

Without that information, without Alec's help, it would be near impossible to figure out a solution. A way to get my control back.

And until then, I wasn't safe near anyone I loved. That long list of people who had saved me or who cared about me. I'd have to keep my distance from all of them. A new cell without visible bars.

Alec knew this would happen.

He knew I would try to solve this on my own. He knew I wouldn't be able to. He planned all of this.

"He won," I said, even though I wanted to scream.

"No, you can't talk like that. We won. We were the ones that got you out. We'll find a way to beat this too. We're together now, and nothing can stop us." Kylan smiled.

His hand reached for me, to stroke my cheek, to brush my hair away. His fingers nearly grazed my open skin but halted in the air just before it touched me. He moved it down to my clothed shoulder and rested his hand there.

I glanced at him, at his hesitation. As long as I was like this, we couldn't be together like I wanted. I knew it. Kylan knew it too. I was sure that somewhere in a dark corner, Alec was laughing.

Pristine, soft snow fell outside. I gazed around at the beautiful home that was every dream I had ever had. I dropped my eyes to the cup of hot chocolate warming the table and spreading a frosty ring across the glass. I couldn't look at Kylan or the smiling pictures surrounding him.

Because I knew I had everything. But I couldn't keep any of it.

My hands fell into my lap. "I have to go back."

THE END

TO THE READER:

I'm unspeakably grateful that you chose to read this story and that you made it to the end. Know-ing this story has a place in your mind or heart is more special than I imagined it would be. Now that you've read through all the fantastic heartbreak and twists, I hope you love these characters even more.

You are the reason that more books like this can come out and the third book is already in creation because of your support. Whether you loved this book or hated it or didn't finish or thought it was a let down, make your thoughts heard. Leave a review on Amazon or Goodreads. Every review, no matter how small, is helpful for budding authors.

Thank you for supporting the Legends & Shadows Saga, and I hope you're along for the ride until the final end.

ACKNOWLEDGEMENTS

Oddly, this is the hardest part about writing a book. So many people contributed along the way that it's hard to name only a few.

To my amazing husband: Thank you for all the unending support. You stayed up a lot of nights and let me talk out a plot for hours even though none of it was connecting for you and half the time I wasn't even talking about this series. You're a true champ and I love you.

To Suzanne Johnson, my editor: I am loving working with you and I can fell how much you care about these characters with me. Thank you for your thoughts and your seemingly endless passes over the manuscript. Thank you. Thank you!

To Sarah Hansen, my cover designer: You never cease to impress me with what you can do with design. You are talented and creative and do such a great job capturing the thoughts in my head. I adore these covers and can't wait to see what you come up with next.

To my family: Memo, Mothy, Meow, Mames, BB Wee, and A Single Bean, you guys are everything to me. I love your quirky moments and humor that helps me create characters with fun personalities. You will always be important to me and I highly doubt anything could tear us apart at this point. I love all of you.

To my friends: I needed a lot of support this year and you were always there for me. The main reason this book is a reality is because you encouraged me and never let me fear failure. You mean more to me than I thought friends ever could. Thank you.

To my readers: You will always be on my list of people to thank. Getting to talk about my characters and discuss the story with you has been such a rush. I love that you are a part of this world I created. It means even more that you love this world too. Thank you for your support.

ABOUT THE AUTHOR

Angie Day found her love of writing while in college where she studied psychology and eventually went on to a master's degree. She noticed the need for romantic and fantastic adult stories that were still wholesome and clean. So, she took matters into her own hands with her debut series. When she's not devouring the next book, she is spending time outdoors with her husband.

To follow along with her journey, find her on social media or check out her website.

www.angiedayauthor.com
@angiedayauthor

DON'T MISS

THE FIRST BOOK IN THE LEGENDS & SHADOWS SAGA

www.ingramcontent.com/pod-product-compliance
Lightning Source LLC
Chambersburg PA
CBHW020556310726
48979CB00008B/1233/J

* 9 7 8 1 7 3 3 8 1 4 4 3 0 *